Contents

The Order: Chasm of Wicked Sins

Author: Katerina St Clair

Edited by: Kira Marie

Revised Edition

Copyright © 2023 by Katerina St Clair

Revised Copyright © 2024 by Katerina St Clair

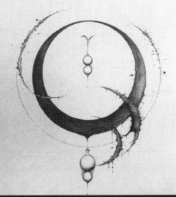

DEAR READERS,

Let this world be your refugee.
Let these characters be your warriors.
For we are all fighting our own battle.
Now, let the war begin.

Playlist

Start a War- Klergy & Valerie Broussard

The Untold- Secession Studios

Arsonists Lullaby- Hozier

Too sweet- Hozier

How Villains Are Made- Madalen Duke

How Far Does the Dark Go?- Anya Marina

KATERINA ST CLAIR

A Little Wicked- Valerie Broussard

Black Magic Woman- VCTRYS

House of Balloons- The Weeknd

Love and War- Fleurie

Take Me to Church- Hozier

FOREST- THE DARK DAYS

He stands in solemn wait, watching Andrew with an observance I have only seen in the cold, dead gaze of a Shifter seconds before it has made its final kill. The gold locks of his hair are tinged with the presence of dye, concealing the vile nature of the hunger he no doubt tries to suppress each time he smells the blood of a Marked.

Dictating Andrew like an animal, he infiltrates the man's mind with his Call, working past my defenses in Andrew's headspace in ways even the Prophet has struggled with. New Haven thought they had successfully altered Andrew's mind more times than I can count, turning him into the subservient empty shell of a human the rest of this society has become.

They couldn't be more wrong.

Now, the Prophet has adopted yet another puppet to dictate. Another soulless Marked, ready to kiss the glove of the Prophet's filthy hands, waiting at their feet like a kicked dog. This new Commander is not like all of the rest before him. He stands with confidence, watching the world around him as I watch him.

For weeks, I have been following his every move, watching the patterned nature of his day-to-day life. After my brief glimpse of weakness in the Prophet the moment I slashed their calf and watched them stagger each time they moved days after the injury had been delivered, I knew it was only a matter of time before they started exhausting their resources to start tracking me, and all of the others I have allowed to infiltrate this vile city.

I savor the feeling of the Prophet's fear that rolled through me that day. The way they clutched their wound, painting the Earth with their red paint while blessing my ears with their blissful scream. Even now, I know they question why they were unable to fully heal, blatantly unaware of the power my blade can create on an entity like them.

They were born to create the Marked.

I was born to bring them down.

There is no greater purpose than that of saving mankind from its own demise.

The blonde, *Xavier*, whispers silently to Adam, putting fear in the man's mind, making the Official question his job choices. Tugging up on the hood of my robe, my silver hair remains braided, spanning down my front, begging to fly free from its constraint. Watching Andrew observe his old companion from the other side, a man with the last name of Markswood, the annoyance created within me by Xavier's ability to give Andrew a sudden lapse in memory is nothing short of frustrating.

"Just another thing for me to undo," I whisper coldly, biting my inner cheek to try and distract myself from the mindless thought pattern of exposing myself just to make the blonde twit feel a sliver of pain he and his dictator have unleashed on the Marked and Unfortunates under this ward.

Cocking his head as he watches his mindless mutts work through the crowds of dirtied Unfortunates, he stays still, observing the world as if he is invisible. So few know him to be the one running the show behind the scenes. The Prophet has appointed an Elder to be the face of this society, letting Xavier come and go as he pleases, pushing him to do whatever vile sins he is instructed to carry out.

Xavier is nothing more than another pawn for the Prophet to dictate.

Creeping closer toward the open clearings in Xavier's mind, I sense a lingering presence of dread, only surfacing in the moments he thinks he is truly alone. It consumes him, eating away at his every waking thought. A sense of loss clings to him. His family has been taken from him, one that he has spent a great deal of time trying to protect.

"So the Devil's pawns do have souls?" I question, inching closer to the wall, poking my head a little further out.

What could the Prophet have done to his family to get a Marked of this magnitude to submit? Unlike many of the other spineless puppets the Prophet has scouted out, this Marked is different. His energy courses through me every time I am near, begging me to get a little closer. I hear his strong heart beating quietly in my ears each time I allow my thoughts to quiet down. Even now, I should be running, hiding from the one person who has been able to sense me despite my efforts to stay concealed. I should be running for the hills, waiting until I have a way to kill this man before I get this close.

Instead, I watch him, wondering at what point I have pushed too far.

Watching the man run his hands along his throat, his thoughts of the Prophet's "rat" creep into my mind, reminding me of the true danger that lies in being this close to him. Wincing in pain, he shakes his head, trying to distract himself from the lesions swarming his skin.

His voice is bound.

"No wonder you are so adamant about finding me," I whisper, my mouth pulling into a sinister grin. "Yet, you continue to hunt me, blatantly unaware of who I am or what I am capable of," I scoff, humored by the ignorance *my* new Commander carries. "How foolish can one man be?"

I've heard the stories of what Xavier has done to those the Prophet deems a threat. Crushed skulls, broken bones, bodies with throats ripped clean from them. Those who question him lose their tongues, and those willing to listen to slander on his name lose their ears.

He's ruthless, begging to have the tip of my blade kiss his cold heart.

In many ways, I am supposed to be afraid of the man. He spends hours hunting me, hoping to get even a glimpse of the pest the Prophet fears so deeply. Perhaps he thinks I am a large man, one someone of his size could easily beat in combat. Or maybe he thinks I am a ghastly Shifter, something he deems as inferior.

Everything about this man is telling me to run.

So why is it I want to run my finger along his jaw and trace the most delicate features on his face?

His haunting beauty eats away at me.

How could someone with such a delicate grin conform to such wicked ways?

Lost in my train of thought, my focus diverts away from the man and to the ground. Keeping my head down, the hood conceals the parts of my face my mask fails too. Hearing the distant cries of Unfortunates lined up for public punishment, my mind diverges back to the goal at hand.

Find the Marked, save the innocent.

Snapping my head up, my body moves quicker than I can react. The blue-gold eyes, once patiently observing the wave of Unfortunates working in and out of the crowds, now barely get a glimpse of my searing golden gaze. Watching my hair barely keep up with my body, any reassurance that I moved before he could catch a glimpse of me quickly fizzled away the moment my hair flew free from its braid.

Pressing my body against the closest wall, my heart beats out of my chest, my body flooding with the adrenaline a single glance has created.

Unable to control my abilities, my veins flood with energy, the beat of my heart infuriatingly loud. Clutching my chest, I gasp for air, my body and mind consumed with emotions that are not my own. It shatters my focus, forcing me to run despite my need to Winnow away from all of this. Stumbling as I make a break for it, the brooding presence of his large figure takes away the light from the entrance of the alleyway.

Feeling the momentary lapse of dysregulation fade, I try to focus on finding a way out, facing the oncoming brick wall ready to make or break me. Keeping my head lowered, I hear his footsteps catch up, his need for Winnowing not needed in a vicinity this close to me. Ready to force him back with my Hold, I bare my teeth, reminded once more of the blood that paints this man's hands the moment he grabs my hood.

Yanking down my hood, his hand coils in my hair, stopping me dead in my tracks the moment the space around me begins to shift during my Winnow. Wincing as he tugs, his strength is undeniable, his body something even those with the strongest Hold would cower at. Feeling him control me with his grasp, he forces me backward and into the closest wall, shoving me as hard as he can into the solid brick barrier. Hitting the wall so hard it begins to crumble, I brace myself for what's to come, kicking into fight or flight mode with little hesitation.

Still struggling to focus in the presence of his swarming energy, I try to take a full breath. Moving away from the wall, he tugs once more, forcing me to keep my back to the wall. Shakily breathing, I close my eyes, forcing up my walls before he can make his way inside. Feeling my blood drip down my forehead, his grasp tightens, his hand forcing my head back to get a better look up at him.

Suffocated by the energy flooding through his veins, he breathes shakily, equally as caught off guard by the energy running down my face. Feeling the barriers solidify in my mind, he tries to find a way in, angered by the defiance brewing in my demeanor. Keeping my eyes shut, I release a shaky laugh, pleased by the low growl that exits his throat.

"Open your eyes, *rat*," he hisses, his voice low, kissed with a maturity that is years older than what he presents to be.

"Quite the nickname," I taunt with a grin, keeping my eyes closed as the cold metal of his blade runs beneath my shirt, begging to pierce my skin. Keeping my robe open, his free hand stays coiled in my hair, his body pressed against mine, stopping me from moving a muscle.

"Open your fucking eyes before I spill your guts in this alleyway," he warns, all playfulness void from his voice.

Trying to strategize my best way out of this, I can't help but acknowledge the thrill that encompasses me having him this close. Feeling his warmth radiate through my clothing, the chill of the blade becomes extremely tolerable. Once I have confirmed my mind is safe, my eyes begin to pry open, both of us flustered and stoic, his eyes widening the moment he sees my gaze up close. Unable to look away from his crystal blue irises scattered with gold flecks, I gulp, scolding myself for not immediately showing this man what kind of Marked he has backed into this wall. Clenching his jaw, he releases my hair, his hand pulling down the edge of my mask, exposing the devious smirk painting my expression in light of the red hue entering his cheeks.

"You're a woman," he whispers, his grasp on the blade loosening the longer he observes me.

Feeling the odd presence of something entirely unknown drawing me closer to his mind, I feel his confusion, as much as he feels my defiance. His mind is not an open playground, yet-

"You can get inside," he finishes, his finger touching my temple, coating in my blood. "As easily as I can get into yours," he finishes.

Startled, I feel around for the barriers in my mind, confused once I sense their presence. Unbothered and unscathed, they remain as prevalent as they had only moments ago.

"How the hell are you in my mind?" I question, my voice low and cold.

"I could ask you the same thing, love," he snaps, his voice kissed with an accent time has taken away from him.

Sheathing his blade, he leans closer, every single one of my instincts forcing me to reach for my own knife. Creeping closer to my side, his breath dances over my skin, warming my already hot cheeks.

His scent smells of pine and cinnamon, his bright canines flashing every time he pulls his mouth into a taunting grin.

"I was going to kill you," he whispers, his lips grazing the side of my face. Gathering my ear lobe between his teeth, he bites, chills rolling down my body at the feeling of his hands forcing themselves onto my hips. "Perhaps torture is a much more divine fate for you."

What am I doing? I could have this man begging on his knees for mercy in five seconds. Why am I allowing him to touch me like this?

Why does it feel this good to have his hands on me?

"Torture?" I question, feeling my lips pull into a wide grin. "You'll have to think of something more creative than that if you want to harm me."

Shoving him back with my Hold, my grasp on my abilities returns, allowing me to force him into the submission he so desperately wanted to inflict on me. Watching him slam into the wall behind him, I push away from the wall, cocking my head at his flustered demeanor.

"I will admit, this is the first time I have given one of the Prophet's minions enough time to even debate harming a hair on my head," I say, shaking my head in frustration.

"I'll kill you," he snaps, his hair in disarray from his large movements.

Moving toward me, he reaches out, ready to force me into the wall once more. Grabbing his wrist, I stop him, coaxing his body into a still position, my Hold far greater than his Call.

"You are an interesting specimen," I say gleefully, finally allowing my finger to trail down his jawline, feeling the warmth of his skin. Wincing away from the touch, I grab his face, forcing him to look at me as he had done to me. "You'll be seeing me. You are, after all, my Commander," I grin, watching his eyes widen with the heat of anger.

Trying to move, he thrashes, his face still settled in my hand.

"I found you once. I'll find you again," he barks, my throat releasing a joyous laugh.

"For your sake, I hope you're wrong," I mutter, releasing his jaw. Backing away, I keep my Hold latched to him, watching how he struggles to escape. "Next time you see me, I advise you not to hesitate if you want to harm me," I warn, facing away from the brooding Commander.

"You won't mind if I get a head start."

Winnowing before he can protest, the space around me dissipates, leaving the man to pry himself away from my Hold. Dissipating too quickly for him to keep up, I let my body melt into the transition away from this reality, settling into the imagery of my next point of destination.

Commander or not, that man is broken, fighting for a cause much deeper than politics or authority.

He has someone or something he cares for.

Something he loves.

Sadly, love is a weakness.

Perhaps that's why I've never entertained it.

CHAPTER ONE

XAVIER

Nothing prepares you for the silence that death brings.

It creeps in, infiltrating every moment of quiet you share with your thoughts, pulling you deeper into the spiral it has created and farther from the light in your life. Grief is inevitably the true marker of one's resilience in the presence of pain.

Some may sink, and some may swim.

There is no in-between.

In all my years walking this planet, I never thought the vile nature of what all Marked hold within their souls could suffocate the light within her. An empty shell of what once was roams this compound, begging to feel something other than the surface level of pain she has forced herself to remember.

The moment she killed Hunter, something within her shifted, something deeper than the pain that Fallan's death had brought on. She craved the power she felt and reveled in the fear that scorned every face surrounding her. In that moment, the power triumphed over the pain, creating a high within her mind that she had subconsciously been chasing. I feel it every time she allows me to be near her, even in moments she thinks I am no longer watching. She avoids what she used to find comfort in like the plague, isolating and grieving, surrounded by reminders of the man she loved and the urn that houses his ashes.

She was not able to say goodbye to Fallan.

She was not able to tell him how much she loved him.

Even worse, she was not able to get the answers from him she needed, and as much as I try to think of a way to give her the clarity she needs, I only add physical pain to the load of mental strain she already carries.

Forest Blackburn changed that day.

Something new infiltrated her soul, something that Elyon wanted her to feel.

Fear.

Fear of loss.

Fear of losing.

It's a mistake she has sworn to never make again.

It has been six months since the death of Fallan Markswood and all the others caught in the crossfire of Elyon's sick games.

Six months of silence.

Six months of grief.

Six months of lies.

If I'm not lying to Forest in the scarce moments she allows me to be near her or justifying her actions to her estranged friends who can hardly tolerate her, then I am lying to Kai, the one person still genuinely clueless as to who killed Hunter. Given the narcoleptic state Forest had managed to put her brother in before she went for the kill, Kai awoke in a med unit, shaken and inconsolable the moment he saw not only his mother's urn but Hunter's too. He cried so hard that I swore he would stop breathing once he let it all out. Once his eyes met mine, there was no way to explain to him why his sister had done what she did.

Hunter, Rae, and Jeremey were traitors, keeping information locked away from us. It's a concept I understand, one I would have implemented myself had I been in her position. Sadly, getting the others to understand that thought pattern has been nothing short of impossible.

Rocking on the legs of my chair, I hold the sketchbook between my legs, carefully dragging my brush across the canvas despite my utter lack of creativity. Teetering on the back two legs of the chair, I anticipate the moment my balance falters. Despite Forest's avoidance of me, I have tried to find some way to get the woman to acknowledge my presence. If forcing myself to partake in the one thing she has an interest in gives me a way in, perhaps it's worth the paint now staining the front of my shirt. Leisure days come once a week, and each week, I lock myself in this room, never finding the courage to see who or what Forest is doing. As far as I know, she's the farthest thing from comforting to be around, and lord knows I have very few ways of dealing with my frustrations toward her in a healthy manner.

Trying to make out the imagery decorating the paper, I do my best to get a mental picture of what it is I am trying to create.

"Evermoore, you decent?" Aaron's annoyingly optimistic voice yells, startling me enough to drag my brush across the canvas in an aggressive streak.

Watching the dark paint scorn any progress I could have made, disdain settles in my mind, making it that much harder to look pleased once the man invites himself in unannounced.

Swinging open the door, I toss the sketchbook at Aaron, watching his eyes widen as it smacks him in the chest.

"I didn't say you could come in. What if I was not decent?" I question, narrowing my eyes at the man.

Inviting himself to sprawl across my perfectly made bed, the ash from his uniform settles on the sheets, reminding me once more how much I hate the company of others.

"Good thing you weren't indecent," he mutters, making himself at home.

Holding back every urge to explore his mind after the comment, my curiosities surrounding why he chooses to spend time with me can remain to myself.

"I'm sure you wouldn't mind," I spit, forcing my chair back to the floor with a heave. Watching his body perk up, he pulls himself up, watching me with a wide-eyed expression I know is fueled by embarrassment.

"You know some people are able to look past your looks and realize how much of a jackass you are?" he says, pointing to me with a long finger as if I am not already aware of the effect I have on people.

"Says the man sprawled on my bed when he could be with his friends?" I question, shaking my head as I peer at my dirtied shirt.

"Every Sunday I come here, and every Sunday you act like I'm supposed to be someone else," he prods, once more trying to get me to speak about Forest.

"I'm not doing this with you again, Aaron," I warn, keeping my gaze on the ward outside.

"It's been six months, and you've yet to even try to get near her, let alone speak to anyone about the very apparent history you two have," Aaron mutters, doing his best to stay calm.

"Did you forget the part where, If I tell you anything too extensive, I am bound to the thought pattern of making sure your head is ripped clean from your body?" I question, watching him roll his eyes.

"I remember. The issue is I don't think you'd actually do it. Only one person I considered a friend ended up following through with something as gruesome as that."

Wincing at the mention of Forest's actions toward Hunter, I can't help but turn around.

"What would you have done?" I question, moving closer to the arrogant bastard.

Sitting up fully, his eyebrows rise with curiosity.

"What kind of questions is that? I would have forgiven-"

"No. Suppose you were in her shoes. If your mother lay dead at your feet and the man you love was killed before he could explain the pile of lies thrown onto you, knowing damn well it would not have happened had Hunter and the others stayed silent, what would you have done with that grief and the opportunity to avenge them?" I question, keeping my pace toward the man. □

"I wouldn't have killed Hunter," Aaron says, finally allowing himself to stand with as much anger as I have thrown onto him.

"Maybe that's true," I say, getting closer to the man. "The problem is, Aaron, you're weak. She wasn't. That's a reality none of you are willing to come to terms with," I snap, my face inches away from the freckled one before me.

Pulling his lip up in a grin, I feel my frustrations rise.

"All of that defense, you'd think she doesn't hate you."

"I'm not defending Forest," I warn, grabbing the front of the man's shirt. "I'm being realistic. If you start speaking like you have any advantage over her, then you are as good as dead. I can live with the hate she has given me. Can you live with the sorrow she has given you?"

Staying silent, he swallows slowly.

"I can live with the hate. How long can you hold onto a part of her that was once there?" Aaron questions, my chest pinging with pain at the comment. "Whether you like it or not, you allow me to come in here and speak to you as I do because you know deep down, without me, no one else could give two shits about you. Kai can play nice, and Valerie can tolerate you, but the one person you want to look you in the eyes has never been farther away."

Holding onto his shirt, I tug harder.

"You think I fear being alone?" I question, feeling the smile engulf my expression. "If that were the case, I would have driven myself to madness long ago."

Shoving him back, I wipe my sheets clean, taking the spot he had allowed himself to indulge in.

Resting my face in my hands, Aaron moves toward the sketchbook, tossing it on the bed.

"Says the man painting in hopes of getting a little closer to her," Aaron scoffs, the sketchbook open to one of my many hideous paintings. "You know, maybe, if you-"

"Six months," I mutter, keeping my head down.

"What?"

"For six months, I have tried to find a way to explain the truths that Elyon revealed, a way to justify all that I know. I have mapped out every scenario in my mind and only hit dead ends. She sees me as the reason Fallan is dead and the reason Elyon got to any of us in the first place. It doesn't matter what Elyon or anyone else said about Fallan; he is still dead, and he took her with him."

Laughing at my own comment, I shake my head.

Pulling my chair from the window closer, he finally settles into a more appropriate spot.

"Enlighten me on why that's funny," he says, crossing his arms angrily.

"He didn't take Forest with him when he died," I say, shaking my head with frustration. "He got rid of the parts of her that you knew to be real. The woman walking around this compound now is one I've seen before, one that I hardly could understand. You keep asking me why I care, why I even try," I say, staring the man down intently. "There was a time when I was as broken as her, and you know what she did?" I question, feeling the urge to hurt Aaron escalate.

"What did she do?"

Laughing in defeat, I ram my fist into the nearest wall, distracting myself with the endorphins of my pain.

"I can't fucking tell you, Aaron. I can't tell anyone anything that matters," I say, watching the skin of my knuckles come together, healing as quickly as it cut. Keeping her locked away from my feelings has been effortless, given the concrete barrier she has forced between us. If isolation is what she wanted, then she has sure as hell accomplished it.

"He's still in New Haven, you know?" Aaron questions, eyeing the streak of blood left on my wall from my outburst.

After Elyon's quick slip away from the madness he created, it took little to no time for him to comfortably slip his way past New Haven's wards, taking his rightful place as the Commander he so desperately tried to create. After years of running the show from behind the scenes, it would seem he was no longer satisfied with dictating from a safe distance.

"Why are you telling me this as if there is anything I can do?" I gripe, still confined by the bind controlling my every action like a ticking time bomb.

"You know she will go after him," Aaron says, rolling his fingers over his tired eyes.

Despite the fear that consumed the citizens of both compounds after the chaos that unfolded, New Hope and the Sanctuary managed to rebuild, forging stronger borders meant to keep Elyon and any of his resources out. Regardless of the pain she carried, Bekah took over Elyon's role, growing colder with each passing day. In a matter of hours, she lost her closest companion and mentor, both stolen from her for reasons beyond her control. If it weren't for the smile Valerie plasters on every time she sees the brute woman, I'd say all hope for happiness within her would have faded. She will never admit it, but I know the appreciation she has for the blonde runs much deeper than what the naked eye can see.

Regardless of the hate the people of this compound might have once harbored for me, it began to fade the moment Bekah decided to be civil toward me. After the rage Forest displayed, I went from enemy to ally in the blink of an eye.

Foolish bastards.

No amount of kindness they show me now will make me forget the way they treated me like an animal.

To our surprise, Bekah allowed us all to stay in the compound, promising to house Forest so long as one of us kept her in line and did what was needed to if she ever had a deadly outburst again. Everyone but her brother and I agreed to those terms without hesitation. Deep down, I know Bekah fears the cold stare I gave her in response to those terms.

The day everything went to hell, it took no time for Bekah to go back to the underground portion of the sector, alleviating all those souls trapped beneath the compound. Most of the bodies below us were rotting, dead weeks before we had the opportunity to find them. A few elders and some children remained, starved beyond recognition. The girl Kai and the others swore to have seen did not return, leaving us with an abundance of questions rather than answers. Thankfully, Bekah saw to it that our wristbands were removed, knowing now it was merely a way for Elyon to keep track of his energy supply.

"She isn't leaving this compound without being noticed," I say, sensing the rampant thoughts of yet another approaching body ready to disturb my peace.

"Because you've been able to keep such close tabs on her recently?" Aaron questions.

Sighing, the anger I might have had begins to fizzle away, replaced with the looming presence of unsettlement each time I think of Forest's coldness.

"I'm trying, Aaron. I'm trying to do better. I'm trying to be better so that she can finally look me in the eyes for more than five seconds. I won't ever tell you I am trying for any reason other than her, but please try to see I'm not against you," I say, watching the man's cold expression drop into something much more foreign.

"I don't come in here because I hate you, Xavier," Aaron states, shaking his head, his red locks falling in front of his eyes. "I come here because, after all the shit that happened, I really do consider you a friend."

Pausing, I can't help but scoff.

"Save yourself the trouble and find someone else."

Swinging open the door without announcement, the second body peers into the room, eyeing both of us with curiosity.

"Nyla?" I question, looking over the compound leader with a great deal of confusion.

"Bekah said you'd be in here. I was hoping to discuss a few of the defensive measures you had implemented in New Haven that I could carry out to my compound. We are nearly done rebuilding, but our ward is our final step, and the last thing I need is anyone from New Haven coming in and destroying it once again."

Avoiding my eye contact, she looks down at the floor.

"Is there a reason you aren't looking at him?" Aaron questions, sensing the tension from a mile away.

Grabbing my jacket, I put on the warmth, moving past the woman with little to no acknowledgment of her aversions.

"I slept with her daughter," I state, recalling one drunk-fueled night that caused me to stumble into their sector a few weeks ago. "Let's just say she wasn't a fan of how she looked afterward."

Glaring at me, her eyes finally meet mine. Covering his laugh, Aaron avoids the woman's searing gaze.

"She got what she wanted, love," I say, guiding the woman to follow me. "Now, are you going to walk with me, or did you just come here to disturb me?"

"Like I said, we have managed to figure out how to keep the wards up. The problem is we can't seem to create anything stronger than what New Haven already has. Even this compound has created some form of defense with the electricity in their borders," Nyla states, keeping her distance as the two of us walk.

"Our scientists utilized thermal radiation to automatically sense when to accelerate the ward's protective measures. It sounds like you need an extra step of defense before the problem is able to walk right in."

"Does that apply to whoreish men who lay hands on your daughter?" she questions, her temper hot.

"Was she complaining?" I question, looking down at the woman with raised brows.

"Well, no-"

"Then neither should you," I snap, watching her mouth snap shut.

"Excuse me!" Kaiden's familiar voice shouts, pushing past compound members in front of us, his walk filled with determination. Eyeing me with a wide gaze, he apologizes to each patron he pushes, only calming down once he is facing me. Barely acknowledging Nyla, he rocks on his feet, easing up a little more once Aaron finally decides to join the conversation after spending an uncomfortable amount of time alone in my room.

"What?" I question, watching the man fidget with his hands.

"Kaiden?" Aaron questions, now entirely focused on the conversation.

"What is it?" I push again, watching the man's eyes shift behind him.

Gulping, he grabs the sleeve of my wrist.

"I think it's better if I show you."

CHAPTER TWO

XAVIER

The redhead's fist comes down on her cat-like grin, busting her lip and cutting her cheek. Devouring the pain from each blow, Forest barely attempts to hold back Bekah, savoring the way Bekah's frustrations grow each time she manages to heal herself in a mere few seconds. Watching her blood paint the mat, Forest looks pleased each time the woman is able to deliver a blow that leaves any trace of injury. Raising her fist for a third time, I move closer to the glass, horrified by my first real look at the woman in what feels like months.

Her hair is bright, her face hollow, as if she hasn't been eating. Bruised and worn, her knuckles are raw from her combat training, and her arms are covered with bruises from places she has been grabbed too hard. Feeling the faint tether to our bond surge with energy, Forest's smile drops, her eyes quickly scanning the room. Using her disorientation, Bekah manages to hit the side of her face.

Pulling her brows in, a look of anger washes over her expression over the move she was not anticipating. Shoving Bekah off with a simple nudge of her head, the woman goes flying backward, Forest's eyes wide with rage. Healing the wounds along her face, the bruises on her body remain. Staring down at Bekah, she crouches down, her frustrations grow while the weight of our connection forces cracks in the barriers between us.

"She's been allowing Bekah to violate her face all morning, and I have no clue why," Kai says, flustered with adrenaline. "I don't know how much longer Forest can keep up this performance before Bekah starts trying to make her attacks more permanent," Kai says, watching his sister taunt the redhead, pushing her to get back up and finish what she has started.

Bekah's thoughts are rampant, each one more aggressive than the last. Too focused on pushing the woman to fight, it hasn't even occurred to Forest to glance up and find the source of her sudden disorientation.

"You psychotic bitch," Bekah's mind whispers, watching Forest with shock.

"What are you doing, Forest?" Aaron questions, fogging up the glass from how close he has chosen to watch.

"You need to intervene," Kai pleads, tugging me closer to the entryway door. Holding my ground, I yank my hand, narrowing my eyes at the woman's older brother.

"No, I don't," I smile, eyeing the door with curiosity. "In fact, I think I'll watch," I mutter, nudging my shoulder into its front.

Maybe now she will finally be forced to face me instead of cowering like a wounded animal.

She might have everyone in this compound fooled, convinced she is nothing but a stone-cold face.

Deep down, I know she has hidden a much deeper feeling, one she feels every time she faces me.

Confliction.

And it petrifies her.

Slipping my way into the training room, all the other Marked gawk at the sight of Forest and Bekah, silently placing bets on who will get the upper head. Smacking away Forest's hand to help her up, Bekah stands, forcing her fist forward and into Forest's jaw. Eating the hit as if it were nothing, Forest turns away, her hair covering her eyes as she pants heavily. Feeling the cracks continue to falter in her mind's stronghold, my chest feels heavy, her wave of depression suffocating me from the inside out. Watching Forest keep her head down, Bekah raises her hand, ready to deliver another blow.

Grabbing the woman's clenched hand without looking, Forest stops the red-head from getting a decent hit, squeezing her knuckles until the skin has turned white. Slowly pulling her head up from its slumped position, Forest's lip is painted with blood, her tongue licking the wound clean. Ever so slightly watching me from the corner of her eye, her anger festers, her hand squeezing harder.

"My turn?" Forest questions, Bekah's face pale with fear.

Like flipping a switch, Forest is on Bekah, moving quicker than anyone can react. Taking several steps back, the other Marked give the two women some space, allowing them to sprawl out across the floor, becoming a tangle of black-clad clothing. Slamming Bekah's head to the floor, Forest has her pinned, her hand digging into the woman's side as her legs force down her thighs. Keeping one hand in the woman's short hair, Forest watches her, patiently waiting for her to submit.

"For two hours, Bekah has been trying to get Forest in that position. It took Forest seconds," Valerie chimes in, her voice coarse as if she has been crying.

Leaning into her cousin's open arms, Aaron holds Valerie, urging me to stop Forest from continuing with her actions.

"This is how she lets it out, Aaron," Valerie mutters. "Whether I like it or not, this is the only way she knows how to cope."

Despite the anger Valerie holds for Forest, there is no denying the proof of our friend's betrayal. Pages upon pages of Hunter and Jeremey's intricate notes of our ins and outs were found in Elyon's study, giving the man direct access to the details of our day-to-day lives. Any question Elyon had was quickly answered by one of the two or solidified in passing by the woman Forest once considered one of her closest friends. No matter how we look at it, Hunter betrayed us. All who followed in his step were just as guilty in the eyes of Forest.

Still, some question whether or not Forest's reaction should be feared or admired.

In the silent moments after Forest's actions, she decided to shut me out, excluding me from the feelings she had managed to hide within the depths of her mind. Getting her to look me in the eyes has been impossible. After receiving Fallan's urn, there was no way to get her into the same space as me, let alone tolerate my choice to reside in the same compound that had, by some miracle, allowed her to stay too.

The countless questions she needed answered were locked away with her emotions.

Her mind is closed off, meant for her and only her.

I want nothing more than to tear down those barriers and find the true face of what really nestled in her soul the day she lost what she thought was everything.

"Mark is worried for her," Kai whispers, observing his sister with a confusion none of us have the courage to clarify.

Thankfully, Bekah agreed to let Mark take residency here, allowing him to enjoy what time he can of his elder years in this compound's version of retirement. Having lost so much family, Kai and Forest cling onto the man, guarding him with the protection they would have given to Kai's parents had they been given a chance to live. Jolie refused to leave New Haven before the new wards were established, hoping that eventually, Hunter would show face, easing her terrified mind. Kai and Mark tried to tell the woman the truth, begging her to follow Mark's lead.

Denial is sometimes much more comforting than reality.

As much of an advantage New Haven has received in Elyon's control, Mason still tries to get the upper hand, showing face every few weeks to speak separately to me and Forest about his plan of action. Talks with his people have begun. Their requirements to aid us in the liberation of New Haven are all reliant on Forest's willingness to trust their need to revert back to human is stronger than their fear of Elyon's control. Getting her to side with anyone has been daunting, causing Mason's visits to become less frequent.

So long as Elyon is in New Haven, we all have a reason to fight.

"Strike me down as many times as you'd like, Bekah," Forest taunts, pulling me away from my blank stare. "It won't bring Jeremey back," she warns, finally releasing her Hold over the woman.

Standing up to look her over, Bekah rolls onto her back. Her eyes are narrowed with rage.

"I could say the same about Fallan," Bekah snaps, only smiling once Forest's has faded.

Reaching toward her leg housing a blade, my body jolts at the aggression unfolding in front of me.

"You talk too damn much," Forest hisses, ready to test Bekah's reaction speed with the point of her blade.

Tugging my arm harder, Kai's eyes fill with emotion.

"Help her," he pleads, my jaw clenched in frustration.

"Kaiden," I beg. "I only make things worse."

No longer taking my sorry excuses to avoid the conversation I am about to have, he tugs more aggressively, forcing me forward with all the strength he has.

"Good thing there is no point in you trying to gain her favor."

If only he knew how wrong that statement is.

Say too much and force her into a spiral she can't come back from. Make her remember what she needs to and force us both into a state of pain that only ends with both of us six feet under.

One slip up, and the damage I create will be irreversible.

Tell her the truth and lose the only thing in this life I have cared for as much as the family I lost.

How the hell do I justify that?

Love is pain.

The love I have for her is deadly.

Perhaps a one-way pass to hell is worth the risk.

Moving quicker than I can think, I surge toward the woman, wrapping my hand around her shaky hand, forcing her blade back down into its sheath, feeling the warmth of her skin for the first time in what feels like a lifetime.

Finding myself between both women, her eyes meet mine, forced to look at nothing but me as those around us watching in disbelief. I put my hand on her wrist, her eyes narrow, her hand smacking my chest, trying to get me as far away as possible.

"Get the hell out of my way," she whispers coldly.

These are the first words she has said to me in months, yet I'd listen to them on repeat.

Forcing her hand off of her blade, I yank her closer, returning the anger she so desperately wants me to feel.

"Don't tell me what the fuck to do when you have done nothing but make selfish decisions for weeks," I warn, moving closer, taking in her familiar scent. "She has had enough," I clarify, scolding the woman as if she is a small child.

"She has had enough when I have deemed that to be true," Forest hisses, her energy surging to life in light of my presence. Regardless of her hate for the bond, there's no way to stop the feeling that floods both of our chests, forcing the blood in our veins to pump at a rapid speed. Without asking, I grab the back of her neck, tugging her closer, watching her wince at my brash movements.

"I have spent far too long allowing you to run your damn mouth and act like an entitled brat. Step the fuck back, Forest, or so help me god, I will make you," I warn, tugging the hair on the back of her head.

Laughing in my face, she smiles.

"You're right, Xavier," she utters in a tone meant to mock me. "She has had enough," her smile deepens. "But you haven't."

Winnowing back a few feet, she grabs my arm, forcing my hand free from her hair. Anticipating this reaction, I move forward, feeling her Hold consume me, forcing me to stay in place. Moving toward me, she reaches for her blade, her eyes lowered with drive. Ready to pounce on me as she did Bekah, my frustrations reach a tipping point, the hands of my mind driving into the walls of hers so hard, I feel a crack.

Got you.

Reaching out once she is close enough, I tug the waistline of her pants. Letting her blade clatter to the floor, I turn her around and drag her into my chest.

Wrapping my arm around her throat, I close her airways, slipping into the minor breach of her mind, filled to the brim with nothing but pain. Startled by my sudden entrance, the strength of our connection is impossible to shove down, leaving her pressed against me, her hands clawing at my arms. Feeding into my ability to distract her, I reach my hand beneath her shirt, feeling the skin of her mark, pressing firmly on her lower stomach, listening to her silent gasps.

"Did you forget I could get in?" I ask, holding her close to me as she keeps me in place.

"Did you forget how much I fucking hate you being this close to me?" she spits, gasping in between words.

"Maybe I wouldn't need to be this close if I wasn't always cleaning up the messes you leave in your path," I warn, pulling my mouth closer to her ear. Feeling her shudder beneath my touch, her hands resort to squeezing my arm, her airways beginning to falter. "Your mouth says one thing, Forest," I mutter, feeling the hair rise along her arms the moment she feels my lips beside her ear. "Your body is saying another. Do you want me gone, or have you been waiting for me to come in here and scold you for a while?" I question, no longer needing to break into her mind to feel the anxiety the question had created.

Forcing herself to face me, she raises her fist, aiming for my nose with a strong swing. Grabbing her wrist, I stop her, squeezing harder than usual to get her attention. Keeping one hand positioned under her shirt, my nails drag across her lower stomach, unable to keep up with her quick movements.

"Cut it out," I hiss, watching her hand shake in my grasp. "You're acting like a damn child." I hiss, observing the room filled with gawking eyes.

"Get the fuck out!" I yell, no longer offering anyone the opportunity to witness what might happen. Backing away, Bekah whistles, forcing the group out of the room and away from the show of power in front of them.

Keeping my eyes on her, she stays still, watching me with a look I can't quite decipher.

Trying to writhe away from my grasp once the room is clear, I squeeze harder, no longer mindful of the bruises surely tracking her skin. Shutting out her pain, a flood of enjoyment from the discomfort rolls through me, her mouth hiding a smile of pleasure.

"You fucking like when I hurt you?" I question in disbelief, dropping her wrist, finally feeling her Hold release. Taking a step back, she rubs her wrist, watching it heal while the other bruises on her body remain.

"I might have broken some bones a week back," she says, already mindful of my observance of her beaten figure. "The pain reminds me I still have a shroud of humanity."

"Is that the pile of shit you have been telling everyone else?" I question, watching her scowl at the statement. "You're being ridiculous."

Scoffing, she grabs her blade, sheathing it with a hefty shove.

"Trust me, I would have been much happier had things gone my way," she hisses. "You're not the one I wanted to be here."

Hit with a wave of pain at the comment, I remain cold, my mind racing to the feeling of relief I felt knowing Fallan was gone.

No matter what he was to Forest, he ensured the parts of me Forest knew would remain locked away.

They both did.

"Well, given that you are the one who gets to dictate who lives and who dies around here, I'm sure you'd love the opportunity to have a do-over," I say, crossing my arms as I watch her move toward the door. "Maybe Hunter would have gotten a second chance, and you wouldn't have to lie to Kai about what happened."

She stops, her head slowly craning back to me.

"I'm sorry, Forest. Did you get comfortable with people telling you what you wanted to hear?" I ask, her guilt seeping through the cracks.

"It should have been you."

I pause, my words caught in my throat.

Smiling at my reaction, she moves toward the door, forcing it wide open, barely acknowledging her brother patiently waiting on the other side.

"Not now, Kai," she warns, moving away from the man before he can even speak.

Stuck in place, the weight of her words hang over me, my mind past the point of taking in any more pain. Filled to my max with undeniable anger, I watch her move past the observatory window, her gray hair pulled back into a tight braid. Slowly approaching me, Kai moves closer, his gentle hand patting my shoulder, his ears far too useless to hear any of the truths that were laid out. Watching her sulk away, my jaw is taut, my hands clenched tightly.

"She'll come around. At least she did not Winnow away immediately. She needs time to grieve. She sure as hell gave me the time I needed to come to terms with Hunter."

This poor, clueless optimist.

There is no way I can stand here and force myself to carry out her lies.

Not now.

Guilt twists my stomach.

"I need a drink," I mutter, moving away from the man, my body fuming with an excessive need to drown my sorrow in a cheap bottle of whiskey and a compound tramp, forcing me to forget the woman I really want to be around.

Like it or not, she wants me this way.

She likes me this way.

Angry, unpredictable, vicious.

I no longer have the patience for self-control.

If she wants me to be her villain, fine.

I can be the fucking villain.

CHAPTER THREE

FOREST

I never thought I'd see the day flowers bloom once more, embracing the land in spots of color only seen during the warmest months of the year. Running my finger over one of the countless wildflowers surrounding me, the rich smell of lilies and pansies swarms my nose. Keeping my focus on their little dances in the wind, the smell overpowers the ash, the clouds considerably less dense as the year moves along. Taking in the mostly clean air, I sigh, keeping my legs tucked to my chest, my focus on anything but Mason.

Seated next to me, he wears a large robe, one meant to conceal his slowly shifting figure. Once large and inhumane, he now presents as tall as Kai, his body much more recognizable to that of a human rather than a ghastly creature. Still foreign in the face, his eyes are dreary, his skin sickly. With clawed hands and thick skin, he looks like a creature from a mythology textbook, his body rigid in every way it can possibly be.

Looking back to the ward of New Hope, only a few inches behind us, it's tempting to leave it all behind.

Ever since I started slipping Mason my blood, he has decided to keep our interactions more private. He does not want to burden either of us with the conversation it would take to explain our actions to Xavier. He values the man's respect tremendously, and I value my sanity. Both would be compromised if Xavier ever caught wind of mine and Mason's isolated conversations.

There's no way to be around Xavier without feeling everything all at once. I worry about what will happen if I am given the opportunity to truly be alone with him.

Will I kill him for what he did to Fallan? Or will I spit on the grave of the man I love and allow myself to feel the bond Xavier has led me to believe was far from false?

"What happened?" Mason questions, breaking my silent concentration.

After Xavier's blowup inside the training room, I felt absolutely defeated. All morning, I was able to stow away anyone Bekah threw at me, devouring the pain they delivered with open arms. The moment his hands were on me, all of my defenses came crashing down. My ability to block out my emotions faltered, and any face of strength I was able to uphold began to crack.

"I tried doing what you recommended," I say, touching my bruised arms. As much as I like helping Mason, the ability to convert a Shifter back to a human is not as simple as slipping them your blood. It takes a toll, draining you for hours, possibly even days, making it considerably harder to allow myself to heal. "I began utilizing an outlet for my pain."

"By getting into fights?" Mason questions, touching my neck with the point of his claw.

Flinching away, the pressure of Xavier's arm left bruises, ones I could only semi-heal.

"By releasing my anger in a few quarrels," I clarify, rubbing my throat. "Xavier is the only reason that is there."

"He pissed you off again then?" Mason questions, reading between the lines. "You'd think given how little you have chosen to interact with him, or anyone but me for that matter, you wouldn't have so much pent-up anger toward him."

Giving me a sideways expression, a question lingers on his tongue.

"Say it."

"Why do you talk to me anyway?" he questions, fully aware of the answer.

"Like it or not, you don't judge," I clarify, watching him roll his eyes.

"I do judge, Forest, just not in the ways most do. You like the fact I don't see you as a monster. You like it even more that I am one of the few men who can look at you without fantasizing about what you look like naked," he clarifies, urging me to shove him.

"You know, I'm starting to take that as an insult," I smile, watching him shake his head with a sharp tooth grin.

"You're not my type. I like a woman who isn't in love with two other men."

Snapping my mouth into a straight line, I stop laughing.

"I'm not in love with Xavier," I hiss, his eyes narrowing.

"As if you could remember. I don't know how many times I can go over this with you as subtly as I have. Your memories were locked away. Only you can unlock them. No one will be able to clarify anything until you have every part of your old self once more."

"And you assume some part of me that's locked away loves Xavier?" I hiss.

"I never said it was the part of you that's locked away that loves Xavier, Forest."

Staying silent, I bite my inner cheek.

"So, I was right in assuming Xavier is the reason you contacted me so suddenly? He did anger you?"

"When doesn't he?" I exclaim, tearing away the top of one of the hundreds of flowers. "And Kai's always hanging around, acting so accepting, fully unaware of what I did. It's impossible to look at him without seeing Hunter."

"Isn't that what you wanted?"

"No," I say, running my fingers along my eyes. "I never wanted to lie to Kai. I thought what I did was for the best."

Sighing, Mason's mangled hand lands on my leg, diverting my focus back to him.

"Have you ever stopped and asked yourself why you did it?" he questions, waiting for me to respond.

"Why I did what?" I question.

"Why you killed all of them?"

"Rae, Jeremey, and Hunter were all contributors to Fallan's death."

"Have you ever tried to ask Xavier about-"

"About what? The fact he knew Fallan was sent after me, or the fact Fallan clearly had as many lies as Xavier. My mother is dead, and Mark is hardly holding it together. It doesn't matter how much redemption Xavier seeks. He is the reason the Prophet was thrown into our lives."

Biting back his words, Mason shakes his head, letting the air consume itself with silence once again.

"Do you hate Xavier, Forest, or do you hate the way you feel when you're with him?" Mason asks, his question flooding my chest with a wave of unsettlement.

"I do hate the way I feel when I'm with him-"

"Because he brings you a comfort you could not find in Fallan, and you hate yourself for it."

Saying nothing, I try to find my best argument against the man's point. Staying silent, the frustration within me builds, my focus only on the field in front of me, the ability to contain my Hold dwindling.

Clenching my hands, the space in front of me uproots, dozens of flowers forced free from the ground, the grass sinking in as a divot forms in front of us. Shakily containing my energy, Mason scoots a few feet away, no longer willing to see how much more he can prod me on this conversation topic.

"Are you still getting the dreams?" Mason asks, fully aware of my escalating inability to control the damage I create in light of my rage.

Ever since Fallan's death, my mind has struggled to cope, forcing countless thoughts into my mind that only end in bloodshed. A power that once felt manageable now comes over me, threatening to destroy everything within its vicinity. Managing my emotions on my own has been hell. Trying to throw anyone else into the mix, especially Xavier, only makes my actions much more unpredictable.

Every night since Fallan's death, the same dream has come over me, painting my mind so clearly that I sometimes question if I am still asleep. Waking up outside a cabin, one made from the materials of the land, a roaring fire lights the windows of the quaint building, its front decorated with an array of potted plants and furnishings to make it feel like a home. A body of water settles in front of the home, its premise surrounded by the very pines Fallan spoke of seeing frost in the winter. Delusionally, I have made myself believe he sent me the imagery to sleep, to dream of a life we could have had.

A life that was stolen from us both.

Every night, I awake on the cold ground, and every night, I am torn away from the blissful peace before I can open the front door.

It has turned into torment.

Feeling the warmth radiate from the home, and seeing the shadows pass over the window.

My hand clasps the cold handle of the front door, always ready to embrace whatever lies on the other side, only to watch it all come crashing down.

When my eyes open, I face nothing but the cold, lonely dorm room, my body still huddled on my side of the bed, expecting to feel his warmth or feel his hands pull me closer.

More recently, I have found myself staring at the body of water in the dream, questioning whether or not jumping in, and taking a large breath might ease the suffering my mind has created.

"Every night," I mutter. "I almost miss having nightmares."

Looking over the destruction I had managed to make, Mason sighs.

"You need to let people in, Forest," he warns, touching my bruised arms. "You're destroying yourself and allowing it to happen."

No longer wanting to talk about me, I focus on the parts of his skin returning to the youthful fleshy color he once had.

"How are you feeling?" I question, grazing my fingers across his arm.

"You mean, how do I feel after allowing you to use me as your own personal science experiment?" he asks with a smirk, giving me the humor I so desperately need to hear.

"Why else would I ask?" I question sarcastically, giving the man a nudge.

"I feel the same," he sighs, pointing to his semi-human face. "Clearly less hard on the eyes," he smiles.

Despite having so many features of the creature, some aspects of his past facade have shown through. Once black sockets for eyes, now the starts of an iris form in their center, the color something rich and dark, flecked with a ring of gold. His hair has begun to grow back, sporting a head of brown, slightly curled hair, much similar to my brothers. Decorated with scars, his skin struggles to stow away the damage he has faced in his lifetime. Able to wear clothes, he can conceal most of his rugged identity with his robe and mask, moving more freely with each passing day.

"I can't keep avoiding Xavier every time I come to see you," Mason utters, avoiding my eyes as he speaks. "You seem to forget he was my only companion when New Haven decided using my kind against their will was a bright idea."

"I'm not asking you to avoid him."

"You and I both know that the moment he sees me walking on two legs again and standing at a normal height, he will come looking for you. It's clear your experiments have had a toll on you physically. When's the last time you had three solid meals?" Mason prods.

"Last time I checked, I don't need you lecturing me," I warn, shooting him a look he knows better than to question. "The only thing Xavier will do when he finds out we've been conversing is lecture me on how much 'wasted energy' I've expended trying to convert you."

"Forest?"

Whipping around, Mason and I are startled, both of us shooting to our feet as we observe the redhead in front of us. Eyeing down the both of us, he throws us a confused expression, keeping his focus on Mason.

"W- what the hell is going on?" Aaron questions, keeping his distance from Mason.

"I would say that's my queue, Blackburn," Mason smiles, Winnowing before I can get a word in.

Watching him dissipate, I silently utter my curses, letting my focus land on the man who has made it his priority to replace Fallan and Hunter with the Commander he used to consider his biggest threat. Whatever Aaron has to say to me, it is nothing more than regurgitated bullshit fed to him by my friends or Xavier.

"So now you're following me?" I question, moving past the man.

Grabbing my shirt, he stops me, giving me a solemn look.

"So, you *can* look me in the eyes?" I question, watching his brows furrow in frustration.

"I'm not here to argue with you, Forest. I'm here to make amends. Whether I like it or not, what you did is a decision none of us had the strength to make. If it wasn't you, it would have been Xavier. At least I can acknowledge the life those three would have lived here in light of their betrayal would have been just as miserable as the fate you delivered them," he says, dropping his hand. "Your brother is miserable without you, Forest. Everyone is. Kai has no one left other than Mark-"

"Then he is not alone," I hiss, moving past the man once more.

"Do you even care how much we have sacrificed?" he yells, getting as close to my face as he can. "Have you seen Mark? Like really seen him? He's suffering from withholding your secrets. We all are. Your brother holds onto the faith that you are healing when all you are doing is trying to find a way to refine your abilities in private so that you can what? Try to go after the Prophet? You're growing weaker every day, Forest-"

I can't contain it.

I can't keep it in.

"Don't you think I know that?" I yell, my eyes blazing with fire. Stepping back from me, I grab his shirt, keeping him within arm's length. "I'm not an idiot, Aaron. I am the reason we lost that day. I am the reason all of those we care about are gone. I thought I was strong enough to take on the Prophet. I thought I was three steps ahead of his plan when, in reality, he was three steps ahead of mine. I am the reason all of your lives have crumbled, and I am faced with that every fucking time I look you all in the eyes. My brother, my mother, my father, all of them would have fucking been fine had I never gone to your sector. And now, there's a whole other part of my life that I can't fucking remember without killing myself in the process! So yes, Aaron, I am weak. I'm weak in every possible way. I hate myself for what I did, and there's no way to fix it. You may think I am out here with Mason for my own self-gain, and maybe I am. But at least helping him is one kind thing I am able to do without destroying everything around me," I shudder, glancing at the patch of ruined ground behind me. "Or so I thought."

Silent, he drops his facade of anger, observing me with wide eyes.

"I didn't come here on behalf of anyone but myself, Forest. I came here as your friend. As angry and pissed off Valerie and I are about what you did, we understand. Regardless of what happened, you're shutting out the people who are still here, Xavier included. Every day, Elyon's whereabouts become more unknown inside New Haven, and we get no closer to bringing him down."

Reaching into his pocket, he pulls out a note, pressing it to my palm.

"Xavier has been holding onto this, waiting for you both to tolerate one another before giving it to you... it's from your mother," he says, shaking his head in disappointment. "I no longer have the patience to wait with him," he says, squeezing my hand to draw my focus away from the letter. "Do not let their deaths be in vain," he says, letting go of my hand. "So, grow the fuck up and be our Apparatus. We need a leader, Forest." Turning away, he moves in the direction he came from, his back facing me. "No more running."

Waiting until he has left, I grip the note, hesitantly opening its worn front. Finding a set of coordinates sprawled on a page, Xavier's familiar handwriting stands out, my eyes gravitating toward the message.

"The Shifters refugee coordinates?" I question silently, glancing farther down the paper, my eyes landing on her handwriting.

> *He put faith in me.*
> *Now, I put faith in both of you.*
> *Your mind is your greatest strength, Forest.*
> *Unlock the door and set yourself free.*
> *I love you.*
> *- Momma*

Blankly staring at the message, I pan back and forth between the handwriting, startled by the difference in ink. One is old, the other much newer. Keeping my breaths shallow, I carefully fold the letter, forcing it into my pocket before I can reflect too deeply.

Watching the sun kiss the sky in bright waves of red and burnt orange, the colors sprawl across the land, creating a hue of color the ash had blocked out for so long. Feeling the roll of hunger consume my stomach, I bite back the pain, no longer willing to entertain my spiral of thoughts without a sufficient meal in me.

"I'm so damn hungry," I whisper, my focus on the compound behind me.

No more running.

It is finally time to face the noise.

CHAPTER FOUR

XAVIER - THE DARK DAYS

Feeling her breath brush the back of my neck, all of my senses are on high alert, my mind struggling to focus on anything but the lifeless corpses of my parents at my feet. Questioning whether or not I am imagining her presence behind me, my body stiffens, my shoulders barely holding me up. A few more hours hanging like this, and there is no guarantee I can stow away the deadly effects sure to follow. Feeling every protective measure in my mind come crashing down, my mother's still eyes watch me, my heart beating out of my chest. Looking at my father's mangled heart, my stomach churns with nausea, my body shaking from shock.

I am the reason this happened.

I am the reason they ever came to New Haven in the first place.

Years of researching who and what I am, while I was off creating trouble of my own.

All the love they showed me, all the kindness they gave me, even when I didn't deserve it, and for what?

It was all for fucking nothing.

Tensing up at the feeling of a hand touching my scarred back, my body flinches away from the touch.

"I don't know how the hell you managed to communicate with my mind from so far away, but it looks like me looking further into it was in your best interest," she whispers, her voice finally registering.

The Prophet's rat.

The very woman they so desperately wanted to see in my mind.

The woman they killed my parents for.

This isn't the first time I have been near her, or even the fifth. After that interaction in the alleyway, she continued to watch me, telling me bits and pieces of her plan, keeping me within arm's reach, only letting me remember what she wanted. It became a game for her, and a puzzle for me. Who was this woman, and why did she seem to follow me everywhere I went? Each day feels like a hunt, one where I never get the upper hand. Even now, she taunts me, my mind and body able to bend at her will.

Time and time again, she would seek me out, trying to cover up her obsession with the Prophet with the facade of a woman trying to gain knowledge. Each time, I swore I would kill her, yet every time her smile would breach her lips, the energy flooding between us became enough to knock any man senseless.

She wears the face of an angel but hides the secrets of a devil. Frustrating is a generous word to describe the hold her presence has had over my mind.

It doesn't matter how much hate I harbor toward the woman.

The moment she is near me, I can't harm her.

It's impossible to make her bleed, no matter how many times I have fantasized about it.

It's infuriating.

Making her way from behind me, her mask is pulled up, her eyes wide at the horrific mess of bodies before me. Looking over the pain inflicted on my body, I see the horror lining her eyes, my body flinching away the moment her hands land on my face. Ready to snap at her, she keeps me still with her Hold, her eyes scanning my face repeatedly. Rolling her thumbs over my cheeks, her hand reaches behind my head, gently massaging the skin of my neck, easing my horrific thoughts.

"Stop moving, you're only going to make your wounds worse. Take some shallow breaths and listen to the sound of my voice. The more you panic, the worse it will get," she whispers, her voice calming.

She is soothing me.

"I wouldn't have concealed your memories of our interactions if it meant it led to this," she gasps, her thumbs continuing their roll over my cheeks. "I thought I was keeping you safe from the horrors that come with knowing who I am."

Settling into her touch, the warmth from her hands helps distract me from my pain. Focused on nothing but the golden flecks lining her rich green eyes, she watches me with genuine sorrow, looking at me as if I am a person worthy of sympathy.

"They are- they *were* my parents," I plead, my voice coarse from my screams. "The Prophet killed them because I couldn't tell them who you are," I grovel, biting back my emotion. "And I had to let it happen. I had no choice. Why did you do this?" I snap. "Why do the people I love keep dying?" I question, as if she can actually give me an answer.

Bringing in her brows, she looks hurt.

"I didn't know they had your parents, Xavier," she says. "It's a mistake I won't make again," she mutters, my shock too high to register inflicting any pain on her. "Let me help you."

Up close, she looks frail, as if I could snap her, even with my torn shoulders. In most scenarios, I would have to crane my neck down to speak to her, her figure meant to conceal the power within her.

Saying nothing, she squeezes the metal binds with her hands. Watching them break free, my body becomes dead weight the moment my arms are let loose. Screaming with pain, my arms are useless, my body slumping onto her much smaller one, her strength alone not enough to keep me up. Kneeling to the floor, we are both crouched, her body cradling my head close, my ear settled above her heart. Holding me like a small child, she rocks me back and forth, holding me with a firm grasp. Debating whether or not I can find her knife, the appeal of injuring her and yelling out to the Prophet is so enticing.

Does anything I do really matter now that everyone I love lies dead at my feet?

"Do that, and you'll forever question what fealty to me could have meant for you," she warns, already rooted in the depths of my thoughts. "I won't stop you from cutting me or shouting out to that demon. Know one thing, Evermoore: the life the Prophet has in store for you is a life of loyalty that only ends with your suffering."

"I am loyal to no one," I warn, baring my teeth toward the woman.

Hitting me with a smile that is impossible to look away from, she looks me over with thrill. Running her thumb along my lips, she gives me the opportunity to snap at her finger, something telling me she would find more pleasure in the action than she would pain.

"I'm counting on it."

Watching another body Winnow into the space, she remains calm, her hands still holding me upright. Taking a few blinks to register what I am seeing, the second body moves closer, our eyes locking as I finally process who is standing before me.

Andrew Blackburn.

Green eyes and all, he looks over the space, his eyes wide at the sight of my parents. Covering a gag, he shoves down his disgust, his eyes on the woman, impatiently tapping his foot. In this light, he looks far from naive. Sternly watching the woman, his eyes shift around the space, taking in as much as he possibly can.

"Was this their reaction to not getting a glimpse of you in his mind?" Andrew asks, shaking his head in disbelief. "Sick fucking bastard."

"I clearly underestimated their temper," she hisses, glaring at the man. "As much as they have underestimated mine."

"We don't have much time, Forest," Andrew whispers. "Get rid of the pest and let us be on our way. No more loose ends."

Forest.

Her name is Forest.

"Trust me, I'm aware. I wouldn't have found him so quickly if he wasn't so adamant about trying to follow me," she mutters, keeping her focus on me. "Do not tell me what to do with him. If your plan was to watch me sit here and carve his heart out, you will be very disappointed. Touch a hair on his head, and we will be having a very uncomfortable conversation," she warns.

Why is she doing this?

"How the hell are you in here?" I question Andrew, spitting up blood. Wiping my lip with her thumb, she ignores how dirtied I have made her. Casually raising her hand close to her mouth, she bites back the urge to lick her finger clean, her thoughts quietly circling my mind. "Your chip's code is active. The Prophet and I have been in your mind-"

"You forgot that the two of you tampered with one of my men," Forest says with a grin, remaining calm despite the chaos unfolding around her. "Wrong move on both of your parts," she says, moving closer, her nose brushing mine. "Perhaps it's a good thing I have a fascination with you."

Apparently, Andrew holds more weight to the woman than she is willing to let on.

Fully focusing on the weight of the situation, the blood from my parents wafts in my nose, my mouth stifling yet another gag as my limp arm attempts to reach for them. Stopping me from moving, I let out a groan, its sound echoing throughout the space. Forest's hand quickly lands over my mouth, stopping me from making more noise than I already have. Running her hand through my hair, she continues to be gentle.

"You're going to have to be quiet if you want to live," she warns, finally pulling on a face of determination. "Let me help you, Xavier," she says, begging for me to give her trust.

Trust is the last thing I can give anyone.

"He's injured. There's no way to transport him in this condition," Andrew warns, only addressing the woman. "Plus, I'm sure he'd love to deliver your head to the Prophet on a stick."

He is protective despite how much authority she seems to hold over him.

"I am aware," she mutters, looking over my injuries.

"You have the Prophet petrified," I gasp, blinking back the haze of my vision.

"That is just one of the things I make the Prophet feel," she smiles, pulling away from me to observe my beaten torso. "They are just as confused by my presence as you."

"The ligaments in his arms are torn," she mutters. "The cuts have begun to infect. His blood loss is eating away at his cognitive functionality."

"That sounds like a death wish waiting to happen," I mutter, glancing over to my parents. "How bad could that really be?" I question.

Listening to the distant echoes of footsteps, both Forest and Andrew narrow their eyes, both of them on high alert.

"There is no time to play doctor, Forest," Andrew scolds, his posture defensive.

"Do not scold me, Blackburn, as if you are my father," she hisses, keeping her focus on me. "We both know that is the last thing either of us needs right now."

Familiarity is all that surrounds the pair.

Despite the bickering the two partake in, she trusts Andrew, and he trusts her.

Had her hair been three shades darker, it would not have been hard to convince me the two were actually father and daughter.

Reaching toward the knife tucked away in her waistband, she moves it closer, my body anticipating yet another wound to add to the collection.

Pausing, she raises her brows at me, the knife hovering between us.

"I am many things, Xavier," she warns, sliding the sharpest edge over her palm, the smell of her blood flooding my senses with sweet ecstasy. "But a woman who harms manipulated souls is not one."

Raising her palm to my mouth in the same fashion as the Prophet, I flinch away, her blood pooling in the palm of her hand. Not forcing me to feed, she remains still.

"What are you doing?" I question, her hand moving closer once again.

"I am healing you if you allow me to," she says, keeping her gaze on mine. "Accept the offer or suffer the consequences. Either way, you're leaving here with me. I'd rather you do it in comfort rather than pain."

Without much effort, I slip into her mind, ready to sense the lie buried in her statement. Finding nothing but honest truths, I eye the blood, both of us watching each other with hesitance.

"Time's running out, Forest," Andrew says in a panic, the footsteps now much closer.

"I'm not the Prophet, Xavier," she pleads. "Let me help you."

Against all my better judgment, I move forward, landing my lips on the intoxicating gift she has provided. Feeling the strength of her blood consume me, she drags me closer, my arms slowly gaining motor function as I grab her waist, pulling her as close as she has me. Squeezing her side, her front brushes up against me, my hand grabbing her wrist, pressing her hand to my mouth. Not knowing what to do with her free hand, she lands it in my hair, gently massaging the back of my neck as I feed, her body so fragile in moments like these. Feeling the connection between us grow, her power becomes my own, my strengths flooding through her, both of our minds defenseless in the presence of one another. Letting her hand fall from my mouth, our eyes lock, an entirely new feeling surging through both of us. Our hearts are a beating mess.

"Can you feel that?" she questions, her voice barely a whisper.

Giving her no verbal response, all I can do is nod.

"What do you want from me?" I question, finding the strength to keep her held against me, voices finally latching to the sound of the oncoming footsteps.

Smiling as joyously as she did before, her lips curl, her focus on me and me alone.

"You, Xavier, are the Prophet's most treasured Commander. Not once have they clung on to one as they do you," she says, easily prying away my hand's forceful grasp. Leaning closer, her lips hover near my ear. "That makes you my leverage."

Pulling away, her tongue grazes the corner of my mouth, licking clean the remnants of her blood coating my skin. Startled by the action, the unknowns surrounding this woman grow, her eyes burning with a power she has only let me see the surface level of. Holding her hand up, she locks the doors, grinning at the sound of the Officials now pounding on the doors with loud shouts. Looking up at Andrew, he crouches down, his hands moving toward my parent's heads.

"What are you-"

"Bring them with us," she commands, bringing me to my feet. Tugging up her mask, she pulls up her hood, her arms wrapping around my neck, dragging me down to her eye level. "Time to go."

With no warning, the doors break open, the countless eyes of the Officials landing on the sight in front of them. Already in motion, Andrew has dissipated from the space, the bodies of my parents now gone, leaving nothing but puddles of blood. Pushing through the crowd, the Prophet's silver mask catches my eye, my body filling with adrenaline.

Pausing at the sight of Forest, she smiles at the figure, her eyes lowered with rage.

"Consequences," she whispers, looking at no one but the Prophet.

Winnowing before anyone can act, the room around me shifts, her body pressed to mine, both of us closing our eyes as the shouts of men trail off into the void of darkness. Keeping my hands on the woman, she stands on her toes to keep her hands around my neck, her grasp tightening as she continues to Winnow us. Hesitantly, I wrap my arms around her waist, forcing her up and onto my feet, giving her the leeway she needs to hold on tight. Feeling her head press into the crook of my neck, her smile moves across my skin, both of our bodies drained from exhaustion.

"I knew I liked you," she whispers, the space around us finally settling into something entirely new.

I want to protest.

I want to slam her to the ground and have her beg for mercy.

There's no explanation for what prompted my smile.

CHAPTER FIVE

FOREST

K eeping my hood up, the smell of rich meats permeates through the air, breaching my nose hairs in a satisfying wave of savory aromas. Feeling the grumble in my stomach, the urge to eat is quickly stowed away by the imagery of Fallan's beating heart, his eyes filling with the presence of death. Forcing my hands together, I squeeze hard enough to manage the shaky tremors bound to follow every time my mind wanders to that place. Keeping my head down, I keep my hair tucked in the jacket, making sure to follow my feet with my eyes as I walk. Silently moving through the hallways, I nudge shoulders with a few patrons, not taking the time to apologize or even acknowledge anyone standing in my way.

Moving through the main doorways that lead to the massive space, my eyes avert from the area Fallan took his final breaths, the floor still tinged from the bleach it took to rid the space of the sheer amount of blood. Continuing toward the large window nestled in the space next to my friend's table, a few catch a glimpse of my presence, quickly looking away the moment I decide to make eye contact. Raising my head the closer I get to my companions, their smiles begin to drop once we all make eye contact. Forcing on the familiar front of coldness, my flat expression grows cold, my hand prying away the hood that felt like an escape from judgment. Scanning the table, I catch myself looking around for Xavier, sensing no surge in our connection like I generally do when he is within the vicinity. Keeping a smile plastered on his face, Kai is thrilled to see me, making it that much harder to smile back, knowing damn well I am undeserving of his kindness.

Neglecting my friends has been a task I would not wish on anyone. After forcing myself to stay in this compound to refine my abilities, I started to realize just how hard it is to tolerate a space where the person you thought loved you has passed. For as much admiration I have for Fallan, I can't help but be angry with the list of questions he left me with, unable to be answered by anyone but Xavier, who can hardly speak without injuring both of us.

On top of my inability to deal with grief, I am left with the knowledge of the pain I have inflicted on all of them, forced to know that every time they are pulled into a dark place in their thoughts, I am the reason for that thought pattern to a certain extent. The want to treat my body with kindness dwindled quickly, making it easier to avoid dining and my friends entirely. My hunger for power has grown, making it impossibly hard not to slash the throats of every Marked who looks at me funny, taking as much of their energy as I like in the process.

It's a vile and sinister thought pattern. One I am far from proud of. All of our friends, though angry, try to convince me that what I am feeling is normal, as if I am not a monster they all fear will snap one day. It's exhausting to pretend I believe them; it's even more tiring to try and convince myself Xavier's brutal honesty is not what I need to hear. For every kind word they say to me, he tells me five unkind ones. His hatefulness is justified and needed.

It's the only way to keep him away.

The last thing I need is to try and explore what the true nature of our relationship really is.

I'm no idiot; I know we have a past with memories that have yet to resurface. I worry the more I push, the farther away from Fallan I become.

I'm not ready to know who the man was when he was not loving me.

Locking away the need to look for Xavier, I try and track another body in the crowd, suddenly reminded why I pushed myself to come here in the first place.

"Hey," I mutter, creeping closer to the table. Half expecting most of them to avoid eye contact, they awkwardly ask me to join them, regardless of the fact that it is the last thing they want to entertain.

"So, she does eat?" Kai questions happily, scooting away from Aaron, allowing me into the space between them.

Unlike all the other times, Aaron slides over, offering me the spot with no resistance. Giving me a small smile, Valerie eyes me as I sit down, prompting me to give her one of my own. Feeling foreign to the gesture, I touch my mouth, startled by the feeling suppressing those facial muscles for so long can create.

"Not used to what that feels like?" Valerie questions, gently nudging my foot beneath the table with a playful push. Sliding over a second plate of food, Kai smiles, letting his lips land on the side of my head with a sweet touch. Leaning into his body, his warmth is comforting, his curls longer than the last time I had been this close to him. Seeing the stubble lining his face, he looks much older, his age finally starting to show, transitioning him from a young-looking man to something much more similar to that of our father.

"I'm not used to much of anything anymore," I admit, poking at the pile of mashed potatoes with my fork, struggling to get the mush down my throat once it has landed in my mouth.

"Well," Valerie starts, the ice in her tone fading away. "I know Kai is glad you're here."

Easing up, she continues eating, finally lowering her rigid shoulders. Returning to her conversation with her cousin, I tune out their words, focusing on the pile of food before me.

"She looked you in the eyes," Kai says, smiling as he squeezes me. "That's progress," he beams gleefully.

Feeling the food churn in my stomach at his optimism, Valerie and Aaron casually glance up, both fully aware of how little I deserve his kindness. Trying to form the right words, I catch a whiff of bleach waft through the air, breaking past any pleasure I might have had from the meal in front of me. Glancing backward toward the warped wood, I begin to shake, his blood painting my eyes as it pooled on the ground. Envisioning the way his heart looked plastered on the floor, his sullen blue eyes came next; his dead expression of fear burned into my eyes.

This was a mistake.

Feeling the food threaten to make a return, I rapidly scan the room, pulling away from my brother's touch. Locking eyes with my reason for being here, I yank my hand away before anyone can try to grab it, moving farther away from the table. Grabbing my brother before he can follow me, Aaron urges Kai to stay sitting, his eyes fixated on the area of the room that sent me into a panic.

Turning around, I lock eyes with Aaron, unable to hide the look of anguish threatening to tear me apart. Finally piecing together the root of my avoidance, he says nothing. Forcing everyone to focus back on the conversation, he gives me a nod, letting me leave without another word. Pulling on my mask of strength, he waves me over, urging me away from central dining, and closer to the one thing that has brought me joy in light of the darkness seeping into my soul.

Still wearing his lab coat, his eyes shift, his hand pulling me toward an empty hallway. Listening to the clank of cups and plates, he jolts, clearly still unsettled by our interactions.

Keeping his hands tucked in his pockets, Jonah gulps, his head wet with sweat.

"You're late. You forced me to resort to searching through central dining to find you," I say, leaning into the wall closest to us. Clearly tired from his most recent shift, his heart beats rapidly, his thoughts of fear rolling through both of our minds.

"Do you have it?" I push, only feeling the fears in his mind escalate.

Tugging at his collar, he pulls his hands from his pockets, both clearly void of the one thing I need.

Blood.

For months, Jonah has been supplying me with a fix of Marked blood, allowing me the opportunity to push my abilities to the absolute limit regardless of how much real food I am consuming. I could eat one meal every three days, so long as I down a few ounces of the rich liquid a week. Initially, it was disgusting. Every time I let the liquid touch my tongue, all I could think about was Fallan. Eventually my abilities began to improve, making it that much easier to feed the fire burning within me. With this extra boost of motivation, forcing myself to go to central dining was no longer needed, giving me the opportunity to have seclusion from Xavier and anyone else trying to figure out what was working through my mind.

"Where is it?" I question, lowering my eyes with displeasure.

Gulping, the man takes a step back, still fearful from our interaction that day I awoke in his care all those months ago. He still guards his neck when I get too close, as if a syringe is the way I would choose to put him down this time.

"I did-"

"You did?" I ask, suddenly much more interested in the conversation. "Where did it go?"

His thoughts answer my question long before he can.

"Xavier said he'd hold your supply for you-"

Fighting back the urge to grab this man's neck, I settle on driving my fist into the concrete wall, letting it crack beneath my emotional Hold. Letting my violent tendencies melt away into the action, Jonah steps back, knowing better than to make a run for it. Pulling my hand away from the wall, I observe the tattered skin, watching it heal with amusement.

Xavier is angry at me, and he will make sure I know it. Dictating the route of my quick fix is only the first step. Next, he will torture me with it, ensuring I know how much control it has over me.

"Why would you do that?" I ask, keeping my tone neutral, watching the man's eyes shift from the wall, then back to me.

"He told me you know where to find him if you want it back," he sighs. "Between the two of you, I'd rather not see what he is capable of," he says, a scoff rolling free from my throat.

Moving forward, I stop him from taking another step back. Creeping closer, I fix the collar off his shirt, smiling up at him with a large grin. Suddenly much more fearful, reality sets in, my hands running down the man's chest. Moving closer to the side of his head, he shakes, my nose grazing his neck.

"Wrong move," I warn. "If you can't provide what you promised me, perhaps you can find another way to repay me." His face goes blank. "You are Marked, after all."

Grabbing his neck, I tug him forward, ready to take what I'd like from him. Reaching for my blade, my Call calms his mind, his ability to scream stifled by my hand's grasp.

Ready to slice his wrist in a non-lethal stroke, I feel a hand tug me back, forcing me to release my grasp on the man. Watching him gasp, I shake off the hand. Backing away, the doctor looks panicked, his eyes wide with surprise. Tucking my blade away, I watch the man with a lowered gaze.

"I'm done helping you and your blonde psychopath," Jonah exclaims, letting his panicked jog turn into a sprint. Turning on my feet, Aaron's angered expression faces me, his eyes shifting to the tattered wall.

"Ten minutes you are gone, and I find you threatening one of the doctors?" he questions, my eyes rolling.

"Technically, he is the one who stole my blood for Elyon. Why not let him repay that treason?" I question, looking around for the others.

"I walked over here for your brother. He was upset after you left. I happened to hear you when you decided to attack this wall. It's only me if that's why you are so paranoid," he mutters, crossing his arms.

"Walking Kai back to his dorm?" I ask, taunting the redhead. "A little too happy Hunter is gone, are we?" I ask, seeing the fleeting image of my brother tucked in some of Aaron's more safeguarded parts of his mind.

Growing red, his pale skin lights up, his annoyance rising.

"Don't turn this around on me, Forest. You're the one fucking feeding on people to avoid dealing with the fact Fallan is gone, and Xavier is still here. Like it or not, you have a past with Xavier, so you can either fucking deal with it, or move on like the rest of us."

Staying still, I try and think of a rebuttal.

Once again, my words continue to fail me.

"I use the blood to hone in my abilities," I sigh, letting the hate in my tone die down. "I can't go into central dining without seeing it all over again. I can't do anything without feeling pain. They won't let us bring food into the dorms, and as twisted as you think I might be, I can't look at Xavier because I *want* to be near him, not the other way around," I admit, hearing it aloud for the first time ever.

"How so?" Aaron pushes, easing up on his defensive position.

Sighing, I rub my eyes, trying to make sense of my thoughts.

"When I am away from him, I can only think of every reason I hate him—why Fallan hated him. It feels like I am upholding Fallan's livelihood, keeping my distance from the man who threw our lives into chaos, the man who made me lose Fallan."

"And when you're with him?"

"I can breathe," I shudder. "I can forget, for even a moment, what grief feels like. He sees past my bullshit, and I see past his. It's not admiration, or love, or anything close to it. It's survivor's guilt, something he and I both carry. I want to be near him, because he makes me forget Fallan's gone, and in some ways, I question if that is worse than feeling the pain."

Staying silent, the man watches me, his mouth downturned, his eyes filled with sorrow.

"Then be selfish," Aaron mutters. "Fallan would not want you to live this way. Hate Xavier so much that all you wish to do is scream in each other's faces. Let him feel your pain. Let it out, Forest, because no matter what you do, Xavier will still be there."

Confused by his defense of the man, I raise a brow.

"Well, someone had to keep him in line while you decided to spiral," Aaron smiles, his body moving closer as he whispers. "You drove the man to paint," Aaron says, my heart pinging with pain.

"He hates art," I say, shaking my head.

"Almost as much as he hates your avoidance. It's funny what desperation does to a man. It makes you rethink why Xavier did most things."

Letting his words settle, I take them in.

Touching the rings around my neck, the cool metal of the three rings brings me back to reality, forcing me away from the spiral that was sure to follow.

Three rings.

My mother, my father, and Fallan's mother, all settled above my heart.

"Just because you can forgive Xavier, does not mean I will," I say, watching the man shrug his shoulders.

"I don't expect you to, Forest," he smiles. "Besides, I think he has something that is yours. That jackass really does think he can dictate everyone still," he says jokingly, reminding me of my anger.

"Xavier is not in dining on Monday night," he says. "He retires early-"

"Convenient," I snap.

Scoffing, I turn away, eyeing the sign pointing toward the dormitory units.

"Out of our way!" Bekah's voice yells in a horrified command.

Turning to face her, the woman dictates her men, forcing them to make a barrier with their bodies, hiding the massive weight she now drags across the floor. Smelling the strong scent of smoke, the mangled mass is tarnished.

"Help me out, Danvers," she hisses, motioning Aaron over to help.

Moving before he can, I help her grab the mass, my stomach recoiling at the burnt and deformed boy in front of us. Stuck in a petrified state, the body is burnt beyond recognition, its skin still warm from the horrific torture. Clothes melted and jacket barely hanging on, we both pant, my hands sooted with a mix of ash and soiled skin. Giving up the labor-intensive method she has chosen to utilize, I force my Hold over the body, picking up on her thought pattern and the direction she wants to follow. Dragging the body closer to the communications room, Aaron holds open the door, giving me space as I navigate the body into the open room with a few twists of my hands. Hitting the floor with a thud, Bekah's men shut the door, guarding the outside of the room with rigid postures. Taking a moment to digest what lies in front of me, I shakily breathe.

"What the fuck is this?" I question.

Aaron avoids the body, doubling over with a gag.

"Is that one of our men?" he questions frantically, barely able to look at the body.

"One of our perimeter guards. One of our men found him once he went to alleviate his shift," Bekah mutters, glancing up at me with concern. "I think it's best you leave."

Baffled, I scoff at the notion, narrowing my eyes.

"Forgive me if I have no want to follow your lead," I hiss, watching her brows furrow.

"Forest, the last thing you need is to be here for this conversation-"

"Why?" I question. "Worried I might snap your neck?" I prod, her mind unable to hide the truth my statement carries.

"Unbelievable-"

"You have no authority here, Blackburn," she warns, her voice finally finding its valor.

Moving closer, I step over the man, my focus on the fearful redhead.

"Don't speak to me about authority when we know damn well where you've been slipping off to in the middle of the night to betray your duties as this compound's lead," I snap, fully aware of the late-night visits the woman takes to Valerie's quarters.

Snapping her mouth shut, she backs down.

"What happened to him?" Aaron questions.

"Isn't it obvious?" I start, nudging the body with my foot. "Our wards are electric; he got too close. He's new to the position," I start, glancing over to Bekah. "Right?" I finish, concerned by her lack of agreement.

"One of my men found this with the body," she whispers, too shaken by my comment to continue pushing me. □

Pulling a note from her pocket, I grab the paper, my eyes scanning its front.

The clock is ticking, Xavier.
The bloodshed has no end.□
First, I come for the innocent.
Then, I come for her.

Staring down the paper, the sound around me dissipates, my eyes hyper-focused on the sinister handwriting.

"Forest, what is it?" Aaron questions, my throat swallowing nothing.

Giving the door a quick glance, I move, shoving the note in my pocket.

He's still taunting us.

Even when we can't see him, he taunts us.

"I need to go," I whisper, reaching for the handle.

"Where are you going?" Bekah questions, the panic in her voice one she no longer has the energy to suppress.

"To find my damn Commander."

CHAPTER SIX

AARON

After several minutes of conversing, it was easy to conclude that leaving Forest to deal with Xavier on her own was in everyone's best interest. As sickening as it was to inhale the burnt flesh of our fallen comrade, intervening in the interaction that is bound to happen between the pair sounds considerably less desirable than dealing with my own emotions. After taking scans of the body and informing family members of the man's passing, Bekah had her men haul the body off to cremation, only adding to the pile of stress the woman carries daily.

Hesitantly joining me to return to dinner, we plant ourselves at the table, both of us an exhausted mess just waiting to implode. Pressing my head to the table's wood surface, I sigh, doing my best to force on a calm demeanor.

Staying calm has begun to feel like a foreign concept. For every moment of peace, I feel the inklings of fear and self-doubt seep in, making me question how long I may hold onto the things I love before it is all violently ripped away from me. For several months, I have questioned why I have found it so easy to accept Hunter's passing despite the grief it has brought Kai. Traitor or not, the man was one of my closest companions, someone I had the pleasure of getting through my worst years with. ☐

I can't help but feel relief every time I reflect on his absence.

Taking a seat next to Valerie, Bekah smiles at the blonde, being sure to hide the small squeeze of the woman's leg beneath the table. Even when I want to be angry at Forest over her assumptions, she is never far from wrong. The two have been careful about hiding their growing favor for one another, still as hesitant to explore the idea of a relationship as Kai was with Hunter. Looking over, I had expected to see Kai watching me, waiting for me to elaborate on my sudden exit. Nowhere to be seen, I force myself up into a seated position, glancing around the space for the curly-haired man.

That's odd, he normally always stays at the table.

"Were you off trying to see why she had yet another meltdown that could lead to someone's death?" Valerie questions, pulling my focus back to the table.

Cold as ice, the blonde holds her ground with her avoidance, twisting the knife in her displeasure toward Forest every time Kai is out of earshot. The brunette may be in pain, but he is one of the few whose emotions are still intact, leaving us the burden of safeguarding what light is left within him as best we can.

Eating silently, Bekah does not interject. I'm sure she is also curious as to why I was with Forest in the first place.

Following Forest was a risk, one that could have ended much differently. As much as I can acknowledge that she is a friend, I can equally acknowledge how much of a threat she really is. In some way, I think that's why I have had no issues growing closer to Xavier. The farther he strays away from Forest and isolates himself, the less grasp we have over her and her sometimes explosive actions.

"How long do you plan on icing her out?" I question, not wanting to explain how Forest has managed to keep her energy up with so few meals.

"Until she decides to tell Kaiden the truth about what happened to Hunter. I'm getting sick of carrying around that lie for her," Valerie grovels. "Do you know how hard it is to listen to him defend her when she has little to no shame in killing the man he loved?"

Once more, I feel annoyed by Valerie's hateful statement, unsure why I can't bite back my words when it comes to defending Forest's actions.

"Last time I checked, Hunter betrayed us," I snap, watching her mouth pull into a deeper frown. "Hunter turned his back on all of us, and we lost Fallan's life because of it. Whether Fallan was truly who he said he was, or a man seeking revenge, at the end of the day, he loved all of us, Forest included, and he died unable to defend any of his actions. Now, all we have left is Xavier, and his inability to give us any information that is worth a damn," I hiss, snapping at my cousin furiously.

Looking to Bekah for support, the woman does not budge.

Given Valerie's expression, I'm sure there will be consequences to that avoidance later.

"Hunter and the others were funneling information to Elyon behind all of our backs. I would have preferred a trial, but in light of her grief, I can't say I don't understand her actions," Bekah says, looking defeated once the blonde scoots herself a few inches away.

"Someone in the med unit told me she's been sneaking vials of Marked blood," Valerie says, finally urging Bekah to look up at me.

Shifting uncomfortably, I avoid her gaze.

The woman may be love-struck, but foolish is the last thing I would ever associate with her.

"Do you have proof?" I question, ready to drag my cousin across the floor for pushing me as much as she has.

"I don't need proof. She eats maybe one meal a day, and her strength is still unreal. She is fully capable of manipulating someone into feeding her fix," Valerie states.

The link between Marked longevity and blood consumption was off-putting initially. As Xavier's blonde hair faded to its natural gray, the longer he left it undyed, the more questions he allowed me to ask. He took no pride in anything he had to say. The blood he consumed came with the cost of life. Lives he had taken for himself.

Initially, I thought spending time with the man would make it easier to see that he was anything but human.

Imagine my surprise when it did the exact opposite.

"Now I'm going to have to lock down my med unit's blood supply," Bekah hisses, clearly unaware of the goods Forest was receiving from one of her doctors.

"The person who told me put their life on the line to leak that information. Perhaps it's best to keep it between us three for now," Valerie says, now the one landing her hand on the woman's leg.

That was a short dry spell.

"She's been running her own experiments on Mason as well. A few of my men have caught them conversing at our border, only they are beginning to no longer struggle to see the differences between Mason and a Shifter. It would seem Elyon was not wrong about her ability to convert the Shifters," Bekah says, clearly pissed off enough to spew any information on the woman she has.

As off-putting as Mason initially was, he became a great resource to get to know his kind. Scarred by the abuse his kind receives under the ward, talks of peace between the compound and the Shifters have been difficult. Mark had managed to make his way into their home with Katiana, but since then, the Shifter's security measures have gone up, giving no one enough time to explain their reasoning for stepping on their grounds before being torn apart. If what Bekah is saying is true,

Mason's transition only makes him that much more of an outsider, leaving us fewer resources than we started with.

"That's a good thing!" Kai blurts, moving closer to the table with a dessert, cheery and optimistic as usual.

Everyone grows silent.

It's almost sickening how much the world has taken from a soul like his.

Taking a seat next to me, he smiles, clearly aware of his sudden entrance into the conversation. Trying not to question everyone's sudden silence, he slides a plate of sweets before all of us, serving himself the smallest piece.

Squeezing my own leg, my heart twists in the presence of his kindness. Why couldn't Forest have let him stay the boy from behind the shops, the one filled with nothing but an urge to complete his Judgement Day?

"The closer she is to converting the Shifters, the closer we are to having a whole new group of allies willing to take Elyon down," Kai says, all of us quiet about degrading his sister in front of him.

Or is she his sister?

He knows all the truths that Elyon laid out, festering within Forest's mind like a poison. In some ways, the denial we all choose to hold onto is considerably better than facing the truth.

"Do we have any leads on what could harm Elyon?" I ask Bekah, still as shaken as she is in light of what we both just saw.

That man was almost beyond recognition, having no part in any of this.

Innocent or not, Elyon has no empathy.

"Not much. Mason has tried to give me what information he can, but we are still reaching dead ends. We only have one lead, but the chances of it going anywhere are slim," Bekah says, now fully leaned over the tabletop.

"Well, what do we have to work with?" I question.

"There is talk of waters older than New Haven or any of the sanctuaries. If whispers prove to be true, the water is years older than the new world, but traces of Marked DNA linger in the water. I'd say a body of water containing remnants of something older than society itself is worth exploring." Reaching into her pocket, she pulls out a paper. "The problem is no one has been able to find it. It's settled deep within the unmanaged parts of the thicket outside of the Sanctuary. The trails are rigid, and the forest can be cruel once night falls."

Handing me the set of coordinates, I look them over before tucking them away.

"Maybe I can go check it out with you," Kai says, softly smiling at me. "I haven't been outside this compound in weeks."

Just as avoidant as his sister, Kai has kept his social interactions minimal, only speaking to Valerie or me in passing. Checking on Kai as much as he can, Xavier spends the most time with the man, reassuring him that his sister will one day be in a place where she can look Kai in the eye.

"I see no issue with that," Bekah intervenes, clearly just as tired as the rest of us about keeping Forest's secret.

Smiling back, I sigh.

"So, we are looking for-"

"Reflecting pools," Bekah states. "Supposedly, the water Elyon's gifts originated from."

Shaking my head, I add the body of water to the never-ending list of shit I have to deal with. No longer hungry, I nudge away my food, watching Kai pile his dessert into his cheeks.

"It's a win-win, really," Kai says, smiling gleefully. "Either we find the Prophet's creepy bathwater, or we can utilize it for ourselves and enjoy a dip in some water that hasn't been filtered nine times over," he says, once more remaining optimistic.

Wishing now more than ever I could rant to Xavier about my escalating frustrations, I bite my tongue, easing Kai with yet another smile.

Letting him enjoy his meal, I dread the journey with him I can't avoid.

How the hell am I going to keep Forest's secret from him when it's the one thing that might bring him some clarity?

Could I be any more selfish?

"I spoke to Xavier today," Kai mutters, speaking after everyone has returned to their private conversations.

Looking his way, I raise my brows, curious about what the pair could have spoken about.

"Did he give you the cold shoulder too?" I question with a laugh, shaking my head with frustration.

"He notices things about her I never thought twice about," Kai says, his eyes gravitating toward the large window.

Focused on the conversation, I scoot a tad closer, giving Kai the opportunity to keep his voice as silent as he'd like.

"Like what?" I question, finally getting the man to speak about something other than his forced optimism.

"He pointed out that every time she admits a truth to herself that she does not want to hear, her cheeks go so red that it travels to her nose. When I tried to rebuttal him, he told me I do the very same thing." Kai smiles, my own grin creeping along my lips.

"What caused a conversation about you and your sister's deep-rooted psyche?" I ask, resting my head on my propped-up hand.

"I suppose, I wanted to know how to read my sister better, and..."

He trails off, poking at his food.

"And?" I push.

"Why have you been so nice to me?" Kai questions, my words catching in my throat.

Looking around, half expecting someone to be watching us, I tug on my collar, meeting Kai's stern expression.

"You lost someone-"

"Before everything, all that time ago, when Hunter was hanging that man in my face, you went the extra mile to be kind to me, throwing yourself into a scenario that would make anyone uncomfortable. Why are you being so kind to me?" he questions, a wave of self-doubt circling the question.

Saying nothing, I narrow my eyes, wondering where the punchline is to his question.

"Because I care about you?" I say, looking around the table. "I care about all of you."

Saying nothing, his eyes drop to his plate, his hands fidgeting with his sleeves.

"Hunter cared about me. He loved me, yet he still hurt me. I'm not asking you this to validate me; I'm asking you this to reassure me. Are you being kind to me because you want to, or because you feel sorry for me?" he questions, his pain finally breaching the surface of his facade.

Unsure of what to say, I look over the man, wondering what has prompted my hand to move.

Touching his leg, his body flinches, my hand staying in place. Looking down at my hand, his hazy eyes dart to me, his lips parted, ready to ask a string of questions that can't seem to leave him.

"If you're asking me if I am being kind to you for an alternative motive, Kai, I'm not," I say, pulling my hand away as quickly as it had arrived. "Nothing I've said or done with you has been for show."

Looking down at my plate, I let the realization settle between us.

"When you were trying to make Hunter jealous-"

"Even then, Kai," I say without thinking. "I don't do things unless I want to. Like it or not, I'm not Hunter," I say without thinking, both Valerie and Bekah's eyes on us.

Feeling my cheeks fill with heat, I ready myself to walk away from this conversation, too embarrassed to find a good enough justification for anything I have said. Turning my legs away to swing them over the bench, Kai touches my back, his gentle eyes watching me like a hawk.

"Your face," Kai says, his finger gently grazing my cheek before quickly pulling away. "Your cheeks and nose are red, " Kai mutters. My hands run along the surface of my skin, feeling the lingering effect of my truths.

Focusing back on his food, his eyes avoid mine, his shoulders much more rigid.

"I wasn't asking Xavier about my sister," the man whispers, clarity washing over me.

"Why would you ask Xavier about me?" I question, his hand rolling over his eyes.

"I was trying to figure that out myself." His legs swing over the bench, his hands grabbing his tray of food. "You're not the only one with internal conflict."

Saying nothing else, the man tosses his items into a bin, lowering his head as he walks, completely avoiding any eye contact. Hearing a scoff, I glance at my cousin, ready to hear her snide remark.

"What?" I bark, her fork snapping up toward me, pointing with raised brows.

"First time in your life you have feelings for someone," she says, shaking her head. "And it happens to be your dead best friend's boyfriend. No wonder you didn't shed a tear for Hunter."

What the hell have my feelings gotten me into?

CHAPTER SEVEN

FOREST

Standing in front of Xavier's door, I tap my foot, debating how angry I should be when interrogating him about his fixation on intervening in my life. Feeling the note from Elyon crumple each time I move, the internal debate about prioritizing giving Xavier vital information over yelling about his meddling is insufferable. Pressing my head to the metal door, I try to suppress my anger, debating whether or not turning around might be in everyone's best interest.

Ever since Fallan's death, I have barely allowed either of us the chance to have a conversation, let alone deep dive into the relationship Fallan clearly shared with Elyon's daughter. Every interaction I have with the man is confusing, forcing me to face truths I can barely process on a good day.

I know how this conversation will go.

He will be pissed about what I said in the training room, and I will be pissed about his intervening with my blood supply. The conversation will only end in an argument, and the feelings that implode after that will make it impossible to get anywhere even remotely productive.

"This was a terrible idea," I whisper, pushing away from the door.

Stopped by the sound of quiet gasps on the other side of the door, I focus on the noise, unable to decipher what is going on. Carefully creeping closer to the handle of the door, the gasps grow more pained, the heartbeat of whoever is making the noise painfully loud in my ears. Feeling a mix of pleasure and anger roll through mine and Xavier's connection, I feel flustered, my hands shaking with adrenaline.

I'm going to regret this.

Undoing the locks of his door with my Hold, I quietly slip into the poorly lit room, unable to adjust quickly to the light the candles provide. Silently shutting the door, I smell the familiar scents of his space, unsettled by the presence of something new lingering in my nose. Blinking back the darkness consuming the space, I sense another body in my presence, its heart so loud, it's hard to think straight.

Hearing their breathy gasp once more, my eyes gravitate to the bed, my eyes finally focusing as I startle myself backward at the sight in front of me.

Bound to Xavier's bedframe with paracord, the woman gasps in pain, her chest rising and falling rapidly, any mobility stolen in the entrapping knots holding still her wrists and ankles. Coated in new bruises moving down her sides, legs, and breasts, her body is mangled, her blood void of the energy a Marked might carry. Slicked back into a tight ponytail, her brown hair is a mess, her lips parted as a giddy smile paints her expression. Watching her legs shake, her undergarments are lazily thrown on, her makeup smeared down her cheeks, her eyes covered by a satin black mask. Moving herself up, she rests her back against the headboard, her bra straps falling down her arms. Not sensing his energy, I creep closer.

So, this is the outlet for Xavier's anger.

Fucking women into submission.

Focused on the sheer amount of vulnerability he has forced onto the woman, my stomach fills with heat, my cheeks growing flustered at my body's reaction to seeing something like this. Looking over the woman, I can't help but feel annoyance at her presence in the space, my hand gripping my temple, forcing down the hateful thoughts toward the woman.

He used his Call.

This isn't something a woman would willingly want.

"Jesus Christ," I whisper, biting my bottom lip.

"Xavier?" the woman questions, her voice dripping with anticipation. "I'm not done letting you play with me," she smiles, prodding the fire to my annoyance once again.

Fuck this, time to give her back her free will.

Moving forward, I prepare myself to rip off the woman's mask, easily stepping into her mind. Flustered, I find no sign of his Call anywhere. Every thought pattern inside of her mind leads to a conclusion she willingly reached on her own.

She wanted this.

She wanted him to do this.

Feeling his large hand grab my wrist, I pause, too lost in my train of thought to entirely focus on what was around me. Stopping me before I can remove her mask, our connection suffocates me, his feelings of pleasure and rage jumbling in my mind. Tugging me toward him, I brace myself against his bare torso, his pants just as lazily thrown on as her clothes, his sweats loosely hanging on his hips. Feeling my free hand land on his scarred front, I glance up at him, his eyes burning with rage at my sudden intrusion.

"What the fuck are you doing in my room?" he questions coldly, his hand squeezing tighter.

Prying back his fingers with my Hold, I shove him back, giving the woman a wide-eyed look.

"Apparently, I'm stopping you from murdering her," I hiss, fully aware of the bloodied streaks along her inner thighs.

"Xavier," the woman pouts. "Who is that?"

"Forest," he warns, grabbing my shirt as he begins to escort me out. "Get out of my fucking room-"

Shoving him away again, I hold him back with my Hold, tearing off the woman's mask. Looking bewildered at first, her eyes adjust, her face dropping to a look of disappointment.

"Oh, it's you," she mutters with disgust, looking past me and smiling at Xavier. "Xavier, take these binds off and kick out the compound murderer so I can finish you off myself-"

This fucking bitch.

Using my Hold to tear away her ankle restraints, I grab the cord around her wrists mid-sentence, yanking it free from the bed frame with little to no resistance. Wrapping my hand around her ponytail, I drag her off of the bed, watching her stumble to get her footing with her shaking legs. Trying to swat me away, I glare at her with my burning gaze, watching the woman easily submit as I toss her into Xavier. Letting go of my Hold on the man, I cross my arms, cocking my head at the sight of them.

"Go ahead and finish him off," I snap, tearing off my coat and tossing it on the nearest chair. "I'm not leaving until I've had a conversation with him."

Lowering my eyes at Xavier, he has full access to my mind, utterly aware of what I will do to her if she chooses to piss me off again.

"Xavier, maybe we should just-"

Silencing the woman by grabbing her neck, his focus stays on me, his hand squeezing her throat, stopping her words.

"Stop saying my name." Grabbing her clothes, he tosses them at her.

Lab coat and scrubs.

So that's how you weaseled your way into my supply.

"Get the hell out of my room. I'm done with you," he warns, shoving the woman away from him.

Simply nodding, she lowers her head, unwilling to look at either of us right now. Standing still, she pulls on her lab coat, concealing her mangled body as she moves past us. Mistakenly looking up at me, I hold her focus.

"Speak to me that way again, and you will find out why they call me a murderer," I warn, motivating her to leave the space as quickly as possible. Slamming the door shut, Xavier clenches his jaw, tearing his sheets away from his bed and putting them into the laundry basket.

"I see you are handling your anger well," I scoff, looking over the nail marks plastered across his back. Turning around, he moves closer, his voice low and cold.

"As well as you are," he hisses, fighting every urge to grab me and force away my defiance toward him. "Not all of us partake in an endless blood supply from the med units to avoid facing reality," he barks, the muscles of his front prominent in this lighting.

"I see. So you fuck her into submission to make yourself feel powerful? Is that right?" I question, hearing the scoff roll off of his throat.

"Better than snapping her neck," he hisses, digging where it hurts.

Glancing at the ripped binds hanging from his bed frame, conflict stirs in my stomach at the sight.

"Want a go?" he questions, catching me off guard.

"And share a bed with you and every other woman you've been dragging in here? No, thank you." I gag, listening to him laugh at the comment.

"Don't worry, you wouldn't be able to handle it," Xavier gripes, crossing his arms as he watches me. "Fallan conditioned you to accept gentle touch in the bedroom."

Filling with anger at the mention of his name, I move forward, getting in the man's face. Holding myself up on my toes, I point my finger in his chest.

"Don't say his name-"

"As if you know him!" Xavier snaps, leaning in closer. "I see your ability to lie to yourself has not faltered."

Stepping aside, he moves away from me, finally pulling on a shirt.

"I'm sorry I scared off your way to finish," I scoff, watching his canines gleam as he pulls his lips into a smirk.

"Don't worry, the night is young. My hand will do just fine," Xavier says with a grin, forcing yet another wave of heat through my cheeks.

"You are supposed to be at dinner right now," Xavier says, acting as if what I walked in on is not something he wanted me to see.

"Right, thank you for the insight."

"You've been avoiding it."

"If I wanted someone nagging in my ear about it, I would be spending free time with my brother."

Without warning, he moves closer, lifting up my shirt with little to no care about asking. Unable to stop himself from looking away from my body, I feel the chill of his room, his eyes slightly widening at the sight. Moving me backward, I stumble, feeling his hand shove my torso down, my back meeting his mattress. Dragging my shirt farther up, he grabs my wrists with his hand, forcing them above my head as his free hand travels down my side, dragging his fingers over every prominent rib.

"Look at it, Forest," he warns, my eyes still avoidant. Grabbing my chin, he gets me to look down, my skin covered in bruises along my sides every place I have been hit. Letting his hand continue his soft touches, he keeps my legs pinned, my energy too low to fight him on this. Had I gotten my fix, perhaps the position I have myself in would be much different. "You haven't been eating," he states.

"Haven't been eating food," I gripe, unsettled by how comforting the warmth of his hands is. Putting more pressure on my wrists, he leans closer.

"I could do whatever I want to you right now, all because you are being too childish to care for yourself," he whispers. "What if it wasn't me holding you down like this? What if someone wanted to hurt you, and you were too weak to stop them from touching you as I am now?"

"How do I know you won't hurt me? You are clearly willing to do it to others," I snap, recalling the woman in here moments ago.

"That was not pain, Forest," he mutters, moving his head away from my face, his nose trailing down my stomach. Releasing my wrists, I lean upward, his knees on the ground as he drags me closer by the loops of my pants.

I could push him away with my Hold.

I could slap him across his face.

Feeling the warmth settle between my legs, I shake my head, angered by the way my body reacts around him. Stopping his exploration above my belly button, his lips touch the skin, gently kissing before pulling away.

"It was pleasure," he clarifies, rising to his feet. "Clearly something you need, given what you just allowed me to do," he says, my body begging me to ease the warmth escalating between my legs.

Observing how easily he got me to submit to his touch, I force myself up and away from the bed, moving past him with anger.

"I didn't come here to have you play doctor with me," I snap, my cheeks crimson with embarrassment and shame.

"Then why are you here? Other than to ruin my fun," he questions.

Moving toward my jacket, I grab Elyon's note, tossing it in his direction. Feeling the lingering touch of his kiss along my front, the cold metal of Fallan's ring pressed against my chest feels like a hot prod.

How disappointed would he be with me right now?

"Elyon is killing our men and sending the bodies back to us. It is a warning for you and me," I say, watching him observe the note.

"When did you get this?" he questions, my focus no longer on the blood he stole from me.

Perhaps he's right.

Perhaps it's time to face reality.

"Bekah got it moments ago," I say, finally looking him in the eyes. "There's more."

Keeping his interest, he takes a seat, watching me with complete focus.

"I overheard a conversation Bekah was having with Aaron and Kai."

His interest escalates.

"They have a lead."

Chapter Eight

Xavier- The Dark Days

The crackle of a roaring fire fills my ears, my face flooding with warmth. Feeling the cold ground beneath my aching body, I keep my eyes shut, unsure if I ever want to open them again. Feeling the much looser constraints around my wrists, the space around me is warm, unfamiliar in the way it smells. Taking a moment to roll over onto my back, I groan, finally allowing myself to open my eyes.

Looking up, the roof is decorated with shadows from the light of the fire, my eyes taking several moments to adjust. Finally able to look around without spots in my eyes, I take in the quaint home, its furnishings what you'd see in a traditional Untouchable household. Staying quiet, I focus on the movement in front of me, watching her gray hair brush against her lower back as she observes her blade. She is too focused on sharpening its edge to notice my cognitive state. Positioned in front of the fire in a leather chair. She has ditched the black tactical gear I have always seen her in, now sporting an oversized sweater and soft sweats.

In this setting, she looks the farthest thing from deadly, perhaps even gentle.

No wonder the Prophet has struggled to seek her out.

If it weren't for the gray locks she so proudly wears, she would easily be able to blend into this society.

Looking down toward my feet, my words are caught in my throat, my focus on the two perfectly wrapped bodies positioned along the floor. Wrapped tightly with pale gauze, their eyes are covered with gold coins, flowers tucked into their cold hands. Washed clean of their blood, and put into new clothing, their wounds are stitched shut.

If it weren't for their complexions, I would think they are sleeping.

If it weren't for the traditional burial attire clinging to both of their bodies, it would be impossible to tell they were ever mangled to begin with.

Clearing his throat, I hear Andrew. Pulling up a chair next to Forest, he looks over a Re-Regulation device, her eyes finally pulling away from her blade.

"I can't stay for long. Katiana is still a wreck, and Kaiden is not helping ease her anxieties with his crying," Andrew says, watching the woman with a respect the Prophet would kill to have.

"Do you think she'll be able to perfect it?" Forest asks, ignoring the man's urgency to be home with his family.

"If this Re-Regulation device doesn't work on you, then the medicine will surely finish it off. Katiana has been working on an altered chip, one that should keep your Marked traits under control. So long as you follow the rules, all will be well. Although, it's getting harder to lie to her about why I need devices and medication. She will only believe it's for work for so long before I have to start utilizing her chip," Andrew sighs.

"You will have to use her chip if she is to believe I am her child. You are the one who suggested we hide in plain sight. The Prophet has yet to fully see my face, only the brief glimpses of it the few times they have caught me Winnowing in their vicinity. The only way to hide is to lock away the parts of myself that make me dangerous. Once opportunity strikes, then you will be the one to bring me back to the light," she smiles, patting the man on the shoulder. "Have faith in your Apparatus."

Smiling, the man shakes his head.

"What's so funny?" she questions, smiling at the man.

"The idea of you living in my house, pretending to be my child," he gasps. "What's even worse is you'll have no clue. Do you know how aggravating it will be to not sit down and have a drink with you, explaining all the progress I've made with the resistance inside these walls?" he questions, her smile only growing.

"You know I see you as a father now, correct?" she asks. "You are the only man I've met willing to give me guidance while also being foolish enough to question me."

"A father to a woman older than I?" he questions.

"A father to a woman who needed to not feel alone. The debt I have to you and your family is not light. I will see to it Kaiden is taken care of, as well as Katiana and you. The Blackburns are the reason I may carry out my duties. You three are the reason our people will find peace."

Unable to stop the cough from escaping my throat, I feel a surge of pain move through my front, my body jolting upward into a seated position the moment her gaze snaps back to me.

"Blondie's waking up," she whispers. "Enjoy your night," she pushes, waving Andrew off with a grin.

Accepting the offer to exit, Andrew hugs the woman, giving her a kiss atop her head.

"I'll see you tomorrow."

Saying nothing else, he Winnows, leaving nothing but me and her confined to the unfamiliar space.

Creeping closer, she is careful with her steps, dragging over Andrew's and her own chair and taking a seat once she is in front of me. Crossing her legs, she watches me, pulling free a sketchbook from beside her, sketching along the pages, as if she has nothing better to do.

"What are you doing?" I question, looking at the empty chair.

"Drawing you. As I said, you interest me a great deal. It's quite frustrating for me... I figured you'd like a seat rather than the cold floor," she smiles, speaking so casually, you'd assume we are friends.

"Would you rather I torture you, Xavier? You think so low of me. I would assume you know better than accepting the Prophet's words as truth," she smiles, the gentle upturn of her mouth something many would love to see.

"You think I should just give you trust?" I question, forcing myself up and onto the seat.

Considerably less damaged than before, her blood seems to have done the trick. Still sore, the wounds are nowhere near as unbearable as they were before.

"Trust is the last thing I expect from you. Trust is earned. It's not something you can force. If I wanted you dead, Xavier, you would be. Trust me when I say I do not normally allow anyone associated with the Prophet to be so close to me."

"Why allow me?" I snap. "I still have every want to kill you. Your little trick inside my mind to block your image from my thoughts is the reason my parents are dead," I hiss, glancing at their wrapped figures.

"I am aware of the part I played in your parent's death," she whispers, pulling away from her drawing, her eyes on me. "I suppose that is why I have allowed you to be so close to me. If injuring me repays my debt for the pain I caused you, it's a price I'm willing to pay."

Groggy and disoriented, I weigh the offer, debating whether or not harming this woman does any good.

"Harming you would only temporarily ease my pain," I mutter, looking over their cold bodies. "It doesn't bring them back."

Trying to stand up, I stumble back down and into the chair, frustrated by the weakness that has overcome my body.

"Don't move too fast. My blood was able to heal you, but the healing process is still in motion. Your body took quite the impact," she mutters, tucking her sketchbook away once more, hiding its contents from all to see.

"Where am I?" I ask coldly, still not convinced by her kind demeanor.

"Inside my refugee in New Haven. As far as anyone knows, I am a secluded elder wishing to spend my years in isolation," she smiles, wincing as she speaks.

"You do realize telling me that information gives me the ability to ensure you are found once I am out of here?"

"I am fully aware," she sighs. "I suppose selfishly, I hope you'll find it harder to leave after a few days with me." she glances at me, her eyes filled with emotion. "There is always more than one side to a war. I just hope you fight for the right one."

Scoffing, I shake my head.

"And I suppose that's your side?" I question.

"It's the side you choose to fight with, not the one you have been forced to submit to. I am many things, Xavier, but I do not believe in taking away a person's right to choose."

Leaning forward, she catches herself with the armrests of her chair, stopping herself from slumping forward. Instinctively moving toward her, I grab her arm, stopping her from falling out of her chair.

Looking at my hand, I quickly pull away, settling back in my seat.

"Healing your lesions was draining. I had to give you more blood while you were unconscious to finish healing some of your internal bleeding. I am a bit out of it."

What the hell is she thinking? Allowing me to be within her vicinity with such weak defenses?

"You're their rat," I clarify, now hearing her gentle scoff.

"You willingly call a woman that? No wonder you were in your situation," she says, humor lingering in her tone.

"My name is Forest, in case you didn't catch that. No need for the dehumanizing nicknames."

"Forest? Just Forest? No last name?" I question, her name one most would consider odd.

"That would require knowing what poor souls willingly allowed their DNA to be used in my creation, and Katiana's parents ensured that information would stay under lock and key. So, no. No last name."

"Andrew-"

"I undid all of the damage you and that bastard did on his mind. No more manipulating my men into killing those he cares for," she says, finally showcasing a lick of anger in her tone.

"The Prophet will know-"

"Nothing. The Prophet will know nothing," she snaps, daring me to continue questioning the influence she has.

Looking at my parents, I narrow my eyes at the woman.

"Why did you take them?" I question, her head shaking.

"They were your family. You lost them. You deserved to bury them properly."

Reaching into her mind, I try to find an alternative motive, one that can give me a reason to hate this woman as much as I have been trained to. Finding only dead ends, she raises her brows at me, waiting for me to come up with my next line of reasoning to hate her.

"You won't find anything. The Prophet used them to torture you. It doesn't matter who you are. You didn't deserve that."

I pause, her words stuck in my mind.

You didn't deserve that.

Never in my life has anyone uttered those words.

"Who are you?" I question.

"A woman who doesn't know when to quit."

Sliding off her chair, she moves closer, my body pressing into the back of my chair. Taking a seat on my armrest, she gently grabs my wrists, guiding them into her lap. Massaging the tender skin rubbed by the binds. Close enough that I could snap her neck, she remains still, her warmth radiating off of her.

"What are you doing?"

"Probably something idiotic," she mutters, her hand waving over the binds. Watching them snap, they fall to the floor, her fingers continuing their motion to ease the pain. Watching the fire's light dance across her face, she looks peaceful, my heart beating right out of my chest.

She's so close now.

I can end all of this.

Moving faster than either of us can react, I grab her neck, forcing her to the ground, my body towering over her as I pin her in place. Watching her eyes grow wide with bewilderment, I tighten my grasp, feeling her place her hands atop my own, her words struggling to leave her closing throat.

Not fighting back, I push harder, her gentle touch only growing that much more aggravating. □

Raising her hands, it takes all that I have not to physically shove myself away from her the moment her hands cup my cheeks. Rolling her thumbs along my skin, she gasps for air, her hands gently gripping the sides of my face.

"Breathe, Xavier," she says with pain. "I won't hurt you."

Startled by her words, I force my hands away from her, leaning back as she begins to gasp, coughing until her airways are clear. Feeling a lingering pain around my throat, I rub my neck, suddenly much more aware of how restricted my air really was. Leaning upward, I remain positioned above her, my legs still pinning down the lower half of her body. Licking her thumb, she wipes my skin with her finger, collecting remnants of my blood still coating my face. Landing her thumb in her mouth, she cocks her head, letting the bruises on her neck heal in a matter of seconds.

Forcing myself off of her, I stand, pacing around the space like a madman.

"What do you need from me?" I question hesitantly, keeping my focus on her as she stands.

"It's simple," she smiles. "I need you to tell me everything you know about the Prophet."

My body fills with fire.

"And then, I need you to help me kill them."

CHAPTER NINE

VALERIE

"You want me to join them?" I question Bekah, still trying to process how she could think I would so willingly accept any invitation that involves me being civil with Forest for more than an hour at a time.

Crossing her arms as she watches me pace the dorm room. Her brute nature fizzles away the moment she is behind a closed door, leaving a broken woman tormented by the life she has been forced to live. Nervous to give me the torturous invite, she looks fearful of my response, filled to the brim with a shame I wish she would shake.

"You're making it seem as if I will not be there at all," she grovels, taking a seat on her bed, waiting for me to stop moving around the space.

"It's one thing to act civil with the woman in small spurts. It's completely different to ask me to travel with her to a place we don't even know exists," I shout, my pent-up anger surrounding Hunter and Fallan's death just as confusing now as it was six months ago.

Every time I see Forest, it's as if I am looking at a different girl, one teetering on the brink of a mental breakdown. Her actions in the compound within the past several months have been risky and, even worse, isolated.

Isolation has driven the woman into a short-tempered state, one that could ultimately lead to more casualties than it does solutions to our Prophet problem.

"I'm not asking you to braid her hair and tell her how much you missed her. I'm asking you to accompany me to a place I have only heard of in passing. And maybe I don't want to go without you."

Laying out the true nature of her asking me to come, I stop, finally letting my anger melt away. Keeping her head down, she avoids looking at me, her cheeks red with embarrassment.

"You... you don't want to travel without me?" I ask, her head craning up to look at me.

"I can't say I feel safe with the idea of you being here alone," she whispers, fidgeting with her hands anxiously. "I'd rather have you within arm's length, and having Xavier and Forest with us is more protection than what anyone here could provide, not that I'd ever tell Evermoore that."

Letting my frown shift into a smile, my hand gravitates toward the woman's, her shaky grasp happily embracing my firm one. Trailing my hands to the sides of her face, I hold her in between my palms, feeling her fingertips trail up my sides, snaking their way beneath my shirt. Studying the intricate features of her face, every freckle that dances across her skin is yet another thing for me to marvel at every time I am this close to her. Falling deep into her green-blue eyes, she watches me with raised brows, uncomfortable by people looking at her for too long.

Holding her chin up, I stop her from getting the opportunity to look away. My smile deepens, her cheeks only growing redder against her pale skin.

"I will go," I whisper, leaning closer. "I won't miss a chance to finally get out of this compound and spend some time with you."

Smiling at the comment, she allows herself to pull me onto her bed, embracing me with a touch I value more than she knows. Pressing her lips to my temple, I let myself straddle the woman, feeling a weight lift off of my shoulders at the sight of her so gleeful.

"We don't have to hide in a dorm like this. I am not as timid as Kaiden," Bekah sighs, once more reassuring me how little she minds people seeing us as something other than close friends.

"I'm not embarrassed by you, if that's why you just said that," I sigh, pushing my hands through my hair. Now, avoiding her gaze, she sits up, her smile quickly leaving her face.

"Val," she sighs, cupping my face, forcing me to look her way.

"You can talk to me-"

"It's Forest," I whisper, my tone shaky in the deliverance. Saying nothing, she watches me, waiting for me to go on.

"I don't want her knowing what I hold close to me. I don't want you around me so often that you become..."

"A target?" she questions, raising her brows. "I'd like to think Xavier and Forest have enough respect in the fact I let them stay here to not snap my neck," she begins to joke, the reality of how possible that really is stopping me from breaking my cold expression. "But it seems you don't have the same faith in them that I do."

"Can you blame me?" I question, sighing in defeat. "Hunter fucked up. He sold us out in hopes of keeping us all safe, and it cost him his life-"

"Keep you all safe? Or push Forest and Xavier in the fire to save people's asses?" she questions, being the voice of reason, even when I wish she wouldn't.

Saying nothing, I let then logic settle in my mind, unable to find a rebuttal.

"It was easier to not fear her when I knew she had limits."

"Everyone has a breaking point, Val," Bekah sighs, her hand rubbing the back of her neck. "Some of us choose to take the emotional approach, rather than the violent."

Glancing at her arms, I see the red marks from the rubber band she wears, some of the welts larger than others.

Ever since her mother committed suicide, thoughts of the occurrence swarm her at random, forcing her to go into a place she struggles to get out of. Sometimes, she will hear the woman's voice; other times, she sees her at random, throwing herself into a panic that is nearly impossible to pull away from. Getting her to start snapping her wrist with the band was a good diversion from her thoughts, but since Forest used Deception to get back at the woman by showing her the imagery of her mother, the fear-inducing thoughts have only seemed to escalate.

"Was it a bad day?" I question, raising her wrist up to my eyes, her head nodding in defeat.

"Like I said, some people choose a different approach," she sighs.

Pulling the rubber band off of her wrist, I move her arm closer to my mouth, her eyes tracking me closely. Letting my lips land on the warm skin of her wrist, I place gentle kisses in every spot reddened by the band, taking my time on the more painful-looking ones. Saying nothing, another smile begins to pull across her lips. Kissing her skin until every square inch of her pain has been tended to, I drop her wrist, her arms wrapping around me so tight that I can barely breathe.

Resting her head on my chest, I run my hand through her fiery locks, keeping my cheek pressed atop her head.

"I'm scared of what Forest may be capable of," I whisper, keeping my body wrapped in her arms.

"We all are... except Xavier. Perhaps that's why she avoids him the way she does."

The blonde Commander, as hard as he is to tolerate, truly is the one thing keeping her in line. Parading around this compound like nothing can touch her, she turns the other way the moment she sees Xavier, unable to look the man in the eye long enough to hold a conversation. To most, that would be a comfort, knowing she has some form of fear. To Xavier, it's torment, pushing the man closer to a breaking point Forest should be wary of. Despite all the fear I have toward Forest, the pain she must feel is indescribable. Ever since Fallan sought her out, all in the name of fighting for a love that was not his to take, her life has been nothing short of hell.

What could she have done to his Dove to make him step on so many people's toes to get his way?

Did he really love her, or was fear of her wrath much worse than pretending to love someone you truly hated?

"You know, as much as I love Fallan, he lied to her, and she's in denial about it."

Scoffing at the comment, Bekah squeezes tighter. □

"Seeing Fallan as anything but a saint poses a few problems for Forest."

"Like?" I question, anticipating the redhead's response.

"If Fallan is no saint, then what would that truly make Xavier to her? She holds onto the hate Fallan helped her create about the man. Take that away, and what is there really?"

"A man who does not know when to quit," I scoff, amused by the lack of intelligence the male species seems to carry.

"A man in love. A man driven by the love to the point he allowed her to be with another."

Hitting my heart deeper than I expected it to, I think of what it would be like to have someone I care for so deeply be paraded around in front of me like that, unable to say a word without facing the repercussions.

"We can paint who we want as a villain for as long as we want, but, at the end of the day, everyone lies."

Looking down at the woman, I raise my brows with amusement.

"And what lies are you keeping from me?"

Throwing on an expression I have come to know well from every debate she has conducted for her soldiers, the playful banter she allowed me to see quickly fades away.

"I lied when I said I was okay hiding out in this dorm like this," she says. "I've done many things in my life, but the one thing I promised myself I would never do is be fearful of being open about the things that make me happy. So few times has anything in this horrid life made me want to live it. Then you come into it one day and make me feel like something other than a Marked spending every day fighting for a life I did not choose to live."

Buzzing with what can only be a dozen alerts, her pager goes off, requesting her immediate presence far away from me. Moving me off of her, I sit in silence on her bed, tucking my legs into my chest, watching her scowl at the device.

Readjusting her clothes, she shoots back a quick reply, rolling her fingers over her eyes.

"I have to go," she says, grabbing her jacket, making her way closer to the door.

Pausing before she can open it, she clenches the handle.

"I'm not okay with hiding you. I'd rather take the risk of others knowing how important you are to me and walk hand in hand with you in the hallways than conceal myself like a coward. I'm no better than Forest if I run from what brings me fear."

Saying nothing else, she leaves the room, slamming the door more aggressively than I'd like to admit.

Keeping myself positioned on her bed, I take in a shaky breath, left with nothing but the presence of my regrets and the shame tethered to them.

CHAPTER TEN

FOREST

Taking in the cool summer air, I inhale deeply, embracing the serenity with open arms. Feeling the heat of the liquor settle in my stomach, I take a long swig, handing the bottle over to Xavier, watching the judgment linger in his expression every time I take more than he has. Keeping his distance from me, we sit side by side, both of our legs dangling through the balcony bars, my head pressed to the cold metal of the railing.

Unable to look at the two papers he has laid before me, Forest Blackburn's birth certificate and death record cling to my soul, the need for alcohol a necessity after fully processing what I am seeing. Unable to paint me the full picture, Xavier settled on accompanying me outside, too shaken by Elyon's message to admit being alone was the last thing he wanted. Feeling dizzy from the liquor, I try and recall my earliest childhood memories, no longer able to see them as I once had. Thinking of no one but Kai, I feel immense guilt over the truths he will have to know. Tucking the documents back in his coat, Xavier sighs, taking a drink large enough for the both of us.

"He's still your brother-"

"You think he will believe that once I tell him what I did to Hunter? As far as reality goes, I am a stranger who took residency in his home and preyed on a vulnerable woman who lost a child, and the shittiest part is I can't remember why. I can't remember anything fucking useful without going through you," I grab the bottle, downing the clear liquid. "Worst of all, you can't tell me anything useful without getting both of us killed," I shudder, powered by the alcohol's ability to loosen my tongue.

"The Prophet's message was a warning. It's clear that he wants you in his confines," Xavier says, leaning back into the wall, his shirt ridden up. "It's not something anyone will let happen."

Scoffing, I run my hands through my hair.

"You underestimate how much they fear me. If sacrificing me means this compound's internal threat is lifted, they would hand me off in a heartbeat," I say, looking over the man. "Don't tell me you wouldn't like to be rid of your reminder of how little you can say."

Glaring at me, he pulls his legs upward.

"You have gathered no clarity on what you really mean to me if you think there is any scenario in which I choose anyone in this compound over you," he warns. "You are choosing to be blinded by your ignorance. You don't need me to fit together the pieces for you, Forest. If your hate was as adamant as you pretend it is, you wouldn't be sitting out here right now stealing glances at my bare skin every chance you get."

Flustered, my stomach surges with warmth the alcohol has not created, my body once more betraying Fallan.

"So long as you see those feelings as a betrayal to Fallan, you will never gain clarity. Your mind might be closed off, but there are remnants of what was. Fallan lied. I didn't. That truth drives you mad."

Letting silence consume the conversation, Xavier clears his throat.

"They expect you not to go to the reflecting pools," he says, picking up on my thought patterns.

"They are afraid of me. Of course, they don't expect me to go," I mutter, feeling my body sway as my balance depletes.

"But you will go regardless?"

"A lead is a lead, Xavier," I snap. "Mason-"

"Mason? You've been conversing with Mason?"

Pausing, I shut my mouth, kicking myself in the ass for having such a low filter.

"You've been feeding Mason in exchange for information?" Xavier asks, fully able to piece together the full picture with such lowered guards on both of our ends. Staring forward, I ignore the man's searing gaze.

Reaching into his mind, something much deeper than annoyance touches his thoughts.

He is jealous.

"Mason's fealty to you is unshakable. Whatever information I thought I could take from the man was quickly diminished. All I am doing now is trying to help him. Nothing more, nothing less."

"Have you fully converted him?" Xavier questions, biting back his anger.

"I've tried," I sigh. "Something continues to hold my abilities back-"

"You're holding onto what happened with Fallan," Xavier interrupts, his voice cold.

"Xavier, don't-"

"Don't what, Forest? You need to talk about what happened."

"I'm not-"

"You're in denial!" the man snaps, forcing himself into a standing position, his hands running through his hair. The sooner you accept that, the sooner-"

"I'm not in denial!" I yell, using the railing to stand as aggressively as him. "You want me to sit here and wallow over the fact the man I love is dead, or even worse, the fact that I supposedly killed his first love, Dove, Elyon's daughter, and no one can even remember it."

Staring at me, he narrows his eyes.

"No one?" he questions, his mind an open door. "I've told you countless times you can look."

"It hurts the both of us if I look," I whisper, reaching my hand below my shirt, touching my ribcage. "Weakness is the last thing either of us can afford right now."

"Since when do you care what hurts me?" he questions.

The cool air begins to morph, growing increasingly warmer the longer we are outside. Still kissed by the gift of summer, the nights are long, the stars painting the night sky.

Raising his shirt to wipe the sweat from his forehead, I catch a good glimpse of the man's tattoo, its lines intricate, spanning farther down his side than I had previously noticed. Painting his front and the beginning of his shoulder, I see the beast consume his skin, his eyes wavering over to my watchful eyes.

"You've yet to tell me what the hell that is-"

"I have told you," he whispers, his jaw clenched. "You just don't remember."

Feeling my chest flood with pain, I look away in embarrassment, trying to regulate the flood of emotions rolling through me.

Sighing, Xavier moves closer, his hand grabbing my own, his shirt tucked behind his head, leaving his torso out for all to see. Gently pulling my hand closer, he massages my wrist, letting it touch the painted skin, tracing the lines of the tattoo with light touches. Ignoring the nail marks on his sides, his face softens up, his eyes watching me explore his skin.

"It's a dragon," he clarifies. "It's one of the most feared creatures in the fairytales the old world had. Misunderstood creatures often kept in confinement," he says, the correlation between him and the creature prevalent.

"The art style looks familiar," I smile, enthralled by the intricate lines.

"I would hope so," he pauses, stopping my hand from tracing any longer. "You are the one who drew it."

Pulling my hand away, I cross my arms, forcing myself to gaze up at the stars.

"I know you say I knew you-"

"You did," he mutters, wincing at the statement, his throat flooded with pain.

"How close were we, Xavier?" I mutter, my eyes unable to look at the tattoo any longer.

Clenching his jaw, he shakes his head.

"Hardly," he mutters, pulling his shirt back down. "We had a common interest at the time. Still do."

"Which is?" I question, watching the man fiddle with his pocket watch.

"Taking down Elyon to save our people."

Absorbing his words, I run my hands over my arms, suddenly consumed with a chill feeling. Thinking back to how I got here, the woman's vulnerable position paints my mind.

"Were you hurting that woman?" I question, watching his mouth upturn at the statement.

"Only in the ways she wanted. I can't exactly go on a killing spree to satisfy my blood lust. Tying up women and having my way with them has to do."

All of that pain, yet she was so eager to have him continue.

Could pain like that truly ease something as large as grief?

"Can I ask you something?" Xavier questions, taking a step closer. Forcing my focus away from the sky above, I hesitantly nod, finally meeting eyes with the man. "Why only now are you speaking to me? For months, you have avoided me," he states, his body inches away from my own.

"Every time I look at you, I think of Fallan." My fingers graze my temple. "And I think about how he is gone. We clearly have unfinished business from our past that you can hardly tell me about... and honestly, Xavier," I pause, my emotions choking my throat. "I need him, and I can't have him, and all that's left is you, which makes things that much more confusing."

Stepping closer, he pushes my arms down, allowing his hands to run up and down them. Warming my chill skin, he leans closer, his voice low.

"Why is that?"

"Something about you keeps me close. The false bond... the bond."

I can't even bring myself to call it false in his presence.

"Why not feed into it?" he questions, his hands moving away from my arms and to my hips, his fingers grazing my lower back.

Fighting every urge to pull him closer, I keep my arms at my sides.

"Because Fallan will truly be gone, and after the dust has settled, I still see you as the man that caused his demise."

"You hate me?" he questions, keeping himself out of my mind.

He wants to truly hear the answer from me.

"I have no choice. If I don't hate you, then what I am left with is much worse."

Feeling his anger roll through me, he forces his hands away, biting back his words as he creates space between us. Pacing around the deck, he grabs the bottle, allowing himself to finish off what's left, his hand clenching the drink.

"Remember that hate next time you decide to interrupt a good fuck and drag me out here to listen to you wallow about a reality you had just as much a part in creating," he pauses, pointing his finger toward me. "You blame everyone else for what has gone wrong when you should be looking in a mirror."

Feeling the tears well in my eyes, a look of regret paints the man's face. My pride quickly forces back the emotion, my anger taking control.

"Why come out here with me then?" I snap, moving past the man and closer to the door.

Grabbing my arm, he stops me, his voice as cold as ice.

"Perhaps I was hopeful you could pick up where she left off."

Hit with anger by the statement, I pry my arm away, shoving his chest with as much force as my body can provide. Watching him stumble, he looks flustered, his emotions a mix of sorrow and frustration.

"You're horrible-"

"So are you!" he snaps. "The difference between me abd you is that I don't hide it."

"I hate you, Xavier," I mutter, a scoff leaving him.

"I know."

Reaching for the door handle, I can't control my sobs. Looking back at him, he crosses his arms, his hand still holding the bottle.

"I thought-"

"You thought what? That I could be kind and sincere like your Fallan? He's gone, Forest, and you're just as responsible for his death as I am."

Feeling the pain flood my chest, I say nothing, too filled with emotion to say anything remotely logical. Forcing open the door, I push myself inside the building, letting the sound of the bottle shattering against the wall drown out my sobs, both Xavier and my mind filled with nothing but pain.

CHAPTER ELEVEN

ELYON

I rifle through the stack of papers on my desk, my eyes fixated on the numerous potential Marked still roaming through the Untouchable sector, unscathed by my hand. Crossing off every name we have already dealt with, the list grows smaller, the possibility for a new, divine breed of Marked growing more possible with each passing second.

I failed the first time.

Free will has made it impossible to truly have control over the Marked that scour the lands. So long as free will is taken, there is no other choice than to submit to my wants. Surrounded by all the finest luxuries, my silk suit is tailored to perfection, the liquor in my cup aged years older than most of my Officials. Taking in the luxuries of the Untouchable sector, I smile at the layer of dust still being cleaned by my Unfortunate service workers in my once very lively home. For years it has sat vacant, doing nothing but collecting dust, patiently awaiting my return. Glancing over to the metal chains still hung from the rafters of my roof, I crave the day Xavier hangs from them once more, wallowing like a child as his beloved Forest Flower lies a mangled corpse at his feet.

Perhaps then he will know what disloyalty truly costs.

Sensing a nervous mind, I glance up at the two large doors, my interest finally focused on something other than the abundance of Marked I can't wait to get my hands on. Lingering on the other side of the door, the body anxiously taps its foot, still unnerved by my presence.

Fear is good.

Fear stows away the thoughts that defiance breeds.

Waving my hand, I force the doors open, my eyes landing on the frazzled figure of one of my younger Officials, Josh, one of Forest's former classmates she acquired when she was off playing dress up in New Haven.

Had I known how defiant her mind could truly be, the likelihood of anyone in the Blackburn family living another year would have been slim.

Cautiously taking a step into my study, Josh keeps his hands tucked in his pockets, his body filled to the brim with nerves he can't seem to shove down. Carefully stepping in my direction, he clears his throat, his mind still trying to process Xavier's sudden exit and my sudden arrival.

"Is there a reason you are disturbing me?" I ask light-heartedly, extending my hand to the seat before my desk. Taking a seat, Josh clasps his hands together, his eyes carefully observing the room.

"I figured you might want updates on our deviants," Josh says, hiding the fear in his voice with a low tone.

"You ensured they got the body?" I question, smiling at the imagery of the compound guard screaming in agony.

Poor fool, he still had a full life ahead of him. It is always unfortunate to be at the wrong place at the wrong time, but so long as Forest and Xavier are in my compound, I see it best fit they understand just how little time they really have.

"As you instructed, sir," Josh says, lowering his head with respect as he speaks.

"Good," I smile, leaning back in my chair. "And how are preparations going for our special event?" I question, raising a brow at the boy.

"Everything will be in line by the time our guests arrive in New Haven sir," Josh says, my night getting better with each passing second.

"And my Shifters?" I question, thrilled by the sheer number of creatures trapped behind these wards.

"The ones within our borders are subservient. The group taking residence in the refugee will need extra motivation to follow any of our commands," Josh says anxiously, finally delivering me my first bit of not-so-good news.

"Perhaps it would be wise for me to pay them a visit," I ponder, tapping my fingers along the oak desk.

"Now is not the time. Regardless of the upper hand you may have on them, they won't give up information by force. You need to find their rogue, the one that Forest has managed to nearly bring back to his human form."

"Human form?" I question, my smile dropping. "She has truly managed to convert one of the Shifters back into their original form?" I question, narrowing my eyes at the man.

"A few of our men have reported seeing a mostly human creature navigating between New Haven and the Shifter refugee. Over the past few weeks, it's become much harder to distinguish whether the entity is man or creature. If he is a Shifter, he no longer walks on four legs, and his body is much smaller. Human clothes fit the creature once more," Josh says, my smile dropping further.

"So, she can convert my Shifters?" I question, feeling a vein twitch above my brow the longer I allow my annoyances to fester.

"Possibly," Josh says, being cautious with his words. "But, knowing how much blood a conversion takes, it has weakened her no doubt."

Breaking the tension with three loud knocks, the presence of more than one heart lingers behind the slightly ajar door. Waving once more, I urge the men into the space, putting a pin into the less-than-desirable conversation that was about to ensue.

Clearing his throat, one of my older Officials waits for my command to speak. Giving him a nod, I cock my head at the ground.

"Sir, it's here."

Smiling, I clap my hands, taking a large drink from my glass.

"Bring it in!"

Shoving past the men with brute force, one of my robed loyalists moves forward, their face concealed with a mask all too similar to my own. Carrying the large, black box, their gloved hands dig into the box's side, gently placing it on my desk with a nod in my direction.

Taking a stand next to me, I squeeze their hand in acceptance, giving the box a wide-eyed stare of thrill.

"You all can leave," I utter to the men, forcing Josh back down in his seat before he can try to slip away.

"I wasn't speaking to you," I snap, listening to the low chuckle of my loyalist patiently waiting at my side.

"Was it hard to have them sewn?" I question, hopeful the handiwork of the Unfortunate seamstress is still up to par.

"I didn't exactly give them a choice," my loyalist snickers, my grin wide in the gleam of their mask.

Tearing open the lid to the box, an array of feathers meet my vision, my focus on the intricately sewn patterns etched into the gown. Pulling it free from the box,

I lay the dress across my desk, looking over the perfectly soft fabric, its size made just for her.

"What is it?" Josh questions, his eyes fixated on the lovely gown.

"My Apparatus's gown. The one she will wear when she finally decides to return to me."

Narrowing his eyes at the dress, a swirl of thoughts formulate in Josh's mind.

"Do you disagree with me, Josh?" I question, his head immediately shaking.

"It's not that, sir," he sighs. "She won't come to New Haven willingly, especially if she has no plan," Josh warns, reminding me of a reality I know all too well.

"I am aware of that, but it would seem leaving Xavier and her brother alive gives me more leverage than I initially thought," I smile.

"Why do you say that?" Josh questions.

"So long as she cares for someone more than her own self-gain, she will always be weaker than I," I smile, closing my eyes as I lean back. "It would seem she has felt that she's gained a lead by finding the reflection pools I originated from. The foolish part of that plan is that she truly thinks she will make it to such a sacred ground without my interference. In order to get to the pools, one must pass through the Sanctuary first. It would seem Forest is eager enough to believe I am not already three steps ahead of her," I exclaim, finally pulling my focus back to Josh.

"What is your plan, sir?" the man questions, anxiously fidgeting.

Already subconsciously knowing I require his help, he waits for a response, his forehead wet with his nervous sweat.

"It's quite simple really," I smile. "The demise of Forest Blackburn of course."

CHAPTER TWELVE

KAIDEN

Moving through the silent hallway, I run my hand along the wall, distracting myself from the swarm of thoughts flooding through my mind every time I am alone. I know the others are keeping secrets from me, whispering to one another in the brief moments they think I have left the conversation.

I am no fool to the deception lies create.

The problem is, I'm not sure I want to know what it is that they are hiding.

Ever since Hunter, Fallan, and my mother's death, life has been nothing short of miserable. Initially, I thought I would be able to manage my grief with my sister, creating some sense of comfort in the mourning we both share. Her isolation came quickly and without warning, shutting out everyone and everything she possibly could.

As easy as it is to pull on a face of strength and act like I have moved forward, I am just as stuck as she is. Unable to sleep most nights, I wander the hallways, envisioning futures and possibilities that will never happen.

I never got to spend a night alone with Hunter. I never got to hear his hopes and dreams. Everything we spoke about, every possibility for the future he wanted once we were out of the grasp of Sanctum and the New World Order's control, now, all a distant memory. He will never speak again.

He will never love me again.

All that remains is an urn, filled with ashes that I cannot hold, cannot touch.

He is gone.

But my sister is not.

Turning a corner, I pull my focus away from my spiral, and down the dormitory hallway. Solidifying my plan of action, I make my way closer to my sister's section, clasping my hands together while nervously fidgeting with my fingers.

How would she feel about my sudden intrusion?

Would she turn me away, avoiding me as she has done for months?

Would she smile, allowing me into her space with open-

Slumping forward, a body lays plastered against my sister's door, using its front to support their back. Wearing a hood, the large body grips an empty flask, tossing it across the floor, watching it skid down the hallway. Clearing my throat, the figure snaps their head up at me, calming down once familiarity settles in both of us.

"Xavier? What are you doing-"

Screams break out behind my sister's door. Xavier's body leans forward, his hands shaking as he covers his ears, his eyes wide with fear. Biting his lip, he closes his eyes, his energy surging to life, my hand already reaching for the door handle. Grabbing my wrist, the man stops me, his eyes like glowing embers.

"Going in there will make it worse. This nightmare has to p- pass," he mutters, slurring his speech every other word. "I- I'm stowing away her fears, stepping into her mind every time she starts screaming to ease her," he slurs, leaning forward from exhaustion. "Her screams kept me from sleeping myself. It's all I could hear in my mind. Normally, we can drown each other out, but-" Glancing at his flask, he pauses. "The alcohol seems to have made that difficult."

Pulling down his hood, he watches me, Forest's room silent once more. Crouching down to his level, he looks broken, his eyes filled with sorrow.

"She has been nothing but hateful to you. Why do you keep trying?" I question, genuinely seeking an answer.

I've heard the whispers of Fallan's betrayal. I know his lies run much deeper than any of us will ever get clarity on. When Fallan died, his secrets died with him.

But, in all of this chaos, has anyone ever asked Xavier the part he plays in the bigger picture?

"Why do I keep trying?" Xavier smiles, his voice giddy at the question.

"If the answer to that is not obvious to you, of all people, then perhaps I am hopeless," Xavier mutters, only able to communicate with anyone in brief statements. Reaching his hand up toward me, I help the man up, watching him stumble, his body like a rock.

If he were to fall on me right now, there's no guarantee I could get him off of me, let alone drag him to his dorm.

Leaning closer, I feel his arms wrap around me, my body still, his voice hot with alcohol. Regardless, I remain still, letting the man give me the foreign embrace.

"Why did you fight for Hunter? Even though you knew it was wrong? Why did you keep trying? " Xavier questions, pulling away from the embrace. The kind-hearted Official I met so long ago stands before me now, his face anything but malicious.

"That answer is simple. I love- loved him. I loved him," I clarify, watching his jaw clench.

"And if he couldn't remember you. Then what? Would you still l-"

Clutching his chest, he is unable to get the word out. Biting back a horrendous pain, he hides his cry of defeat. Turning around, I see the cut span down his back, the blood soaking through his hoodie.

"It would seem," he gasps. "I am asking too many questions," he mutters, shaking his head. "I should get back to my room, I need to rest if I want to keep this pain from her."

Squeezing my shoulder, he begins to move past me, his body shaking with adrenaline.

"You're in love with my sister," I whisper. "It wasn't Fallan. It wasn't Fallan that night of the bonfire, was it?" I question, my mind racing to the night we all danced at the bar in the Sanctuary. Dozens of times, Fallan and Forest had told me the story of their interaction at Josh's party, and not once was Xavier in it. But like second nature, he grabbed my sister and danced with her in ways only someone who was at that bonfire could do.

Staying still, he does not confirm or deny, his fingers prying into my shoulder.

"We've all lost something we l-love, Kaiden," Xavier hisses, his body finally pulling away. "I was idiotic enough to chase after it, and now, I will eternally pay the price."

Grabbing his wrist, I stop him.

"Her memories of Fallan, when they were children, and anything after that-"

"Go to see your sister, Kaiden, before I am forced to rip your tongue out for letting you in on as much as I have. You're no idiot. Don't be foolish enough to push any further than you already have."

Moving quickly, he undoes the lock to my sister's door, slipping a key he no doubt stole back into his pocket. Moving without so much as another word, his figure moves down the dark hallway, only disappearing once he has turned a corner. Glancing at the slightly open door, I see a figure stirring, her body tangled with the blankets. Slipping inside, I shut the door, being sure to latch the locks shut. Hearing her slight groans, her face is blanketed with sweat, her body curled into the fetal position.

Whispering, her voice is shaky, her hand entwined in her hair.

"Momma," she whispers. "F-Fallan," she continues, my heart dropping. "I'm sorry, I didn't want any of this. I promise I have a p-plan-"

Watching her breathing escalate, I reach out, my hand grazing her face.

"Fores-"

"Xavier!" she yells, her eyes flying open, her cheeks coated in tears. Panting as if she ran a marathon, she blinks back her confusion, her eyes adjusting to the dark space. Her hands reach forward, gripping my shirt. Touching my front, her hands shake.

"Who is it?" she asks, finally pulling herself back into reality. Looking over her frazzled state, we both make eye contact, her body finally relaxing. "Kai?" she questions, her voice lined with emotion.

"Hey, kiddo," I whisper, touching her damp hair. Taking a seat on her bed, I pull off her covers, letting her body breathe as I tug her closer. Ready to move away from me, I grab her hand, cupping her face with a frown.

"No more running from me," I whisper, her lip wobbling with emotion. "You were screaming. You're an idiot if you think I am not coming in here if I hear that."

"H- how did you get in here?" she questions, letting her head rest on my chest.

Leaning back into her bed frame, I pull her with me, allowing her shaking body to lean into me. Grabbing one of her lighter blankets, I pull it over us, letting it land over our heads, gathering us up in a bundle.

"Xavier let me in."

Perking up, she looks around for the man, my curiosity about why she said his name only growing.

"He didn't come in. He was waiting outside your door, drunk as shit, but doing his best to ease your nightmares with your mental bond," I say, her hands rubbing her eyes.

"Why did you say his name, right before I woke you up?" I question.

Staying silent, her body begins to shake, my hand landing on her side, feeling her bony ribcage.

"I suppose he was in my nightmare," she whispers. "Or maybe the opposite," she shudders, running her hands through her hair. "I could feel his energy pulling away the facade of the dream, making it easier to look past the fears. I guess, in some way, I was hoping he would be the one to wake me up."

Swallowing nothing, I glance at her dresser, Fallan, and my mother's urns gleaming back at me.

"I knew you were missing meals," I whisper, my focus on her slightly sunken face. "Not like this."

Trying to move my hand away from her body, I keep it still, forcing her to acknowledge the toll of her avoidance.

"How do you do it, Kai?" she questions, her voice shaky. "How are you okay with the fact that they are gone?"

Her pain is eating her alive, taking any hope for life with it.

"I suppose I hold onto the fact we will be able to take down the person who killed them." Her body stiffens. "I hold onto the fact that we will be able to diminish the evil that could kill the people we love so easily."

Silent, she leans closer.

"Did Xavier hear me crying?" she questions, fearful of him seeing any of her vulnerability.

For someone who chooses to hate the man so much, he sure does occupy her mind.

Can I truly say nothing of what I have learned with Xavier without jeopardizing both of their lives?

"You could tell he felt it. He was positioned outside your door, waiting for someone to help his drunk ass up. He unlocked the door before leaving."

Sniffling, she shakes her head.

"I swear he got a new lesion. I felt the pain in my dream. Why would he have a new cut?" she questions, my mind avoiding reflecting on the words we shared. The last thing I want her to do is explore my mind and spiral as much as he has. This is the closest I've been to my sister in weeks. My knowledge can remain mine for a little while longer.

What's a few more secrets? Clearly, no one is seeing the full picture.

All I know is that Forest is my sister.

Nothing can change that.

"Nightmares. It's all it is. he might have been one drink away from alcohol poisoning, but he had no new lesion. At least not one I know of," I say, easing her tense body.

"You've been so cold to me, Forest," I say, finally addressing the one issue I need clarity on. "Why?"

Saying nothing, her hand lands in mine, her voice clear.

"I'm not a good person, Kai," she states. "You are. I will just ruin that."

Looking down at her, I grab her chin, her eyes finally on mine. Puffy and red, her face is drenched in tears, her voice ready to break from emotion.

"You are not their puppet, Forest. You are not evil," I whisper, pressing my forehead to hers. "You are something much greater than all of this. Do not forget the last name you carry, and the people who love you. In life or death, there are those who will return to hell and back for you," I utter, my mind racing to the brief words Xavier had shared.

I was idiotic enough to chase after it.

This was no past event.

He is still chasing after his love.

He is running after *her.*

"And what if I like it in hell, Kai? What if I like how I feel when there is no one around me... no one to care for?" she questions, her thought pattern created by isolation.

"If that were the case, you would not have allowed me to hold you and wouldn't be calling out for the man you seemingly hate while you sleep. It's because you want us with you that you are fearful. Fearful of loss." Both of our eyes avert to the urns. "Fearful of grief."

Planting her head on my chest, I feel the wetness blotch my front, her mouth no longer able to stifle her sob. Feeling her body heave, she grips my shirt, her voice a hoarse cry.

"I'm so sorry, Kaiden," she sobs, allowing me to pull her as close as possible. "I'm sorry for all that I've done to you," she continues, my hand stroking her hair.

Grabbing the sides of her face, I get her to look at me, her tears wetting my fingers.

"The worst thing you did is run from me," I say, my own voice cracking as the tears roll down my face. "You and Mark are all I have left.... Please, please don't leave me-"

Wrapping her arms around my neck, she leans into me, my arm wrapped around her body, both of our legs dangling off the bed. Staying in our seated positions, she stays pressed against my shirt, her tears and mine slipping free from our eyes. Absorbing the moment, we both take deep breaths, our cries fading into small laughs, both of us an emotional wreck of emotions by the end of it.

Continuing her laughter well after the moment has passed, I look over the woman, her head nestled against my arm once her arms have dropped.

"What?" I question, her eyes flying open.

"It's nothing," she smiles, her voice hiding something she wants to say.

"What is it, Forest?" I push, unable to stomach another secret I am uninvolved with.

"You smell like Aaron," she states, my heart dropping.

"He has been helping me readjust to life since Hunter's death-"

Zoning out at the mention of Hunter, her smile drops, her body rigid once more.

My blood runs cold, my skin filling with goosebumps. Every time I mention the man, she shuts down like this, unable to look me in the eyes.

"I'm sorry, Kaiden," she whispers, my heart beating out of my chest.

Clearing my throat, a feeling of dread washes over me. It is a feeling that has lingered in the back of my mind for awhile.

"For what, Forest?" I question, unsure if I want to know the true nature of her avoidance.

Settling back into the touch, she relaxes her rigid posture.

"For all of it," she whispers, her voice coarse with emotion. "I should have never dragged you into any of this. Maybe if I had left things alone, Hunter would still-"

"It isn't your fault," I say through my teeth, wishing now, more than ever, I could ask her the one question eating away at my soul.

Are you the one who killed Hunter and Rae?

The question eats me alive, tearing away at my soul. Could she truly be capable of something as vile as that? Could she look the man I love in the eyes, and watch him take his final breath?

Hugging me deeper, she remains silent, my pain replaced with something much colder. Suddenly much more avoidant of being this close to her, I finally begin to understand how she must have been feeling for months.

Loving my sister is one thing.

Understanding the woman she is now, is something entirely different.

Perhaps the sister I knew really did die with Fallan.

CHAPTER THIRTEEN

FOREST

G roggily forcing my eyes open, the warm presence of a body next to me startles me back into reality, my hands frantically grasping the presence beside me. Feeling a much leaner figure than Fallan, the haze of sleep wears away, my eyes hyper-focused on my brother's sleeping state. Still in his clothes from the night before, he crosses his arms, his head leaning back on my bedframe. Still in the grasp of slumber, I glance at my calendar, already dreading the long list of preparations needed to get done before we can travel anywhere.

In one of the few sleep-ridden conversations Kai and I tried to have last night, he explained the reflecting pools, pulling me further into the conversation, not quieting down until I agreed to go. The journey will bring us to the Sanctuary, giving us at least a day to rest before migrating to the possible location of the waters. Working on nothing but whispers, we are all taking a shot in the dark. It is not surprising the others don't want me to go. I would be confused if there was any scenario in which they find comfort in my presence. Even last night, Kai was biting back words, too scared to ask me the one question that might push him away from me forever.

For now, all I have is this.

My kind, loving brother.

The same brother I would die for in a heartbeat. □

Telling him the truth would change the way he perceives me for good, leaving me with one less family member and only more rage.

It's a rage neither of us are willing to explore.

Nudging his head, he quickly opens his eyes. Focusing on me, he stretches his long arms, releasing a large yawn.

"What time is it?" he questions, giving himself as much space on my bed as he can.

"It's time for you to get moving," I smile, feeling relieved the moment his mouth curls into a smile.

Looking at his position, he shakes his head, rubbing his sleepy eyes.

"I didn't mean to impose by staying the night," he starts. Rolling off my bed, I swat his leg playfully, stretching my arms as high as they go. "The last thing I want to do is make you uncomfortable."

"Kai," I snap, his focus dead set on me. "You're my gay, older brother. The last thing I am worried about is being uncomfortable by your presence," I smile, both of us flustered at the use of his label for the first time out loud.

"No one says that anymore, Forest. The old world took that labeling with it," he says, cautiously rubbing the back of his neck.

"Would you rather I just say, 'Hello, this is my brother Kai. As attractive as he might be ladies, he loves when men-'"

"Don't!" Kai yells, his face red. "What you said the first time is perfectly fine."

Giggling like a child, a loud roar breaks free from my stomach, both of us silent.

"How about I cut you a deal?" he questions, finally excusing himself from my sheets. "I will leave and give you some time to get ready. In return, you eat whatever it is I decide to sneak for you from dining?" he asks, my stomach grumbling cheerfully at the idea of food.

"I'll take that as a yes," he smiles, moving closer to the front door.

Pausing, he turns around, taking a few large strides near me. Craning his head down, he kisses the top of my head, lingering on the touch for several moments. Soaking it all in, the dull pain in my chest I had managed to suppress returns, my stomach rolling, filled with an anxiety I can't control.

"I'll see you in forty-five minutes," he smiles, finally pulling away.

Watching him make his way out the door, I stay standing in place, my hands running up and down my arms. Glancing toward the bathroom, the urge to cleanse my body escalates. Ignoring the guilt, I move closer to the bathroom door, ready to try and wash away my abundance of sins.

Feeling the water work its way down my body, the water runs clear, swirling down the drain in large waves. Working my hands through my hair, it rests above my ass. In desperate need of a haircut, I press my fingers to my rings, my mother's band sticking out more than the others. Every few months, she would trim my ends, reminding me of how vital it was to keep up with the dye. Now faced with locks entirely unfamiliar, their light tone grows dark when damp, my head framed with the wild locks. Running my hands down my body, I carefully trace each scar, feeling the rough skin beneath each fingertip.

All these scars, each one a reminder of what I have lost.

Once clean skinned, now devoured by the whispers of battle.

Glancing around the shower, my eyes gravitate toward the walls, a handrail broke from mine and Fallan's time here.

Fixated on the broken bar, I reach for his mother's ring, feeling the metal erode from where I have repeatedly rubbed it over the past few months.

I never thought I could miss the touch of one person's hands so desperately.

I never thought I would miss the way his lips touched my skin. He knew every single part of me like a map.

He kissed me with fire and loved me with all he had.

Or so that's what he wanted me to believe.

Gripping the chain to the necklace, I tear it free from my neck, tossing it onto the bathroom counter. Panting, it felt as if the metal was choking me, tightening around my neck the longer I tried to force happy thoughts into my mind. Filled with a flood of confusion, the back-and-forth in my mind regarding Fallan's actions haunts me.

Did he truly love me when he was touching me?

Or was he just trying to get inside my head?

Watching the rings roll across the bathroom counter, I feel the tears roll down my cheeks, the water quickly washing them away.

At what point do the lies end, and the truth begins?

Closing my eyes, the water consumes me, my hands traveling down my front, feeling my frail body beneath my hand's touch. Hearing his faint whisper in the echoes of my memories, I touch the back of my neck, remembering the way his lips felt as they pressed against the sensitive skin. Traveling down my neck, I touch my breasts, the feeling of his hands touching my chest lingers, his thumbs rolling over my sensitive buds, his body pressed firmly against mine. Growing heat works its way up my stomach, my body leaning forward, my head pressed against the wall of the shower as I work down my front, my fingertips trailing down to my hips.

Remembering the way his hands held me as he gently braced me for the moment he entered me, the heat escalates, my hand moving farther down. Biting my lip, I linger above my warmth, the conflict within me torturous in every way possible.

"Fuck, Fallan," I sob, letting my hand tremble. "Why did you leave me alone? Why did you leave me with so many damn questions?"

Shaking uncontrollably, I force my thoughts in a new direction, the imagery of Xavier's compound whore flooding my mind. Reminiscing on her restraints, the warmth escalates once again, my mind racing to the anger settling in his voice.

The night is young, my hand will do just fine.

Regrettably aroused by the comment, the shaking stops, my mind focused on something other than the loss surrounding me. Letting my back meet the wall, I sink down, planting my ass on the edge meant for soaps and other bottles. Knocking them to the floor, I take a seat, spreading my legs, unable to contain the wetness slicking my thighs. Gently grazing my fingers over my clit, the touch is stimulating, my mind continuously racing back to the woman in his bed. Thinking about the grin she wore and the bruises she proudly showcased, my mouth stifles a moan, my fingers plunging into me, hard and aggressively. Using my thumb to continue my pace on my clit, I rock my hips into my hand, feeling the water wash away the sinful action. Parting my mouth to release the gasps, I think of the nail marks coating the man's body, the warmth in my stomach escalating, my fingers working in and out with ease. Focused on nothing but the power the man thought he held over that woman, I reflect on the frustrations I created within him, my wants for him to silence me something I am very ashamed to admit to myself. Thinking about the way his lips felt pressed against my lower stomach, the breathy gasps escaping my mouth turn into full-fledged moans. Finally seeing the imagery of his fiery eyes in my mind, I roll my thumb over my clit one last time, wondering what his lips would feel like traveling to other places-

Arching my back, the warmth implodes inside my stomach. Unable to hide the noise, I let out a breathy moan, grasping my breast with my free hand as I do so. Biting back the urge to say his name, I quickly pull free my hand, my face red with embarrassment as I go to reach for the rings. Feeling nothing, it's as if a weight has been lifted from my chest, allowing me for the first time in months to actually breathe. Glancing around, I feel the buzz of the orgasm die down. The water continues on, shifting from its blazing heat to a much colder temperature.

"What the fuck am I doing?" I whisper, turning off the water.

Excusing myself from the shower, I run my towel through my locks, pulling on my underwear and bra. Crossing my arms over my body, I wipe away the condensation on the mirror, getting a good look at the red coating my cheeks. Still wet from something other than water, I fight back the urge to touch myself again, disappointed by the thought pattern it took to allow myself to feel sexual relief. Glancing at the rings, I narrow my eyes, gathering each one up, before gently placing them in my bathroom's side drawer.

"I'm not letting you go," I whisper, biting my lip. "I'm finding myself without you," I continue, slamming the drawer shut with a thud.

Continuing to run the towel through my hair, I step into the cold air, my nipples chilling into points, aching beneath the bra. Closing my eyes, I take a large breath, tossing the towel in the general direction of the hamper, my blood running cold once I realize it never hit the floor.

Prying open my eyes, we both look flustered, his free hand in his pocket, shifting the front of his pants. Holding the towel with a white-knuckled hand, his eyes are wide, his body taking shallow breaths, my body suddenly the most exposed it's ever felt. Watching him scan me up and down, the warmth between my legs flourishes. Stopping his exploration once he lands on my eyes, my hands shake, both of us fully aware of what he might have heard.

Swallowing nothing, I stand still, barely able to get the words out.

"Xavier?"

Chapter Fourteen

Forest

"K ai-"

"He left the door unlocked," Xavier mutters, tossing the towel onto the chair. Trying not to explore my body with his eyes, he looks at anything but me, fully aware of what I had just allowed myself to do.

"How long were you-"

"Long enough," Xavier snaps, keeping his hands in his pockets as he continues to readjust the part of himself clearly straining against his black pants. Aroused by the sight, I scold myself mentally, trying to focus on anything but what he has hidden beneath his boxers. Pushing past the yearning need between my legs, I move past him, forcing open my drawer as I begin to rummage through my array of shirts.

"Well, it's no better than what I stumbled upon last night. Consider us even now," I snap, trying to deflect attention from the larger problem.

I touched myself to the thought of Xavier, and knowing how these connections work, he knows it.

"I wasn't doing that for pleasure, Forest," he says coldly, my hand settling on one of Fallan's black shirts, my eyes avoiding the urns resting above the dresser. "I did it to distract myself."

Still busying myself by rifling, the warmth from his body radiates behind me, my heart rate escalating the longer I pretend to be busy.

"Really good distraction," I scoff, his warmth unbearably close.

Jumping at the feeling of his hands wrapping around my hips, I stay still, straightening my posture. Feeling his fingers touch my bare skin, he leans closer to my ear, his hair brushing the side of my face.

"You don't have to love someone to distract yourself," he says, forcing my chin up with his finger, I face our reflection in the mirror above the dresser, my cheeks so red that I might look sick to some. "You don't have to love someone to feel in control," he says.

Watching his hands work up my sides in the mirror, he flips my body around, our eyes meeting. Regrettably, looking down, I see the strain against his pants up close, my throat swallowing with anxiety at its intimidating length. Once more, feeling that pulse of pleasure between my legs, I narrow my eyes at the man, doing my best to hide how much I'd like to cross my legs to ease my throb.

Moving his hands away from my sides, he squeezes my ass before working up my spine. Trailing his hands over my breasts, one of his hands winds in my hair, yanking me closer, my lips inches away from his. Growing more stimulated each time he tugs a little harder, our breaths mix, his free hand pushing my lower back. Feeling his length press against my lower stomach, I become an uncontrollable mix of nerves, my mind unable to focus on anything but his touch.

"Self-pleasure is no sin, Forest," he whispers.

"What the hell are you doing?" I question, forcing on my best face of anger.

"Testing a theory," he smirks, my legs slick from my own creation.

"You kicked that woman out yesterday because you wanted to be touched like her, not because you were angry-"

"That's not-"

Tugging my hair, he silences me, shoving me hard into the dresser. Gasping at the aggressiveness, I close my mouth, feeling his body lean into me.

"You're tired of people being fragile with you, aren't you, Forest?" he questions, reading me like a book.

Shaking my head, I deny the claim, baring my teeth to his coy expression.

Saying nothing, he grabs the hand I pleased myself with, pulling it closer to his mouth, his nose taking in my scent along my fingers. Unable and unwilling to stop him, his tongue grazes over each finger before landing them in his mouth. Gasping, I bite my lip hard, only making him more excited, his mouth licking my fingers clean from the remnants of my climax. Pulling my hand away from his mouth, the idea of pleasing myself with his spit on my fingers only makes things worse.

"You're fucking sweet, Forest Flower," he mutters. Wincing at the comment, my legs threaten to shake.

"You can't kiss me," I warn, his voice releasing a low laugh.

"On the lips. Kissing is for those who want love."

"I could never love you," I snap, his face pulling into a cold expression.

"Then you will take the touch that hate creates, and you will take it without protest."

Moving too quickly for me to react, he pulls on my hair, dragging me closer to one of the lounging chairs in the space. Forcing me to plant my ass in its soft material, he grasps my thighs, keeping me down as he lowers himself to his knees, his head level with my torso. Gripping my legs so hard, they no doubt will bruise, I pant heavily, my heart beating out of my chest.

"Xavier-"

"Shut your mouth!" he snaps, his Call buried in my mind. Having no want to open my mouth again, he eyes the wetness along my thighs, his mouth pulling into a look of satisfaction.

Forcing open my legs, he leans closer, my fingers buried in his locks, not even trying to force away his head. Watching his tongue trail up my inner thigh, I bite back my moans of pleasure. Watching him lick up every bit of my slickness, a silent gasp exits his throat. Feeling the way the point of his tongue drags across the skin, I cannot stop myself from letting out a silent moan, his eyes snapping up to me in anger. Pulling my hands free from his hair, he forces my wrists down by my legs, his teeth latching onto the soft skin of my inner thigh, biting with no warning. Stopping myself from releasing a yelp, the game he is playing settles in my mind.

If I make a noise, I face the consequences.

Continuing on, he works dangerously closer to my dripping warmth. His lips graze the innermost part of my thigh. Running the tip of his tongue across the crease of my thigh, he takes in what he can of my taste, my lip bleeding from the sheer willpower it's taking to remain silent.

"Say how much you hate me, Blackburn," he mutters, his hands gripping my wrists harder. Pulling his head up to look at me, he taunts me with his smug expression, my annoyance rising the moment I realize how much control he has over me right now.

"I fucking hate-"

Dipping his head down, he bites my inner thigh harder, hard enough to draw blood. Letting the mix of a moan and groan leave my mouth, I watch the red collect on my skin. Licking the wound with gentle brushes of his tongue, my blood touches his lips, his voice cold as he forces me to look at the bite with my chin.

"Good luck healing that, love," he mutters, releasing my chin, his hand back on my wrist in a matter of seconds.

Trailing his mouth along the upper waistband of my underwear, his nose grazes my lower stomach, my warmth betraying me like no other, dripping with anticipation to feel his touch. Hovering his lips above the material above my clit, he smiles.

"Say it again," he growls, my legs shaking with adrenaline.

Knowing damn well where this leads, I cannot resist the temptation.

"I hate-"

Pressing his lips above my underwear, I feel his touch through the undergarment, the pressure above my clit enough to make me bend at his will here and now. Bucking my hips into the touch, he smiles deeper, his hands forcing my hips closer to his face, his mouth torturing me with deep, slow kisses along my warmth. Starting at my clit and focusing above my folds, the material of the underwear grows damp, my breasts begging to be touched.

"Say it again while my tongue licks up every drop of you and your hips are rocking your pretty pussy into my face," he snaps, my eyes widening at the use of such derogatory slang. Latching onto the way the wording makes me feel, I bite back my protests, enthralled with the high his touch brings me.

"I hate-"

Dragging down the top of my underwear, his lips land on my clit, gently kissing the swollen bud with a light touch. Feeling a thousand feelings come over me, the pleasure from his mouth lights me up, making me internally beg for more. Feeling his tongue graze the sensitive point, I release my loudest moan yet, my body begging for him to taste my cum, and force his fingers inside of me whether I want it or not.

This is wrong.

"You hate what, Forest Flower?" he questions, my eyes catching a glimpse of the urns.

I can't crave this.

What the fuck am I doing?

Using my Hold to pry away his wrists, I Winnow, stumbling closer to my bed, staggering as my legs violently shake. Gripping my bed frame, Xavier stands with annoyance, wiping his lips with his thumb as he stares me down. Holding the bedpost, I fix my posture, readjusting my underwear, my inner thighs too wet to ignore. Trying to heal his bite marks, they slowly disappear, some lingering more than others. Hidden by the color of his pants, his large presence aggravates him, his hand tugging at his belt.

"Finish what you started, Forest," Xavier warns, creeping closer, his mind racing with countless ideas that end with me begging for him to touch me. "I dare you to tell me how much you hate me again."

Moving closer to the bed, he backs me up, my legs hitting the mattress. Growing frustrated by the power play the man continues to demonstrate, I bare my teeth. Grabbing the front of his shirt, I force him into the bed with my Hold, watching his back slam into the mattress. Sitting up before I can stop him, the man forces me onto his lap, his hands gripping my hips. Feeling the strain of his length against his pants, I land on top of his lap, my warmth and his length only a few layers of clothing away from something we can't come back from. Keeping his fingers latched to my sides, he forces my hips to rock, allowing me to grind on him, my slickness coating his pants. Releasing the breathy moans, he entwines his hand in my hair once my body has continued rocking for me.

Why does it feel like I am seconds away from begging the man to let him do with me as he pleases? Dragging my head closer, his lips graze up my neck, his teeth gathering my ear lobe, nipping. Tugging tighter once I wince, the yearning in my warmth grows unbearable, my hand reaching to finish myself off once more.

Grabbing my wrist, he stops me, his voice low as I continue my rock on his hips.

"I promise you, Forest, I will hear your soft voice beg me to force my cock inside of you," he whispers, keeping me still, his hand within my own. "It won't take manipulation to get you to land your pretty cunt on top of me and stretch yourself out, struggling to keep yourself from crying," he warns, his hand taking over where mine would have. Gently rubbing my clit from above the material, the warmth swirls in my stomach, the impending presence of a climax approaching. "I will fuck you so hard the flush leaves your cheeks, and you are begging for a god to save you from me."

Grabbing the back of my neck, he releases my hair, his thumb grazing my jaw, forcing me to look down at him as he continues massaging me.

"You feel how wet your pretty cunt is?" he questions, glancing down at his pants, forcing my head down to watch with him. Watching my hips rock, I coat his pants, his thumb seconds away from creating my blissful release. Feeling his length only grow harder, I know he is fighting back his climax, his mind just as open as mine. "You like soaking through my pants like this? Tempting my cock?" Watching him smirk at me, I try and look away. He stops me, forcing my focus back on his eyes. "You want me to bend you over and fuck you until your cum coats me. And even then, you won't want me to stop until you're unable to stand," he says, reading my mind like a book, all of my sickest fantasies emerging from the depths of my mind. "Unlike Fallan, Forest, I have no self-control. I will gladly fill you up and make it damn clear who you belong to."

Pinching my clit above the material of my underwear, the warmth implodes, my body leaning forward into him, my face nuzzled into his neck as I try to hide my moan. Biting the skin of his neck, I stop myself from being too loud, feeling the rock of my hips die down, his length still ungodly hard beneath me. Pulling away from his neck, I see the start of a bruise, my underwear soaked, leaving a very noticeable patch of cum along his pants. Wiping it from his crotch, he licks his thumb clean, his free hand keeping me on his lap.

"I hate you," I seethe, still craving all that he has sworn to do.

"Yet, your cum is all over my pants and settled on my tongue," he whispers, his nose inches away from my own. "So why don't you tell me how much you hate me while I fuck you senseless and make you forget what love even is."

"I'm not too sure I even knew what real love feels like," I whisper, digging the knife of Fallan's betrayal into my heart.

"Hey guys! I come bearing gifts!"

Snapping our heads toward the door, my brother's loud bangs on the door send me into a frenzy. Quickly Winnowing back into the bathroom, I slam the door shut, my eyes glancing in the mirror, shocked by the sheer amount of marks Xavier had managed to leave. Other than my actual mark, the man's love bites and bruises coat my skin, his touch powerful in contrast to my weakened figure. Narrowing my eyes, I hate how weak my body looks, my mind racing with a million negative thoughts. Touching the marks he has left, I half expect to frown, my fingers grazing the smile encapsulating my face. □

Xavier wasn't trying to make me feel weak.

He was forcing me to show him how much power I really have.

And I failed miserably.

Hearing Xavier open my door, I look around for clothes, silently cursing myself for being ignorant enough to forget them. Cracking the door open, Xavier keeps his hands in his pocket, trying to rid himself of the uncomfortable presence in his pants. Looking at the bite mark on Xavier's neck, now a bruise, Kai throws him a look, his eyes scanning the man's body, even more perplexed by the stain on the front of his pants.

"What the fuck happened?" Kai questions, choosing to focus on the bruise.

"One of my compound fucks likes to get a little wild," Xavier smiles, his eyes quickly snapping to me. "Isn't that right, Forest?" He questions, grinning like an idiot.

"I could care less where you're putting your dick," I snap, my legs still trembling from his touch. "Can one of you please just hand me some pants and a shirt?" I question, watching Kai glance around for something.

Kicking open my bottom dresser drawer, Xavier grabs a pair of pants. Tearing off his shirt, I lower my eyes, only looking up once he stands before the crack in the door. Smiling as he peers inside, he keeps my body concealed from Kai, his eyes marveling at his handiwork.

"I said a shirt, not your shirt," I hiss, his head shaking.

"Last time I checked," he whispers, pointing to his neck before tapping his inner thigh. "I marked you, love. And you marked me," he continues, his head leaning slightly closer. "You'd be fucking delusional to think I am allowing you to parade around in your dead boyfriend's clothes after what we just did. If you need a man's shirt, it won't be his."

Stepping back, he leaves me with the clothes, ignoring my brother's suspicious look from across the room. Thinking Xavier has taunted me with the knowledge of his "compound whore" Kai shakes his head, watching the blonde with curious eyes.

Closing the bathroom door, I glance at the clothes, my stomach rolling with nerves.

If I wear this shirt, he wins. He thinks what happened now may be something he explores again.

If I walk out, Kai sees my bruises and pieces together what the hell just happened.

Biting my cheek, I silently cuss, my hand forcing on the man's shirt, his scent consuming the material. Becoming aroused once more, the bond between us grows stronger, my heart yearning to feel his touch in more ways than one. □

Fuck my life.

Forcing my hair into a braid, I swing open the door, tucking his shirt into my waistband. Much larger on me, the shirt is loose. his eyes laced with a look of satisfaction at seeing me in his clothes. Changed from his stained pants, he wears a pair of Fallan's, not asking permission to wear the clothing.

Giving the pants one look, I shake my head, my mind filled with anything but love.

"Forest?" Kai questions. "Is everything fine-"

"I'm fine." I snap, shoving past the two men, my body spilling into the hallway.

Leaving them in the room behind me, I make my way down the hallway, one feeling prevailing through it all.

Want.

A want for touch.

A want for control.

A want for *Xavier.*

CHAPTER FIFTEEN

VALERIE

"You did what?" I question, her head lowered, her legs curled into her body in an attempt to make herself smaller. Sitting in one of the lounging areas, she had pulled me aside, all of my instincts telling me to avoid the conversation. Feeling her hand shake as she pulled me along, I quickly realized how petrified she really was. Barely looking me in the eyes, she laid the events that happened with Xavier in her dorm out on the table, the bruises on her wrists light but visible. After some hesitance from Kai to leave her alone with me, I managed to convince her to eat the plate of food he had brought her, her mouth hungrily devouring the food with no difficulties.

Barely looking up, her face is red, clouded with shame. This is the first isolated conversation we have shared in months. Despite the anger I harbor toward the women, there were countless other people she could have pulled aside to explain this to. She did not need to pull me aside, let alone isolate me as she has now. She knew the risk of speaking to me alone. She knew judgment was sure to follow. Taking deep breaths, I glance at her neck, the chain housing her rings gone.

"You said you wouldn't judge," she snaps, her voice shaky each time she speaks.

"That was before you told me Xavier had you pinned down and begging for more in your dorm!" I exclaim, shaking my head in protest. "What would Fallan think-"

"I don't know, Val!" she growls, her body suddenly less rigid. "I don't even know if he loved me or loved the idea of having the woman who killed the person he really loved at his disposal!" she seethes, the truths that Elyon had shared eating her alive.

"I have no idea what I really was to Fallan. Elyon ensured that would be the case. Fallan is dead, and because of it, so is the possibility of the truth! Xavier can hardly say anything without hurting us both. So I am so fucking sorry if, despite my hate for the man, he can at least distract me from the fact that I may have never been loved to begin with."

Snapping my mouth shut, her pain radiates off of her, the sorrow she has buried imploding within her.

"Judgment is the only thing I can give you, Forest," I mutter, her eyes narrowing. "For months, you have shut everyone out. Now, the only things I know about you are the conclusions I have had to draw myself." I whisper, my voice shaky.

Taking a moment to focus on the elephant lingering in the room, Forest sighs, her legs pulling away from her chest as she finally adjusts her posture.

"Val, he betrayed us-"

"I know that, Forest!" I yell, my eyes clouding with tears. "I know that. But you have failed to do the one thing I have been wanting you to do for months!"

We both pause, our eyes locked on one another. Silently waiting for my response, she keeps her mouth shut.

"I want you to fucking apologize. I want to see you have remorse over what you did."

Seeing a shift in her demeanor, she goes rigid, her body tense with strain. Giving me a cold look, it's easy to tell how little remorse she truly feels about the situation. It doesn't matter what any of us say; the woman truly did think what she had done was necessary, and perhaps she is right. Still, I've needed her. I've needed someone other than Kai or Aaron to help me navigate my own confusion, and she hasn't been there.

My anger is so much more than the death she has created.

Everyone needed her, and she wasn't there.

"I'm sorry I took him from all of you, Valerie-"

"It wasn't just him you took, Forest. You took yourself that day and buried her into the abyss that Fallan died in. You have lied, manipulated, and pushed away the one man who might be able to bring you back from all of it. Do you have any idea how many nights Xavier spent outside your dorm listening to your screams? Do you know how many times he had the cooking staff make meals they didn't even know how to make, somehow knowing you enjoyed them? Do you have any idea how many times Kaiden got excited to see your face, knowing damn well you had no intention of speaking to him? You shut everyone out because you thought you were helping, when in reality, the only fucking person you were helping was yourself. We have all lost people, Forest, but you're still here. So, if you could take a moment to stop being a selfish prick, perhaps, things can go back to something semi-close to normal!"

Growing silent, the sound of my deep breaths fills my ears.

Perhaps she will say nothing-

"You're right," Forest whispers, her eyes filling with the first sign of emotion I have seen in months. "Youre right about all of it."

Landing her face in her hands, she takes a deep breath.

"Sometimes asking for your forgiveness, knowing I might never be able to get it is more terrifying than shutting you all out completely. I'm not an idiot, and neither is my brother. I know he has an idea of what I did. I'm scared. He and Mark are all I have left, and even then, Mark is still so torn up from what has happened, there's no guarantee I say one wrong thing and don't send him over the edge. I'm scared, Valerie. I know I have fucked up, and Xavier-"

She pauses, letting out a defeated sob.

"I fucking straddled and teased myself with our Commander in my dorm and did it with no shame," she cries, her hand shaking once more.

Hesitantly reaching out, the girl I once knew breaks through her cold facade. Grasping her hand, I make the conscious decision to scoot onto her couch, allowing my body to lean into hers. Tensing up, she relaxes into the touch, grasping my hand as hard as she possibly can.

"Did you want him to continue with his actions?" I ask, still putting together the pieces of what Forest truly means to Xavier. His obsession with her is not new, that much I have gathered. Given the strains he has in his mind, it's impossible to paint a whole picture, especially if parts of Forest's memories are still buried deep within her mind.

"I didn't want him to touch me lovingly, Val. I didn't want him to be gentle," she says, her hands rubbing her wrists.

"Then what did you want, Forest?" I question.

"To feel the pain. I wanted to distract myself with the pain he could inflict."

Taking a moment to digest her words, I squeeze her hand harder.

"You think that you deserve pain?" I question, her body burying deeper into mine.

"I think I deserve to suffer for what I have done. I thought allowing Xavier to do what I could with me would solve that."

"And?" I push, a tear slipping free from her eye.

"The pain he inflicted felt more loving than anything else I have felt these past six months. It only made me want him more."

Letting that truth linger in the air between us, I sigh.

"What are you to him, Forest?" I question.

"Something that I do not have the energy to explore yet. It doesn't matter how much hate I give him, he always finds a way to push past it. No matter what I do to Xavier, he will always find a way back."

"And how do you feel about that?" I question, her eyes meeting mine.

"If I answer that truthfully, then Fallan's memory is as good as gone. I can't explore what me and Xavier are, because every time I do, the truths said about Fallan only seem to become that much more real."

"Real?" I question, wiping the tear from her face. "Or truthful? Sometimes the truth is the last thing we want to face."

Nodding her head, she says nothing, my eyes glancing at my watch.

"We leave today to settle into the Sanctuary for the next few nights," I utter, pulling her up with me as I stand.

"A lot of things are unknown right now. What I do know is the last thing I want is you being distant in all of this," I say, pulling her in for a hug. Graciously accepting the offer, she holds me tight. "I don't forgive you, but that doesn't mean I don't care about you."

Letting out a gentle laugh, she squeezes tighter.

"I can work for your forgiveness," she whispers, keeping me close.

"I'm counting on it."

"He really made the chefs prepare new meals?" she questions with a sniffle, blatantly unaware of the softer side of our brute Commander.

"Oh, Forest," I smile. "That was only the beginning."

Chapter Sixteen

Kaiden

Strapping the ropes down on our truck, I pull the chords with all that I have, stumbling backward once my hands lose traction. Bracing my lower back before I can topple over, Aaron smiles, his freckled cheeks creasing with his dimples as he watches me try to pull my weight. Only needing one vehicle given our group's size, we pack as much as we can into the bed, only leaving a few gaps of room for those of us riding in the back.

"What's so funny?" I question, watching the man cross his arms.

"You, trying to pull your weight. I will give you credit for being able to pack the bags like a pro, but your dismount while trying to tighten down straps could use some work," the man says. Playfully nudging him away, I scowl at him.

"Last time I checked, all you were doing to help is standing there and watching me," I warn, pointing my finger at the man with accusation.

"Perhaps it makes me smile to see you trying so hard," he mutters, my chest filling with a wave of nerves at the comment.

Shoving down the feeling, I scold myself for having a reaction to it at all. Aaron is just messing around. Reading between the lines about a comment like that is idiotic. All he does is mess with others. I am no isolated instance of him trying to be something more than playful.

Keeping his large bag slung across his back, he patiently waits for me to try lugging it into the bed. Stepping aside, I roll my eyes, not wanting to embarrass myself with my utter lack of upper body strength.

"Wise choice, Blackburn," he smiles, moving closer, my body instinctively moving in front of him.

Glancing at me, he raises his brows, another smile pulling across his face.

"For the record, if needed, I could totally beat your ass," I warn, growing redder the moment a laugh escapes his mouth. Slamming his hand over his lips, he grins, my stomach flourishing with nerves once again.

What the hell is wrong with me?

"If that's what you need to tell yourself, Blackburn," Aaron smiles, moving past me, easily tossing the bag into the back of the vehicle. Playfully scruffing my hair, I shove him away, listening to his joyous laugh at my annoyance.

This is the banter he and I have created over the past several months.

He pushes me past my comfort limits, I force his ego back down to reality. Initially, I was quite annoyed by the relationship we had created. Now, given how long he knew Hunter, it almost feels welcoming.

"Who is driving?" I question, looking at the empty driver's seat.

"Xavier took the initiative," Aaron states, pulling himself into the back of the truck. Offering me a hand, I swat it away, pulling myself up with a little less ease. "Although I doubt Forest will trust him to do anything alone."

Taking a seat next to Aaron, our legs brush, my mind already mentally prepared to watch him pull away as Hunter always had. Leaving his leg where it is, he settles into his seat, glancing at my observance of our legs with a cocked head.

"Not a fan of my pants?" Aaron questions, both of us wearing the same dark tactical gear.

"Funny," I state, rolling my eyes at the man.

Standing abnormally close, Bekah and Val approach the vehicle, both of their hands grazing one another as they walk. Leaning forward to get a better look at the pair, Aaron smirks, his lips pulling closer to my ear as he whispers.

"How subtle do you think they think they are?" he questions, my head turning to face him.

Not backing away, his face is inches from mine, my hand gripping my pant legs as I try to focus.

"You really think they are an item?" I question, his smile growing.

"They are constantly around one another and always feeling each other up. I'd say their willingness to hide whatever is going on between them is about to be void," he whispers, leaning away as he spreads his legs, getting into a more comfortable position. Letting my leg continue to press into his, he sighs. "I wouldn't have the energy to hide what I want."

Processing his words, I swallow nothing, my eyes snapping in his direction.

"I don't see you parading around with any woman. I would say you're keen on hiding your wants," I scoff, his eyes narrowing at me.

"Yeah? Who told you I was going after women?" he questions, my stomach threatening to force breakfast back up.

Grabbing my leg, he squeezes, his laugh breaking through the air once again.

"I'm fucking with you, Kaiden," he laughs, letting go of my leg, the touch lingering. "I haven't found a connection worth exploring," he admits, a wave of disappointment washing over me, quickly followed by a wave of regret over the thoughts I am allowing myself to have.

"Right," I say, my mind racing back to Valerie and Bekah.

"Your cousin needs something to distract herself from the fact she lost two childhood best friends at the same time," I mutter. "As do you," I continue, his interest suddenly perking.

"You have any ideas, Blackburn?" he questions, his tone forcing another wave of nerves in me.

What the fuck is going on with me?

Lowering my head, Aaron's smile drops, his hand touching my back.

"You lost someone as well. Don't discredit that pain by forcing on a smile," he says quietly.

"Hunter would have loved the flowers that bloomed this summer," I utter, my eyes focused on the sprawl of flowers decorating the compound.

Saying nothing, Aaron's hand drops. His liveliness when around the topic of Hunter is always depleted. Hiding as many truths as everyone else, he shuts down, my annoyances toward the others avoidance something I am struggling to hide.

Startled, a bag goes skidding across the bed, slamming into the other bags with a thud. Looking up, Forest's face is fixated into a scowl, her focus on anything but us. Moving around the vehicle, she crawls into the passenger's seat, slamming the door closed as hard as she can. Making the vehicle shake, I widen my eyes at her attitude, watching the way she crosses her arms, her eyes staring out the window. Much angrier than she had initially been when leaving her dorm this morning, I glance at Aaron, his eyes just as wide as mine.

"What has her so worked up?" Aaron questions.

Clearing her throat, Valerie joins us on the bed, Bekah only a few steps behind her. Settling into the seat across from us, the blonde glances at Forest, making room for Bekah as the redhead slings her arms behind the both of them.

"Xavier," Valerie states.

"When I got her from her dorm this morning, Xaver was already with her. She did seem pretty off," I mutter, wondering what had gone down between them.

"Two sexually deprived individuals with hate for one another alone in a dorm?" Bekah questions. "Put the pieces together. Perhaps her anger is about something a little more physical?" Bekah questions. Swatting Bekah in the leg, Valerie looks pissed off.

Narrowing her eyes at the redhead, it's clear whatever information Bekah just spewed was not something Valerie was supposed to repeat.

"Wait," I question, glancing at my sister. "Did Xavier have sex with my sister-"

"No," Xavier's brooding voice interjects. Carefully placing his bag in the back of our truck, he cocks his head. "Although, I can't say I bring out the best emotions in her," he mutters, glancing at the passenger side of the car.

"They are going to crash this vehicle and kill us," I mutter, watching Xavier smile at the statement.

Hopping in the back, Xavier tightens down our final supplies, making the task look easy compared to me.

"We need to leave now if we want to make it before dinner," Bekah states, receiving nothing but a nod from Xavier.

Pulling free a sketchpad from his bag, Aaron begins to doodle, his drawing very baseline. Clearly new to the hobby, Xavier eyes the sketchpad, crossing his arms as he watches the man.

"You took that from my room," Xavier snaps.

Smiling, Aaron waves it in the man's face.

"It was my turn to find a talent."

Scoffing, Xavier shakes his head.

"I think you should keep searching," Xavier says, eyeing the childlike drawings scattered across the page.

Hiding my smile, Xavier gives me a grin, his lighthearted attitude something all of us so rarely see. Continuing on with his final adjustments to our supplies, I watch Aaron draw, his hands hard at work to create something semi-recognizable.

The sketchbook is Fallan's. Something he left behind that Xavier felt the need to keep, and Aaron felt the need to steal.

"Since when do you draw?" I question.

"I feel like, in some way, Fallan's presence lives on in his work," Aaron states, flipping through the pages, my eyes landing on the drawings Xavier clearly created. It is filled with nothing but different perspectives of my sister's face. The images are painted, crafted with a certain observance Fallan's drawings lacked. "Although, I can't seem to figure out who this is."

Landing on one of Fallan's older drawings, I catch a glimpse of a young woman, her hair straight and long, and eyes narrow. Smiling in the drawing, she wears gear similar to ours. Not quite Forest, but someone entirely different.

"It's Elyon's daughter," Xavier mutters, not looking at the page. "It's Dove."

Saying nothing, the group goes silent, all eyes but Xavier's averting to the page.

"Everyone has secrets," Xavier whispers, jumping down from the bed of the truck.

"I didn't want to believe what Elyon told Forest about Dove," Aaron whispers.

"Sadly, Fallan had more secrets than he did answers and he was killed before he could be honest with all of you," Xavier says coldly.

Saying nothing, he moves into the driver's seat, all of us watching as Forest scoots closer to the window, creating as much space between the two of them as she can.

Sitting in silence, my eyes linger on the paper, Aaron quickly deciding to tuck it away the moment Forest's eyes catch a glimpse of what we are staring at. Locking eyes with me, she looks pained, her head lowering in disappointment.

It doesn't matter what truths are being kept from me.

Forest knows far too many.

And it's eating her alive.

CHAPTER SEVENTEEN

FOREST

Keeping my head pressed against the glass, the motion of the vehicle jolts me every few moments, pulling me away from my blank stare into the great unknown. Forcing my legs as far away from Xavier as possible, his hand grips the steering wheel, his eyes glancing to me every few minutes. Not having the courage to look at my friends in the back through the window, my nails dig into my legs, my mind thinking of anything but the interaction Xavier and I shared in my dorm. Instinctively reaching for the rings, I feel nothing, my fingers grazing my bare skin. Feeling the pulsing pain from Xavier's bites, I focus on healing the skin, unable to fully fix the damage without his blood.

Frustrated, I focus my Hold on a pile of rubble 300 meters out, watching it crumble to the ground the longer I stare at it. Feeling the energy flood through me, I breathe heavily, directing all my anger on every bit of the already broken structure that I can.

"Are you going to ignore me the whole ride and keep shattering what's left of the old world, or are you going to grow up and talk to me?" Xavier questions, utilizing his voice for the first time this whole ride.

Going rigid at the sound of his voice, I straighten my back, keeping my focus outside of the window.

"I don't want to look at you right now," I mutter, blocking away the imagery of his mouth and hands exploring my body.

The last thing I need is to look over at him wearing Fallan's clothes and feel yet another ping of guilt in my chest.

Sighing, his frustrations escalate, the space between us feeling that much smaller.

"It's too long of a ride for you to ignore me the whole time," he snaps, the vehicle jolting, his hand clearly struggling to stay still.

Feeling the burning heat claw its way from the depths of my stomach, the command in his voice does things to me. Wishing I was deaf, I claw deeper into my legs, replaying every single awful thing he has done, settling on the imagery of my father's lifeless body.

"You know I can feel what you are trying to suppress right?" he questions, my cheeks radiating the heat he has created.

Knowing I have all my barriers up, I narrow my eyes, ready to call this man's bluff.

"Fallan couldn't if I locked him out of my mind," I whisper, moving my body further into the passenger side door.

"Maybe that will finally make you question the legitimacy of the bond you shared with him." Xavier scoffs, my head staying pressed against the glass.

Tearing my hand free from its grasp of my thigh, his hand lands on its surface, his fingers brushing my inner thigh as he grabs my leg. Feeling the warmth return, I touch his hand, ready to push him away. Squeezing gently, he stops me, his thumb running a circle above the skin.

"Forest, look at me," he asks politely, my body staying faced away in protest.

Squeezing harder this time, his touch grows more impatient, his hand gripping my thigh as he drags me a few inches away from the window, his fingers buried in my leg. Keeping my gaze out the window, his annoyance forces a smile onto my lips.

"Forest, look at me before I make you in front of all of these people."

Swallowing nothing, I hesitantly look his way, unsure if I want to know what his threat really means. Locking eyes with the man, he keeps his hand on my leg, his eyes filled with frustration.

"What's wrong?" he questions, genuinely seeking an answer.

Could he be that dense?

Can he truly not piece together why I would be so avoidant of him right now?

"What we did. What I allowed you to do. It was-"

"Hormonal," he interrupts, allowing his fingers to grip tighter. "You need someone to make you forget about your feelings, even if it is just for a few minutes-"

"And that should be you?" I question, frustrated by how little I know.

"You've made it clear how you feel about me," he growls. "I figured a hate fuck is considerably more distracting than anything else the men of the compound could have provided."

Internally shaming myself the moment he says "hate," my throat swallows nothing, my hand still hesitant to remove his from me.

"I need clarification, Xavier," I settle on saying after several seconds of quiet eye contact.

"I'll give you as much as I can," he sighs, bracing himself for new lesions.

"Dove.... She and Fallan-"

"Were in love, if that's what you were about to ask," Xavier clarifies, answering my question before I can even finish it. Growing nauseous at the idea of Fallan being in love with another, I shake my head.

"And you knew him?" I clarify.

"Not outside of what I did to his family, and the ties he had to Elyon's daughter. Elyon had taken a certain interest in him, as he did me. Now I know why," Xavier says, wincing as he speaks.

"And us?" I question, his mouth snapping shut.

It's the one question no one can seem to answer.

The possibilities of what his answer could be haunts me, pushing me to do things I would have never done only a few months ago.

Listening to the silence, my need for the one answer I was hoping to have begin to dwindle.

"Did what we do feel wrong?" he questions, patiently waiting for a response.

"Tremendously."

"Beyond the guilt, did the feeling of my hands on you feel wrong?"

No.

That's the problem.

Every second his hands were on me felt right. In the past, every time Xavier touched me, it felt foreign, as if glass was cutting my skin. Still, I could not shy away from the way his presence made me feel. Now, in light of the bond, all I crave is his hands on my skin, touching me in any way he pleases.

In many ways, I worry I crave being the source of his pleasure.

"No," I settle on saying, hoping my silence was enough for him to not pry.

"You're lying to me," Xavier whispers, dragging me just a bit closer. "Do you know how hard it is for me to hold back with you?" he questions, my eyes already on his. "Do you understand how much you frustrate me?"

Scoffing, I lean closer, my expression painted with anger.

"The feeling is mutual," I snap, shaking as I speak.

Quickly scanning me up and down, he focuses back on the road.

"You need to start taking care of yourself if you want to keep sneaking behind my back to converse with Mason," Xavier grovels, something festering within his mind.

It's not quite as strong as anger, but equally dangerous when expressed by Xavier.

Jealousy.

"You're angry I've been spending alone time with Mason."

Letting out a laugh of defeat, he bares his teeth.

"I'm fucking angry, Forest, because I can't touch you in the ways I want, let alone speak to you!" he yells, loud enough some in the back might be able to hear.

"Then how did you back in my dorm?" I question, pushing the man further.

"Our lips cannot touch. It does not mean I can't touch you in other ways," Xavier says, moving his hand farther up my leg.

"If you say the wrong thing, or touch me in the wrong way, you risk both of our lives?" I question.

"Yes," he sighs, looking more defeated the longer this conversation plays out.

"Why risk it?" I question, his eyes avoidant of mine.

"I watched the man who was hired to bring you to me touch you for months, becoming the reason for your smile," he whispers, unable to look anywhere but forward. "Even if you hate me, Forest, being the reason for any ounce of your pleasure is enough for me."

Without much thought, I grab his hand, urging it farther up my leg, his fingers nearly brushing my warmth. feeling that surge of excitement, his eyes finally glance to me, the blood flow between his legs once more causing strain I shamefully wouldn't mind easing.

"What did you hear while I was showering?" I question, the words escaping my mouth before I can stop them.

"I heard you touching that pretty body of yours and rocking your hips into your hand," he starts, his hand creeping closer to my waistband. "I heard that soft moan leave your lips and questioned every single one of my morals when I held myself back from walking in there myself and finishing what you had started," he continues, my warmth already aroused by his touch on my leg. "I questioned why I tied that woman up in the first place when, in all reality, she was the last person I wanted in that position-"

All at once, the guilt of what I have allowed to happen once again comes crashing down. Knowing some other woman has felt the intoxicating feeling of his touch, my own feeling of jealousy comes over me, the validity in his words becoming less apparent. Knowing he has said the same thing to others, my mind races, unable to understand why the imagery angers me so. Suddenly wishing I had snapped the woman's neck, his touch now feels shared with every other woman he has managed to get into his bed. Tearing his hand away from me, I toss it back at him, his eyes widening with surprise.

"You're just a compound sleaze trying to get his dick wet," I snap, moving closer to the window once again.

Scoffing at me, he narrows his eyes, now gripping the steering wheel with his right hand, letting his left try and shove down the strain in his pants.

"If that's how much respect you think I have for you, then you won't mind me exploring the women in this sector."

Angered by the sheer amount of jealousy a statement can create, I speak without thinking.

"Be my fucking guest. Perhaps it's time I branch off as well. I'm getting tired of being touched by men who know me before I even know them!" I seethe.

Both filled to the brim with an influx of emotions, the jealousy festering within both of us is detrimental.

"You're the reason he's gone," I snap, reminding him once again of the reality he has created.

Glancing toward me, Xavier's eyes are filled with anger, his mouth curling into a devious smirk.

"And you're the reason I'm here. I suppose you are as much at fault for Fallan's death as I am."

Focusing his attention on the road for the duration of the drive, silence festers between us, each second more painful than the last. Unable to think of a retort, I push my head against the glass once more, closing my eyes as I think of nothing but the shame I carry.

CHAPTER EIGHTEEN

JOSH

"You want us to move toward the Sanctuary tonight?" I question Elyon, his eyes scanning the three different colors of napkins awaiting his approval.

Hyper-focused on the small details of his extravagant homecoming party, nothing goes without his approval. Watching the man examine each napkin, he focuses on the light creme-colored one in the middle, waving away his other two Paradoxes, pinching the napkin between his two fingers.

"Do you think this will align with the color scheme?" he questions, acting as if he didn't ask me and his men to infiltrate the Sanctuary to force some fear into Forest. Looking over the bland-looking napkin, I shrug my shoulders.

"It looks pretty much the same as the other ones," I admit, knowing there is no point in lying to the man.

Rolling his eyes, he tosses the napkin in my face, pointing a ringed finger toward his closest Paradox.

"Come back when you have found something up to my standard," he hisses, urging the Paradox away from him with his Hold. Finally making full eye contact, he takes a seat in his chair, looking at me with a look of question.

"Was I not clear enough for you? Go to the Sanctuary, find Forest, and remind her what true fear feels like," Elyon snaps, looking at me as if I am the dullest being to walk this planet.

"By that you mean-"

"Torture her for all I care. Do what you please with her. You and I both know she is quite a pretty face; I'm sure you can make use of it," he snaps. It's clear his respect for Forest only extends as far as the power she may provide him.

"Fear is what you want her to feel?" I question, his eyes rolling as if my questions could not be any more mind-numbing.

"I want you to give her a reason to be afraid. Clearly, she and Xavier roam the lands as if there isn't a target on both of their backs. My sorry excuse of a Commander needs a reminder of what's at stake. He has grown comfortable, and she has grown vulnerable. I'd say it's time for both of them to remember what it means to cross me," he hisses, slamming his fist into the armrest of his chair.

"And killing her isn't an option?" I question. It comes as no surprise how willing I am to watch the woman suffer. The Blackburns have been nothing but a vile plague to my people's society. I nearly celebrated the day I became aware of Katiana's death. For every Blackburn that falls, my father comes that much closer to resting easy, knowing I did everything in my power to make the people who stabbed him in the back suffer.

I will savor Xavier's demise the most.

"No. You will not kill her; rather scare her, remind her what it is she is truly running from. I don't care how you manage to scare her, but you are going to need to keep her down," Elyon says, reaching into his robe.

Holding out a large syringe filled with clear liquid and red swirls, I examine the gift, flicking it until all the bubbles have dissipated.

"What am I looking at here?" I question, my eyes scanning the syringe up and down.

"A strong sedative. One powerful enough to keep five men down and then some. I infused my blood into this batch to ensure she stays unconscious long enough for you to drag her someplace quiet." Pulling out yet another syringe, one much smaller, he tosses me the needle, my hand grasping its slim base. "Use this one on her brother, make sure she sees him alive and panicked when she wakes up. The only way any of you are making it out of that room alive is if you have her brother for leverage. I am trusting you not to fuck this up, Joshua," he warns, my name like poison on his tongue.

"Take a few extra men with you. You will need the support," he snaps, looking me up and down.

Could she really be that much of a threat?

Back at the academy, I could break her pretty little nose without so much of a second thought.

"Those foolish thoughts will end with you in the same position as your father. Do not take Forest Blackburn to be anything but a deadly force, one you will navigate carefully."

Of course, he is already in my mind.

Nothing is private anymore.

Dirty Marked.

"Remember how important she is to your prior Commander," Elyon whispers, my hands shaking in light of my ignorant comment within my mind. "The same Commander who ensured your father's brain matter was plastered across your face."

Thrown back into that night of the Lottery, I close my eyes, shutting out the panic that overcomes my chest each time I let it happen. Seeing nothing but Xavier's cold gaze paint my vision, the want to bash the man's head in and hear his cries is the only thought I allow myself to explore. Watching Elyon's smile rise at the anger he has created; he leans back in his chair with a grin, waiting until my anger has reached a manageable level before speaking.

"You done?" he questions, my voice nothing but a whisper.

"How would you like us to torture her?" I question, suddenly much more eager to find a way to make the blonde suffer.

"Cut her, beat her, or even have your way with her. Do whatever you deem necessary to ensure she and Xavier feel pain," he smiles. "Even if that means torturing poor sweet Kaiden, until he is as lively as his parents," Elyon mutters, a second wave of thrill washing over me.

Imagine the pain Xavier would feel knowing his poor little Forest was tortured beyond recognition, knowing damn well, there might have been something he could have done about it.

"Poor Xavier," Elyon laughs. "Always two steps behind, left to watch the people he loves suffer at the hands of the enemies he should have killed."

Scoffing, I tuck the syringes away into my pockets, giving the room an observant glance.

"Is there anything else you'd like to discuss?" I question, feeling less confident the longer I am forced into a space with Elyon alone.

"That will be all. Get together your men and then begin your trek. I will let the ward guards know of your exit," Elyon says, pulling his focus back to the long list of to-dos scrawled on a large piece of paper.

Turning away, the door to the man's study opens, a mask of silver looking me over, ready to escort me from the space.

"Josh?" Elyon questions, my head snapping backward.

"Yes?" I question, my throat dry with anxiety.

"Mess this up, and I will personally rip out every one of your teeth and force you to swallow them until you choke," Elyon smiles, his tone incredibly light in contrast to his haunting words.

Saying nothing, I nod, adjusting the front of my uniform.

Moving past the follower in wait, I keep my gaze forward, fully aware of what a task like this entails.

Forest Blackburn will feel true fear.

That is not a promise.

It's a guarantee.

It has to be.

CHAPTER NINETEEN

FOREST

S urrounded by a glimmering ward, the Sanctuary comes into perspective, its buildings still being pieced back together little by little. Mostly a functional compound once more, a group of guards sits in wait for our arrival, Nyla's kind smile lighting up the moment she sees our vehicle. Waving with a smirk, Xavier looks toward the woman, her eyes growing wider, my mind shutting out the sinful thoughts she carries every time she looks at the man. Pulling her attention toward me, she tugs at her collar, her mind reeling to the night I aided in destroying this compound. Touching her earpiece, she mutters a few commands, a large hole the size of our vehicle opening wide, allowing us safe access past their deadly ward. Since being rebuilt, guards exchange shifts, guarding every possible entrance 24/7.

Considering the casualties they faced, man and child alike, Nyla thought it best to ensure absolutely no one could be at risk should there be another attack. Protocols have been implemented, forcing all untrained citizens to find protection, keeping the innocents safe from the tyranny of war. Moving deeper into the compound, Nyla's guards direct us to park with their other vehicles, my focus on all they have needed to rebuild. Most buildings in the downtown portion of the city needed attention; some I hadn't even realized were affected.

"We managed to destroy this much?" I question, breaking my silent streak with Xavier.

"Can you see why people are wary of you now?" he snaps, his voice as cold as ice.

"Are you?" I question, his voice scoffing.

"No. Perhaps that makes me a fool."

Looking toward the group in the back, I can't help but notice Kai and Aaron's closeness. Their legs touch as they ramble on about whatever mindless topic interests them. Moving toward the window, Bekah pounds the glass, her eyes on Xavier.

"Park it, Evermoore, so we can start unloading!" she yells, kicking the feet of both men, ordering them to start pulling their weight.

Putting the vehicle in the park, Xavier jumps out, his hand already ready to shake the hand of the compound leader eagerly awaiting his smile. It's almost comical how quickly people changed their perceptions of him after what Elyon did. Even those in the compound who tormented him on his birthday have non-stop tried to gain his forgiveness, fully aware of how little he intends to accept. Opening my door, I jump to the ground, feeling a wave of dizziness come over me, my hands gripping anything I can to try and get a stable foothold. Taking shallow breaths, I wait for my focus to return, my body avoidant of joining the others as they pull supplies from the back of the truck.

"When's the last time you've had an actual meal?" Xavier's voice questions, his hands on me before I can stop him.

Holding me upright, he leans me into his chest, my body too weak to argue with him on the topic. Feeling my eyes begin to orientate, he keeps his arm strung across my chest, his free hand pressed against my lower stomach, holding me against him with a great deal of force. □

Sometimes, I question if he holds me like this with fear I will one day disappear.

"Does stealing food off of Kai's plate count?" I ask with a grin, my head resting on his chest as I look up toward him.

Anything but amused, he narrows his eyes.

"I'm serious, Forest," he hisses, keeping his gaze on me.

Reluctantly, I spew the truth.

"It's been a while."

Shaking his head, he lets me go, reaching toward his leg, his hand pulling free his blade. Dragging the sharpest edge over his palm, he doesn't wince, my eyes gravitating toward the pool of rich red collecting on his hand.

Grabbing me with his uncut hand, he drags me closer, leaving little room between us. Still distracted by unloading our supplies, the side of the vehicle conceals us, giving Xavier full reign to do as he pleases. Bringing his hand closer to his mouth, he takes a lick of his own blood, the red painting his lips. Wanting nothing more than to lick his lips clean, the need to consume his energy becomes overwhelming.

"Careful, Forest. You know the rules," he whispers, fully aware of the hold he has over me right now.

Moving his hand closer to my salivating mouth, my body burns with a new desire. Reaching his hand down to graze my inner thigh, he smiles once I wince.

"Your bites would heal nicely," he mutters, my eyes gravitating toward the bruises still on his neck.

Inching his hand closer, his forehead presses to mine, my body buzzing with adrenaline.

"How bad do you want it?" he questions, his voice hiding something much more erotic in his words. Biting my lip, his hand is inches away. All I would need to do is grab his wrist-

Grabbing my chin, he pulls his forehead away, forcing me to hold eye contact.

"I asked you a question," he warns, his impatience prevalent.

Feeling the shameful reaction from my body to his words, a wave of heat festers in my lower stomach, his own body reacting as sinfully as mine. Moving forward, I keep my body pressed to his front, concealing the blood flow between his legs.

"I will not beg," I hiss, grabbing his wrist. "I'm not one of your whores."

Dropping his smirk, he does not move me.

"Is that a challenge?" he questions, both of our bodies buzzing with thrill.

"It's a warning," I whisper, grabbing his knife and slicing the tip of my finger. Too close to stop me, I raise my own hand, watching the blood trail down my finger. "One of us will submit," I continue, landing my finger on his lips, his hand quickly shutting as it heals. Watching the bruise on his neck dissipate, he grows weaker, his eyes wide with confusion. "Temptation goes both ways."

Pulling my finger away from his lips, he wipes what's left off with his thumb, his eyes hot with rage. Backing away, he processes the powerplay I had managed to throw at him, both of our hormones replaced with annoyance.

Looking at his healed hand, the sound of others drawing closer snaps us back into reality. Moving past me, he grabs my arm, unable to hide the anger within him.

"I will let you heal your wounds if you promise to follow me somewhere with no questions," he whispers, his lips inches away from my ear.

Glancing at him, I shove down any excitement the statement might have caused.

"You're manipulating me to get what you want?" I question, his hand squeezing harder.

"I'm giving you the opportunity to heal yourself as you did me. I promise that after that little stunt, the last thing you want to do give me is attitude," he hisses, his eyes hot with rage. "Come with me with no lip, and I promise it will be worth your time. You can't survive on power alone."

Opening my mouth to protest, it quickly shuts the moment Valerie moves to the side of the truck. Having no argument, all I can do is nod.

Hesitantly agreeing, he releases my arm, pulling on a smile as if I didn't have him straining against his gear at the thought of me begging for him.

Two can play at your game, Xavier.

The problem is, nothing is ever just a game between us.

CHAPTER TWENTY

KAIDEN

Watching my sister trail after Xavier, a pit of unsettlement rests in my stomach. As much as I can tolerate their truce between one another, the two of them spending alone time together is a much harder pill for me to swallow, especially considering his and her abrupt reaction to me after I had knocked on the door to her dorm. I have learned my lesson when it comes to barging in, but given the massive bruise on his neck and the shame written on her face when we locked eyes, whatever happened between them is not something either of them is willing to come clean about.

"Fuck this," I whisper, ready to charge after my sister.

The last thing she needs is another man influencing her decisions. If I could rid her of men's wicked nature, perhaps she would be better off. Had I been a better older brother, I could have protected her from all of the evils we faced over the past year. Grabbing my jacket, Aaron stops me, his eyes already bound by a look of judgment.

"You're not going after her," Aaron snaps, tugging me back.

Stumbling, I turn on my heels, shoving his chest as hard as I can.

"Why the hell not? I could care less what kind of relationship you built with Xavier during all the time you spent trying to use him to replace Fallan. You have no idea whether or not she will be safe-"

"Take it down a notch, Blackburn," he hisses, cutting me off before I can continue. "If she is with Xavier, she will be fine, not that she needs the extra support. Last time I checked, Forest is capable of handling her own."

Readjusting my jacket, I move past him.

"Says the man who has no family," I say without thinking.

Scoffing at the statement, I fill with regret.

That is the last comment I should have made.

"Last time I checked, Valerie is still my family, and so are you," he hisses, no longer willing to engage in conversation. "Or at least *I* consider you to be."

Walking away before I can try to apologize, Nyla waltzes over, her hair wound into a bun on the top of her head. Stopping Aaron before he can leave the group, she waves over Bekah and Val. Circling the woman, we all cross our arms, patiently waiting for whatever skew of comments she wants to throw at us.

"So, you all are trying to find the reflecting pools?" she questions, biting back a smile that means nothing good.

"Yes, is there a reason we shouldn't be?" I ask, suddenly unnerved by the woman's demeanor.

"Why are you smiling like what he asked is a joke?" Aaron questions, his eyes wide with confusion.

"Because it is a joke. No one has seen the reflecting pools, let alone dip their toes in one," Nyla scoffs, waving her men off to haul away what's left of our supplies. Rasing their eyebrows, Bekah and Val look less lively, all of us curious as to why our reason for being here in the first place could be so comedic.

"Are you saying they don't exist?" I question, her head shaking.

"I never said that. I said no one has seen them." Extending an arm out, she directs us toward the Sanctuary's main strip.

"Walk with me, will you?" she questions all of us, moving before anyone can react.

Dragging our feet as we follow along behind her, our exhaustion sets in, each one of us eager to partake in the Sanctuary's lovely lounging.

As nice as the dorms are back at New Hope, nothing beats the feeling of goose feather pillows and silk sheets.

"Tell me, what do you know of the reflecting pools?" Nyla questions, her eyes wide with delight, as if the topic is one she could ramble on for hours.

"We've heard the whispers of what the Shifters were willing to tell us," Bekah mutters, finally contributing to the conversation. □

"So you have heard the stories?" Nyla questions, smiling ear to ear.

"What story?" I question, her hands clasping together with delight.

"The waters were told to have been the birthplace of the Prophet, otherwise known as the first Marked. You all know the stories of the great war. Nuclear fallout ravished the lands, the air nowhere near as clear as it is today, and that's saying something," she whispers, our eyes averting to the ward stowing away the thin veil of ash still floating through the air. "The human race as we knew it was near extinct; men and women turned into creatures, unable to make it back to their true form. The nuclear fallout changed their genetic code, fueling them with the desire to feed on anything they could, never able to satiate their hunger," she pauses, giving the group a long glance. "That is until a child crawled into the waters of the reflecting pool, barely able to take a breath, their body already facing the dire consequences of the radiation. Humans had gone underground, yet it never dwindled the spirit of a curious child," she continues, my mind racing.

"How do you know any of this?" I question, my eyes narrowing.

"Do they not teach you the readings of our ancestors in New Haven?" she questions, Aaron now the one to speak.

"They banned the old world's text from all of us," he mutters, shining some light on the knowledge she harnesses.

"Yet another luxury your kind took away from you," she says, continuing on her path. "The child was consumed by the waters, barely able to swim, their body flooded by the energy the Earth could provide. As if Mother Nature herself had breathed new life into mankind, the child emerged from the waters alive and, shockingly enough, still human despite the radiation. The Shifters that had chased the child cowered, filled with a new bloodlust in the presence of a new blood. The blood of the first Marked. Unlike the humans they had been forced to feed on, the blood of the Marked was richer and more satiating. Whereas the Shifters were creatures, hidden in the night, the boy could walk the Earth, dictating power far greater than any Shifter had been able to achieve."

"I thought all Shifters were Marked stuck in a state of Deception-" Bekah begins.

"We're getting there." Nyla continues. "The Shifters were a fail-safe for the altered humans. A guarantee that man could not push their newfound powers to their limits. For you see, a Marked is not a being of power, rather than a being able to blend in with mankind. It's a common misconception amongst your people to consider Shifters Marked, when that is far from the truth. Marked are those who derived from the Prophet. Shifters are those who derived from the consequences of war, all creations of Mother Earth."

"So no Marked can turn into a Shifter?" I question, her head shaking.

"Initially, until the Prophet deemed it a fitting punishment for those of his bloodline who stepped out of line," she warns. "The child grew large, aging with grace. Once the child reached adulthood, the need to expand his bloodline accelerated, and his followers passed on his blood as if it were the next plague. Sanctum's hubs were swarmed with his creations, a new divine race infiltrating the peaceful homes Sanctum tried to create."

"Was Sanctum always evil?" I question, her head shaking.

"Not initially. Unfortunates and Untouchables used to coincide with one another, only divided by pay rather than social status. Once the Prophet found out about the powerful offspring he had created, too much time passed, and the need to feed grew stronger. Some of our ancestors sensed the division that was about to be created. Society began to falter, and once those with gifts began disappearing, the free-willed minds amongst your society began to retaliate-"

"That's why the chips were implemented. Elyon needed control to ween out his Marked," I whisper, fitting the pieces together.

"Not only did he need the energy in their blood to remain youthful, he needed to ensure that he would remain the most powerful amongst his kind," she utters. "We knew the creator in silver to be the Prophet. The creators of the compounds fled the hubs before the New World Order was established, swearing to liberate the lives saved by the Order. Two compounds were established near each hub, promising to house anyone looking for refuge. When I was your age, I was told the stories, and now, I pass the torch to all of you," she says, my mind racing with a million different thoughts.

"Eventually, the need to combat the Prophet's forces was essential. It was said a savior, an Apparatus, would be born one day to be the Prophet's undoing," she says, my mind racing to Forest.

"If the Prophet's skew of words were true, Forest was made in a lab by Kaiden's grandparents-" Bekah starts.

"That's not possible," I interrupt, my thoughts revolving around the Prophet's many lies prevalent. "We've been over this plenty of times. Forest was not made in a lab. She's my fucking sister. The last thing I need is you spouting the Prophet's garbage in my ear," I hiss, the memories of her and I as children considerably hazier as the months have progressed.

"I'm just relaying what we were told-"

"No one asked you to do that," I hiss toward the woman.

Closing her mouth, she backs down, my fists balled with anger.

"No one said she was created by bright minds behind the wards, but if it's true, at the very least, the idea of how to create Forest came to them in the reflection of the waters. How else do you think humans could create power to that magnitude?" Nyla questions, clearly excited about the topic at hand.

Barely listening to her foolish conversation topic, my thoughts divert to one place.

"The Prophet's undoing, what you're suggesting is-"

"That Forest and the Prophet must die at the same time to permanently end the Marked's existence, yes."

My heart stops.

"The end defeating the beginning."

Forcing my nails into my palms, I try and think of something to say.

"Settle down, Kaiden; as I said, these are just stories, some many have turned away from. Not everyone is keen on believing the stories of the elders."

Scoffing at the woman, I relax, letting Aaron squeeze my shoulder, forcing me back into reality.

"They are just stories, Kaiden," he urges. "That's why she was smiling before she even spoke," he hisses, narrowing his eyes at the woman.

"What can I say," she beams, looking over every wide-eyed expression in the group. "Your reactions were more than enough reason to spout that bedtime story all of the elders shouted like scripture."

"Can you be any more insensitive?" Valerie questions, glancing toward my unnerved figure.

Waving my hand, I run my fingers over my eyes.

"Let's leave the cryptic bedtime stories for someone who is willing to entertain them," I hiss, Nyla's eyes rolling.

"Tough crowd," she mutters, finally stopping her tangent. "Perhaps a few drinks will help wash away the anxieties I have given you all?" she questions, all of us eyeing the rebuilt bar, everyone's shoulders relaxing at the sight.

Saying nothing, Nyla pushes past the doors, Valerie and Bekah hot on her trail. Grabbing my shoulder before I could follow along, Aaron stops me, his face pulled into a frown.

"What?" I question, his eyes looking anywhere but me.

"You do know she was just fucking with you right? Stories like that have swarmed these compounds for eons. She thinks it's hilarious to get a kick out of newcomers," Aaron says, doing his best to ease my anxieties.

"Let's just get a drink. I'm tired of thinking," I mutter, my hand reaching out for his without thinking. Startled, we both look at our grasp, my hand quickly retreating, landing behind my neck as I anxiously rub the skin.

"I'm sorry-"

"It's fine, Kai," Aaron sighs, finally looking me in the eyes. "At least to one of us."

Moving before I can speak, he moves past me, my words caught in my throat. Standing alone outside the bar, I have nothing to say, my mind stuck on the words Nyla shared.

Forest and the Prophet must die at the same time to permanently end the Marked's existence.

Bedtime story or reality, the notion is equally haunting.

CHAPTER TWENTY-ONE

FOREST

Taking my time to trail after Xavier, I land my feet in his footprints, trying to match his enormous strides when he is not looking. Smiling at the way he watches the ground as he walks, I quickly drop my grin the moment he looks back at me, his eyes catching a glimpse of my childish behavior. Suppressing his own smile, he makes an abrupt stop in front of an unrecognizable building, my body nearly slamming into him. Stopping in our tracks, I observe the pastel blue structure, its front void of damage from our battle. Looking around for a sign to give myself some clarity on where we are, I see nothing but the white paint-chipped door, a large open sign strung across its front. Looking around for other compound patrons, I see that this area of the sector is dead. If this is all part of some grand scheme to kill me, all the odds are in his favor.

"You really think this is how I would kill you?" he questions with a smirk. "Dragging you to some unfamiliar building with your abilities fully intact?" he questions, already buried inside my mind.

Swatting his arm, I touch my temple.

"Are you going to tell me where we are?" I question, watching his smile grow.

"That would involve me speaking to you, which would mean you have to be civil, and we both know you are incapable of a civil conversation right now, love."

Flustered at the comment, I narrow my eyes.

"You really want to argue that point with me?" I question.

Pulling his lips up, I see his real smile for the first time in what has felt like forever. Caught off guard by the light it gives his eyes, I take several moments to recompose myself. Watching the way his nose scrunches once he has let the grin consume his face, something in my heart flutters, something I'd rather keep shoved down.

Looking toward the door, he shoves it open, allowing me to go in first, saying nothing about the feeling nestled within the depths of my chest. Smelling a wave of savory and sweet baked goods, I close my eyes, enjoying the scents unfolding around me. Taking a deep breath, I let the scents soak in, my eyes flying open to marvel at the small space.

Wood tables, chairs, and a few odds-and-ends sofas crowd the dining portion of the space. Older than some of the other buildings in the sector, its walls are lined with wallpaper made of a print decorated with flowers. A large glass case divides the front counter to the customer's area. A menu filled with items I barely recognize rests above the cashier's station. Seeing another door behind the case, I hear the clatter of plates and cups. Looking at Xavier, his arms are crossed, his eyes watching me take it all in.

"What is-"

"We aren't open quite yet!" a lively voice chimes as the kitchen doors swing wide open.

Stepping behind Xavier, I allow him to make first interactions.

Wearing a nametag that is hardly on straight, the name *Mischa* hangs to the woman's apron. Appearing around the same age my mother was, her gray streaked hair is held back with pencils. Holding a curvier frame, she has a youthful glow to her skin, the natural aging process treating her well. Having a full pout and warm smile, she wipes the flour from her hands onto her apron, moving closer to the counter as she finally processes the two bodies in front of her.

"Xavier?" she questions with a smile, my interest in the small shop suddenly much higher.

"You really thought I would stay away from your shop if I were in this sector?" he questions, his tone much livelier than all the other times he has interacted with the others in the compound.

His tone here sounds natural as if he has been suppressing this side of himself for who knows how long.

Moving away from me, she focuses only on the man. Gathering the woman in his arms, he embraces her with a tight hug, one of the pencils falling free from her hair, her hands cupping his face.

"Of course, you look the same," she exclaims, pinching his cheeks. "While I sit here wallowing away in my own culinary despair," she mocks, poking fun at the man.

Watching his cheeks redden, he clearly is unfamiliar with touch as motherly as that. Swallowing the guilt inside my chest every time I think about how much he must have gone through to get where he is now, the nerves quickly return.

"You're as beautiful as ever-"

"You know I don't need you to kiss my ass," she laughs. "I thought it was you I saw last time in this sector before everything went to shit."

Rubbing the back of his neck, he throws her a look of apology.

"I didn't exactly have time to speak to you-"

Growing still, the woman's eyes lock with mine, her body rigid at the sight of me. Keeping my distance, I hold my ground, unable to look away from her petrified stare. Looking between Xavier and me, she rubs her eyes, suddenly much more interested in me than the blonde standing in front of her.

"Fores-"

Grabbing her arm, Xavier stops her before she can finish. Shaking his head, he places a finger over his lips, his eyes returning to their cold look. Unnerved by the woman's ability to clearly know my name, I take shallow breaths, trying to regulate the flood of anxieties rolling through me.

"Still?" Mischa questions Xavier, his only response a nod.

"Right," she says, forcing away her look of shock. "So, what will you two be having?" she questions, my eyes averting back to the foreign menu.

"I'll have a drip," he says, glancing back at me with a grin. "And she will have the lavender latte with honey."

Scrunching my nose at the order, she nods, moving away from us and back toward the kitchen. Keeping his hands tucked in his pockets as he moves toward me, I scrunch my nose, hearing his quiet chuckle escape him.

"I've never had that. How do you know I'll like it?" I ask sarcastically, his hand reaching out to grab mine.

Gently taking my hand, he guides me to one of the larger sofa chairs, urging me to take a seat. Settling into its soft fabric, my body thanks me for the break, making it impossible to protest once his hand lingers on mine for a few additional seconds.

"Just trust me," he says, leaning back in the chair.

"Is this a bakery? Like Jolie's?" I question, his head shaking.

"A cafe. We had a few in New Haven."

"My father really didn't give me time to explore any of the luxuries inside of New Haven. He was always so focused on keeping me at home and getting me to do my work," I sigh, Xavier's smile dropping.

As much as I'd like to ignore the truths Elyon laid out about my parents, no one else can seem to do the same. Admitting I am nothing more than a test tube lab junkie creation is one thing. Admitting to myself my family is not my own, and I am years older than I can remember is another.

Sometimes, ignorance is the one way to keep yourself sane.

"Do you really believe that?" Xavier questions, his eyebrows raised.

"Would you say otherwise?" I question, his mouth snapping shut.

Taking a few moments to listen to the sound of Mischa hard at work, he finally breaches the silence.

"If you could see anything, what would it be?" Xavier questions.

Pondering the question, I rack my brain with a million different ideas.

"The largest mountains the human eye can see," I smile, watching his grin return once more.

"How about you?" I question.

Looking away as he thinks of an answer, a new liveliness consumes his expression.

"I'd go overseas. I've heard stories of the rolling hills and beautiful pastures of flowers that blanket the Swiss lands," he smiles, eager to speak on the subject. "I heard a few years back they managed to isolate themselves from Sanctum's control, staying true to the roots of their ancestors. Cottages are as quaint as this building and society is void of the control we live in. Their Marked are safeguarded, and people united." His smile drops. "Or so the stories go."

"Why do you do that?" I question, leaning a bit closer. "Why do you get so eager and then shove it down?"

"Do people really care what I have to say?" he questions, his eyes glancing down at the slim amount of space between us. "Do you care, Forest?"

Feeling that familiar flush of red enter my cheeks, I clear my throat.

"Do you really think I do not care about you at all?" I question.

Paying no mind to my words, he shrugs his shoulders.

"You hate me-"

"Not for the reasons you think."

Hating him for what he has done would be blissful.

Hating him for how he has made me feel is nothing short of hellish.

"Then why do you so deeply attest me, Forest?" he questions, pushing me further than I'd like to go.

"You can step into my mind. You know why," I whisper, his body only moving closer.

"I want to hear you say it."

"Hope I'm not interrupting," Mischa interjects, both of us creating space, her hands balancing several things.

"No," I say, waving her over. "Come on over."

Placing down the drinks, my eyes gravitate toward the layer of foam on top of the latte, its top decorated with a tinge of purple and swirls of white. A drink as black as night rests in front of Xavier, its strength meant to keep a person up for days. Sliding a plate filled with treats across the table, Mischa smiles, my stomach grumbling at the sight of food.

"Oh, we didn't order anything to eat," I say politely, her mouth upturning at the comment.

"You look like you need it," she smiles, my head lowering at the realization of yet another person seeing my dwindling state.

Walking away, Mischa squeezes Xavier's shoulder, his eyes only on me.

"Think I'm still being a persistent asshole when I say you need to take care of yourself?" he questions, sipping on the dark drink.

Raising my cup to my lips, the sweet and bitter liquid coats my tongue. Surrounded by the drink's warmth, I can't help but smile at its taste. Grabbing the plate before he can interject, I joyously welcome the flaky pastry. Clearly, I was hungrier than I led myself to believe.

"I'll make you a promise to come here and eat as many pastries as I can while we are here, so long as you try to answer my questions," I whisper, his nod more than enough for me to begin my line of questioning.

"So, you and me... we knew one another?" I question, his shoulders rolling back with discomfort.

"Something like that," he says, cocking his head as he watches me.

Taking another bite, I run through the wording of my questions.

"And Mischa, she knew me?"

"You could say that."

"We were close?" I push, his eyes wavering over mine.

"That is definitely a way to put it," he pushes, throwing me nothing but cryptic answers.

"Why can't she tell me what she knows?" I ponder, watching her organize her case of treats.

"My bind has subconsciously forced me to kill anyone that utters my secrets."

"So it's all a guessing game?" I push, his smile dropping.

"Essentially."

"How do I know you're not lying?" I question, pointing my finger at his chest.

Grabbing my hand, he lowers it from his body, interlacing our fingers and resting it on his leg. Buzzing with delight at such a small interaction, I keep my hand in place, allowing the touch to happen.

"You don't. Trust will have to play into all of this."

Settling in my chair, I pull my focus away from the man and our interlaced hands. Giving the shop a long glance, my mind pictures a large painting on the closest wall, covering the tacky wallpaper with a beautiful landscape piece. Seeing nothing but the faint outline of where a painting once resided, I touch my temple, trying to pinpoint where the imagery had come from.

No, not imagery.

A memory.

"I've been here before," I whisper, my eyes dead set on the wall.

Letting go of my hand, Xavier's focus follows mine.

"The painting," he whispers, gently touching my chin to get me to look at him. "Do you remember the painting? Do you remember where it went?" he questions with a hope I have seen in him very few times.

Dread overcomes my soul, my frown lining my face immediately.

"I remember what it looks like," I whisper, his hand dropping from my face. "Nothing else."

Looking defeated, Xavier runs his hands through his hair, his eyes closed with frustration.

"Of course you do," he grovels, my mind drawing more blanks than I'd like to admit.

"Perhaps this will do more justice than words can at the moment," Mischa whispers, her floured hands dropping a photo in my lap before I can protest.

Facedown, the photo is older, dating from almost two years ago. Opening his eyes, Xavier looks at the photo, his gaze darting to Mischa.

"She's not ready–"

"She'll never be ready," Mischa snaps, silencing the man. "Perhaps it is you who's not ready."

Tuning out their conversation, my hand shakily grasps the photo, turning it with caution. Stuck in a state of shock, my own eyes look back at me, my hair twisted into multiple braids, pinned back to showcase my features. Sipping on the very latte I drink now, I smile with a wide grin, my cheeks flush with pink. As clear as the imagery in my mind, the beautiful landscape piece rests behind me, my hair as gray as it is now.

I don't remember this.

My heart beats out of my chest.

"Who took this-"

Stopping myself before I can start, I focus on the reflection in my cup.

Light gray curls and piercing gold-blue eyes. Distorted in the cup's reflection but so easily recognizable.

Xavier.

"Y- you took this?" I question Xavier, his cheeks as pink as mine in the photo.

"Like I told you, Forest," he whispers, plucking the photo from my hands. Observing it, a blissful smile paints his face, his finger trailing over the features of my face as if the woman in front of him is the farthest thing from the one in the photo. "I can only say so much."

Moving to retrieve the photo, Xavier stops Mischa, his hand already tucking away the photo inside his jacket.

"Can I keep this?" he questions, my mouth opening before hers can.

"Why would you want that?" I push, needing more now than ever to hear him speak.

"You're smiling," he settles on saying, politely waving Mischa away. "I never see it."

Ready to argue against his point, I stop myself.

He's right.

All I do is argue with the man.

If there is a side to me he once knew, I've done my best to avoid revealing it.

Call it fear.

Fear of what I will do once I remember all that has been stolen from me.

Xavier included.

For a moment, the grief weighing down on my chest is bearable, his presence a comfort rather than an avoidance. Settling into the chair, the tether running between us burns hot.

It was foolish of me to think the guilt would not come creeping in.

"At what point did you realize Fallan was lying to me?" I question, unsure if I want his answer.

Glancing over at me, he takes a sharp breath, downing the rest of his drink.

"Forest-"

"At what point, Xavier-"

"The whole time," he answers coldly. "I knew the whole time."

Reflecting on every interaction I shared with the raven-haired man, the memories now feel tainted; the love he gave me was something created by necessity rather than reality.

"You let it happen?" I question, anger ridding my tone.

"It's not like I had a choice-"

"We always have a choice, Xavier," I exclaim, eyeing the man down with conflict. "You would have been my choice," I blurt out loud for the first time, my words leaving my mouth before I can stop them. "It didn't matter how deep Fallan was in my mind because I still came back to you. You were the only thing I had under that ward that wasn't trying to harm me, and even when you did, for some fucking reason, I still loved-"

Stopping myself, his eyes are wide, hazed with a look I can't quite decipher. Covering my mouth, I close my eyes, shaking my head with embarrassment.

"I felt things for you, Xavier, that I shouldn't have, and it ate me alive," I push, trying to hide the well of tears in my eyes. "And the worst part is, I know I would do it all over again." Glancing up at him, the tears blur my eyes. "So don't tell me you didn't have a choice. It sounds like we always find a way," I push, anger washing over me. "Or at least one of us does."

Narrowing his eyes at the comment, the hell I just unleashed paints his expression.

"Is that why you did what you did?" he starts, his body rigid with strain. "Is that why you killed Hunter and ran away with Fallan every chance you got, even when I begged you to stay?" he pushes, his own frustrations finally breaking free. "Is that why you tell me you hate me, and regret every single interaction we have? Are your choices the reason you can allow me to touch you in private but can barely stomach a smile for me in public?" he questions, my heart flooded with pain. "Is that it, Forest?" he pushes, my head shaking. "You feel guilt now because he is gone, and I am all that you have left. If he were here, I know you'd go crawling to his feet and help him drive the dagger into my heart."

Standing up, I stare him down, the energy coasting inside of me reaching an unmanageable level.

"Do you honestly believe that?" I question, his expression only growing colder.

"Wholeheartedly."

Backing away, I glare at the man; my hands balled into fists.

"If you think that's true, then perhaps it's best my memories stay gone," I hiss, turning away before he could interject.

Shoving past the front door, I spill outside, trying to catch my breath. Needing a quick way to drown out my sorrows, I eye the bar, the mask of coldness I wore in the compound one I must force on around Xavier, too.

Pain is weakness.

Weakness ensures the people I love die.

Nothing I do now will make any of this right.

I suppose it's time to do what's wrong.

Chapter Twenty-Two

Xavier- The Dark Days

"So, you're hunting the Prophet?" I question, keeping my hood drawn.

Following behind the woman, she glances back at me with a grin, her beautiful smile enough to make most men fall to their knees. Reaching her hand back toward me, I eye the gesture with confusion, her hand grabbing my own before I can protest. Feeling its warmth radiate through me, that familiar flood of energy every time she is near me rolls through me; her cheeks flush with delight.

"Can't have you trailing off," she scolds, holding my hand as gently as she possibly can.

"You are aware I could twist your neck and leave you and this compound behind?" I warn, hardly able to consider it much of anything given its scarce resources. Large tents are pegged into the Earth, leaving little room for creativity. Dozens of buildings are plotted to be built, each one grander than the next. Large fences and dozens of guards on post help secure the new build. Among the array of tents lies four buildings. The Sanctuary headquarters, lodging, a cafe, and a bar. Despite the countless resources this compound needs to get anywhere near New Hope's magnitude, the priority to have liquor and caffeine has prevailed.

"Twist my neck?" she questions, laughing at the statement with thrill. "The only way anyone is getting their hands around my neck is when they're in my bed forcing me to-"

She pauses, suddenly aware of how open she was.

Feeling my cheeks flood with heat, I clear my throat, letting us both stop our march toward the pub with bewilderment.

"I didn't mean to be so-"

"Open?" I ask, trying not to imagine the woman in such a vulnerable position.

As defiant and cold as she can be, she is equally as exciting, someone most would want to spend a night with. Beautiful in every way a woman can possibly be, her voice is intoxicating, her mind a delight to explore. I catch myself questioning more often than I'd like what she looks like beneath all of the layers she chooses to wear. What would she do if someone truly took the control out of her hands? Would she ever be the type of woman to submit to anyone-

"One slip up from me, and you're questioning what I look like undressed?" she questions, glancing down, my robe thankfully covering the slight blood flow a thought pattern like that has created between my legs.

Keeping my cold demeanor, I ignore her question, ready to move past her. Touching my front, she stops me, her eyes meeting mine.

"I was created to end the Prophet's existence. That is why I hunt them," she clarifies, taking a deep breath. "You may question my actions, and for that, I do not blame you. I am on borrowed time, Xavier, so forgive me if I tend to lack social boundaries," she apologizes, sincerely seeking my approval.

"You say that as if my approval of what you do matters," I scold. "What role do I play in this anyways?" I push, trying to find the real reasons behind her kindness.

The last thing I need is to feel the sting of betrayal the moment she decides to abandon her role as a kind savior.

"He's had more of you in the past. Young, dumb Marked used and abused to be his little poster child. You've given me all that you know. Generally, I would have been rid of your kind the minute I was done getting what I wanted," she answers honestly, waiting for me to keep pushing.

"You sound as if you hate all that have been forced to associate with them."

"I do," she says coldly. "To a certain extent, those under the Prophet's thumb crave their approval, becoming brainwashed and susceptible to the lies the Prophet feeds them. To me, killing their servants brings me one step closer to creating the peace mankind needs."

"Do you wish to kill me?" I question, her smile returning once more.

Taking another step toward me, I hold my ground, not allowing the woman to gain the upper hand.

"If I wanted to kill you, Xavier Evermoore," she whispers, pulling her lips to my ear, her hands flat on my chest. "Don't you think I would have done so already?"

Her lips graze my cheek. "I had no reason to offer your parents a proper burial other than the fact it brought you peace. When you are in pain, I feel it. When you are angry, I feel it," she pauses, her mouth pulling away from my cheek and hovering to my lips. "When you are sexually at odds with your mind, I feel that too. I feel everything you feel when I am near you, as you do me. The problem is, I don't know why. So, pardon me for keeping you alive. Believe it or not, it's easier to care for someone's well-being when your mind and theirs are suddenly entwined."

"Why are you so avoidant about letting yourself trust me?" she asks, reading my mind like an open book.

"Why are you foolish enough to allow me your trust?" I push, baring my teeth to the woman.

Touching above my heart, she rests her warm hand on my front.

"Under that layer of pain, there is a heart that was made to care for others," she mutters. "Perhaps I'm angered by how easily you look past that."

"Hopeful you'll be the one to make me feel something, Forest?" I prod, her smile rising once again.

"If you fell in love with me, Xavier, it would only be your undoing."

"Don't worry; I am not concerned," I scoff, backing away from the woman, her hand dropping. "I don't prefer the woman I have chosen to be with viewing me as a monster."

Watching her smile drop, she shakes her head.

"I've never considered you a monster," she sighs. "That notion is not one you have found in my mind."

Taking several seconds to compose ourselves, we keep our distance.

"And Andrew? How are you so sure he is not one of the Prophet's many pawns?" I question, diverting the conversation away from the fact I truly have found no ill feelings in her mind toward me.

It could all be part of a larger plan to manipulate me.

"Andrew and I want the same thing: peace for those at a disadvantage in this vile world." Crossing her arms, she shakes off a wave of hunger. "Andrew has done nothing but jeopardize his and his family's lives to fight for my cause. The last thing he is, is a traitor."

"This?" I question, taking a look around. "This is not New Hope's doing?" I question, avoidant of the place I used to call home.

"New Hope is a breeding ground for control, as much as they say they strive for liberation under the ward," she says, glaring in the direction we came from. "Between you and I, I am not the fondest of the man running the measly structure.

New Hope is one of many compounds in the same way that New Haven is one of many cities. Larger cities blanket the land. Some even I am wary of. That is why my cause must expand. With no allies, I have no fight."

"Do you believe in the Marked?" I question, her body rigid.

"I believe the Marked were never meant to have the power they do, me included. The Prophet wants expansion of their kind. I want the human race to have a fighting chance. So long as there is Marked, humanity will continue to suffer."

Rolling my eyes at her remark, she narrows her eyes.

"Do you not agree?" she questions.

"Instead of worrying about what has already been done, why not rally the Marked for good rather than trying to find a way to end them all," I question, her brows raising.

"You think the Marked are capable of coinciding with those with no gifts?" she questions.

"I think we are humans at heart. All we want in this world is peace."

Smiling at my comment, I sense deception in her mind.

"What?" I push, ready to shove her into the wall to get her to talk.

"Easy, tiger," she pleads, throwing her hands up with a grin. "The last Commander I asked that question to suggested genocide of the Marked, and all of those who wronged him in New Haven-"

"Why are you smiling?"

"Despite all that has happened to you, Xavier, all that a *Marked* has done to you, you still want peace for our kind," she exclaims, her grin so wide, I'm sure her cheeks are in pain. "I don't test you, but if that was one, I can't say you haven't pleasantly surprised me."

Widening her eyes, her cheeks grow red, my anxieties returning once more.

"What did I-"

"You're smiling," she whispers, reaching her hand out before I can stop her.

Touching the two corners of my mouth with her cool fingers, she marvels at the sight. Something within me shifts at the sight of someone so enthralled with something as simple as a smile. Biting back a gasp, her hands cup my cheeks, her reaction one of the most genuine things I have seen in a while.

"I wasn't sure what it looked like," she continues. "I had to guess when I had sketched you back in New Haven-"

"Forest?" one of her companion's questions, a young man, one far too young to be following a cause as heavy as hers. "Where should I put your bags?" he questions, her hands quickly retracting, an authoritative mask slipping over her kind-hearted attitude.

Giving us as much space as she possibly can, she backs away, averting her attention to the man waiting for her word.

"Go ahead and leave it in lounging."

"I'm sorry if I interrupted-"

"Lounging," she reiterates, off-put by the idea of her men seeing her so vulnerable.

Wishing her hands remained where she had planted them, I mentally hold onto the sweet touch, questioning how something so delicate could warm my soul in the ways she has.

Perhaps it was not the touch alone but the meaning it held in that moment.

A smile meant enough for her to drop her authoritative act.

My smile meant something to someone.

Watching the man trail off with her items, I raise my brows. □

"Servants?" I question, now aware of just how many of her men linger, watching us from a safe distance.

"They believe in the cause. I keep their chips in line, giving them full access to come and go from New Haven as they please."

Waving over one of her men, they move quickly, barely looking her in the eyes as they approach.

"Yes-"

"Remove his binds," she orders, both he and I glancing at the restraints withholding my ability's full potential.

Hesitantly reaching toward the key strapped to his belt, she nods her head toward me

"I wasn't asking," she retorts, the man gaining a newfound energy.

It doesn't matter what these binds are holding back. The respect this woman has from all of those who follow her is considerably more powerful.

Fiddling with the key, the man undoes the locks slowly, his hands shaking as he does so.

"I could kill you," I warn, the man's shakes escalating.

"But you won't," she smiles, silently thanking the man, whose walk away from us was nothing short of a run.

Combing through every torturous way I had planned to deliver the woman to the Prophet in exchange for my freedom, my feet stay planted, the idea of harming her almost revolting to think about. Watching me with curiosity, she waits for me to do something, my hands at wait by my side.

Every time I try and feed into the idea of twisting that pretty neck or draining her body clean of its energy, my stomach rolls, my mind clouded with despair.

"Hard to kill something when it doesn't want to kill you?" she questions.

All I can do is remain silent.

"Humor me, Xavier," she backs away, her body edging closer to the doors of the pub. "Do you know how to have fun?"

Offended by the comment, a small smirk creeps along my lips.

"You know, the thing that makes life a little less miserable?" she questions, finally breaking my streak of silence.

"I am aware of what fun is. It doesn't seem like a logical plan of action for either of us," I hold up my wrists. "Especially given the freedom you have given me."

"By all means, go back to New Haven," she says, extending her arm away from the pub. "I think you will be very disappointed knowing you missed out on the opportunity of seeing me try and act like my life is normal."

"You kidnapped me."

"Yet you're still here."

Surging forward, I grab her arm, dragging her closer. Giving me no reaction, she remains still, a seductive look of thrill plastered across her face.

"Why are you doing this?"

"Because I want to keep you safe," she snaps, my grasp loosening. "And I want to know why that is."

"You're worried about having a weakness?" I realize, her smile dropping.

"I have no weaknesses, Xavier. That's how I stay alive," she hisses. "Now join me or stay back and question what a night of fun with me could have entailed."

Letting go of her arm, she shoves past the doors, the strong smell of liquor and cheap beer hitting my nose. Taking a deep breath, the two paths in front of me unfold, nothing but conflicting guiding me.

Leave this compound and give the Prophet the whereabouts of his rat.

Go through those doors and question why her touch is more addictive than the idea of the blood flowing through her veins.

Perhaps a drink will help me understand my decision.

CHAPTER TWENTY-THREE

AARON

There is a certain eeriness to this bar now, one I never expected to feel.

The last time we were here, we were all alive, blissfully unaware of the lies and betrayal that would unfold only a few hours later. Completely avoidant of the table we sat at last time, Kai has remained silent, drowning his sorrows in his pint, immediately refilling his drink every time he reached the bottom of his cup. The table we sat at is barren. The chairs we sat at are a stark reminder of the dwindling size of our group.

"I do hope what I said did not bring down your willingness to drink with us," Nyla says, paying close attention to Kai's quiet state.

"Whether I am being reminded of our friend's betrayals or the fact my sister is probably not my blood, the time I've spent in this compound is nothing worth celebrating," Kai snaps, the alcohol fueling his drive to yell at the woman.

"Your sister is not your blood," Nyla utters, my eyes narrowing at the woman.

"I don't think-"

"Let her speak, Aaron," Kai hisses. "I don't need you safeguarding my feelings."

Snapping my mouth shut, Nyla sips on her drink, a look of hesitance lining her face.

"How do you know that?" I question, trying to piece together how one woman could have so much knowledge.

"Back when this compound was no formidable force, the people of this sector spoke of the woman in the robe, the Apparatus meant to save us from our demise.

Of course, we knew the story of the reflecting pools and had seen the wrath of the Prophet, but, as the years went on, the hope that there was salvation was slim."

"When was the Sanctuary developed?" Kai questions, putting a timeline on all of this.

"I knew your father, Kai. I'd say around the time you were no older than a year or two old."

"You knew my father?" Kai questions, everyone's silent conversations suddenly less important than ours.

"I knew your father, and in turn, I saw your sister in passing, as well as your Commander. At the time, I was in my late 30's, and by no means was this compound's lead. Whereas age has clearly caught up to me, I can't say the same for Xavier and Forest-"

"So, it's true then?" Kai questions, taking a large drink from his pint. "She's not my blood?" he pushes.

"Not exactly. Katiana's parents were researchers. If the whispers of Forest's followers were true, The Prophet's blood and your bloodline were utilized in her creation-"

"Why are you only now telling us this?" I question, cutting her off before she may continue.

"You know by now Xavier's voice is bound?" Nyla questions, all of us nodding in agreeance.

"Then you know, he has been sworn to execute anyone that whispers his secrets in his presence, especially your sister's."

"Why?" Bekah questions, her focus on no one but Nyla.

"Xavier and Forest are bound—one tie, one soul. If one were to pass, the other would quickly follow. The Prophet ensured Xavier's voice and actions were bound. As for your sister, her mind was locked away, just like everything else in New Haven. If she were to learn too much at once, she'd realize the lengths it would take to fully recover her mind."

"And what lengths are those?" Kai questions.

"Death," I mutter, putting the pieces together.

"No matter what Forest and Xavier do, they are bound to death."

"It's cruel really. Not only must he stay silent, but he must control his urges for the woman. If he were to solidify the love he has for the woman with a kiss, he ensures both of their lives are forfeit-"

"Would that not mean the Prophet's demise?" Valerie questions, asking the one thing no one has wanted to.

"Their deaths must be entwined. Two hearts pierced at the same time with the steel of a blade forged from the waters. Some say it lingers at the bottom of the reflecting pools, waiting to be retrieved."

Narrowing my eyes at the woman, I can't help but question her.

"How do you know so much?" I question, her eyes snapping to me.

Rolling up the sleeve of her arm, I glance at the mark inked onto her wrist, something very similar to the scar on all the Marked. Its design is abstract, each crescent pattern decorated with flowers.

"I am one of the few of Forest's followers that remains," Nyla whispers, all of us going silent. "A follower who must stay silent in order to keep her cause alive."

Looking at Kai, he looks shocked.

"You knew my sister and didn't think to tell us?"

"In front of Xavier?" Nyla questions, downing the rest of her drink. "I am many things, Kaiden, but I am not a woman foolish enough to seek out her death sentence. So long as the Apparatus lives, so does my reason to fight."

Taking several moments to reflect, all of us down the rest of our drinks, no longer wanting to try and enjoy a night of non-sobriety.

"The reflecting pools, has no one truly seen them?" I question, the look on her face more than enough to answer my question.

"What do you think?" Kai questions sarcastically, his eyelids dropping. "Everything else in our life is a fucking lie."

Shoving himself away from the table, he swipes his glass, stumbling toward the counter with a grin, his eyes taking in the bartender with admiration.

"Perhaps he must be elsewhere for conversations like that?" Nyla questions, a scoff leaving my throat.

"Are you only now putting that together?" I ask, moving to join the man at the bar before the bartender drags him outside for harassment.

Hearing the doors to the bar slam into the wall with great force, my eyes catch a glimpse of her fiery ones. Pushing the doors open, she shoves past anyone in her way, heading directly toward her brother and the flustered bartender. Glancing at Nyla, she places her finger over her lips, warning us all to stay silent about our newfound information. Saying nothing, Nyla stands, watching Forest with curiosity.

Standing next to her brother, he looks her up and down, his hand reaching out to grab her, dragging her closer.

"What's up, granny?" Kai questions, his words slurring, her eyes wide with confusion.

Note to self: never let Kaiden get drunk with critical information stored in his mind.

Moving before he can out Nyla for being a follower, I snag Kai, letting him lean onto me for support, his sister crossing her arms as she watches us.

"Is there a reason he is suddenly so keen on bringing up my potential age?" she questions, more hot-tempered than normal.

"Potential?" Kai laughs, my hand slamming over his mouth.

Narrowing her eyes at her brother, my body sweats with the idea she has buried herself in his mind.

"There is nothing but drunk thoughts in his head," she mutters, glancing at the bartender. "And images of you, lover boy," she continues, her hand patting my chest.

Growing tense, I struggle to find my words.

"No fair, I can't call you out for every raunchy thought you've been conjuring up since Xavier slipped back into your life-"

"Aaron," she snaps, her eyes only on me. "Take care of him. Get him some water."

Reaching over the bar, Forest grabs a large bottle of clear liquor. Reaching for his inventory, the bartender tries to stop her.

"Young lady-"

"Do it and see what happens," she hisses, tightening her grip on the man's hand.

Gulping back his fears, the man pulls away, allowing her to take her position on the bar stool, downing several shots in one go.

Approaching with annoyance, Nyla shakes her head.

"Forest, that's not for you-"

"Do you really want to try and take this away from me right now?" Forest questions, Kaiden releasing a laugh at the sight of his sister.

Backing off, Nyla raises her hands, bowing her head at the woman before returning to the table.

Shoving me off of him, Kai moves back over to his sister, his grin wide from intoxication.

"What did Xavier do to you this time?" he questions, poking his sister in the cheek.

Biting back my fears, she finally relaxes at the sight of him, her hidden smile enough to allow me to take a breather.

"Is it that obvious?" she questions, his head furiously nodding.

"I've known you for what? Probably about two real years-"

Stopping himself, she pauses her drinking.

"I'm your brother," he says, her focus only on him. "No matter what anyone says, I'm your brother. No one else's," he says, posing the statement as if he is asking her to reassure him.

"Of course you are, Kai," she mutters, running her hand through the man's hair. "You and Mark are the only family I have left."

Letting her brother wrap his arms around her frame, she rubs the man's back, her eyes glancing at me.

Giving me a look I know all too well, she pleads for me to sober him up, her focus clearly on drowning out whatever emotion she is going through with that bottle.

Pulling Kai off of his sister, I drag him closer to the table, his face hot from the liquor.

"I wasn't done-" □

"You are now," I hiss, forcing him to sit down. "You're drunk as hell and honestly unable to stop yourself from yapping," I hiss, taking a seat next to him. "You need to drink some water, and-"

"Stop saying what's best for me, Aaron," Kai snaps, eyeing me down with anger.

"I'm trying to help you," I hiss.

Watching a man take a seat next to Forest at the bar, his eyes undress the woman, her interest suddenly much more elevated. Striking up a conversation with the man, his hand lands on her leg, her mouth pulling into a grin.

"You're in no place to deal with that tonight," Nyla backs me up, her hands rubbing her eyes.

Glancing at his sister, Kai shakes his head.

"It seems like no matter what I do, I only do more harm than good," he whispers, both mine and Forest's smiles dropping at the statement.

Looking over Kai, I see now the internal struggle the man has been forced to battle alone. Losing all that he has known in such a short amount of time, the weight of his reality is suffocating, his need for his sister higher than ever. In light of Hunter's absence, Kai feels as if he has nothing and no one. Theres no good way to tell him, all I have wanted for months is the man to confide in me. It's selfish and cruel, and honestly, my biggest regret, but it's impossible to act like Hunter's death did not bring me some sense of relief.

Unlike Hunter, I don't question what I want.

I want Kaiden to need me in the ways I have needed him.

I want him to know I'm here, I'm really here.

"Your sister feels guilty, Kai. She knows she is spiraling," Bekah states, observing Forest's flashy display of PDA with the man. This little show she is putting on is not because of you."

Drawing my focus back to Kai, I try and find a way to distract his mind.

"Tell me something about yourself that no one else knows," I whisper, all of my focus on the man.

Smiling as he racks his thoughts, he lets out a sigh of defeat.

"I'm terrified I will be the last one in my family to survive," Kai whispers.

"Forest will not die, Kaiden-"

"I'm worried she will do something that makes her dead to me," Kai reiterates, all of us quieting down.

The image of Hunter's neck being snapped fills my mind.

Kai is no fool; he knows the lies we have told him are far from the truth.

He needs his sister to give him a sign she is still with him.

I worry she has no idea what that looks like anymore.

"Your family is not just the Blackburn blood anymore," I retort, letting my hand clasp his.

Reaching across the table, Valerie grabs the man's hand, squeezing it as hard as she can.

"You will never be alone, Kai, so long as my family exists."

Pulling his focus to me, his eyes are hazy with emotion.

"Let me be the sober one tonight. Enjoy your night and know I will be there when you're ready to throw it back up," I smile, his hand staying in mine well after Valeries had retracted her gesture.

Letting the man drag her away from the bar, groups form in the middle of the space, letting their bodies sway to the sweet sound of music. Grabbing Forest with no cares in the world, the man holds her from behind, his hands exploring her front, her eyes closed as she leans back into his chest. Forcing his fingers into her sides, he grabs the woman like she is delicate, someone he is fully capable of overpowering. Letting the man do as he pleases with her, his hands trail up her body, her smile wide as he flips her around, being sure to give her ass a harsh squeeze. Wrapping her arm around the man's neck, he pulls her closer, Bekah mimicking a fake gag the longer she watches.

"If only you knew what he was thinking right now," Bekah hisses, Valerie's eyes avoidant of the display in front of her.

"You know why she's doing it?" Kai questions, Nyla's interest suddenly perked. "And I have a feeling that reason will walk in at any moment-"

Like clockwork, the doors swing open once more, hitting the walls more aggressively than they did the first time. Giving the room a cold and empty stare, Xavier initially focuses on our group, his eyes constantly shifting, clearly looking for anyone but us. Hearing Forest's soft laugh fill the space, I turn at the same time as Xavier, my stomach flooded with nerves at the sight of the man feeling her up, her focus too distracted to notice Xavier's looming presence. Ready to intervene, Kai tries to stand, my hand grabbing his leg, forcing him to stay seated.

"You have to let this play out," I whisper, unnerved by Xavier's still body observing the sight with balled fists.

"She is getting exactly what she wanted," I push. "She wanted him to see this."

"Why?" Kai questions, Xavier's focus staying in place as he answers.

"I pissed her off. Now, she's pissed me off."

Not saying another word, he moves toward the bar, her eyes finally opening, landing directly on the blonde. Taking a seat at the bar, her grabs a bottle of whiskey, allowing himself to eye the sight of her being felt up. Cocking his head as he challenges her, he takes a large swig of the bitter liquid, his body relaxed, her searing gaze locked on his.

They are challenging one another, seeing who will break first.

"This is going to end terribly," I whisper, receiving only nods of approval from those around me.

"Why do you say that?" Kai questions sarcastically, Nyla the first to answer.

"He is in love with her," she whispers, "And there is no way for me, him, you, or anyone else to help her see that."

Chapter Twenty-Four

Forest

Staring daggers in Xavier's direction, the man's hands explore my body, his hands moving dangerously close to the bottoms of my breasts beneath my shirt. Letting the alcohol guide me, his thoughts of overpowering my seemingly weak figure are loud, infiltrating the minds of both me and Xavier. Letting my mind paint the images of what a night with this man would look like, I daydream the idea of feeling his lips on my bare skin, his tongue dragging down my neck. Forcing these images toward Xavier, a devilish grin encapsulates my face at the sight of him clenching his bottle of whiskey. Thinking of all the ways he could kill the man, he stays still, cocking his head at me without a care in the world. Flipping me around, I press my back against the man's front, his hand riding up my shirt, exploring the warm skin of my torso. Bringing his lips to my ear, he gently kisses the skin, my body feeling satisfaction from anything but his touch.

"My name-" □

Forcing my Call into the man's mind, I stop him before he can finish.

"*I could care less. Now make me feel something other than your boner pressing into my ass,*" I hiss, my eyes glancing up at him, a smile painting my expression.

Nodding with a look of pure bliss, his hand moves higher up my front, his thumb gently grazing the underpart of my breast, concealed by the large dark shirt covering my body.

"I'm surprised you allowed me to dance with you," the man whispers, my smile dropping at the realization Xavier no longer watches with anger.

Feeling the man's hand drag down my body, it shakes as the blonde grasps his wrist, pulling it out from under my shirt. The man is completely startled by the action. Moving away from me, his focus is now on Xavier.

Before, the man seemed like a formidable foe against the man. Now, he looks like a child, cowering at the feet of his father.

"Walk away. That's the last fucking time you're touching her," Xavier hisses, his hand already out, stopping me from moving toward the pair.

"Look man, there's a whole bar full of women who would love to fuck you. So you'll understand when I tell you to fuck off and find some other girl-"

Twisting the man's wrist, he silences his scream, looking at Xavier in pure terror.

"Touch her again, and the only thing you will want to do is jam your dirty hands into a meat grinder," Xavier hisses, shoving the man away.

Stumbling back, the man holds his sprained wrist, glancing between the both of us with wide eyes.

"You two are fucking crazy! What is this? Some fucking kink you both get off too?" he questions, a smirk leaving Xavier.

"You don't know the half of it," Xavier snaps, his Call entwined with the man's mind.

"*Run,*" Xavier hisses, both of us watching the man nearly slip trying to get away. Running past the double doors, the man leaves, Xavier's hand lowering. Finally looking at me, it's clear he's pissed, his eyes filled with anything but amusement.

"Dance with me," he snaps, grabbing my shirt before I can protest. Pulling me toward one of the farther corners of the dance area, he pulls my arms around his neck, his hands gripping my waist much more aggressively than the man before him. Having to step onto his feet to keep up with him, he holds me as close as he possibly can, his eyes locked with mine.

"I didn't agree-"

"I wasn't asking, Forest," he barks, my mouth snapping shut.

Trying to convince myself I want to get away, I bite back my words, his fingers meeting my bare skin as he makes his way beneath the shirt. Touching my hips, I coil my fingers in the back of his hair, our noses grazing as we hatefully stare one another down.

Bringing his head down, his lips graze my neck, tempting to kiss all the areas I wish the other man would have. Feeling that familiar heat fester between my legs,

I allow it to happen, feeling his canine drag up my neck, his lips inches away from my ear.

"You think sleazing it up in a bar with some man who planned on berating you in bed every way he possibly could is what you wanted?" Xavier whispers, his jealousy something I subconsciously know I want.

Trailing his fingers up and down my back, his palms remain on my hips, his hold tight enough that most would consider it painful.

To me, it's nothing short of intoxicating.

"Maybe I did want it," I whisper, his mouth pulling away from my ear.

Looking down at me as we sway, he slowly shakes his head.

"You want someone to take control of you," he says, no longer posing a question.

"I want someone to try," I snap back, getting in the man's face.

Filled with excitement, a surge of energy rushes through me, his body buzzing with adrenaline.

Moving his hand away from my body, he holds the side of my face, using his thumb to prop up my chin to look at him, stopping me from looking away.

"I think it's in your best interest if you stop speaking with that pretty mouth."

Feeling something brush against my lower stomach, my defiance brews.

"Why don't you give it something else to focus on, or would you rather keep standing here pretending like you're not straining against your pants at the idea of doing everything I was going to allow that man to do to me."

Smirking, he lowers his tone.

"I am not a gentle person, Forest."

"I am aware. You're a killer, Xavier. Just like me."

Lowering his gaze at the comment, I can't help but continue.

"Now, are you going to fucking do something about it, or allow one of these other men to do it for you-"

Forcing me over his shoulder before I can finish, he takes advantage of the loud claps of people applauding Nyla offering to pay for everyone's rounds. Utilizing the lack of focus in our direction, I hit his back, his hands firmly grasping me. Doing my best to Winnow away from the man, he grips my thighs, his body quickly moving toward the one place in this bar that offers isolation.

Frustrated, my ability to Winnow is useless with this much alcohol in my system.

"Alcohol?" Xavier laughs. "I hold back tremendously with our connection, Forest. Not tonight. You're not running away from me."

Filled with a mix of fear and thrill, he shoves past the bathroom door, my mind begging for anything but forgiveness.

Forcing me into the bathroom wall, the locks are done, my back nearly meeting the metal bar meant for support. Holding me down, his Call infiltrates my mind, my body begging to feel his touch.

Feeling the alcohol run its course, I smile at his use of force, frustrating him further. Unable to look away from the strain in his pants, the heat rises between my legs.

"Kneel on the fucking floor," he orders, my body reacting before I can stop myself.

Letting my knees hit the ground, his Call sways my thoughts, my frustrations growing the longer I allow him to dictate me.

Trying to get up, a warm, hot sting scorns my face, my mind barely processing the action until my knees have hit the ground once more.

Feeling the burning heat in my cheek, the slap reddens his hand, his eyes watching me with a look of taunt. Unable to stop the smile from spanning across my lips, I glance up at him with amusement, my skin quickly stowing away the pain of his slap.

"I said stay the fuck down. I should have done so much more after you forced all those mental images."

Trying to pinpoint why I did that in the first place, I finally face reality, fully aware of how much I wanted him to be angry.

I wanted him to touch me as he is now.

Watching his hands fidget with his belt, vindictive words touch my tongue.

"It would have been so much fun to force you to watch us having a good time," I mutter, staring him down intently.

Trying my best to get an upper hand, all of his abilities keep me down.

"Why is our bond so prevalent?" I question, his hand tugging free his belt.

"Because it's real," he winces, the rich smell of his blood reaching his lower torso.

Wrapping the belt around my wrists, he forces them behind my back, fastening the belt around the metal bar, my hands unable to do anything in their current state. Slumping forward, he tugs me upright, my anxieties nonexistent with help from my liquid courage.

"You're not fighting this, are you?" Xavier questions, my face reddening at the remark.

There's nothing to say.

He's right.

"You want to see what I am willing to do to you."

Once again, it is not a question.

"You won't kill me," I warn, something unfamiliar entering his expression.

"I don't have to kill you to remind you how much I hold back with you."

Tightening the belt, my arms pull further behind me.

"Should I be scared, Commander?" I question sarcastically, my warmth painfully anticipating touch.

"Depends. How wet is this making you right now, Forest?" he asks, my face immediately dropping, doing its best to hide the embarrassment on my face.

There's no way for me to argue.

Even now, I feel the slickness collecting in my underwear.

Fidgeting with his zipper, he presses against his underwear.

"How do you know I won't bite it off?" I question, warning the man before he can try anything.

Smirking, he flashes me his canines.

"You'll be too busy trying to adjust to focus on anything else."

Feeling my stomach fill with excitement, I bite back my smile.

"I have experience," I spit, driving yet another nail into his wall of jealousy.

"Yeah?" he questions, anything but angry. "And where do you think you got it from?"

Tugging his waistband down ever so slightly, I catch a glimpse of his length, my snide remarks fading away the moment I take in the sight of him. Caught off guard by the length trapped behind his boxers, his veined hand touches his hardened length, his mouth stifling a sound of pleasure. Looking me over, a smirk fills his expression.

"Not quite what you were expecting, beautiful," he questions, my mind forcing itself back into reality.

"I've seen better," I snap, sounding unconvincing to even myself.

"No.... You haven't. Now open your mouth for me."

Ready to protest, I hold my ground.

"No-"

Forcing his thumb into my mouth, he drags open my jaw, squeezing my cheeks between his fingers, his thumb holding down my tongue.

"You're going to take it, Forest, and you will do so until I'm done," he warns.

Closing my mouth, he narrowly avoids my teeth clamping down on his thumb. "That's unlikely," I protest.

It's the last thing I want to say.

Tugging down his boxers further, the red of his cut drags down his lower stomach, kissing his v-line. Truly startled by his length, he takes it upon himself to stroke himself, being sure to slowly drag it on, holding the temptation in my face. Biting his lip, he stifles his groan, his eyes on me. Shamefully, wishing he had let me be the source of his pleasure, my mouth barely hangs open, his hand stopping his motions.

"Spit on it."

Bringing it closer, my grin widens.

Two can play this game.

Moving closer, I allow a trail of my spit to touch his head. Letting my tongue delicately touch his tip, he throws his head back with pleasure, his hand gently coiling in my hair, my lips wrapping around his head, before dragging my tongue down his sides. Feeling his grasp tighten, I mentally process how much of him I could really take in my mouth. Being sure to take my time in the spots he likes touched the most, the sound of his pleasures only makes me that much more aroused.

"Fuck," he whispers, my tongue dragging back to collect the sweet precum lingering on his tip. Licking my lower lip as I pull away, my words come before I have time to process the position he has me in.

"Perhaps you have Fallan to thank for this."

Grabbing my hair tighter, I know I've fucked up.

"Your mouth is wet enough."

Jamming the entirety of his length into my mouth, my words are gone, my mouth struggling to adjust as he hits the back of my throat. Eyes watering and all, I groan against his length, curious at what point the alcohol comes back up. Trying to pull my head away, he forces it back down, allowing himself to thrust as I bite back my cries. Expecting to feel fear, I am filled with nothing but pleasure, slowly adjusting to the feeling of his length pounding my mouth.

"Take it, Forest. Your mouth is dirty enough as is."

Continuing to thrust his hips, my throat is beaten to all hell. Straining against the belt, I listen to the sound of him moving in and out of my mouth, spit dripping down the sides of my mouth, my eyes clouded with tears. Gagging without warning, I bite back my willingness to fully submit, letting my mouth adjust once more.

"Keep going. You look so beautiful taking all of me like this."

Finding a comfortable enough rhythm, the size becomes semi-bearable, my head finally finding a motion. Feeling my tears breach my tear line, the water rolls down my cheeks, my eyes watching him with defiance. Cupping my face with his free hand, he looks down at me with authority, my underwear wet to the touch.

Fucking hell.

I love this.

"I should bite you," I mentally hiss, his smirk widening.

"Do it, and I'll bite you back."

Keeping his pace, I groan with pleasure, his groans only adding heat to my face. Feeling a pulse along his base, I ready myself to pull away, his hand stopping my head from pulling away.

"You're going to taste me."

Feeling my warmth implode, I moan against his length, biting back the urge to break my wrists to feel myself. Giving it one last, good thrust, the sweet, salty, warm liquid coats my throat in a rush. Listening to him gasp, he drags my mouth away from his length, my spit trailing after me. Instinctively moving before I can stop myself, I lick what's left clean from his head, my throat already sore. Watching me with surprise, I lean closer to the blood smeared across his v-line, moving quicker than he can react.

"What are you-"

Nudging his shirt up with my nose, I follow the trail of blood created by his lesion, running my tongue along his skin, licking clean the smudge from his v line up to the bottom of his wound. Watching it slowly heal, a surge of energy rolls through me, his eyes wide as he watches me clean his dirtied skin. Utilizing my newfound energy, I force my wrists forward, listening to the belt snap, his hands pulling up his boxers and pants, leaving his zipper wide open. His hand still in my hair, he gently tugs me back into a standing position, my warmth buzzing from its release. Lifting my ass enough to plant it on the metal bar, my throat screams with pain, my hair a disheveled mess. Toying with my waistband, he focuses both hands on undoing my buttons, leaving no room for protest once he has dragged my pants past my thighs, letting them hang at my ankles.

Looking over the wet mess he created, he runs his fingers over the top of my underwear, my body instinctively feeding into the touch. Reaching his hand below my underwear, my release coats his fingers, his fingers gently massaging my folds, making it that much harder to stay silent.

Slipping his Call back into my mind, my mind is his.

"You like taking me in the bathroom like this, hiding how wet you really are for me. You like being dirty with me."

Saying nothing, he pulls his hand free, observing my climax settled on the tips of his fingers.

"You finished while sucking my cock?" he questions with surprise, my only response a small nod.

Dragging me off of the bar, he turns me around, allowing my ass to face him.

"Well, I can't have that." he whispers in my ear, his voice tempting something much deeper.

Entwining his fingers with mine, he guides my hands to the bars, prompting me to hold on tight. Taking a stand behind me, he rubs my ass, letting his tainted hand pull closer to my mouth, landing his fingers coated with my release into my mouth.

"Can you taste how sweet your cum is? Do you enjoy how good being dirty feels?"

Tasting my sweet release, he drags his fingers from my mouth, grabbing the base of my neck from behind, allowing his wet fingers to gravitate back to my warmth.

"Stay quiet," he hisses, dipping his finger below my waistband, running his fingers along my warmth, before doing the one thing I've needed this whole night.

Allowing two fingers to enter me with ease, I feel the entirety of their length enter me, my mouth releasing a silent moan as I grip the bar for support. Pressing my head to the wall, he continues to hold the back of my neck, pumping his fingers in and out of me mercilessly from behind, curling his fingers every so often, his motion more than enough to keep me on the track to finish once again. Listening to his silent groans and the sound of his fingers moving in and out of me, the action is more than enough to drive any woman insane.

"You like this, don't you, Forest?" he questions, gripping my neck harder. "Do you feel how wet you are? Do you know I can sense how close you are to cumming all over my fingers?"

Feeling a world of pleasure, he thrusts his fingers harder, my throat gasping, biting back its pains.

Running through every possible scenario, I question if I have the self-control to stop him from taking me like this here and now.

"Oh, Forest," he whispers, continuing his pace. "I ensure you will take every part of me tonight, so help me god-"

Cut off by the sound of loud knocks on the door, I am startled, instinctively moving to push him away. Keeping me down by my neck, I catch a glimpse of his smirk, his hands continuing his actions.

"What?" Xavier questions loudly, his fingers still working in and out of me.

"How much longer, man?" a foreign bar patron questions, my hand clamped over my mouth, hiding how impossible it is to stay silent every time he curls his fingers.

Working his fingers in and out more aggressively, he continuously hits my most pleasurable points, finding excitement in the way I try to hide my noises.

"Fuck off," Xavier hisses, my stomach filling with warmth, my teeth latching onto my hand.

"I've been waiting for like fifteen minutes."

Leaning his lips closer to my ear, his words become my tipping point.

"Cum for me again, beautiful, I want to watch you struggle to hide that pretty moan."

Feeling the warmth flood my stomach, my moan drowns out in my hand, my legs shaking as I let my release coat his fingers. Gently pulling free his fingers, I feel empty, his hand already dragging up my underwear and pants before flipping me back over to face me.

With cheeks flushed and skin red, we both look frustrated, my eyes glaring over the mess coating his fingers.

Giving me a smirk, he lands his fingers into his mouth, closing his eyes with a look of satisfaction, licking myself clean from his fingers in painfully slow drags. Tasting every bit of me, he can; he savors the taste, his mind just as open as mine.

Staring at one another, a buried instinct takes over, his hands cupping the sides of my face. Grabbing his shirt, I tug him closer, our noses grazing, both of us pausing seconds before we allow it to happen.

Hovering our lips above one another, we breathe heavily, our minds finally processing how close we really are.

I almost kissed him.

He almost kissed me.

Reality comes creeping in, my heart filling with pain.

If that was the touch that hate creates, then what the hell is this? We've already got what we wanted: release. Why would either of us go for this?

Taking into account my current situation, I step back, his hands dropping immediately.

"What did we just do?" I question, my throat slowly healing.

"Forest, before you spiral-"

"It's only been six months," I panic, running my hand through my hair.

"He was lying, Forest-"

"That's not what matters to me, Xavier, can't you see that?" I question in a cry, his mouth clamping shut. "You think all of this is how I view you?" I push, as the true nature of my feelings fall free from me. "Have you not gathered that I needed you.... That I need you? Fallan was always after me, but you, you made me feel safe-"

My throat is swollen, my words hard to come by.

Feeling the tears roll over my cheeks, my emotions spill-free, my hands vigorously wiping my face, trying to hide my pain from him.

"Fuck," Xavier worries, his hands reaching toward me. "Forest, I'm trying-"

"The way I feel for you has shifted, Xavier," I warn, unable to hide my most safeguarded truth. "I can't hate you, and I'm worried that if I don't stop myself, then the way I feel for you will make you yet another weapon against me."

Clamping his mouth shut, he shakes his head.

"What are you suggesting?" he questions, my mind flooded with emotions, his and mine combined.

"You know what," I warn, unable to form one coherent thought. "I can't touch you with hate I don't have."

Stumbling away from the man, I move closer to the door.

"Forest-"

Unable to focus, I Winnow before he can finish the statement, feeling the cool rush of the outside air slap me in the face. Walking on uneven footing, the mix of alcohol and sexual explorations shakes me, my eyes frantically searching for someplace to get away from all of this. Spotting a shop still with its lights on, I stumble forward, leaving the weight of my sins in the bar behind me.

CHAPTER TWENTY-FIVE

FOREST

Trying to hold myself upright, I stumble into the establishment, my eyes hazy with a film of tears. Rubbing my throat, Xavier's blood helped speed up the healing process of any damage he might have done, my body still buzzing with energy. Despite there being enough alcohol in my system to have me on my ass for days, my body does its best to fight the effects, keeping me wide awake. Taking several moments to compose myself, I glance around the space, dozens of dark inky drawings plastered on the wall. Pulling my attention away from my turmoils, the drawings fill every wall, some simple, others extremely intricate. Six reclined chairs are positioned in the middle of the room, hovered by a large machine with a large light.

Moving closer to the front desk, the name of the establishment is plastered on the booking sign-in.

"Tattoos?" I question, my mind racing to the intricate piece inking Xavier's skin.

Watching a man stumble forward from behind a curtain in the back, he holds a cigarette in his mouth, his focus on the list in his hands. Clearly closing up shop for the night, he's aware of my presence, mentally dreading not locking up ten minutes ago.

"I only have time for one more piece before I have to close up for the night," he starts, keeping his focus away from me. "Go ahead and sign in."

Grabbing the sign-in roster, I flip the book back to its first few pages, finding Xavier's name in a matter of seconds. Trailing my fingers over the older date, I drag my finger up, my eyes landing on the name above his.

"Forest," I whisper, glancing at the last name, my heart dropping. "Evermoore."

Forest Evermoore.

"Evermoore?" I question louder, shaking my head in disbelief.

"Evermoore?" the man questions, taking a long drag of his cigarette. "Haven't heard that last name in years. I remember that couple. The poor girl didn't have a last name, so he filled in his last name for both of them. You should have seen the way her eyes lit up-"

Locking eyes with me, the cigarette falls from the man's mouth, his hands fidgeting with his glasses as if they could help him see me any clearer. Almost running toward the front desk, he leans over in shock, his eyes taking as many mental pictures as he can of my figure.

"You're back?" the man questions.

Taking a long look at his name tag, I glare at the middle-aged man.

"I'm assuming you're yet another person who knows me, yet I am blatantly unaware of who you are?" I question, Leo's head shaking.

Pointing his finger toward a wall of drawings, each one gravitates toward me, the line work so familiar.

"It's a real shame if you have no recollection of who I am, given your sketches are some of the most popular designs I carry," Leo whispers, our eyes locked on the designs.

Taking it all in, one of the designs gravitates toward me.

Having seen this design more times in the past few days than I have my whole life, yet another wave of confusion lingers.

"Xavier's tattoo," I whisper, my eyes locked with the creature's sketch.

"One of my favorite pieces," Leo says, smiling with pride. "How is your fiancé doing anyway?"

Feeling all of the warning sirens sound off in my mind, a deep pain consumes me, my body leaning forward, clutching the desk with shallow breaths. As if every protective measure I have utilized to keep myself together comes crashing down, a painful noise sounds off in my ears, my need to silence it reaching deadly levels. Having the urge to end my own existence to stop the swarming aches rolling through my body, I squeeze my head as tight as I can, letting a scream exit my lips, vivid images passing over my mind.

How is your fiancé doing anyway?

Fiancé?

Letting my head rest on the ledge of the desk, the room shakes, Leo's eyes wide with confusion. Sobbing like a child, the images grow clearer, slowly replacing the lies my mind has forced to be true.

Suddenly able to breathe better, the wounds Xavier inflicted heal, another presence lingering in the space of my mind.

"Forest," *h*is voice whispers, giving me something other than the pain to focus on. *"Where are you? What's happening? Your heart is beating so fast-"*

Finally getting a grip on the noise, I shove everything out of my thoughts, cramming the wave of information into any open door I can. Feeling the pain ease up, I keep Xavier out of my mind, doing all that I can to get a grasp on my body's reaction to information I can hardly begin to understand. Feeling the establishment's shake die down, I am able to regulate the noise, pulling my attention to Leo's petrified expression once I can think without wishing to tear my head off.

"My *fiancé*," I say, choking back the words. "He's not here," I clarify, watching the man nod his head, not wanting to push me on the topic any longer.

Looking at my clean skin, I force the conversation into a new direction.

"I didn't get one?" I question, his only response a nod.

"You didn't know what to get at the time."

"Right," I say, distantly recalling standing in this shop once before, my eyes gravitating toward the first chair.

Focused on one of the farther designs on the wall, a back piece working down the spine filled with numerous flowers, I move around the desk, and closer to the chair.

"You said you have time for one more piece?" I question, waiting for the man's wary nod.

"What will it be?" he questions, laying on a fresh sheet over the chair.

"I want the spine piece," I clarify, counting my fingers silently. "Give the piece six flowers."

One for every person in my life I cared about who I lost or ended in the hopes of keeping the ones who I love alive.

Perhaps this is how I will honor them, wearing their flowers as a reminder.

Nodding his head, Leo grabs his cigarette from the ground.

"It's about time you accepted my services. Let's get started."

Laying stomach down on the chair, my shirt is pulled over my head, tape covering my breasts to hide any parts of myself I'd like hidden. Avoiding looking at the bruises along my skin, Leo's fingers graze over my back, numerous cuts and scrapes scarring the skin in white lines. Hovering the large machines closer to my back, the image on the wall is queued up on the screen. Generating six beautiful flowers into the piece, he lines the top of the machine at the top of my spine, its warm light heating my skin. Leaning back in his chair, he taps the machine's screen, a bearable but uncomfortable sting touching my skin.

"No leg work for you?" I question, keeping my body as still as I possibly can.

"My hands are worn from my time under the ward, trying to free those locked away by their minds," he says, giving me a sideways glance.

There's more he wants to say.

"Did you fight on behalf of the compounds?" I question, fully aware of the liberation act they tried to complete.

Dove included.

"No, the liberation acts always seemed faulty. Once that dark-haired radical started leading the liberations, I knew it was only a matter of time before my side would have to step in," he clarifies.

"Your side?" I question, the sting from the machine worse on my scar tissue.

"The side fighting to bring down the Prophet," he clarifies, shifting uncomfortably in his seat. "Your side, Forest."

Taking in yet another bit of information I have failed to remember myself, I keep a grasp on the wave of confusion waiting to disorientate me enough to cause a brain bleed.

"You were one of my followers?" I question, the embers of his cigarette lighting up.

"Up until you stayed under the ward and Xavier had gone off the grid. Imagine my surprise for you to walk in now, after two years of silence.

Not knowing what to say, the sting has reached my lower back.

"The cause we were fighting, did we ever win?" I question, his face flashing with dread.

"The Prophet is still alive, now with a face I had seen one too many times in this sector. I'd say, our fight is only now beginning."

Sitting in silence for a few seconds, he pulls his focus back to me.

"Where is Xavier anyways?" Leo questions, a much deeper voice ready to answer for him.

"Still breathing," Xavier's voice mutters, both of our eyes gravitating toward the blonde who had managed to silently make his way into the establishment.

Only a few feet away, Leo looks thrilled, Xavier's focus only on me. Standing up, Leo and the man embrace, the shop owner's hand slapping the man's back.

"It would seem your fiancé is finally in the mood to paint her skin," Leo says, both Xavier and my nose scrunching at the comment. "Why the hell didn't you tell me you both made it out of New Haven? Do you have any idea how many people would have liked to know she was okay?" Leo questions, Xavier covering the man's mouth.

"Given the fact I am here because of people's whispers about the building shaking, I am going to tell you to tread carefully about what you say," Xavier warns. "Or else I will have to kill you."

Taking in the information, Leo pulls the man's hand from his mouth.

"The Prophet got to both of you under there," Leo shudders. "That's why she looked at me like a ghost, and nearly had a seizure when I mentioned you were her-"

Giving the man a look, Xavier dares him to keep speaking.

"Close," Leo settles on saying, avoiding the word fiancé entirely.

Now settled at the lowest part of my back, my skin stings, filled with heat from the device.

Creeping closer, Xavier eyes the piece up and down.

"Is it horrific?" I question, his hands pulling up a chair to observe. Smiling at me with a grin he hardly wears, he shakes his head.

"No, I think it's absolutely beautiful."

Dragging himself closer, his finger gently touches the skin, no doubt counting each flower.

"Six flowers?" Xavier questions, his hand resting on the table.

Feeling yet another needle touch the scar tissue, I grab his hand, squeezing as hard as I can. Letting his thumb roll over the knuckles, he watches me, offering a tender touch I thought was foreign to him. Keeping my hand in his, I sigh.

"Six flowers for someone important I have lost."

"Fallan, your mother and father, Hunter, Rae.... Who is the last one for?" he questions.

Seeing her vivid image paint the mind of Xavier at random times, her blonde curls stand out to me, her eyes filled with a light that was taken too soon. Not knowing how or why, the clarity on who the child is brings sorrow to my mind, a sorrow that Xavier carries every day.

"Lily," I clarify, his eyes widening, his hand squeezing harder. "The girl in your mind, Lily. She was your sister," I start, digging into the deepest parts of my mind, faint echoes painting a clearer picture. "She passed away because of my mother. The last one is for her."

Shakily holding my hand, his hairs rise.

"You remember-"

"Only passing images, brief broken conversations. There is no clear picture in my mind." I clarify. "It doesn't mean I cannot try to see the truth.

Letting another warm smile settle on his lips, a warmth buries itself in my chest.

It doesn't matter how hard I try to paint this man to be a monster in my mind.

The true nature of Xavier Evermoore is something my mind has safeguarded.

Anything worth protecting like that is something worth holding onto.

"And done," Leo says, breaking mine and Xavier's stare, his hand dragging away the machine from my skin.

Rubbing a soothing cream over my back, the pain fades. His hand holds up a mirror, my eyes taking in the piece. Spanning down my spine, each flower is unique, twisting and sprouting, holding homage to every lost soul. Moving closer, Xavier's fingertips glide down my back, his fingers chilling.

"The cream will take away any pain you might have had," Leo says, looking away as I begin to rise up. Regardless of being taped, I conceal my breasts with my hands, watching Xavier respectfully look away despite the interaction we shared in the bathroom.

"My shirt's by your feet," I whisper, his hands tucked in his pockets.

Filled with shame by the way he touched me, he glances at the ground, hesitantly bending down to grab the material.

Extending his arm out toward me, he looks at the floor, avoiding my eye contact entirely.

Damn it, Xavier.

Lowering my hands, I touch his chin, dragging his gaze up to mine.

Dipping his eyes down, my nipples are concealed by the tape, nothing but my scarred torso out for him to see. Narrowing his eyes at the sight of my tattered skin and bruises, he clenches the shirt, my touch moving away from his chin, gravitating toward the side of his face. Cupping his cheek, his focus directs to me, something sincere in the way he watches me now. Flooding the connection with a deep-rooted pain, my hand drops, his hands moving for me.

Dragging the shirt over my head, he conceals my body, his hands lingering at my sides.

"It's not your fault," I whisper, speaking before I have time to process what I am saying.

Tensing up, his thumbs gently roll over my hips, his eyes hazy with the fog of emotion.

"You and I both know that's not true," he whispers, the guilt of his actions heavy on his conscience. "You were the one thing I swore to never hurt." His voice chokes up, his mask of coldness replacing the face I see now. "I ruin everything I touch."

Taking a step back, he forces space between us, my body hidden from wandering eyes once again.

Sliding off the chair, Leo waits for my okay before turning back around. Crossing his arms, Xavier stares at the man, tapping his foot anxiously.

"You came at the wrong time if you're expecting a new piece on your skin tonight," Leo jokes.

Staying silent, Xavier remains still.

"How much is it?" Xavier questions, reaching toward his back pocket.

"It's on me," Leo says, taking a deep breath. "Your lady is the reason I keep business in the first place." Glancing at me, Leo grins. "If you ever feel the need to drop off new sketches, please, by all means, do so."

Unable to piece together any moment in my life where I could have stepped foot in this shop before tonight, all I do is nod, promising an interaction I know might never happen.

Smiling, Leo glances at the door, ready for us to leave him to his wares.

Picking up on this, Xavier nods, turning away before I can question him.

Following behind him; I wait for him to speak, my hands buried as deeply in my pockets as his.

Nudging open the door, he holds it wide for me, both of us taking in the glimmering sight of the stars above. Rubbing the back of his neck, his focus on the stars is short-lived, his gaze only on me.

"What?" I question after several moments of silence, my body chilling with nerves once more.

Looking at him now, it's hard not to see the imagery he left me with in the bathroom. Knowing how much strength the man bottles up, his violent urges are both terrifying and enticing.

"What did Leo say to you?" Xavier asks. The faint whispers of the words we shared cling to my mind.

Fiancé.

My fiancé.

"Nothing that makes any sense," I warn, my finger rubbing the empty space surrounding my ring finger.

Taking notice of my anxious fidget, Xavier sighs.

There's nothing he can say right now to bring me clarity. The pain one context-less comment alone could create was unbearable.

Almost like-

"I'm bound too, aren't I?" I question, Xavier's mouth pulling into a deeper frown.

"Worse than I," Xavier sighs. "At least I am aware of what I can't say. You? One wrong word from anyone and it could be game over."

Is this truly our reality?

"What now?" I question, internally at odds with where we stand.

Closing his eyes, his head cranes up to the stars, the light casting a perfect shadow across his face. Just like that night at the solstice dinner and the night we shared on the deck, he looks blissful, a sight I am now seeing as if it is the first time.

I should have never run from him that night.

I should have listened to what he had to say.

So many things might have happened differently-

"I need to show you something. I cannot keep listening to your spirals," Xavier says with a plea. Grabbing my hand, he moves, pulling me farther away from the shop. "I need you to see there is more to me than what I have let you see. I keep expecting you to already know. I tried to get you to hate me because it was more bearable for both of us. It's time to remind you who I really am."

Pausing, he glances toward me.

"Who *you* really are," he mumbles.

Clarity in exchange for the chance of death.

I can only hope Xavier knows what he's doing.

CHAPTER TWENTY-SIX

FOREST- THE DARK DAYS

Feeling the burn of alcohol trickle down my throat, it's hard to stomach the harder liquor. Xavier's preference for the rich scotch is somewhat surprising. Trying to keep my neutral face as the alcohol settles in my stomach, I slide the shot glass over to Xavier, watching him fill and down the drink with no hesitation.

It's been a month since Xavier took residency with me. He has been observing and learning, his mind once tinged by the Prophet's poison now enlightened by the hope for a world much better than the one we currently live in.

"It's awful, isn't it?" he questions with a faint smile, watching me try to stomach the drink.

"I can't say it's the easiest thing to stomach," I admit, my mouth salivating.

"I'm not really sure why I drink it," he admits, taking yet another shot. "I think if it didn't work so damn quick, I'd take a mixed drink with as much juice as I could stomach," he says, finally giving me a smile.

"Not to mention, you look much more intimidating when downing a bottle of scotch," I tease, his smile curling higher.

Distracted by a large thud, we both turn, observing the large, modernized jukebox being placed in the farthest corner of the room. Gathering around the once ancient artifact-like vultures, the bar patrons flip its switches, clapping with joy once the calming tunes begin to drown out the bar's lively chatter. Watching people clear the center of the bar, couples go hand in hand, moving their bodies to the rhythm of the music, dancing as if there is no care in the world.

"Have you done it before?" Xavier questions, his eyes on the couples.

"Done what?" I question, focusing back on our conversation.

"Danced," he clarifies.

"Most people don't consider me the dancing type," I admit. "How about you, Commander?"

Smiling at the question, I sense the lingering intoxication creeping up on the man. Equally as disoriented by the rich liquor, the sight of him so lively is somewhat enthralling.

Standing up from his chair, he extends his hand out toward me, his cheeks growing flush at the gesture.

"Try it," he whispers, his hand shaking as he holds it out.

"I don't dance," I clarify, pointing my finger at him with a grin.

"Neither do I," he smiles, grabbing my hand before I can protest. "Fake it 'til you make it, right?"

Letting him drag me toward an opening in the middle of the floor, we both stumble. Placing his hands at my sides, the warmth from his touch ignites me, my arms wrapping around his neck before he can stop me. Struggling to stay at eye level with me, our heights contrast, both of us laughing like schoolgirls.

"You're too tall to dance with," I clarify, his eyes rolling.

"Leading a rebellion, yet your critical thinking has seemed to falter," he teases, grasping my hips tighter, lifting me off the floor momentarily before placing me on his feet, our noses grazing in the process.

Startled by being so close to him, my stomach floods with warmth, an unfamiliar need to be near him registering in my mind. Taking a moment to center myself, I get a good look at the small scars decorating his face. They are small cuts healed by time, his gray-blonde curls falling into his face. Pushing back his hair with my hand, I get a good look at his blue-gold eyes. Watching me intently, he does not flinch away from touch as he has in the past. Swaying to the music, I grasp onto him for support, letting my body guide me as I pull myself closer, my head resting on his shoulder as his arms support my weight.

Slowly dancing to a song whose tempo was meant for fast movements, we silently drown out the noise, both of us entirely content with the moment we have caught ourselves in. "Why haven't you used me as leverage yet?" he whispers, breaking our streak of silence.

Trying to find some half-assed excuse, the truth slips free from my lips.

"I didn't want you to leave," I admit, keeping my head on his shoulder. "Can I admit something to you?" I question, his focus gravitating toward me.

Saying nothing, he moves his hand away from my hip, gently touching the side of my face, urging me to look at him.

Wanting nothing more than to keep my head down, I look at the man, his eyes soft, no longer trying to uphold his generally cold expression.

"What is it?" he questions, my words for the first time, struggling to resonate.

"I don't feel alone," I admit, forcing myself to look him in the eyes. "With you here, I don't feel alone, and I know that sounds foolish-" □

As if I am seeing the world for the first time, his lips silence me, everything around me going dead silent.

Feeling his lips touch my own, his hands cup my face, tilting my head up to hold onto the kiss. Sensing the spark of something much deeper spanning between us, I feel his anxieties over the touch, and the longing need he carried to know what my lips felt like. Kissing back harder, something I didn't know I needed to feel floods my mind, my hands grabbing his shirt, pulling the man closer. Pulling away from the kiss to take a breather, we both look disoriented, our noses hovering near one another, his mind flooded with fear over my reaction.

"I'm sorry-"

Unable to stop myself, I am now the one grabbing his face. Kissing him back harder, his arms wrap around my body, pulling me up and into his grasp, our eyes finally level. Fighting me back with equal resistance, the kiss lights a fire between the both of us. Trying to pull away from this kiss, my bottom lip gathers between his teeth, stopping me from getting too far. Devouring me in yet another kiss, our teeth nearly clatter from the need hidden within the touch. Feeling a warmth flood between my legs, I gasp, doing my best to hide how far I want this to go. Running his tongue along my bottom lip, he seizes the opportunity to slip it into my mouth. Letting the kiss evolve, his tongue grazes my own, the kisses turning from innocent to something much more sexual.

Pulling away from one another, we both pant, our foreheads touching. Keeping my hands on his cheeks, his hands are no longer holding me up. Taking a moment to register what has happened, I feel my legs tighten around his waist, his hands cupping my ass, the other patrons eyeing the sight with whispers of confusion.

At some point during all of that, I had managed to wrap myself around Xavier, pushing myself to feed into the touch as much as I could. Equally flustered and aroused, Xavier's mind is no longer just a space I may glimpse into. Able to come and go as I please, dictating and seeing whatever it is I need.

"Why did you do that?" I question, unable to hide the smile curling along my mouth.

"I'm not sure," he mutters. "I'm sure I'll regret it."

"Why?" I push, keeping my mind out of his.

"Because I told myself I was unable to tolerate you and could leave if needed," he admits, my heart dropping at the statement. "Now, I don't know if that is still my reality."

Lowering myself from his hips, I take a step back, grabbing his hand before he can spiral about what we both just allowed to happen.

"There's one more place I think you should see," I whisper, unsure why I am entertaining more time with the man.

This is not my first stolen kiss.

This is not my first time feeling the hands of another on me.

So why am I wishing to never feel the touch of another ever again?

Giving me a slight nod, I seize the opportunity, dragging us both away from the bar, and the moment we shared within it.

Trying to think of the best thing to say to the man, I draw blanks, shivering as we approach the lively building. Keeping his hand in mine, he does not pull away, his focus on me, and me alone. Still giddy with the presence of alcohol, I feel his presence lingering in my mind, the faint whisper of the touch we shared the only thing warming my skin.

"Why can I feel you?" he questions, finally addressing the thread tethered between us.

"I assume it has something to do with the blood I gave you—"

"I felt it before this," he interrupts, drawing conclusions I'd rather not try and understand. "Never this strong, but I've felt your presence, ever since you started watching me—"

"I don't know," I blurt out, embarrassed by how little knowledge I have about the topic. "I have no clue why I feel you as adamantly as I do."

Dragging him past the building's doors, I hope to silence the conversation, petrified of what a connection like this means in the long run.

How the hell am I supposed to carry out any of my responsibilities so closely tethered to another soul?

Even worse, I have no idea how that tether was created.

"Leo!" I yell, looking around the tattoo parlor for the lively man.

Popping his head up from behind his desk, his wary eyes lock with mine, only easing up once he registers who is before him. □

"Forest," he clarifies, glancing at Xavier with raised brows. " Is that-"

"The Commander I was tracking down?" I question, smiling with delight. "Why yes, it is."

Dropping my hand, Xavier extends his out toward the man. Eyeing the man with suspicion, Leo looks Xavier up and down, internally judging the man before he's even had the chance to speak.

"You'll have to sign in before I offer you any of our services," Leo says, speaking only to Xavier.

Turning toward one of the few clients chairs the man has, he leaves the sign-in roster before both of us, clearly offended by Xaviers' presence.

"I don't think your friend is too fond of me," Xavier whispers, Leo's ears on high alert.

"That's an understatement," Leo whispers, mumbling under his breath.

Holding back a power I know Xavier carries, he balls his fist, mentally debating the ways he could torture the man. Rolling my eyes, I smile at Xavier, watching his tense shoulders drop.

"No need for violence."

Reaching into my large inner coat pocket, I pull free the small sketchpad, tossing it in Leo's direction. Grabbing it before it can hit the floor, he flips through the work, his eyes widening with each passing page.

"You are willing to give me all of these sketches?" Leo questions, my arms crossed.

"So long as you treat our new friend with some respect," I warn, Xavier's mouth now the one curling into a smile. "And give him ink on the house."

"Ink?" Xavier questions.

"You didn't tell him this is a tattoo shop?" Leo questions with surprise.

"I figured he'd run away before I could convince him to look at your wares," I smile, Xavier's eyes finally panning to the images along the walls.

"These drawings, they're for your skin?" Xavier questions, both Leo and I nodding.

Fixating his focus on one of my sketches of a mythical beast, a dragon, his eyes grow wide.

"Is that one of yours?" he questions, Leo now the one nodding.

"Forest's sketches are one of my best sellers. Thanks to this little sketchbook, I should expect to see nothing but customers for the next few months."

"I don't even know where I'd put it, Forest," Xavier whispers, my eyes glancing over his large figure.

"Leo," I ask, my finger tracing down the man's upper arm and moving over to his chest. Can you make the piece span from chest to arm?"

"Of course I can," Leo mutters, clearly offended by my lack of trust in his skills. "I'll prep the chair, but you both still need to sign in."

Covering Xavier's mouth before he can protest, I grab the pen, watching his smile grow as he tries to pry away my hand. Pushing him away, Leo eyes the interaction, a small smile touching his lips, fading the moment Xavier looks his way. Messily scrawling my first name on the sign-in roster, I hand the pen to Xavier, watching him with a devilish grin.

"I signed, it's only fair you do the same."

Rolling his eyes, he takes the pen, taking his time to create his signature, his name easy on the eyes.

"Not sticking with Hayes?" I question, nudging his side.

"Where's your last name?" Xavier questions, my smile dropping.

Glancing in our direction, Leo listens in, fully aware of how little I know about my biological parents.

"I don't have one," I mutter. "I have guesses as to who they are, but given I was developed by lab rats, the luxury of having a last name is beyond me," I smile, his eyes on me.

Bending back over the roster, Xavier continues writing, both Leo and I exchanging a look.

Pulling away from the roster, I look over our names, my heart pinging with pain once again.

Scrawling his last name next to mine, there's something haunting about the way it reads.

"Forest Evermoore?" I question, grinning like a small child.

"For tonight, it isn't just you," he says. "I know what being alone is like. At least this way, even for a night, neither of us are."

Flooded with the feeling of sincerity, something threatens to breach my emotions, something I have failed to feel in years.

Longing.

"Are my newlyweds ready?" Leo questions, both of our eyes rolling.

"Jumped right past partner and went straight to marriage?" I question, prompting Xavier to move closer to the chair.

"Newlyweds is too far for you?" Leo questions, tapping the chair, signaling Xavier to pull off his shirt.

"A bit too formal," Xavier says, tugging up his shirt.

Caught off guard by his figure, my cheeks flood with heat, the imagery of his bare torso enough to silence anyone. Coated up and down with scars, his skin is damaged, the pain he has endured painting the man like a mosaic. Touching the center of his chest, Xavier watches me, his body reactively flinching away before settling against my hand.

"The Prophet did this?" I question, unable to see how extensive his wounds were the night we pulled him from the Prophet's grasp.

"I suppose my bind did a lot of the work, but yes," Xavier whispers, his hand landing atop my own. "It's fine, Forest," he says, his eyes filled with sorrow. "It wasn't your doing."

Swallowing back a pit of emotion, the Prophet's silver mask illuminates my vision, something much deeper than vengeance entering my being.

I want the Prophet to feel pain.

I want the Prophet to feel the pain they have forced on every innocent soul.

If I must repeatedly drive the knife into both of our hearts, I will do it time and time again.

The Prophet's end is inevitable.

For every scar Xavier bears.

For every innocent life lost.

Mine and the Prophet's blood will end the tyranny this world created-

"Hey," Xavier says, shaking me free from my reverie. "You okay?" he questions, my only response a nod.

Hardly accepting the gesture, he settles into the seat, Leo's machine at the ready. Hovering over his chest, Xavier anticipates pain, his hand shakily slung off the chair.

I can't feel remorse for Xavier.

I can't allow myself to see the kiss as anything more than a physical want.

Xavier's emotions must not be in my thoughts.

"I hate pain," Xavier whispers under his breath, so quiet, most would not hear.

Biting my lip, I try to force down my need to soothe him, the creeping feeling of care swarming my soul.

If I do nothing, I can remain neutral.

If Xavier were to be harmed, it would not affect me.

This is all just hormones caused by the alcohol.

It is simply a fun night.

Wincing as the needles prick his skin, his hand shakes, my thoughts of avoidance fizzling away.

"Fuck," I whisper, unable to control myself.

Grabbing his hand, I allow him to squeeze, watching his eyes dart to me. Feeling the warmth of his skin, the tether between us is strong, my mind wavering back and forth between his and mine.

"She regrets tonight," he whispers silently, both he and I startled by the noise in both of our minds.

"No... she doesn't, Xavier. That's the issue."

A dance.

A kiss.

A name.

A bond.

And now, a connection I can hardly explain.

Xavier Evermoore may have been my Commander, but now, he very well might be the Prophet's biggest leverage against me.

And I'm terrified.

Chapter Twenty-Seven

Forest

C radling my legs into my chest, I press my chin to my knees, watching Xavier pace around the space. Biting his nail beds, he looks at me every so often, only able to look at me for a few seconds before shamefully bowing his head.

After our moment in the bathroom, and my revelation within the tattoo parlor, Xavier thought it best to drag me back to his room in the Sanctuary's lodging quarters, internally tormenting himself every time he looks at me. Despite being healed, the shame of how aggressive he was with me infiltrates his mind. Unable to say anything to ease him, I remain quiet. Biting back words he cannot share, we both are frustrated, unable to navigate to the truths in each other's minds. Regardless of whatever memories Xavier may have of me, my own mind prohibits me from seeing them, putting a film over each recollection every time I try to slip into his mind.

"I'm healed," I whisper, hoping the comment will get him to look me in the eyes.

"If you were healed, you would remember who I am to you," Xavier says coldly.

It doesn't matter what I say to Xavier.

No matter what I do, he will always see me as the ghost of someone who meant too much to him.

The loss he feels when he looks at me is a pain he carries for the both of us.

Rolling my hand over my throat, I sigh, still struggling to swallow despite the flesh being healed.

Pausing his pacing, he looks me over, his hand running through his hair.

"I didn't mean to take it that far," Xavier says with full sincerity, a vulnerable side to the man seeping through the cracks of his cold facade. "That man was touching you and the imagery you were showing me-"

"I wanted to see what you would do," I admit, biting back my pride. "I wanted that side of you," I clarify, wondering at what point I had grown so reliant on touch.

Shaking his head, he moves closer, watching me with wide eyes.

"I throat fucked you in a bar bathroom all because I couldn't stomach the idea of another man getting his filthy hands on you again," he snaps, his eyes hot with rage. "Why the hell would you allow me, or anyone to touch you like that-"

"Because I am not blind Xavier!" I yell, forcing myself to my feet, getting as close to the man's face as I possibly can, our noses grazing. "That touch, as violent as it may have seemed, was not meant to claim me, it was a way for you to reassure yourself that a part of me you once knew was still there. Don't stand here and act like gentle touch and loving gestures are in your nature. You love control. You love control more than anything, and the only way you can do that with me is in the brief moments my hormones overcome my mind," I hiss, narrowing my eyes at the man.

Saying nothing, he throws me a cold expression, his lips pursed in a straight line.

"You have an utter lack of self-control," I prod, waiting for him to say something.

"You made your point letting that man touch you, Forest," he seethes. "And I made mine."

"By having your way with my throat in a bathroom?"

"I told you, Forest, I am no gentle person, and if you knew the strength you carry, you'd know that very same truth applies to you."

"Is that so?" I question, a smirk rolling off of his lips.

"You wanted that touch just as bad as I did. You wanted to feel the pain and pleasure I could bring you. You know, deep down, your mind and body craved the experience I could give you because at the end of the day, Forest, I don't treat you like you break," he moves closer, his hands grabbing my hips. "I treat you as if you are the strongest thing in the room."

"So, violence is all we knew?" I question, my hands shaking against his chest.

Seeing something flash across his expression, I narrow my eyes.

"There was more," I shudder, creeping into the spaces of his mind. "But re-membering anything other than the aggressiveness we shared is breaking you."

Lowering his expression once again, the true nature of the force he tried to scare me with comes to light.

"You wanted to scare me away from you."

Shaking his head, his voice comes out a mix of a cry and laugh.

"Anything is better than feeling the way your kindness makes me feel knowing there is no fucking way for me to return any of it."

"There is no way for you to be gentle?" I question, his eyes finally pulling up to mine.

Shocked at what lines his eyes, the buildup of tears threatens to breach his tear line. Fogging his eyes with the haze of emotion, he looks defenseless, my heart dropping at the sight of him so distressed. Never gazing upon the sight of emotion like this in the man before, pain floods my chest, one deeper than the grief I felt six months ago when the world felt like it was ending.

This pain is different.

This pain was not meant for anyone but him to see.

It eats us both alive, making it impossible to take a full breath.

Grabbing the sides of my face, the tears stay trapped in his eyes, his nose pressed up against mine, his lips inches away from touching mine.

Feeling the lesions try and rip both of our torsos, he tries to stow away his past memories, my mind a blank slate, while his is a cluttered chalkboard.

"I'm trying, Forest," Xavier sobs, all of his vulnerabilities on full display. "I'm fighting with all I have-"

"Show me," I whisper, looking past the moment of pain I felt in the tattoo parlor when Leo said too much.

"Show me what I lost," I reiterate, his eyes blinking back the haze.

Reaching into Xavier's pocket, I feel the familiar metal casing of his watch, rolling its surface along my thumb. Pulling it free before he can stop me, I grasp the artifact tightly in my hand, both of us looking down to observe it.

"Show me why this mattered so much," I push, his head already shaking. "I know I've already opened it-"

"No. You really haven't," he whispers, his jaw clenched with strain.

Confused and fearful, I take a step back, Winnowing far enough away he can't stop my actions. Flipping open the top of the watch, he moves across the room, ready to tear the time device away from me. Once again seeing nothing but the watch's interior, and the faint scribe lining the inner rim, I draw blanks, pulling my hand back before he can take it from me.

"There's nothing here, Xavier!" I yell, his arm reaching farther than mine, stealing back the watch.

"It has to be nothing!" he yells. "If I caught a glimpse of what resided inside every day, I would never be able to function."

"Then suffer with me!" I yell, shoving his chest. "I have lost everything, yet you're still here! I need you here with me! Let go of what is inside of that eating you alive and help me find a way out of this!"

"It always humored me that you saw me as a man with no soul when the one part of me I actually gave a shit about was ripped away from me so long ago."

Opening the watch, his finger flicks the underpart of its top, a circular layer of metal clattering to the floor. Holding the watch out, he looks away from what resides inside, my body slowly creeping closer, locking eyes with the horrifying sight.

Frozen in time, looking back at me like a ghost, my eyes land on the photo, the woman captured in the shot all too familiar. Looking over my wide grin and bright eyes, the liveliness of the photo is surreal.

"H- how did you get this picture of me?" I question, a pounding headache building up in my head.

"I took it," Xavier whispers, the headache reaching the back of my eyes.

I can't stop. I need more answers.

"The cabin in the background-" □

"Our cabin," he clarifies, hissing through a pain we both feel.

"That was our home," he pushes. "Or it was going to be."

Looking over the worn engraving, I focus on anything but the feeling of my insides being torn apart.

"You've had this for years?"

"Forest, that's enough questioning-"

"Answer me!" I yell, embracing every painful pulse working through my body.

"You're the one who got it for me."

Ready to double over, I grip my torso, the headache so strong, I might rip my own eyes out.

No.

I have to keep pushing.

Putting the pieces together, it feels like acid is in my throat as I speak.

"We- we were lovers," I cough up, fleeting images passing over my mind, each one more vivid than the last.

"It was more than that, Forest. You were my best friend. I keep waiting for your memories to resurface-"

We both grasp the bed frame, our throats coughing, tightening as our airways betray us.

It's so much pain.

"I keep waiting to see the shift when you look at me-"

Gasping, I clutch my throat, doing my best to stow away the bind we both carry. Hitting the floor with his knees, I sense him stealing my pain, his arms crossed over his torso, his throat gasping for air. Following him to the floor, I grab his face, gravitating all of my focus onto the man, his face settled between my hands.

"You were everything to me. You still are-"

Pushing past every warning sign to stop speaking, something detrimental patiently waits for him to slip up, both of our hearts beating out of our chests. Feeling blood trickle free from my nose, the pains turn deadly, my body struggling to heal in light of our shared pain. Knowing damn well he feels it too, I bite my lip, funneling all the strength he and I have, forcing our hearts to regulate their beatings.

Pulling his head into my chest, I hold him close, letting myself absolve his pain, trusting the strength I carry in the ways that he has.

I am stronger than this.

I am stronger than the Prophet.

No longer will I be a prisoner in my own mind.

Closing my eyes, I focus on every ounce of pain we share, fueled by the truths and the binds that have entrapped us. Letting my arms wrap around him, his large body feels delicate to the touch, my skin burning with heat. Flooding out every horrific feeling trying to work through the both of us, I focus on the sound of his regulating heart, my Call bringing up every line of defense in our minds it can. Imagining a wall shielding us from the bind tightening around our life force, I take my first real breath, his lungs expanding, my mind opening doors once locked.

This strength is mine.

This life is mine.

And it was stolen.

Everything was stolen.

"Forest," Xavier snaps, my eyes flying open, my blood trickling down my lips. Processing what has happened, his thumbs roll over my lips, both of us blinking with wide eyes.

"What happened?" I question, his voice shaky.

"You forced back the bind, even momentarily-"

"Touch me," I blurt out, the moment of opportunity slim.

"What-"

"Not like you did the night of the Lottery, and not like you did in the bathroom. Touch me so I may remember," I sob, his eyes filling with determination.

Grabbing him, I Winnow us to the bed, letting my back meet the mattress. Hovering over me, he watches me close.

"Show me the Xavier that was taken from me."

Needing nothing more, the man wastes no time, our hands gripping at our shirts, forcing the fabric over our heads. Casting the clothing aside, the chill air hits my breasts, his torso filled with healing lesions. Glancing down at my own torso, I see a few scarce cuts, ones Xavier was unable to stow away. Fiddling with my pants, I help him take them off, letting them hit the floor, his eyes taking in the sight of me.

"I don't know how long I can-"

Landing his lips on my breast, he silences my warning, his tongue swirling around the nipple gently, my mind anticipating a bite. Waiting until he has created a sensitive point, his lips gently press down on the sensitive point, his free hand trailing down my side, before moving his mouth to my next breast. Continuing this pattern of landing gentle kisses on my skin, he works across my chest like a map, hitting every sensitive point he can with precision. Moving closer to my neck, his hair brushes my skin, my fingers coiled in his hair, letting his touch consume me. Looking past the aching warmth between my legs, I feel his length brush my thigh, his nose hovering past my own, his lips dangerously close.

"I can't risk it-"

"I know," I sob, rolling my thumbs over his cheeks. "It's okay," I mutter, gently placing my hands over both of our mouths.

Saying nothing, his eyes shift from sorrow to lust. Pulling my hand away from his mouth, he pushes on, letting his lips land on my sternum, his touch trailing down to my lower stomach before trailing above my waistband. Kissing my throbbing warmth above my underwear, the growing need to feel comforting touch grows, his eyes glancing up toward me, his mouth pausing its gentle touches. □

Watching his eyebrows crease inward with concern, I feel the wetness roll down my cheeks, my wrist wiping away a mix of blood and tears, the yearning need to feel safe eating me alive. Struggling to stow away our pain, I close my eyes, letting my head hit the sheets as reality sets in.

No matter what we do, the Prophet's control will linger.

Moving back up toward my face, Xavier moves off of me, his back hitting the mattress. Grabbing me before I can protest, he drags me onto his front, letting my legs lay over his own, my chest pressed against his. Resting my head on his chest, his fingers work through my hair, his hand massaging the back of my neck, his body holding mine close.

"Why did you stop?" I question in a sob, my eyes finally opening.

Watching me with a frown, he stops himself from kissing the top of my head, my energy dwindled down to nothing.

"The Prophet thought I was many things. One being a lust-hungry fool whose most detrimental bind would be my need to feel your lips against mine," Xavier says, keeping me as close as he possibly can. "Eylon never stopped to think that what we had was more than sexual. He took away many things but never considered that holding you as I do now means just as much to me as anything sexual we might have done."

Keeping my head pressed against his chest, I allow myself to let go of our guards, waiting for the pain.

It never comes.

"Tell me a story. Tell me something to distract my mind," I whisper, several seconds of silence ensuing between us.

"There once was a bird," he begins, my interest perking up at his willingness to tell a story. "The bird loved his nest and everyone inside of it, even when they didn't particularly deserve it. The bird lived in peace until the gardener made his appearance. He clipped the bird's wings, breaking him and repairing him over and over again. With time, the bird grew cold listening to the gardener's every word," he continues. I pull myself upward, staring at him with confusion. "Forced to seek out a pest, the gardener tasked the bird to hunt his mouse, not expecting the mouse to be two steps ahead. Trapping the bird, the mouse isolated the bird, stealing the gardener's one advantage. With time, some of the bird's and mouse's feelings for one another grew in ways the gardener did not like; he was angry at the possibilities that these bonds could create with his unmanageable creatures. One night, he decided to change the animal's worlds, tearing each one of them apart, altering how they see one another," he says, his eyes now open as he stares at the ceiling. "The animals cried out in pain for one another, tortured by the gardener's actions. When everything was said and done, the bird remembered the atrocities, and the other remembered nothing except the new life the gardener had implemented for them in their minds. The bird promised to stay good, to follow his rules if it meant he got his mouse back. The gardener took away the animal's voices and locked away the key, forcing the bird for years to watch his mouse look past him," Xavier continues, his voice a bit shaky. "Each time the bird finds his mouse, he sings for her, but no sound leaves him. She looks past him, often hating him," he says, now looking at me. I feel my eyes begin to water. "Now the bird fights every day trying to reverse the gardener's actions, but the gardener was tricky and devious, creating a labyrinth that no one can escape from." Xavier finishes. I shakily draw in a breath.

"What am I to you, Xavier?" I question, a pained expression forming on his face.

"The mouse was everything to the bird," he says shakily, my eyes filling with tears.

Cradling my head, I sob into his chest, the words I wish I could say trapped in the void of my mind.

"I won't leave you again, Xavier, I whisper, his hands holding me tight.

"You will once morning breaks and the alcohol has left you," he whispers, pressing his forehead to mine. "Good thing I always find you."

Chapter Twenty-Eight

Kaiden

Taking a seat on one of the benches positioned outside of lodging, I warm my chill hands, looking to the night sky above, my mind running wild with a floodgate of thoughts keeping me far away from the sleep I so desperately need. In most scenarios, I would say setting aside my emotions for logic was one of my best traits. Now, my emotions eat me alive, threatening to tear away any sense of sanity I have left in me.

Trying to stow away the one thought that has been eating me alive for months, it comes creeping in, settling into every avoidant thought I have tried to force onto myself. Covering my eyes, I try to piece together a reason behind my feelings, something that will make it all feel like less of a betrayal on my part.

Aaron's presence around me over the past few months has eased my pain, making it easier to stomach the person I loved being taken from me. Initially, I thought what Aaron was doing was only bringing me comfort, but after our interaction on our ride in, and our moments in the bar, I question if I am starting to see the man in a new light, one that only pulls me farther away from Hunter.

Trying to decipher if Aaron feels the same way is impossible, making it even harder to justify any of my thoughts. As much as I'd like to talk to Forest, or even Xavier, about the matter, I know trying to speak to them after their abrupt exit together is far from the right move.

At least I can face my denial head-on. Forest lets her denial hang over her, making herself clueless about the truths in front of her. I am no idiot. I know what was said all those months ago. The more time we spend here, the more time I am left to question how related Forest and I really are biologically.

If what is theorized is true, she is a grown woman, one who ruined my family for a cause she can't even remember. Initially, putting together our childhood was clear and easy to pick out. Now, it's all hazy, jumbles of a life that seems so very foreign, like a faint dream you can hardly recall after you've woken up.

Would I still love her the way I do now if I knew she was not my blood?

Would I start to reflect on the reality that she, and only she, had shed innocent blood that day Elyon killed Fallan?

Despite her rage, her hand laid claim to Rae's and Jeremey's lives, breaking their necks like it was nothing. How much longer can I pretend that Hunter's death was not by her doing?

Same broken neck, same unspoken betrayal.

Initially, I might have shunned her, keeping her away from me, questioning if she deserved the same fate as the other three.

After seeing the pages of information that was leaked and feeling the distance from her, it became increasingly clear how much I needed her in my life.

Blood or not, she is my sister.

I just wish she could see how much I need her right now.

After the bar, Aaron tried to get me to come over to his room to play some card games, still giddy from the liveliness of the night. Wanting nothing more than to entertain a bit of fun, my mind stopped me, once more making it impossible to see any interaction with the man in an isolated setting as anything other than a betrayal to Hunter.

I had walked into Forest's lodging first, surprised to see she was nowhere to be seen. Quickly piecing together the fact Xavier never came back, it was easy to draw a conclusion on where she was.

So long as she is with Xaver, then I know she is safe.

Yet here I am, alone on a resting bench, wondering at what point my life became so very tangled.

Seeing a flash of motion in the distance, the tail end of a dark long coat darts behind a building, my eyes blinking past the film of darkness the night brings. Cocking my head, the coat looks very similar to the wardrobe found back in New Haven, specifically by Officials.

"I'm seeing things," I whisper, pulling my knees to my chest.

Feeling a warmth beside me, I slowly turn my head, a large body beside me, concealed by the very cloak I thought I saw. Wearing a mask that hides distinguishable traits, I scoot away, my heart beating out of my chest at the sight of Sanctum's emblem stitched into the coat pocket of the jacket.

Keeping my head down, I count in my head, wondering how quickly I can make it inside the lodging quarters before this person grabs me. Staying silent, I try to formulate a strategic plan, keeping my breathing as quiet as possible.

"Beautiful night," the man says, something eerily familiar in the tone.

Josh.

"I would say so," I whisper, doing my best to fluctuate the tone in my voice.

"No stars like this in New Haven. Too much smoke," he says with a laugh, turning his head to meet my petrified state.

Watching me with his bright eyes, I keep myself backed into the bench's arm rail, taking notice of the other two figures waiting in the shadows, watching the interaction closely.

"What are you doing here?" I question shakily. "I thought you were-"

"Dead? Like Max?" he questions, tugging down the bottom of his mask, his face exactly how I remember it. "Who can I thank for his death? That blonde betrayer or the whore of a woman you call your sister?" he questions, my throat dry with nerves.

Debating screaming, Josh scoffs.

"Do that and I'll cut off your ear. I'm sure you will do just fine in the relationship department without one," Josh sneers. "You are still pining after men? Right?" he questions, mocking me right to my face.

"What do you want from me?" I question shakily, ready to make a break for it once he has reached into his pocket.

"I have been tasked with something very important," he smiles, pulling free a fresh syringe. "I need to ensure your sister gets Elyon's message. Can't have too many powerful Marked roaming around unchecked."

Ready to make a break for it, he grabs my shirt, forcing me back down, the sharp end of the needle plunging into my thigh. Filling my veins with the liquid, the haziness comes over quickly, my body slumping into Josh, his hand delivering my face a hard slap. Biting back a gasp, he holds my head against his leg, pulling his lips to meet my ear.

"Leverage for big sister to come without question."

Shoving me off of the bench, I hit the ground, all of my limbs becoming useless.

"F- Forest!" I try to scream, my voice raspy, my mouth growing numb.

"Save your screams, Kaiden," Josh smiles, looking down at me with joy. "You'll need plenty where we are going."

CHAPTER TWENTY-NINE

FOREST

Letting my legs drape through the gaps of the balcony railing, I take shallow breaths, my body buzzing with an energy I can't stow away. Seeing nothing but fleeting images in my dream, the life I once thought to have lived melts away, replaced by fragmented whispers of a reality buried deep within my mind. No memory is coherent. No face is recognizable. Voices and conversations, stolen by time and the altered chip once planted in my head now resurface, making it impossible to quiet my mind.

Rolling my fingers over the cigarette I had managed to steal from Xavier, I fidget anxiously, peering back at his peacefully somber figure sprawled out on the bed. Deep in sleep, I tugged the blankets higher up his body, watching the way his chest rose and fell as he indulged in his sleep. Grazing his face with my fingers, it was hard to walk away from his sleeping figure, his face peaceful for the first time in what seems like forever. Fixated on the image trapped within the pocket watch, I hold it close to my face, looking it over repeatedly as if some form of clarity will make its way into my mind. Peering at the void of darkness swarming the night sky, the stars that painted the horizons the night the winter brought in its first storm touch my mind. Remembering his wide smile and dark hair, pain swarms my chest.

"Why did you lie to me?" I whisper silently, pressing my head to the railing. "Why did you lie to me, just like everyone else?" I sob, half expecting to feel his hand ready to soothe me with gentle massages of my neck.

"I needed you to be on my side, Fallan," I sob, wondering where all of this is coming from. "And instead, you were hunting me, only truly caring for a woman who apparently hurt many," I push, pain creeping into my mind. "You knew why Xavier went after me. You knew it wasn't your love that I held closest to my heart-"

I stop, finally hearing the word out loud in the same context as Xavier. Bracing for whatever painful consequence the bind might create, my hands shake, my eyes glancing back at the sleeping giant.

"You took him from me," I whisper hatefully, wondering how I could have been so wrong. "You, and the Prophet, took him from me, and I didn't even know it."

Pulling my legs free from the gaps, I stand, shakily holding the watch.

"All anyone ever does is take what matters most from me," I seethe, a feeling much deeper than grief driving my mind. "Does anyone not fear the consequences of breaking a woman who has nothing left to lose?" I question to no one in particular, snapping the watch shut.

"You may have crossed me thinking I was foolish enough to torment myself with the hate you created in my mind for Xavier," I seethe, reaching into the pits of my mind. "You may think you broke me with Fallan's death, eating away at the strength I hold," I feel for a connection, something only blood can create. "Kaiden and Mark, blood or not, are mine to protect." I feel the presence, one meant not to be tampered with. "Xavier is mine to protect," I push, feeling the small surge of energy a mindful eye can sense. "You think playing games with me has a happy outcome?" I question, my voice shaking. "Mark my words. Your society will crumble beneath my feet, and your blood will pave the way for a new beginning."

Sensing his presence, every thought of revenge powers the connection I have forced.

"Oh, Forest," he whispers, my body tensing with adrenaline. ***"For me to die, so must you,"*** he hisses, his tone dripping with authority.

"That should scare you, Elyon," I whisper back. ***"I'm not afraid to die."***

"You should be. For Xavier's sake."

Letting go of the forced connection, I take a deep breath, wondering how I was able to force mental communication from such a far distance. Feeling the buzz of energy fade away, and the heat of my power fizzle, I look around, half expecting Elyon to be standing beside me. Calming myself once I only see Xavier, I tuck his watch in my pocket, debating how much longer I can pretend to sleep when, in reality, all I'm doing is watching him.

"H- help!" a familiar voice tries to scream, my senses on high alert.

Peering down from the balcony, my heart stops at the sight in front of me, all of my senses going into hyperdrive. Watching the flailing figure of my brother limply thrash against the two bodies dragging his dead legs, I drop the cigarette, my eyes glaring at the two men dragging Kai. Gripping the railing, I glance down at my measly excuse for tactical gear. A coat, one of Xavier's large shirts, boots, and a pair of leisure pants meant for comfort rather than mobility. Taking one look into the room, I silently slide the glass door shut, ensuring whatever is about to happen, Xavier is far from it. Taking a mental note of the drop from the balcony to the ground, I brace myself for the two-story drop needed to get to my brother the quickest.

"Save me, Sanctum," I whisper under my breath, fighting back the urge to laugh at the pitiful statement the Untouchables loved to use.

Swinging my legs over the balcony railing, my stomach drops at the feeling of my body heading toward the ground. Using my Hold and bracing my legs, I land on the ground, my body rolling, giving me enough momentum to swiftly recover. Doing my best to stay as silent as I possibly can, the Sanctuary is dead, patrons tucked away and sleeping peacefully, unaware of the vermin that have invaded their lands once again.

"Did you hear that?" one of the masked men questions, barely turning their head toward me.

Darting behind one of the first buildings I can, the night offers the protection I so desperately need, my palms sweaty with adrenaline.

"H- help-"

Slapping my brother across the face, one of the men silences Kai, his body too drained to fight back. Barely mobile, his long legs drag across the ground, his body doing its best to fight whatever the hell they have forced into him.

"Some insight on how much this one talks would have been nice," one of the men hisses.

Killing these two will be easy.

But that's part of the problem, isn't it?

They knew someone would hear Kai, they hoped it would be me. Now, they drag my brother like a white flag, expecting me to step out from concealment, ready to take their bait.

Listening to Kai's weakening heart, the ability to look at any of this logically dies down.

Fight now.

Think later.

Stepping out from the shadows, I Winnow behind the men, only giving myself a few feet of space away from the duo. Tugging my brother back from their grasp with my Hold, his body slumps toward me in a harsh drag, my arms gripping his arms before he can hit the ground. Gently lowering him to the dirt, my eyes narrow at both men. Smiling at me with glee, the pair's eyes go wide.

"Forest Blackburn," one of the men hisses, not an Official I recognize.

With their features shielded with masks, these men are newer to their positions, their uniforms hardly tainted by the blood of the Unfortunates.

"Two, cowardly, New Haven mutts," I hiss, pulling my lips into a vindictive grin.

"We were wondering when your brother's incessive yelling would finally catch your attention," the other Official says, his tone filled with delight.

"My attention is the last thing you want," I warn, evaluating every way I can torture these men.

"Elyon said you were a feisty one," the man to the right laughs.

Slowly slipping into each man's mind, I see nothing but their killer needs to torture us in every way they possibly can. Filled to the brim with fear, the men shake, something off-putting about the hard expressions they force.

Why are they not running?

"Elyon failed to tell you how little patience I have I see," I seethe, the men's heads shaking. Looking at one another with confusion, their fleeting thoughts roll through my mind, only adding fuel to the fire the men have lit within me.

"Where is the blonde Elyon swore would be with her?" one of the men wonders, repeatedly glancing around the area.

"For a killer, she sure does look-"

Raising my hands, I feel the energy of their chips calling to me, my anger reaching its tipping point. Touching the backs of their ears, the men's smiles drop, my head cocking with delight.

"I look what?" I question toward one of the men before turning my head to the other. "Touching one of the men I care about was more than enough. Blondie is off limits."

"Wait-"

Forcing my hands down, the men's chips tear free from their bodies, the skin ripping clean open as the tendrils fly free from the brain, taking any chance at life with them. Watching the bodies hit the ground in a matter of seconds, their chips meet my palms, stropping their tendrils flailing the moment I crush the devices within my hands. Watching the pool of blood collect around the men's heads, I glance down at my brother's still figure, his body twitching every so often as he continues to fight what they gave him.

"Kai," I whisper, nudging my brother, holding his face between my hands. "Kaiden," I whisper again, his eyes barely opening.

"What a great distraction," a sinister tone hisses, my blood running cold.

Josh.

Already preparing myself to Winnow, I turn my head, barely getting a glimpse of his golden eyes and olive skin. Feeling a gut-wrenching pain on both sides of my neck, he plunges two long needles into my largest veins, my throat biting back a gasp as my body tries to fight the anesthetic now working through my veins. Letting my knees hit the ground, I breathe heavily, feeling his hands force my shoulders down.

"I have prayed for the day I face you like this-"

Forcing my head down, I focus my Hold on his body, watching his back scrape the ground as he is tossed backward. Shakily trying to rise to my feet, the drug Kai no doubt has fallen victim to makes my legs useless. Watching Josh recover quickly from the toss, he barrels toward me, his hand grabbing a knife free from his side.

"Fuck bringing you back unscathed," he hisses, my hand instinctively flying up, his blade slicing straight through its center. Staring at the point of the blade now poking through the top of my hand, blood travels down my wrist, both of our teeth bore for all to see. Using his delay to my advantage, I grab his wrist, twisting enough for him to let go of the blade, tugging it free from my hand.

Now with the advantage of a weapon, I use what bit of energy I can deviate to my Call, ready to scream into Xavier's mind.

"Xavier-"

Feeling yet another needle enter my body, I stare down at the syringe of red, now fully injected into my arm. Petrified by the feeling that washes over me, I gasp for air, thrashing my bloodied hand toward Josh, my nails dragging across his face. Breaking a great deal of skin, he yells, his foot flying toward my face, getting a good kick to my jaw.

Hitting the ground with my head, the ability to fight the third syringe is impossible. Grasping my throat, I gasp, doing my best to stay awake.

As if every one of my abilities is being forced into submission, I take a deep breath, staring up at Josh's bleeding face, his mouth upturned into an unsettling smile.

"Elyon's blood," Josh whispers. "To keep you down."

Watching his hand wave through the air, the sound of more footsteps approaching kisses my ears. Hearing faint whispers, the men have varying reactions to the sight in front of them.

"Holy shit, she actually killed them."

"They knew they were bait. It was their fault for taunting her," Josh spits, my eyes droopily opening and closing. "Two double doses of sedative and a vial of the big man's blood, and she's finally down."

Focused on the circle of men now looking down at me and my brother, everything becomes bleak, my body forcefully touched, settled in the hands of faceless men, their nails digging into my skin. Hauled into the arms of a very familiar body, I smell Josh's cologne, his mouth pulling to my ear

"Now you may feel my pain."

Unable to say anything, my voice is gone, my head settled in the crook of the man's arm. Closing my eyes, I try and reach Xavier, hitting nothing but dead ends.

"Consequences," the Prophet's cold tone whispers in my mind before nothing at all.

CHAPTER THIRTY

FOREST

B urning hot pain travels up my body, the smell of burnt flesh kissing my nose every time I sharply inhale. Taking in as much oxygen as I possibly can, my throat is burning, my eyes letting loose a stream of tears down my cheeks every time I try to blink. Unable to look past the mask shielding my eyes, the loud grunts of another keep me awake, my body yearning to free itself from the confinement it has found itself in. In most scenarios, it would be easy to snap whatever binds they have me in. Given the sheer amount of sedatives working through my system, any chance of easily slipping free from the situation I have found myself in has quickly faded.

"Taking it much better than big brother did," Josh's vindictive voice sneers, the hot weapon prying further into my skin, my mind fully registering the pain.

"Fuck," I cry out, lurching forward, his hand forcefully shoving me back into the splintered wooden chair.

Tearing off my mask, his hand strikes my face before I can fully adjust, my eyes barely able to focus on Kai's gagged and bloodied figure watching me with fear. Looking down, Xavier's shirt is tattered, nothing but a bra stopping these men from seeing as much of me as they'd like. Staring at my burnt flesh, my ability to heal has faltered, my mind nothing but a jumbled mess of thoughts I am unable to sift through. What I thought to be a dream now bleeds into reality, eating away at my every waking thought.

"I spoke too soon," Josh snaps, his hair pulled back into a tightly wound bun atop his head. Significantly more worn than the last time I saw him, he watches me with hate. Despite the healing properties of a good Cure-All, my scratches along his face were too deep, the light white scars from my nails traveling across the man's face. Locked away in a place I hardly recognize, the smell of moss and decaying wood protrudes through the smell of flesh. Looking around, the room is concrete, the ceiling composed of wooden boards. Smiling like a drunk fool, Josh places the searing hot blade into a bowl of water. Four men linger at every possible exit, each one entirely concealed by a dark mask, leaving nothing but peepholes.

Bruised and beaten, Kai's lip quivers, his tears rolling down his cheeks. Already covered in lesions, my stomach rolls at the sight, my wrists tugging violently at the dark leather surrounding each wrist.

"You weren't waking up. I figured you wanted something pretty to look at during all of that struggle," Josh smiles, my teeth snapping at him the closer he gets.

"I'll fucking kill you!" I yell, glaring at every person foolish enough to linger in this room and watch.

"Not unless I kill him first," Josh says gleefully, something familiar in the way one of the men holds himself.

Same awkward shifts, and small little eyes.

Colton.

"So, your tag teaming with dipshit now?" I question toward Colton's figure, Josh's tongue clicking in response.

"Such a dirty mouth you have, Forest," Josh sighs, snatching a bottle from the tray filled with one of his many torturous devices. "No wonder you went after an Unfortunate."

Taking a long drink from the bottle, I glance at my brother, his eyes only on Josh.

"No, don't-" Kai begins, my voice releasing a violent scream at the feeling of the liquor being poured over my skin, the pain from the tattered skin mixing with the alcohol enough to make anyone implode.

Screaming so loud, I fear my lungs will burst, Josh pries open my skin, his fingers creating a much deeper lesion, the alcohol seeping into the cut. Screaming harder, I tug as hard as I possibly can, doing everything I can to scream out to Xavier in my mind. □

"Elyon's blood gave him the control to cut off your bond to your new bed buddy," Josh says, dropping the bottle once it is empty, the glass shards scattering across the ground. "And your ability to snap those binds in one clean sweep," he smiles.

"Elyon wants her functional," one of the men mutters. "He can't sacrifice any more of his Marked beneath New Haven to keep her well fed."

Glaring at the man, Josh shakes his head.

"We are not here to make sure she is comfortable," Josh snaps, grabbing one of the shards from the ground. "We are here to reminder her who she has fucked with."

Turning to Kai, he tosses the glass in his hand, eyeing the clean parts of my brother's skin with hunger.

"No," I mutter, pulling at the binds with as much force as I have.

"I believe it's your time again, Kaiden," Josh says, his voice a trembling mess.

"Please, it's getting harder to stay awake, Josh-"

Hearing a loud tear, the binds snap, my shoulders blazing with the heat of a tear within my ligaments. Forcing my legs to move, I barrel toward Josh, his body turning quicker than I can react.

Shoving the glass shard into my thigh, I scream out in pain, his hands forcing me to the floor, dragging me over the pile of glass settled onto the ground. Letting go of his grasp once four more shards have found their way into my skin, he flips me over, my throat panting for air.

"Send a message to blondie," Josh utters, kneeling over me with a look of pure terror.

Running his finger down my front, I flinch away from the touch. Ready to vomit, he pulls free a blade from his side, pointing its tip dangerously close to my heart.

"How do you plan on doing that?" Colton questions, my brother's eyes watering from pain.

Dragging my head upward by my hair, he holds it taut, slicing the blade through the strands he has managed to grab, my head slumping toward the floor. Getting off of me, he waltzes over to Colton with my hair, settling it in the palm of the man's hand.

"I'm sure he can piece together where that came from.

Looking at Kai, I roll onto my side, focusing on the man's binds. Eyes watering and face puffy, I drain my body focusing my Hold on his restraints, his eyes hazy with emotion.

"Forest-"

"You run. First chance you get, you run as far as you can and find Xavier," I whisper, feeling some sense of satisfaction once the binds begin to snap.

The only way Kai will get out of this is if I keep Josh distracted. With what leeway I have given him, he will be able to wiggle free; he just needs time.

Turning back toward Kai to steal a few of his locks, my voice comes out a shaky mess.

"You're punishing Xavier for what he did to your father during the Lottery," I spit, Josh's focus fully on me.

Biting back my tears, he walks over to me, pulling me up from the ground. Shoving me back into the chair, his eyes scan me up and down.

"Do you feel remorse? Do you feel guilty about how quickly you choose to lie with another man after Fallan's death?" he questions, my head already shaking.

"I loved Fallan," I whisper, moving closer to the man. "But I was something he loved out of convenience. That was never the case for Xavier. Xavier looked for me for god knows how long, and when he found me, my memory was gone-"

"You remember nothing-"

"I remember too much!" I hiss, the swarm of memories funneling through my mind, enough to drive most mad. "And nothing at the same time."

"You have fallen in love with him once more," Josh whispers, the words sounding foreign coming from him. "The Prophet was right in assuming you are the leverage to keep Xavier in line-"

"Do you think this ends with me?" I question, a thought rolling through my mind.

"What-"

"Do you think anything ends for the Cleansed so long as the Marked roam the Earth?" I question, genuinely seeking a response.

"Your death will terminate your kind's existence-"

"Not just my death," I warn. "Or has the Prophet failed to tell you the whole picture?" I question, his eyes wary.

"You're lying-"

"Am I? Do you think my dying will stop Elyon from creating more of our kind? Do you think my death will bring the peace you so desperately want? The only way to end any of this is to end the chances for any Marked to be born. We tried eradicating the problem in New Haven the Prophet's way and look where we are now," I laugh in defeat, looking around the space. "You are just another piece on his game board, and the sad part is, you know it."

Narrowing his eyes at the statement, I hear a loud snap, my brother's eyes going wide.

Grabbing Josh before he can react, I pull him down and into me, letting our limbs become a tangle on the floor, my hand reaching out, shoving back the two men standing in the way of Kai's closest exit with my Hold. Making a run for it, something cold and painful lodges itself in my lung, my hand shaking as my eyes grow wide. Looking down, one of the glass shards sits in Josh's hand, its point buried deep into my side. Gasping as I try to breathe, he pulls his lips closer to my ear, my brother seconds away from reaching the door.

"If you leave, Kaiden, I will ensure none of you are able to recognize her once I am done with her," Josh warns, Kai's hand grazing the handle. Staying in place, Kai can leave any second, his foot anxiously tapping the ground.

"Then again, she isn't really blood, is she? She is a woman who infiltrated one of her follower's families, feeding them nothing but lies. The killer of your sweet Hunter."

Burying the glass deeper, I gasp for air, my sins swallowing me alive.

"K-Kai.... Go," I whisper, his body shaking.

"Yes, go, Kai. We both know I'm doing you a favor."

Staring at the door, Josh's men begin to regain footing, my brother's eyes hazy as he looks my way.

Debating running right out of here, our eyes lock, a long list full of apologies running through my mind. Looking at the men approaching him, his window for opportunity is closing.

"She is my sister," he whispers. "Family is a concept you will never have the luxury of understanding again." □

Angered, Josh plows the shard as deep as he can, the feeling of the glass piercing my lung excruciatingly painful. Grabbing my brother, they drag him over to me, forcing the man into the ground, letting him gather me up in his arms. Barely able to breathe, I gasp, Josh's foot crushing my hand as he walks by, his men already forcing a new round of sedatives into our blood.

"Bad move, Kaiden," Josh smiles. "I would have given you a head start."

Trying to speak, my throat is silenced by the blood forcing its way into my airways. Taking all the strength I have, I try to repair the tear in my lung. Enduring yet another round of needles being plowed into our veins, the rich red of the Prophet's blood eases its way into my system, any progress I made on the repair quickly faltering.

Forcing another round of sedative in Kai, he grips me as hard as he can, both of our cheeks pressing to the cool and dirtied floor, my body slowly bleeding out.

"That's enough for now," Josh mocks, making his way toward the door, a set of stairs leading upward.

A basement.

Perfect.

"We'll be back in an hour. Let's hope your strength proves to be true," Josh smiles at me, waving his men after him, each one of their eyes lingering on the bloodied and mangled state of me and my brother.

Watching the door slam shut, Kai stares at me, his eyes wide, his hand barely grazing my cheek. Clutching every open wound I can, his hands hold what I cannot, my eyes spilling with a flood of tears. Joining me, he sobs uncontrollably, our tears mixing with the blood streaking our faces.

"I'm sorry," I whisper, petrified at the position I have put him in yet again. "I'm sorry I hurt your family," I continue, buried memories of a younger Kaiden looking at me, his eyes lined with confusion, reflecting a version of myself I hardly recognize. "I don't know who I am, Kai, but I- I'm not your sister-"

"Yes, you are," he whispers, holding me as close as he possibly can without harming me. "Are we going to die, Forest?" he questions, my lungs gasping for air.

"No," I mutter, pressing my head to his. "I can't die," I sob, my voice shaking. "I can't let you die," I continue, thinking of nothing but Kai and Xavier's well-being.

"It's my job to protect you, Kaiden, that much I know," I wallow, his voice releasing a laugh of defeat.

"That's all you've ever done," he smiles, his tears pouring more rapidly, "That's why you killed Hunter, right?" he questions, my heart dropping.

Ready to throw him my first line of defense, he cradles my head, now allowing me to spiral.

"There's a time for me to be angry, Forest, but it's not now," he sobs, pressing his lips to the top of his head. "Now, I'm just tired, Forest."

Feeling his head droop, his blood spills out of one of his larger wounds, staining the front of his shirt. Watching his hands drop from my skin, I begin to panic, my voice far from me. Screaming as hard as I can, I cry out in pain, my mind hazy.

"Xavier!" I yell in my mind, spots clouding my vision.

"Xavier!" I half-heartedly scream, Kai's body now still.

Trying to drag myself closer to the door, I wail out in pain, my nails scraping the ground.

"Dad?" I question silently. "Mom?" I push, wondering at what point they come to take me away from this hell. Will death be the peaceful terrain and blissful lands we were told of growing up? Will Xavier feel this pain? Perhaps the Prophet's blood will keep him safe from all of this-

No longer having the will to fight, my lungs have lost the war, my throat gasping for air. Rolling onto my back, I glare up at the roof, fearful of what has happened and all that has yet to come.

Death is peaceful.

Fear is something else entirely.

CHAPTER THIRTY-ONE

XAVIER

*"X**avier,"* Her voice faintly whispers in my mind, my body jolting free from its somber sleep.

Taking several moments to compose myself, I take deep breaths, wondering how I was able to sleep so long, for the first time in what has felt like years. Letting the dream state fade, my body aches, as if I had run a marathon after years of not using my body. Still hearing her fearful whisper in my mind, I take a deep breath, scolding myself for yet again letting my mind shift from a peaceful sleep into something much more horrific.

Ready to pull her back onto my chest and watch her peacefully dream for hours, my body tenses up the second my hand drags across the empty space where her body once was. Frantically flipping on the lamp, her body is nowhere to be seen, her energy entirely cut off from me. Suddenly much livelier, I grab my pants, tugging them on as quickly as possible, trying to find my shirt somewhere in my hazy state.

"Forest?" I question out loud, wondering if she managed to get a head start for her day.

Waiting for a response, I hear nothing, my chest filling with a fear I'd rather not have.

Watching the sunrise bleed bright oranges and pinks into the room, something on the balcony catches my attention. Making my way outside, a dead, barely smoked cigarette sits unbothered. Peering over the balcony, I catch sight of disheveled dirt, my worries escalating once I see a few patches of dark red in the places where a struggle clearly ensued.

Backing away from the balcony, I move quicker, grabbing one of the first shirts in my bag I can. Expecting to see some of Forest's gear gone, her bag remains the same, nothing touched or out of place.

She wouldn't leave without any of her things... would she?

Reaching my hand toward the nightstand to grab my final asset, my fingertips collide with the surface of the wood, feeling nothing close to the casing of my pocket watch.

Staring at the sight with confusion, the watch is long gone, my mind finally allowing myself to start to panic.

Grabbing my blade, I march forward, swinging open our lodging door, slamming my fists into the neighboring doors of all of our companions.

"Forest?" I question again, my voice carrying through my mind as if I am shouting down an empty cavern.

"Forest Blackburn?" I question more aggressively, knowing damn well if this was some game of hers, she would at least respond to her full name.

Bewildered and all out of sorts, Aaron walks down the hallway, his eyes heavy, as if his consciousness kept him up well later than the rest of us.

"Hey-"

"Kaiden is gone," Aaron mutters, the doors to our companion's rooms finally starting to open.

"What do you mean Kaiden is gone?" I question, looking the man over with confusion.

"I mean, Kaiden is gone, and I have no clue where the hell he is," Aaron says, crossing his arms as he speaks.

There's too much urgency in his voice, there's more to it.

"What aren't you telling me?" I question, taking a step closer to the man.

"I have searched the whole sector for him. I wanted to see if he was okay after he left the bar last night. He is gone," Aaron clarifies, his eyes narrowing as he speaks.

No, there's something else.

Watching Aaron fidget in this pocket, I move closer, grabbing his arm as hard as I can.

"What else are you not telling me?" I question coldly, his eyes closing.

Shakily pulling his hand from his pocket, my heart drops at the sight in front of me.

Two clusters of hair, one silver and one brown and curled, both blotted with blood.

"It was on the bench outside the bar this morning," Aaron whispers. "It's a warning."

Groggily walking out of her room, Bekah rubs her eyes. Valerie is too caught up in our words to acknowledge the fact she left the same room as the woman.

"What's going on?" Bekah questions, pulling on her regular cold demeanor.

"Radio Nyla," I command in a tone that most would rather not combat.

Whispering to Val, the redhead waits patiently for her radio, glancing up at me as she holds down the button.

"Nyla?" Bekah questions, her arm extending out to me.

Taking the walkie, I hold it close to my mouth.

"Were there any breaches in your ward last night?" I question angrily, only receiving static on the other end.

Swiping the walkie from me, Bekah continues on with a sense of urgency.

"Nyla?" Bekah questions again, tapping her foot as she waits.

"There was a breach last night," she whispers silently.

"What kind of breach?" Bekah questions, clearly becoming as angered as I am.

"They found a weak point in our wards, Xavier, we didn't know-"

"Didn't know what? Who the hell are you talking about?" I snap.

"New Haven found a way in," she says, all of our hearts dropping. "One of the few, newer cameras we installed on lodging was able to pick up a struggle last night-"

"A struggle?" I ask, swiping the walkie away from Bekah, my anger heard from a mile away.

"Kaiden was being dragged away by Officials, and Forest-"

"What happened to Forest?" I question, wondering at what point the sound of static became one of my least favorite things.

"She swooped in to help her brother, and I thought she would have the upper hand-"

"What happened?" I question, no longer willing to allow Nyla to dance around the topic so blatantly.

"She was comforting her brother when one of the men injected her three times. One of the vials was different, a much red than the others-"

"The Prophet's blood," I hiss, shaking my head in disbelief. "That's why I can't feel her, why I can't hear her," I mutter.

"We're in the compound for six months and she is safe. She is in your shitty refugee for one day, and the Prophet gets to her?" I question, dripping with anger.

"Xavier, we are trying to track her down, figure out where they went-"

"If anything happens to her, so help me, Sanctum, Nyla, it's your head I will come for next."

"Wait-"

Slamming the walkie into the wall, it shatters into multiple pieces, my chest rising and falling rapidly. Taking a few moments to compose myself, I run through a list of regulation tactics in my head, finally looking to Bekah.

"You heard her, Xavier. They have no idea where Forest and Kaiden are," Bekah says, her face as cold as mine.

"I do," I whisper, knowing what point the Prophet is choosing to make.

No matter where they are.

No matter where we are.

He will always find us.

"Where are they?" Aaron questions, his eyes lively once again.

"The one place we have been searching for this whole time," I hiss, turning on my heels, ready to tear out the throat of anyone who chooses to cross me.

Closing my eyes, I focus on what's left of our connection being suffocated by the Prophet's presence within her. Listening to the sound of my breathing, I continue walking, forcing myself into the deepest parts of my mind, just as I had during my time in New Haven, looking for the wide-eyed and bright Untouchable girl that Andrew Blackburn had brought into his home. Feeling that slight pull of her presence, I feel a heavy sense of pain each time I gravitate closer, the smell of old wood and moisture clinging to my nose. Taking a deeper breath, the distant voices of men fill my ears, my mind pushing past the Prophet's fortress in her body, words finally formulating in my mind.

"This was a home?" one of the men whispers close to her, her body still in an unconscious state, only one of the two of us listening to the men.

"Her home, if Elyon is right."

Pausing, my eyes fly open.

I know that voice.

I know that voice better than most.

"Josh has them," I whisper, Valerie and Aaron both wide-eyed.

"Where did he take them?" Valerie questions, my legs moving for me.

"The reflecting pools," I march forward, looking back at Bekah. "Grab whatever resources you can, take a few of Nyla's guards, and meet me by their exit in ten," I warn, pushing past the glass doors.

Following close behind me, Bekah breaks off, leaving Valerie and Aaron to hit me in their line of questioning.

"Xavier, what the hell is going on?" Aaron questions, narrowly avoiding getting in my face.

Marching toward the vehicles, I ignore the man, mentally mapping the quickest path to where Josh has dragged them.

"Xavier?" Valerie adds on, becoming just as impatient as her cousin.

Grabbing my shoulder, Aaron begins to drag me back. Grabbing his wrist, I shove him into the closest vehicle, holding him down with enough anger to fuel an army.

"They're at the reflecting pools," I hiss, taking a deep breath. "The only reason I know where that is, is because I have been there," I warn, fighting every urge to rip the man's head clean from his body. "Elyon is sending a message to me. He's sending a message to all of us. What he didn't consider is Josh's hatred for me and the Marked runs much deeper than any loyalty he has pleaded to Elyon," I grovel, forcing myself away from the man. "So, before you ask me any questions and make it impossible not to kill you, can you just trust me, and help me get them back?" I question, glancing at the pair.

Saying nothing, all they do is nod their heads, staying as silent as they possibly can.

Honking a horn, Bekah backs up a vehicle, two guards pulling themselves into the bed, urgently awaiting us. Walking away from the Danvers, I gravitate toward the driver's side door, watching as Bekah shifts over to the passenger side. Pulling myself in, a small hand stops me, tugging harshly on my shirt.

"You can't go like that," Nyla pleads, my impatience growing.

"This wasn't up for debate," I hiss, tearing my shirt free from her hand.

Taking control of the driver's seat, the engine rumbles with life, my feet impatiently waiting to get us in motion. Locking Nyla out of the vehicle, I begin backing away, letting her frowning face fade out in the rearview mirror, Bekah's hands fidgeting anxiously.

"What are we driving ourselves into this time?" she questions, my body unnerved by Forest's silence.

"If they are there and safe, then an interrogation," I hiss, her throat bobbing as she swallows.

"And if they're not safe?" she questions, my hands gripping the wheel. "It seems like a good day for a massacre."

CHAPTER THIRTY-TWO

FOREST

"**R**ise and shine, Blackburn," Josh's manic voice hisses, my eyes flying open at the noise. Feeling something forced into my mouth, the dirtied cloth used as a gag forces itself down my throat, preventing me from crying out in pain. Still depleted and void of energy, Kai lies in front of me, his body weak from blood loss. Feeling the cuts along my skin violently burn each time I shift, dirt collects in each open wound, my clothes dirtied and torn, my pants shifted down my hips.

Looking around, the golden hue of the sunrise dances over the scenery, my eyes struggling to adjust to the serene sight in front of me.

Nestled away in the woods, a small, desolate cabin sits in wait, its windows nailed and boarded up, its interior void of light. Surrounded by dense greenery and distant mountains, the sky is clear, not a sign of a single ward in sight. Smelling the aromatic scent of moisture, I pull my focus to the body of water positioned next to me, its surface clearer than most glass. Feeling an immense pull toward the pond, my lungs barely retain air, my mind hazy from the energy exerted keeping me alive. Bobbing their heads in the water like the koi fish back at the academy, Shifters watch me with their sullen stares. At least five Officials surround the water, their weapons pointed straight at me. Standing over my brother and me with a smug expression, Josh looks pleased, his mouth pulled into a devilish smirk.

"Nothing quite like home," he whispers, crouching down to become more at level with me.

Forcing my chin toward the cabin, he pulls my eyelids back, making me look at the structure until my eyes water.

"You've really let the place go, Forest."

Staring at the cabin, the image inside the watch clings to my mind: my hands grabbing the side of a cabin similar to this one.

Feeling an immense pain radiate through me, one deeper than the lesions Josh has created, one of my hazier memories forces itself forward, the smell of cinnamon and pine wafting into my nose. Seeing what the interior of the building looks like, I see a quaint home, one meant to be filled with love and cherished deeply. Seeing a wave of gray flash over my vision, something about the way the figure moves through the cabin without a care in the world, makes me smile, my legs tucked into my chest, a sketchbook settled on my bare thighs. His large shirt runs down my body, the same shirt he has chosen not to wear this morning. Pacing around the space, he causally sips a cup of tea, his black-inked skin and toned body out for anyone to see. Glancing my way, a smile curls along his lips, the imagery of him inspiring this likeness touching the paper of my sketchpad. Setting his cup on a side table, he inches closer, trying to steal a peak at my work.

"You still hiding it from me?' he questions, my hand instinctively closing the work, tucking it beneath my leg.

Smiling wider at my action, he takes a seat on the couch with me; my back pressed close to the window, now boarded up. Dragging me closer by my ankles, his body leans over mine, countless laughs leaving me.

"I told you; it is a surprise," I whisper with a smile, my arms wrapping around his neck.

Bringing his lips down, they gently touch my own, quickly developing from something innocent to something much more passionate. Running his tongue along my lower lip, I push him back, letting the man drag me into his lap, his hands exploring my bare ass. Kissing him with as much fire as I have in me. Grabbing the back of my neck, he tugs me closer, his thumb toying with the waistband of my underwear.

"You're making it hard to have chivalry, Forest," he whispers, dragging his lips closer to my ear. I will wait a lifetime for you, that much I can promise you, but so help me, God. If you keep kissing me like this, I will not be able to hold myself off for when you finally allow me to call you mine forever," he whispers, my heart fluttering with joy.

"Perhaps I am tired of waiting," I whisper with thrill, my heart guiding my voice. ▢

Pausing, he pulls away, cupping my face between his hands.

"You said-"

"I know what I said. I told you I wanted to live to end the Prophet," I whisper, my fingers trailing across his face. "I think there is something else I'd much rather live for-"

Screaming despite the gag, my back arches, deeper lesions scorning my skin, only adding to my blood loss. Watching me with fear, Kaiden's eyes plead to Josh, his mouth equally as occupied as mine. Forcing my head into the ground to stop my thrashing, Josh shakes his head, his hand pulling free a chain, the watch dangling peacefully from his finger.

"So many suppressed memories within that little head, just driving you and Xavier closer to death once the Prophet's blood has bled free from your system. I'm sure lover boy can feel it now, eating away at him, making it that much harder for him to breathe-" □

Kicking Josh hard in the ankle, Kai yells, watching the man stumble to the ground, dropping the watch in the process. Clutching his now bruised ankle, he waves a hand, stopping his men from moving any closer than they already have.

Trying to reach to utilize some part of my energy to move, I claw at the ground, dragging myself further away from Josh and closer to Kai. Screaming through the pain, I choke on the gag, looking around for anything that may be able to be used to defend myself.

"You nasty Blackburns," Josh hisses, forcing himself back into a standing position, limping the closer he gets to me.

"You never know when to stop," he shakes his head, waving one of his men over.

Grabbing my hair, I scream frantically as he begins to drag me closer to the water's edge. Soon after, one of Josh's men yanks Kai's head, both of us inches away from the water, the Shifters gradually moving closer. Smiling wickedly, the creatures wade through the depths, moving fast once their legs have touched the ground.

"The Prophet wants you alive... wants to use you for some greater purpose," he whispers, the smallest flood of energy working through me. "I think he failed to realize just how much I fucking hate your kind."

Trying to focus on the Shifter's minds, I narrow my eyes, Josh's hand forcing down my gag. Coughing, I glance up at him, his hand shaking one long finger.

"That blood may give you strength, but the Prophet ensured it would give him some control."

"Rot in hell," I hiss, my brother now fully unconscious, his blood loss too great.

"Pity," he sighs, glaring at the Shifter. "Drag her in."

Grabbing onto my ankle, one of the creatures pulls me across the ground, my body colliding with the waters, its hands forcing me down. Feeling the water sting my cuts, I force my head back up, gasping for air. Lifting up Kai, Josh and the man toss his body into the water, a Shifter taking on the task of dragging him further down. Taking one final breath of air, my head dives under the water, the Shifter prying its nails into my skin, Pulling me closer toward the bottom of the lake. Trying to focus on my Hold, my blood swirls the water in clouds, my lungs barely able to stow away the liquid. Watching my brother's limp state be dragged further down, I focus solely on him, his arms floating in the space above him.

Looking down, the Shifter smiles at me, its face hard to make out in the depths of the water. Raising my foot, I kick it as hard as I can in the face, taking advantage of its moment of falter, pushing myself to swim as hard as my body will allow.

Creeping closer to Kai, I raise my hands, using all the energy left in my body, forcing my Hold onto the Shifter clinging onto my brother. Latching onto its mind, I sway every single one of its thoughts, urging the creature to let go of Kai, watching its hand uncurl from around his ankle. Watching my brother's body begin to move, it floats toward the top, his eyes barely blinking, watching me sink further down. Pushing the creature further, I watch as its own taloned claw drives straight into its heart, its voice screaming, drowned out by the presence of water.

The water fills my airways, the fire within my chest escalating with each passing second. Feeling its clawed hand dig into my ankle, my bones shatter the harder it grasps, forcing me deeper down into the dark abyss of the water. Listening to the sound of my own scream fade away with each expansion of my lungs, the light above me grows hazy, my mind slipping deeper into a state of unconsciousness.

I have felt fear before.

I have felt pain.

Never have I felt the hand of death hold onto me as it does now.

Fighting with all I have, the sedatives pumping through my veins weaken me, making it impossible to get a grasp on anything real. □

Watching Josh cock his head as his reflection dances across the surface of the water, a wicked grin spreads across his face, his eyes hot with desire at the sight of me slipping further into death's grasp.

Feeling the burn fade into something much more tolerable, my body feels weightless, the pain fading as quickly as it had arrived.

Death is closing in.

The light is slowly fading.

God help the fools who allowed this to happen.

For the part of my soul that was Forest Blackburn is fading.

All that remains is the Apparatus.

And she will come for **blood.**

"Xavier?" I whisper, fearful he may hear the thoughts.

So long as the Prophet's concoction runs through me, he has a chance at living.

Hearing nothing, my mind fills with some sense of relief.

"I'm sorry we lost our life."

Embracing the silence, darkness clouds my vision.

Time to wake up.

CHAPTER THIRTY-THREE

XAVIER

"Fucking move!" I yell toward the vehicle, slamming my hand down on its wheel, forcing the gas pedal down as far as it allows me. Watching the barren lands shift to lush greenery, dust turns to dirt, the thick mass of the forest waiting to embrace me once again. Barreling through the woods, I urge those in the vehicle bed to hold on, their hands positioned by their weapons, ready to attack the moment they sense danger.

"How far away are we?" Bekah questions frantically.

"No more than six minutes-"

Pain worse than anything I have experienced before floods my chest, my lungs burning as I breathe, clinging to any air they can absorb. Gasping, my skin feels hot with lesions, the feeling of glass shards pushed into every open wound exploring my skin. Feeling my throat close, I jolt the vehicle to our left, only able to keep the vehicle on track thanks to Bekah's quick hands. Clutching my throat, I spit up blood, feeling a puncture in my lung, my voice releasing a shrill sound of pain.

"Xavier?" Bekah frantically questions, the others in the back of the vehicle equally fearful. "What the hell is happening?" she asks, my energy fighting back all of the pain.

"I- it's Forest," I gasp, forcing my hands back on the wheel. "S- she's dying."

Widening their eyes in the review mirror, all of those lingering in the back look fearful, the vehicle pushing through the shrubbery as fast as it can. Thinking of every selfish thing I have ever done, I silently pray for enough fight to get to her, wishing now, more than ever, for once something I do keeps the people I love alive.

Feeling the link from the Prophet's blood bind to Forest weaken, I take a sharp breath, taking in enough oxygen to stay cognitively alert.

"The bastard injected her with his blood. It weakens her but also weakens the link he created between our lives," I hiss, shaking my head. "Her bind to him is faltering."

"And the connection you share?" Bekah questions, holding onto the hope that so long as I feel it, Forest's heart beats strong. "Was that not the Prophet's doing?"

"That was never by design," I mutter, seeing the vague outline of the place I once considered a home, five men standing in wait with malicious grins. "Nothing I feel about her is or was made by anyone but us. He has touched what is mine for the last time."

Saying nothing, the woman smiles.

For the first time in our lives, she sees me as something other than a monster.

"So the devil does have a heart?"

"You don't know the half of it."

Parking the vehicle with great impatience, we all move quickly, staring down the men, ready to tarnish the ground with their bloodshed. Leading the group like a ringleader, Josh smiles at us with a wide grin. My eyes scan the tree line, only feeling some ease once Mason's ghostly figure peers at me through the tree line.

He heard my Call.

We have an advantage.

"Xavier Evermoore," Josh exclaims, all of us frantically looking around for Forest and Kaiden. I would have expected you to at least look me in the eye, given what I have in my possession," Josh grovels, snapping his teeth as he speaks.

Focusing my gaze on him; the pain seeps back into my body, the Prophet's blood wearing off.

"Forest?" I question, unsettled by the silence in my mind.

"There is so much fight within you, boy," I hiss, glaring at the man. "Do you have any idea how many lines you have crossed? Do you have any idea what I am capable of?" I question, trying to catch the man in a fearful state.

"So long as the Prophet's bind holds true, you are nothing more than a worthless puppet. As is your woman, god rest her soul."

Seizing up, I stop, my heart racing at a million miles an hour.

"Where the fuck is she?" I yell, gripping my blade so hard that my fingers have begun to grow numb.

"I'd say, fifteen seconds away from taking her final breath. Perhaps she would have lived longer if she wasn't busy trying to save her brother from the water," Josh says, all of our eyes averting to the reflecting pools.

Big mistake, Joshua.

Forcing my Call into the man's mind, I stumble, feeling the thoughts of his torturous actions toward the siblings. Filled with enough hate to overcome the pain, I push forward, hearing the echo of our blades rattle the isolated space. Josh's hand barely grabs his weapon in time, the others already hot on the trail of the other men. Looking to the waters, Shifters wade through the water, their focus on anything but us. Creeping out from the tree line, Mason looks at me, my voice carrying across the small body of water.

"In the water," I yell, his response simply a nod.

"Kill the traitor!" Josh screams toward his minions, watching the Shifters direct their attention to Mason, his body diving into the dark blue waters.

Pulling back my arm, I take another full swing at Josh, watching him stumble, my hand gripping his blade before he can get a good blow in. Kicking him hard in the chest, I push past the lesions trying to hinder me, filled with a mix of pain from the bind and mine and Forest's connection, now hindered by the looming presence of death. Prying the blade free from Josh's hand, I feel satisfied each time one of our own gets a good slash on one of his men. Swinging the blades in my hand, I savor the way his blood will look painting the blades, the urgency for me to get in the water higher than ever.

"You think this ends when you kill me? Do you have any idea what is going on?" Josh questions, finding every excuse he can to drag himself out of this situation.

"Your dad was a weak and pathetic man," I taunt, driving the point of his own blade into his lung, the very place he harmed her. "You are even more of a disappointment than he was," I push, forcing my blade into his lower stomach, letting my wrists twist both hilts. Watching him double over, Mason is nowhere to be seen, Josh's blood slipping free from his wounds.

He will slowly bleed out, giving me all the time in the world to torture him for what he has done. Too fixated on the others to take notice of me, the other men stay occupied, my body barreling toward the water. Struggling to stay conscious, Josh grabs my leg, my foot raised, ready to kick him square in the jaw.

"This only ends with her and the Prophet's death-"

No more talking.

No more lies.

Forcing my boot so hard into the man's face it leaves an indent, he plummets to the ground, his nose flooding his face with rich red.

"Xavier!" a voice yells, my head snapping to the surface of the water, Kai's arms flaring, Mason struggling to swim faster than the Shifters. Forcing off my shoes, I ready myself to dive in, listening to Kai's distant yells as Mason drags him closer.

"Forest!" Kai yells, gasping for air. "She's still under there!"

Swallowing nothing, I glance behind them, my mind unsettled at the lack of Shifters swimming behind them.

Where the hell did they-

Yelling out in pain, a clawed hand wraps around my ankle, dragging me leg first into the water, moving quicker than anyone can react. Too occupied with Kai, Mason continues on, trusting my ability to hold on for a few more seconds. Feeling yet another hand tug my free ankle, the creatures pull me farther down into the waters, the skin of my body healing everywhere but the places the creatures have grabbed me. Feeling a fading light within me, my lungs burn well before I have stopped holding my breath. Blinking past a haze, I try and utilize as many of my abilities as I can, my energy far from me.

Catching a glimpse of the only thing that has given me a reason to fight in this life, her body lingers at the bottom of the lake. Screaming so loud, even the water struggles to suppress the noise, I look at her motionless body, the Shifters only dragging me closer to the one place I want to be. Watching the silver of her hair light to life, her eyes are wide and sullen, clouds of red surrounding her body, the Prophet's blood fleeing from her system.

Feeling the suffocation catch up to me, I frantically feel around my waist, uttering a silent thank you the moment I feel a small dagger.

Forcing my body forward, I drive the blade into the closest Shifter's forehead, feeling its grasp release, before driving the knife into its companion's skull. Hearing their muffled screeches, I force myself to swim closer to the bottom, feeling her now clean skin beneath my touch, the properties of the water healing all that it can. Looking at the weights tied around her ankles and hands, I cut as quickly as I can, watching her body begin to float the moment all of the weights are off, my legs kicking so hard they burn once she is wrapped beneath my arm. Struggling to get us both up, I urge her ahead of me, watching her body move upward, my legs doing their best to keep up with her.

Changing from murky dark to bright light, her body breaches the surface of the water, Mason's figure grabbing her as quickly as he can, dragging her closer to the water's edge, all of our friends glancing down at the waters in passing moments. Now the Prophet's blood has drained from her system, water fills my lungs, the connection snapping out of place, forcing me closer to an unconscious state. Peering his head back into the water, Mason reaches down, his hand inches away from my own, my fingers just barely grazing his-

Taking a painful jab in my body, a claw protrudes through my torso, one of the Shifters I had managed to hit still functional enough to attack. Watching my blood surround the waters, its healing properties cannot move quickly enough, the combination of the wound and the water in my lungs all too much. Dragging me back down from where I came from, Mason begins to yell, diving into the water, my eyes barely able to stay open.

Coughing, and only taking in more water, my hand stops reaching, my body becoming weightless.

Moving quicker than Mason can keep up with, the Shifter pulls me down, my mind holding on for as long as it can before all the light has faded.

"Come on, you fucking asshole," Aaron's voice frantically yells, the feeling of hands forcing themselves down on my chest extraordinarily painful.

Coughing on the third go, a mouthful of water forces its way from my throat, my lungs taking a raspy breath, my eyes flying open.

Looking to Aaron's frantic and bloodied figure looming over me, his eyes are wide with adrenaline, the others fighting off Josh's men, as more Officials blanket the land.

"Jesus Christ, I thought you were both gone," Aaron grovels, my mind racing to Forest.

Struggling to hold back the swarm of men, the other's blades collide furiously, Kai hovering over Forest's body, clutching his wounds.

Only Marked may heal in the waters.

Only Marked may reap their benefits.

"Both gone?" I question sporadically, forcing myself up and onto my feet.

Watching Mason force his clawed hands down on Forest's chest, she remains still, my knees scraping the ground as I kneel next to him.

"Go fight!" I yelled at Aaron, waving him away.

Narrowly avoiding an Official barreling toward him, the man steps aside, forcing his blade into the Official's gut, Josh's kneeled figure watching in dismay.

"She's not waking up, Xavier," Mason hisses, something entirely empty in the way I feel right now.

"That impossible, if I'm alive-"

"You both died," Kai hisses, glancing down at me in fright. "Your hearts stopped within seconds of one another."

Saying nothing, I glance down at the woman, feeling nothing but utter fear.

"That's not fucking possible!" I yell, shoving Mason away, his body flailing with surprise.

"Go help them!" I yell, taking over his chest compressions. "She's not fucking dying here"

Expecting to feel the looming presence of the Prophet's bind, I stare at her blue lips, a single thought passing my mind.

It doesn't matter if I'm alive.

If she is gone, I'm a dead man either way.

Bind or not, she does not get to die.

Taking every chance in the world, I lean down, the feeling of her cold lips pressed to mine enough to send anyone into a state of shock. Forcing air into her lungs, I watch her chest rise, listening to Mason's distant yells, his focus only on us.

"Xavier!" Mason yells, just as panicked as I am by what I have allowed to happen.

Continuing frantically with compressions and breaths, I anticipate the pain the prophet has planned for me, my mouth holding on a little longer each time I feel her lips. Feeling nothing, not even our connection, fear settles in my body, my hands ready to break her ribs so long it means she has a chance.

Readying myself to press down again, a cold hand wraps around my wrist, the sound of gagging flooding my ears.

Watching her turn her head, water exists her mouth, her eyes blinking rapidly, a golden hue surrounding each iris. Opening her eyes as if it is the first time she has done so, her eyes settle on me, her mouth gaping open. Moving her body upward, Kai's mouth releases a sob of relief. Watching me with wide eyes, her words are caught in her throat, her eyes taking in the fight developing around us. Raising her hand to touch my face, I am unable to find my words. Rolling her thumbs over my cheeks, she blinks back her confusion, something solidifying in her mind.

Unlike any of the other times I have felt it, our connection floods to life, suppressed by the barrier the binds had created for us. Watching her with confusion, she looks at me as if she knows me, her throat releasing a raspy sob.

"The Prophet's bind," I whisper, unsure of what to say. "It's broken ."

"Xavier?" She questions silently, a name she has said many times before.

Unlike every other time, there is no hate behind her words, no fear or resentment.

This is not the Forest Blackburn I held so close last night.

This is not the Untouchable from New Haven.

This is Forest.

My forest.

The woman I would spend every lifetime chasing after.

"Forest Flower?" I question silently, fighting back every urge to release my emotions.

"Years" she mutters. "Years I have been waiting to hear those words once more," she grovels, her pain quickly changing to a look I know all too well.

Fight.

Years of torment and pain, countless nights spent wondering if life was something worth living. Lesion after lesion. Nightmares with no end. It all was for this moment.

It all was for her.

Heaven forgive me for what I am about to do.

Standing up, I scruff Kaiden's curls, easily slipping my Call into his mind.

"Stay away from the fight," I warn, sending off the same message to our companions, watching them back away from the Officials, circling closer to Forest. Still blood-hungry, each Official watches us with bloodied blades, ignoring Josh's gasps for help. Sensing the Shifters creeping out of the water, those not killed by my blade seek revenge, staring down Mason with jealousy they may never satiate. Keeping his position near Forest, Mason watches the woman with curiosity, wondering at what point she moves.

"We already got some good licks on your friends, Xavier, why don't you-" Josh begins.

"Pull out your own throat," I whisper in Josh's mind, not even bothering to turn around.

Hearing his shrill cry, it is quickly silenced by a loud tear. Forest's stifled laugh breaches through the air, my heart singing from her praise. Hearing a loud thud, the men in front of me gasp, the Shifters behind us whispering with panic.

Looking toward one of the closest men, Aaron's blood paints his blade, his hand shakily holding up his weapon.

"Kneel," I order to all the men, watching them hit the ground, their knees buckling at my will.

Becoming attune with a power that is no longer under lock and key, I take it all in, finally looking back to the Shifters.

To my surprise, their heads are bowed in submission, Forest's eyes hot with fire as she looks them over. Craning her head back toward me, the creatures raise their heads, every single one of them bending at her will.

"Are they forgiven?" She questions, a smile pulling along her lips.

Glancing at the men and Josh's lifeless figure, I release a large sigh.

"Not in the slightest."

Lowering her head, she clicks her tongue, forcing the creatures directly toward the men, allowing them to tear at flesh as frantically as they'd like. The sound of the men's screams is close to euphoric. Tapping into the mind of each Shifter that moves past me, I coax their thoughts with ease, urging them to wait patiently once they have completed a kill. Staring at the men with equal amounts of hate, our friends' faces are lined with cold expressions, each one watching the hunt with equal amounts of admiration.

A year ago, had you asked any of them to watch the sight as they do now, they would call you crazy. Now, they watch the sight with thrill.

"Bring me their chips for a reward," Forest whispers, her eyes growing wider.

Glancing at Mason, Forest grabs his dagger, sliding it sideways over her wrists. Whispering in a dialect, she brings the red liquid toward Mason's mouth, watching him cock his head in confusion.

"She was being kind trying to convert you, but, she needed all of her energy to complete the job. You've done your job, and you've done it well. Now feed, and live the life you've lost," She warns, gravitating her arm closer to the man.

Saying nothing, he grabs her wrist, allowing his mouth to take in as much of her energy as he can. Whispering under her breath as he feeds, his hand grabs her waist to tug her closer, a million jealous thoughts doing their best to force their way into my mind. Watching his skin begin to shift, the taloned hands for fingers begin to fade, his hand releasing her arm after several seconds.

"Go," Forest warns, nudging her head toward the woods. "You will be changed soon enough. The last thing you need is to be here when your companions are completed with the kills."

Saying nothing, Mason nods his head, hesitantly backing away from the group.

Watching the Shifters turns their heads, the neuro-chips hang from their mouths, their feet slowly dragging the closer they move to Forest. Dropping their heads in submission, she cocks her head at the creatures, observing them with genuine curiosity.

"You are bound?" She questions, watching them all nod.

Smiling, she stares them down, watching them with raised brows.

"See to it the Prophet receives these chips. Then, you shall be rewarded," I smile, my Call buried deep into each creature's mind.

Watching Mason observe from the treeline, something about his look is distant, some part of him unnerved seeing Forest in the state she once was. Giving me one look, he backs away, disappearing into the thick of the woods.

Nodding, the creatures bend at our will, grabbing the mangled bodies of the men, leaving nothing but pools of blood in their place.

Taking a moment to truly look at her, her face softens, the hard expression she has been wearing since she woke up melting away.

This is no dream.

This is no facade.

She is truly awake.

We are free.

CHAPTER THIRTY-FOUR

FOREST

Unable to look away from the man, every suppressed memory comes rushing in, filling every empty space in my mind. Recalling the feeling of his hands exploring my body, the fire he burns within me was suffocated, snuffed out by the Prophet's bind, and my own selfish need to hide from the evils that have never truly stopped hunting me.

Once forced into submission, the parts of myself trapped in the deepest parts of my mind are free, leaving nothing but the woman I was before all of this. Looking toward the cabin, the sense of loneliness fades away, every hidden memory shared in the space coming back to me. Looking back at Kaiden, he looks at me with confusion, his skin only now healing with the aid of a vial of Cure-All Aaron had brought with him.

"What the hell is going on?" Bekah questions, my focus back on Xavier.

"Is it really you, Forest?" he questions, his eyes hazy with the emotion he works so hard to hide.

Locked away in my own mind, I screamed for her to set me free, sending every message to the clueless part of myself I could. For months I felt another man's touch, forcing myself to be as naive as all of those around me. This whole time, Xavier was in front of me, waiting for me to look at him as I do now.

He could have left.

He could have gotten far from the Prophet, starting a new life for himself, one void of loss.

He could have allowed Fallan to do as he pleased with me, he could have never intervened.

He would be rid of me.

Yet he stayed. □

He stayed even when he shouldn't have.

In no lifetime am I deserving of the love this man has.

"Well, let's see," I say with a smile, taking a step closer to the blonde. "Xavier Evermoore," I scold, looking to the cabin. "I do believe you are behind on keeping up with our garden," I tease, looking at pots filled with dead flowers. "To think, you spent so long teasing me about my lack of a green thumb-"

Shaking his head with a grin, the man moves forward, his hands flying forward, gathering my face between his hands. Wrapping my arms around his neck, the movement is synched, not a single action out of line. As if it were second nature, he dips down, his hands moving from my face to down my sides, pulling me closer. My legs wrap around his waist, his nose grazing my own.

"I-"

Cutting me off with as much force as the touch allows, his lips slam into mine, the need driving the touch unbearably painful. Feeling my words catch in my throat, my sobs come soon after, each press of his lips to mine pushing me closer to the point of emotional release. Coiling my fingers in his hair, I kiss the man like a starved woman, both of our skin hot, the energy coasting between us a connection I have yet to feel with anyone but him. Settling my body into his, he brings me peace, reassuring me that so long as I am with him, I am safe. Pulling away for air, he cups the back of my neck, dragging me back to him, his forehead pressing to mine. Lowering my legs from around his waist, he closes his eyes, keeping me wrapped in his arms. Shuddering as he exhales, he opens his eyes, watching me as close as he possibly can.

"I love you," he whispers with shock. Watching the tears fall free from his eyes, I try to hold it together, feeling nothing but admiration for the man. "I love you so much, I no longer know anything but you," he continues, cupping my face once more. "I have spent what feels like a lifetime questioning if I may ever feel your touch the way I have now and see these eyes that watch me so close." His finger trails over my cheeks, his thumb rolling over my eyes, urging my eyelids shut. "There are years worth of pointless nothings I want to whisper, so much loss and love I wish to share with you," he continues crying; the only other time I had seen it was when he lost his parents. "I will follow you till the ends of the earth, and bow at your feet. So help me, Sanctum; you are mine, Forest Evermoore and I will never let you go," he finishes.

"Do you love me?" I question, finally letting the emotion breach my voice.

"For as long as I draw breath," he whispers, pressing his lips to the side of my head. "And well after my heart has stopped beating."

Hearing shifting behind us, we pull ourselves back to reality, wiping our faces clean from the tears, his fingers rubbing away anything I missed. Looking at us all with shock, the group's mouths hang open, each one more confused than the last. Moving in front of the group, Kai looks the most off-put, nothing but confusion clouding his mind.

There's no good way to explain any of this to anyone.

How does one approach telling a young man just how much I infiltrated his family's life?

I swore to keep Andrew and Katiana safe.

I swore to keep Kaiden safe.

All I have done to the Blackburns is hurt them, all because of Andrew's foolish blind faith in me.

I've let them all down-

"He is your brother now," Xavier whispers. *"Do not look at it as anything else for a moment longer."*

"And if he hates me?" I question, a small smile touching his lips.

"His hate will never outlive his love."

"Speaking from personal experience?" I question, his hand massaging the back of my neck.

"I am almost a goddamn expert in the matter."

Taking a deep breath, I look at Kaiden, his eyes glossy with emotion.

"Explain," Kai whispers, barely able to look at me.

"My name is Forest Evermoore," I start, everyone's eyes averting to Xavier, a small smirk lifting his lips.

"And I've been asleep for the past two years."

CHAPTER THIRTY-FIVE

KAIDEN

Sitting inside the barely up-kept cabin, Xavier pries boards free from the windows, Aaron blankly staring into the fire he had to create nearly a half hour ago. Dispersed amongst the cabin, years of neglect have left the structure to become desolate, the floors coated with a layer of dust. Knowing exactly where things are, Forest works through the quaint home, lighting candles and flipping on lights once Xavier has given her the okay that the breaker still has some use. Digging through the cabinets, she finds an old bag of coffee grounds, letting the cups of the rich liquid steep as she runs her hands through her hair. Glancing over at her every so often, Xavier is clearly speaking to her through her mind, doing his best to ease her at a time when no one feels secure. Taking a long, hard look at the wall, a few scattered pictures of the pair are hung up, shattered picture frames, and broken tables still sprawled across the floor. Counting to herself silently, Bekah clasps her hand over her head, not even accepting Valerie's touch meant to comfort the woman. Watching Xavier and Forest like a hawk, Aaron stands in place by the door, patiently waiting for one of the two to speak up.

Shaking as she grabs the coffee cups, Xavier moves away from the windows, allowing himself to take over Forest's hospitality as she takes a seat across from me. Not even looking my way as she approaches, the woman takes a seat, finally locking eyes with me the moment the tension has become unbearable.

I'm trying to think of the best thing to say before she can get the first word in.

"You're not really my sister," I whisper, her eyes finally focusing on me.

Almost dropping one of the cups, Xavier starts placing down drinks, hiding the nasty stare he surely wants to give me.

"By blood?" Forest questions, happily accepting the drink. "No, I'm not your sister. I have no siblings, or real parents for that matter," she sighs, clearly uncomfortable by the topic. "Katiana's parents, your grandparents, were scientists inside of New Haven. It would seem that they became aware of Elyon's origins much before anyone else. On a whim, they decided to visit the waters, finding them after a few days of searching and a violation of rules."

"How does that lead back to you?" I question, her head shaking.

"I can't explain it, but they said the idea of creating a child strong enough to defeat the Prophet came to them in the reflections of the water. They thought it was Earth's way of trying to find balance. Not too long after they got back to New Haven, they were able to isolate the Prophet's true identity within New Haven's walls, asking the man to come in for a routine check, taking his blood during what he thought was a blood draw to test for disease. Not thinking twice about what it could mean, they had his sample and needed an egg. My mother, if you want to call her that, was a donor. A woman willing to carry out the surrogacy and the birthing process." she sighs, shaking her head. "She was an Unfortunate woman; nothing special about her, which is perhaps why the pregnancy went the way it did. Throughout the whole pregnancy, she struggled to keep herself well, up until the day she had me. Minutes after she gave birth to me, she was pronounced dead and thrown into the incinerator, all in the name of research."

"Her name-"

"Was Forest," she interjects. "My name, had I not taken hers, would have been just number Thirty, a way for no one to get attached to me," she clarifies.

"After years of isolation, listening to their countless rambles of my true purpose, I reached my prime years, twenty years of isolation, only being asked to leave when it meant I was helping an Unfortunates or a Marked in need. All the while, Andrew and Katiana were gaining more attention toward us than anyone wanted, defying rules to explore the love they had for one another. Eventually, Katiana's parent's research was infiltrated, and so was my isolation. That is the day I first tasted the blood of the Marked, and my run from the Prophet truly began. Officials and Marked alike raided the research facility on a tip that Katiana's parents had been abandoning their morning duties. I managed to slip free, tearing into the throats of three Marked in Official uniforms, avoiding the Prophet entirely. He was too preoccupied skinning Katiana's parents alive to notice when I had slipped out, or what I was to begin with." Xavier takes a seat next to her, pulling her closer. "I continued to feed, building up my strength, having one driving force. To kill the Prophet. I knew Andrew's family and any other Marked, were at risk, which is why it was impossible to leave things as is. I started a group of followers, being sure to pull Andrew in once I found out he had you. I started a plan of action, one to kill the Prophet once and for all and shatter Sanctum's rule. I was finally ready to carry it out-"

"When she met me," Xavier whispers, hiding the small smile lining his lips.

"When I met him," she repeats, landing her hand in his.

"Initially, Xavier was a piece, someone who knew everything there was to know about the Prophet that I could not figure out. I was so sure I was going to kill him, and every other follower the Prophet had-"

"You fell in love with him," I put it together. "You two ran away to this place," I clarify, finally registering just how much of a home this was supposed to be.

"It wasn't running away, Kai," Xavier clarifies, rubbing his tired eyes. "We were trying to find an alternative, and we almost did, had Fallan not been trailing us the whole time after Dove's death."

"They came in the night," she whispers, looking around the space. "The plan was to have me blend into the society, take on a new alias. Andrew was not on Elyon's radar, and the birth of Forest Blackburn was deemed legitimate. Katiana's parents ensured that my mother would live on, even if it was through convincing their daughter to name her firstborn after the woman. Xavier would go on as an Official, and I would play my part from the inside. All I needed was the child," she stutters, looking at the broken frames. "Elyon ensured we would suffer for what we had done, watching me like a test subject once more, my mind blatantly clueless to the person I really was, forcing Xavier to watch in silence."

Taking several moments to digest the information, Aaron moves closer, his hand dropping Xavier's pocket watch onto the table.

"I figured you wanted this back," he whispers, saying nothing else.

Nodding his head, Xavier graciously accepts the watch, tucking it back into his pocket.

"Mom-"

"Our mom. Her plan was to isolate the parts of myself detectable by the Prophet. It was all set up. We were on our way to leave this cabin to go to New Haven when they came. They tore down the door and dragged us free from the space, getting the upper hand in a way we thought not possible." Forest sighs, emotion festering in her throat.

Taking a long look at the old cabin, Xavier speaks for me.

"This was our home," he clarifies. "It was the place we thought we could always come to." □

"Kai," Forest whispers, her hand grabbing mine. "No matter what has happened, no matter how you view me, I will always be your sister. I watched you grow up, whether you realize it or not. You protected me when I was at my lowest and did so with no complaints. Nothing about this situation is just, and I understand if you want nothing more than to hate me for as long as you live. I know that what I stole from you was great-"

"You being my sister does not come down to blood," I mutter, squeezing her hand a little harder. "It comes down to the fact that you won't leave me," I admit, unsure where this emotion is coming from. "I have lost everything. Everything I have ever known was taken from me, and it's fucking eating me alive. I keep waking up, thinking I know how to deal with this guilt, then every night when I close my eyes, it comes crashing in, threatening to break me more and more every with every passing day. I need you to be honest with me," I start, taking a shaky breath. "If it came down to it, can I trust you to be my sister or the woman who used my family to hide from the demon that brought it all down."

Saying nothing, she blankly looks toward me, her eyes hazed with the mask of confusion.

"If it came down to me or you, Kai," she whispers, squeezing together. "I choose you every time."

Saying nothing, I close my mouth, biting back the wave of emotion ready to spill free from me.

"I have a question," Aaron finally speaks up, all eyes averting in his direction.

"Fallan?" he questions, a smile pulling onto Xavier's expression.

"How much liquor do we have saved up here?" Xavier questions, a smile finally reaching everyone's face.

CHAPTER THIRTY-SIX

FOREST- THE DARK DAYS

The smug look of power rides her expression, only adding to the mask of evil she carries in her dark, soulless eyes. Her black hair spans down her back, enunciating her high cheekbones and watchful eyes. The blood of my people clings to her shoes, wiped away by the cloak of the uniform she thinks conceals her from my searing gaze. For months I have been watching her work in and out of this city, targeting my kind, using them for her own personal gain. She may act as if she belongs to that compound and as an ally to all the souls trapped beneath the ward. She and I both know she is one of the Prophet's mutts, painting the streets in the blood of the Marked and crushing the Unfortunates beneath her boot, ready to wreak as much havoc as the entity in silver.

If all theories are right, she is their kin.

A vile, wicked-natured woman, poisoning this city from the inside out.

Xavier has told me the horror stories of his compound and the treatment he and his family suffered. Now, he sleeps peacefully in the cabin, expecting me to be at his side, ready to stow away the nightmares.

Can I ever truly rest until the people I love are safe?

"I told you she was here," Andrew whispers, watching as closely as I.

We hide in plain sight, wearing traditional Unfortunate attire, my hair concealed by a hat meant for warmer days like this. Keeping her hands locked with an attractive man, his blue eyes watch her in awe, his raven locks dancing in his vision.

"How many?" I question, keeping my focus on the woman.

"They found four of our people, mangled and bloodied. It would seem she tore into a few lingering Unfortunates that witnessed the atrocities, every one of them Marked," Andrew whispers, keeping a low profile.

"And the boy she's with?" I question, his shoulders sulking.

"That's Fallan Markswood-"

"The man whose father you were forced to execute?" I question, his face pulling into a look of pain.

"From what I know, he has been on and off with her for a few years. Ever since she slipped into our wards. I know she has tried to convince him to go to the compound, but he has wanted to stay back for Mark, and his companion Hunter-"

"Has he participated in any of her treason?" I question, narrowing my focus on the pair.

"You are days away from a procedure that is meant to keep you away from the Prophet's eye, Forest," Andrew snaps. "You should be at home with Xavier before your contact is limited to nothing. The last thing you need to be is out here tracking down a lead that may lead nowhere," Andrew grovels.

"She is Marked. She is a Marked willing to work for the Prophet and has become cozy with a compound that is just as corrupted as New Haven. You and I both know New Hope is nothing more than another landing pad for the Prophet. The Prophet can only force their sorry excuses for Commanders to be their poster children for so long. My best guess is they have their puppets run the show here while their true life hides behind New Hope's walls," I whisper, directing his attention to the girl. "I'd say she is much closer to that pile of shit than we think."

"Her name is Dove," Andrew says, sliding over a tablet. "Dove Morgan. One of our people caught wind of her name one of the nights she and Fallan were in a bar in the Unfortunate sector," Andrew whispers, both of us watching Fallan load baking supplies onto a cart, the woman watching in awe.

"Thank you for giving me something to put on her headstone," I snap, ready to end this conversation.

"You and Katiana have all the preparations ready. I am cleaning up any loose ends that might come back to bite me well after I am too confined by my own mind to know why they have come back for me," I start, Andrew's hand wrapping around my wrist.

"Does Xavier know how little you will recall?" Andrew questions, my heart sinking at the statement.

"I will remember him and the memories we have made, even if they seem faint. There are some things that can't be altered, Andrew. One kiss from him and any protective measures Katiana puts in my brain can easily be overridden by the feeling his touch brings me," I smile, patting the man's hand. There's no scenario in which I could reject his touch. So long as he has faith in the memories I have of him, then there is hope."

Saying nothing, Andrew lets go, my focus in only one direction.

"Where are you going?" he questions, my hand waving him away.

"I'm going back home," I smile. "You should be, too. Katiana and Kai need you right now. You've been absent for days."

I take no pride in pulling the man away from his home life. The last thing he needs is to worry about my actions on top of keeping his family safe. Andrew has done more than enough for the cause and deserves nothing but a life of peace. I do hope he finds his way back to his father, maybe then he will finally take my offer for him to be rid of this place and all of the evil that resides here.

Moving away from the man, I assure his mind with my Call, keeping my smile plastered on my face until his back is turned away. Finally leaving the resting area inside the Unfortunate sector, he takes his time walking by the bakery, being sure to glance inside for his father, looking away the moment the man might notice him. Letting my face drop once Andrew is out of my line of sight, I inch closer to Dove and her lover, feeling a great deal of satisfaction once they start making their way to a more isolated part of the sector.

Creeping behind the pair, I lower my hat, keeping my focus on the ground before me. Stepping over every massive crack in the concrete, my energy coasts at a high, my Call easily slipping into both of their minds, hearing their varying thoughts.

"Only need to crack a few more necks of the scum running amongst the sector before I can drag him out of this shit hole and have him all to myself in more civil living quarters," she thinks as she looks at the man, clearly off-put by his way of living.

"Her eyes always seem to glow golden in this light. It makes me forget how much blood is clinging to her shoes right now. I wonder how many Marked she killed this time," he thinks with awe, clearly as okay with her actions as she is.

Both are vile in thought, justifying the hideous actions she has allowed herself to partake in.

Murdering for freedom is one thing.

Murdering for power is another.

Slipping inside one of the buildings meant for housing, the whispers of a unit number formulate in my mind, the imagery of the apartment settling into my perspective.

"Hopefully, they don't mind company," I smile, allowing myself to Winnow myself into their place of tranquility.

Taking a look around the space, the mirage of herbs, spices, and houseplants is alarming. Looking at the perfectly made bed, and an array of lit candles, I assume the man, Fallan, was expecting to have a peaceful night with the woman.

For shame.

Hearing their approaching thoughts of ripping one another's clothes off, my suspicions are confirmed, my hand already rummaging through his kitchen cabinet, settling on the biggest knife he has in stock. Pulling off the hideous hat and robe concealing my body, I take a seat on his kitchen counter, letting the flame of every candle go out with the use of my Hold. Feeling the room paint me in darkness, I run my finger over the edge of the blade, peering toward the door, now slowly creaking open.

"Shit, they all went out," Fallan laughs, the woman stumbling inside with him, her hands already working their way under his shirt.

"It's fine. I don't need light to enjoy what I am going to do with you," she purrs, her voice like nails on a chalkboard.

Name of an angel, voice of a devil.

How ironic.

Staying as still as I possibly can, their hormones cloud their ability to notice me, my hand balancing the tip of the blade on the countertop.

Hearing bumps and pictures fall to the ground, the sound of their lips on one another is nauseating, causing my stomach to twist with disgust.

"I think I have a bottle of contraband champagne still in my fridge," Fallan mutters, creeping closer to where I sit.

"Turn on the lamp, Dovey," he coos, completely enthralled with the woman.

Feeling his warmth gravitate toward me, my skin is cold as ice, my eyes able to track him, even in the dark.

Had it not been for his pitch-black curtains, the light would have exposed me long ago.

Stumbling to a lamp, Dove flips on the light, Fallan's eyes immediately growing wide once he notices my figure.

"Shit-"

"Guess the light doesn't scare away the monsters," I seethe, forcing my leg forward, hitting the man directly in the chest. Slamming into the floor, his air is knocked out of him, his precious Dove readying herself to Winnow.

Wagging my finger, I stare the woman down, tossing my blade back and forth in my hand.

"Careful, Little Dove," I warn. "I bite."

Forcing my hand forward, the blade goes through the air, slamming into her shoulder, merging her into the wall behind her. Crying out in pain, I dig the blade deeper into her skin with my Hold, savoring the sounds of her screams as the blade wedges itself into the wood of the wall. Looking at his woman with fear, his eyes snap to me, my eyebrows raised with curiosity.

"Get your filthy, Marked Hold off of her-"

Slamming him to the floor with my Hold before he can try to get up, I slide down from the counter, slowly lowering his head to the floor with the tip of my boot, watching him bare his teeth, his limbs glued to the floor. Looking at Dove, she tries to pry the knife from her shoulder.

"See, as much as I despise you for willingly following someone like the likes of her, you have shed no innocent blood, which sadly, makes it that much harder to harm you, Raven Hair," I say, watching the woman painfully pry the knife from her arm. "Her, on the other hand, I wouldn't mind harming."

"Who the hell are you?" he snaps, his spit flying everywhere.

"The Prophet's rat!" Dove answers for him, a smile creeping along my expression.

"So you do know the bastard!" I say with a thrill, giving them both a sarcastic expression. "Well, doesn't that make this that much more fun?" I ask the pair, sliding a chair closer. Taking a seat, I marvel at the sight of her struggle, fighting back the urge to clap once she had pulled the blade free from her arm.

"See, now was that so hard-"

Forcing the blade toward me with her Hold, she stays in place, my hand quick to grab the blade before it can collide with my skull. Grabbing the weapon, blade and all, I admire the strength she put into the toss, feeling the skin of my hand tear, the point inches away from the center of my head.

"Predictable," I whisper, taking the hilt once more, the cuts on my hand quickly healing. Taking a long lick up the side of the blade, the energy of her blood is phenomenal, my Hold on Fallan only growing that much stronger. "Predictable gets people killed."

Winnowing in the middle of the sentence, she lands behind me, her hand coiling in my hair, ready to break my neck.

"Better, but still too weak."

Grabbing her arm, I move aside, forcing her over the chair and onto the floor, twisting the wrist of the hand that had coiled into my hair until I hear multiple cracks. Slamming onto the ground at my feet, I raise my foot, forcing it as hard as I can into her side, letting the sound of Fallan's yells and her screams fuel my fire. Feeling my foot sink into her side, the bones of her ribs shatter like glass, forcing themselves into her organs, her mouth gasping for air. Boring myself so easily, I use my Hold on her as well, dragging her into a seated position between my legs, my hands fidgeting with her long dark locks. Continuing her silent gasps, her broken wrist rests in her lap as her wobbling lip silences her thoughts. Keeping Fallan down on the ground, he thrashes like a wild animal wanting to gnaw off his own foot.

"Dovey, it's okay, just keep breathing-"

"She's bleeding internally," I smile, tugging her head back with her hair, forcing her to look up at me as I look down at her. "Hurts like a bitch, doesn't it?" I question, her energy growing far too weak to challenge me.

"W- why are you doing this?" she coughs, blood spilling free from her mouth.

"Fuck you, you stupid bitch! Take me. I'll do what you need, just take me. Feed her your blood, torture me, just leave her the hell alone-"

"Why am I doing this, Little Dove?" I question, silencing Fallan's pathetic spew of love.

This part of myself is one I do not take enjoyment in.

It would kill me to allow Xavier to see me like this.

Then again, his own demons are not the cruelest partners in bed.

I often shame myself for believing in the concept of abstinence.

The man makes it so damn hard.

"You're angry she killed a few of your fucking Revolutionists and a few dirty Marked?" Fallan questions, my eyes fully snapping to the man.

"You speak of the Marked as if they are not your own kind, boy," I hiss, his eyes widening.

"Our kind is vile!" he snaps, thrashing more aggressively. "The sooner the Marked have left this plane of existence the better-"

"You know it's only a matter of time, right?" she questions, stopping the man from speaking.

Focusing back on her, her eyes watch me close.

"Do enlighten me on what you mean," I say, keeping her head still with my thighs.

Laughing at me, blood paints her already pink lips.

"I know who you're protecting inside and outside these walls. You think I don't know about blondie?" she questions, narrowing her eyes. "Do you have any idea how easily I could send someone to that little cabin you two have nestled away, and torture him in ways worse than what the Prophet did to him," she starts, her mind flooded with the imagery of Xavier's torture, a recording of a previous time he had stepped out of line before I found him the day of his parents deaths. Hot metal prods drag down the man's back, his sobs silent as he pleads with the Officials to let him take a breath. Doing nothing but preventing a child from being taken out during an Expulsion, he receives physical torture, the sound of his screams elevating my heart rate. "Can you see it? Do you see what light punishment from the Prophet is?" she questions, a malicious smile spanning across her face. "There were dozens of recorded videos I had the honor of watching, learning just how to torture the man when I get my hands on him," she continues, bloodlust clouding my judgment.

"When some weren't looking, a few of the female Officials would do what they wanted with him, torturing him further if he ever chose to reject their advances," she pushes, whoreish woman inside of his quarters during his time with the Prophet fill my mind. Working in a set of three to keep him down, they forced him to do as they pleased, only growing happier once he had begun to sob.

"The Prophet recorded all that Xavier did during his time with them," she whispers. "It makes what I am going to do look like child's play."

I can't keep listing.

"First, I torture that little Andrew Blackburn you hold onto so desperately. Murder his wife, tear his child's ears clean from his curly little head. And then, I go for your Xavier, reminding him what life the Prophet has waiting for him-"

Grabbing her hair, I silence her, arching forward as I hover over her. Widening my eyes, I focus my Hold on her neck, holding back my urge to tear her ear off.

"You shouldn't have shown me any of that," I whisper. "Now, I'm angry."

Pulling her head upward, she tries to scream, my Hold too great for her to fight against. Imagining the skin of her neck tearing, I listen to the sound of the flesh ripping, her throat drowned out by the sound of blood flooding her throat.

Thrashing and jolting, she tries to break free from my grasp, Fallan's eyes wide as he watches the sight in shock. Yanking as hard as I possibly can, I don't stop once I have reached muscle or bone. Forcing myself to stand up from the chair, her body stays down, her head moving up with me. So angered I see red, I pull until there is no resistance. Feeling my arms fling back, a great weight collides with the floor, rolling to a dead standstill.

Peering down at her twitching body, I release my Hold on her figure, watching it slump to the side, the bloodied stump where her head once resided landing inches away from Fallan, his throat already filled with vomit. Crying and screaming at the sight, I slowly peer at her severed head, her eyes wide, hazed with the presence of death. Feeling nothing as I look at her, he swallows the bile, gasping for air, too frozen with fear to move.

"Y- you... sh- she's-"

"As dead as the innocents she slaughtered," I answer for him, creeping closer to her lifeless head.

Grabbing it by the hair, I force it into the bag I had brought with me, finally letting up on his Hold, knowing damn well he knows better than to get near me right now.

Turning on my heels, I grab her shirt, dragging her closer to the door, leaving a trail of blood in our path.

Watching the tears fall down his cheeks, he grovels in pain, the loss he feels far greater than what I am capable of understanding.

"I- I will fucking kill you," he whispers, narrowing his eyes at me.

"If you were smart, you would stay far away from me," I warn, my voice cold as ice.

Looking at the dozens of fallen portraits on his wall, I creep toward his coffee table, grabbing a piece of paper settled beneath it. Grabbing a crayon from his stack of art supplies, I sketch something simple; the end result comparable to a child's drawing. Tossing it on his figure, he looks over the paper with confusion, avoiding looking at Dove's deadweight body.

"Consider that my apology, Picasso," I say with malice. "If you come after me, I'll ensure your life is nothing short of hell," I seethe, his eyes hazy with tears.

Looking at the drawing, his hands shake, his eyes got with rage.

"If I come after you, it won't just be you that will suffer," he whispers, the name Xavier circling his mind.

"Unless I develop dementia," I smile. "Then that will be a fatal decision."

Saying nothing else, I drag Dove with me, excusing myself from his quarters, moving until a window comes into perspective. Pulling it open, I position her body on its edge, looking down at the ground below, I whisper silently.

"Stupid games, stupid rewards, Dovey."

Shoving her out the window, her body collides with the ground, a few Unfortunate citizens screaming out, no doubt alerting any close-by Officials of the commotion.

Glancing at her head in my bag, I think of where she came from and the twisted fucks lingering behind New Hope's doors.

"I think it's time we take you home, Little Dove," I smile. Who doesn't love a good surprise visit?"

Dropping her head onto the steps of the compound, I watch it hit the pavement, my hands shoved deep within my pockets, my mask pulled high above my mouth. Leaving a large red stain, the severed body part is a sight for sore eyes.

Having easily slipped past their defenses, knocking out the guards was trivial, making it that much easier to march my way to the front of the steps.

Knowing how mistreated Xavier was during his time here, I think of every person who looked past the torture he received from others, constantly taunting him, trying to convince him he was nothing but a monster.

Xavier's soul is pure. I don't mind his carrying the burden of being the monster everyone expected him to be.

Keeping my hair concealed by the hat once more, I pound on the door, already aware of the cameras trying to get a good look at my image.

Forcing open the door, an unfamiliar man looks back at me, nearly screaming once his eyes gravitate toward the ground.

"Jeremey, what is it?" a female questions, my finger landing above my lips, forcing him to be quiet.

"Make an excuse."

"Nothing, Bekah. It's just one of our men requesting some extra break time," he says, keeping away from the figure on the other side itching to come observe.

Saying nothing, he swallows dryly, his hands shaking.

"I believe she belongs to you all," I say, kicking her head closer, his throat holding back a gag.

"Consider this mercy," I say, patting the man on the shoulder. "The last thing you want to do is piss me off."

Saying nothing else, I leave the man to wallow in his shock, wanting nothing more than to wash away the blood and bury myself under the covers with the only person that makes me feel like something other than a vile monster.

In this lifetime and the next, no price will ever be too much for him.

Perhaps the concept of love has brought some light to my soul.

Or even worse.

His love is the only way I may feel that light.

Without it, all that remains is the dark.

CHAPTER THIRTY-SEVEN

FOREST

Quietly, I make my way to the room that used to be ours, silently locking the door. After the truths that came out, most were ready for sleep, too intoxicated to focus on anything but a good night's sleep. Still buzzing from the presence of alcohol, I stumble with my steps, sensing Xavier's energy lingering in the room. Untouched by time, the furniture is dusty, the bed still unmade, as if we had never left. Watching the gleam of moonlight filter through the window, I tear off my shirt, allowing my chest to breathe, my breasts constrained by the wire bra I would love to rip off. Going for my pants next, I drag them off of my legs, kicking them aside, allowing my hair free from its tight confinement. Taking a deep breath, my body is filled with energy, the chill air kissing my bare skin, only making the bra that much more uncomfortable.

"No one would be complaining if you kept peeling off layers," his voice mutters, the presence of alcohol lingering in his tone.

Glancing to the side, he is seated on one of the chairs I used to sit in to paint, my art supplies still balanced on the dresser. Holding the bottle of whiskey he had claimed, he sets it next to the paint supplies. His legs are spread, his eyes hungry for me.

Peering at him with a smirk, I turn to face him, watching the way his eyes devour my figure.

"Has it ever been that easy for you to take my clothes off?" I ask, creeping closer to the man's brooding figure.

Saying nothing, his lips pull into a smirk, his body relaxed in the chair.

"Come here," he mutters, patting the empty space on his lap.

Shaking my head at him, I take another step closer, anticipating what is to come.

"Take off your shirt," I bargain, watching the man's eyes narrow.

"Dictating me now?" he questions, a strain working its way into his pants.

"Do it," I push, flicking up my wrist, helping him begin the process.

Pulling up his shirt the rest of the way, he pries it free from his body, giving me a good look at his enticing figure. Watching the way the moonlight casts shadows on his strong frame, the scars and black ink of his tattoo come together to form a blissful image. Creeping close enough that he could reach out and touch me, he leans forward, his nose inches away from my stomach.

"I wouldn't mind-"

Silencing me, his lips touch my skin, gently kissing the sensitive spots above the waistband of my underwear. Grabbing my hips tightly, he yanks me forward, allowing his tongue to trail up my body as high as he can go. His hands grab my ass, being as aggressive as he knows I want it. Watching the strain intensify in his pants, one of his hands fidgets with the buttons and zipper, giving his length some breaking room.

Already wetter than I am willing to let on, my body yearns for his touch, the strain against his underwear enough to drive anyone mad. Stopping his kisses, he lingers on the cut he gave me, smiling once his lips press down on the white scars.

"I would fucking cut you every time if it meant it kept everyone's hands off," he whispers, his eyes finally pulling back to me.

"I'm not breakable," I whisper, dipping my head down. "So fuck me like it."

Taking the verbal cue, he drags my underwear down, letting them land at my ankles, yanking me toward him once more. Dragging down his underwear enough to expose his large length, I try and hide my thrill, letting my knees land on both sides of his legs, gripping the back of the chair for support. Guiding me over his length, I anticipate the feeling of him entering me, letting our eyes meet in the gleam of the moonlight.

"Someone else took your first from you," he whispers, both of us angered by a reality we cannot change. "Either way, with me, you will bleed."

Forcing his hands onto my hips, he pushes me down onto his length, my air leaving my lungs at the feeling of my body trying to stretch around his length. Pausing before I am even halfway down, I open up for him, his eyes watching the sight with thrill.

"Fucking hell, do you feel how wet you already are?" he questions, pushing me a little deeper. "Do you feel how much your pretty cunt wanted me inside of you?" he questions, pushing me to the halfway point, my body begging to feel all of him.

Staring at him, my words come out in a pant.

"Are you going to fuck me or keep playing around like a foolish, love-struck teenager?" I question, his eyes darkening.

"Oh, Forest," he warns, forcing me down the rest of the way, my body barely able to take it. "I'm not stopping, even when you're done."

Grabbing the back of my bra, he undoes the claps, tossing aside the undergarment with little to no care. Rolling my hips, he starts a small thrust, my teeth biting my lips to stop the breathy moans from escaping my mouth. Feeling him fully fill me, I let go of the back of the chair, letting my hands gravitate toward his head, guiding his mouth closer to each breast.

Hiding his own groans of pleasure, he grabs my chin, forcing me to look at him.

"If you let out a noise, there will be consequences."

Saying nothing, his thumb toys with my lip, my body moving before I can react.

Letting his thumb land in my mouth, I roll my tongue over his finger's point, biting back yet another moan once his lips meet my nipple, his free hand toying with my other aching breast. Licking and sucking on the sensitive point, he trails kisses around the skin, biting in the places he knows I will have the loudest reaction. Keeping his finger filling my mouth, his length keeps me stretched, his mouth gravitating toward the next breast, while his fingers pinch the nipple of the other.

Unable to hide the moan that leaves my mouth at the feeling of the pain his pinch brings, he pulls away from my breast, letting his thumb leave my mouth, my warmth a dripping mess along his length.

"Was that a noise, Forest?" he questions, my face flush with the heat of sex.

Barely able to process his words, he guides my hips off of him, the sudden emptiness both painful and pleasurable. Pushing me further, I slide off of his lap, his length a dripping mess. Shaking, I hold my ground, watching him stand as he kicks off the rest of his pants, his body looming closer.

"Was that all?" I question, his body moving toward one of the more pleasure filled dressers we own.

"Get on the bed, Forest," he orders, my defiance at full blast.

"No-"

Moving before I can stop him, he grabs what he needs from the dresser, his hand wrapping around my throat, my words caught in a gasp. Dragging me closer to the bed, he forces me down onto the soft sheets, keeping me flat with his knees. Working quicker than I remember, he works with the paracord effectively, twisting my wrists together, forcing them above my head, straining them against the headboard. Trying to kick him off of me, he goes for my ankles next, forcing my legs to spread, being sure to make the chord extra tight.

Sprawled out in front of him, the strain is too tight for me to wiggle away from, his eyes dancing over my exposed body, taking in every inch of me. Reaching toward the nightstand, he pulls free one of his favorite methods of sexual frustration, the gleam of the knife still bright, despite the darkness around us.

"Stay quiet," he warns, dragging the tip of the weapon down my chest, nicking me once he has reached my lower body. "Or I cut," he continues, his head bending down, licking the already healing wound clean.

Picking up where he left off with the kisses, he moves farther down than just my waistline, gravitating closer to the one place I need him most.

For years he tempted me with these touches, never allowing himself to take me as he had in the chair. Despite the fire he has in the bedroom, he is a man of virtue, one who was more than willing to wait until I was bound to him by marriage to take me all the way. My mind is haunted by the thought I unknowingly allowed myself to give away something meant for him and him alone. Now, he has come to reclaim what has always been his right to take.

Kissing along my inner thigh, the tip of the knife keeps me from bucking my hips forward, its point hovering over my lower stomach. Hovering his mouth above my warmth, I try to contain my excitement.

"Not a sound, Forest Flower," he whispers, my voice biting back every noise of pleasure.

Landing his mouth on my warmth, my body implodes, his tongue hitting every pleasurable point he can. Wanting nothing more than to risk getting cut in order to lean my hips further into his touch, I raise my hips, feeling the point of the knife dig into my skin. Letting out breathy moans, his eyes glance up at me, his knife tearing the skin once more.

"Fuck it," he whispers. "Come here, angel."

Dropping the knife on the side of the bed, he uses both hands to pull me closer to his mouth, allowing the small trail of blood to roll down my stomach, his jaw working vigorously, licking slowly along each fold. Taking his time to focus on the clit, he swirls his tongue in a circular motion, my arms straining against the paracord. Tipping me closer to a breaking point, he plunges his fingers inside of me, working eagerly and mercilessly, the sounds of my own body's slickness louder than any noise either of us can make. Gasping and biting back noise, his hand works in steady deep motions, his focus on my clit drawing me closer to my limit.

Feeling my stomach fester with warmth, I reach my climax, my legs shaking, trying to squeeze his head despite the restraint. Smiling like a fool, he looks up at me, watching me closely as his tongue rolls over the sensitive point one final time.

Imploding, my release coats his fingers, my back arching as I allow one of my louder moans to escape past my lips. Curling his fingers as I finish, he continues licking after the climax, my body unable to get away from the overstimulating touch.

"Xavier-"

Continuing on, he grabs my hips harder, moving his arms under my thighs, hooking them around my legs, allowing himself to continue on. Shaking so hard, I fear the room is moving with me, my wrists strain against the chord vigorously, the blood trailing down my pelvis and touching the man's mouth.

"Xavier," I gasp again, struggling to avoid using my Hold.

Feeling an overwhelming amount of stimulation, my wrists yank forward, the chord snapping, my hands reaching for his hair, dragging his head away from my warmth, my release and blood touching his lips. Giving me a grin I know he is proud to wear, he licks my cut once more, snapping the remaining chords with his hands, moving further up my body.

"You broke so many rules," he warns. "My turn to cum."

Grabbing my body, he flips me to my stomach, guiding my hips upward, forcing my back down into an arched position. Wrapping his hand around my hair, he keeps my head up, positioning himself between my legs, running his hand over my ass.

"You may expect me to pull out," he whispers, positioning himself close to my entrance. "That's the last thing I am going to do."

Sliding himself inside before I can give him an answer, his hips meet my ass, my body stretching around him, his length filling me up. Hearing his own moan, he tugs tighter on my hair, my mouth parted open, releasing breathy gasps.

"You see how easily your pretty cunt allowed me inside?" he questions, only adding to the ease of my body allowing him inside.

Thrusting hard and vigorously, the sound of our bodies on one another is intoxicating, each thrust from him taking my breath away. Grabbing one of my hips as he yanks, my slickness coats my thighs, the wet sounds of him pounding into me only adding to the layer of moans suppressed by the sheets covering my mouth. Going in and out again and again, my stomach feels full, his hand striking my ass, before rubbing the tingling skin.

"You like when I fill you up, Forest Flower?" he questions, my only response a gasped yes.

Taking it over and over again, my knees threaten to buckle, a small twitch from him my biggest indicator of what is to come. Using my hair to guide me further upward, he contains his thrusts, his hand grabbing my breasts, his head dipped down against my ear.

"Tell me how much you want my cum to fill you," he growls, bringing himself seconds to release.

"I want-" I start, silenced by one of his harder thrusts. "I want you to fill me up and remind everyone whose last name is mine," I shudder, his lips pressing to my neck. Turning my head to be closer to his mouth, the words leave me with full confidence.

"I love *you*," I whisper, his grip tightening. "I will always love you."

Feeling his release implode inside of me, he buries his mouth in my shoulder, stifling one of his largest moans. Taking several moments to slow down his thrusts after he finishes, he slowly pulls himself from me, my legs shaking uncontrollably.

Turning me around to face him, he guides me into his lap, letting himself hold me, my arms wrapped around his neck, his nose touching mine.

"I have loved you every day since I met you," he whispers. Life will forever haunt me for what it has taken but reward me with the reality that you are the best thing that has happened to me," he whispers. "There will never be enough words to tell you how much I love you," he continues, emotions clouding his voice. "Even the poets would be mute in your presence."

Smiling like a fool, my thumbs roll over his cheeks.

"You are my infinite forever" I whisper. "The only life I want to live is one where you are by my side."

Saying nothing else, I press my lips to his, his mouth hungrily devouring mine. Kissing the man until my air has run out, we pull away from the touch, our foreheads pressed to one another.

"I choose you," I continue. "Nothing else ever really mattered."

Easing his anxious soul, he smiles, glancing toward the bathroom.

"I'm not ready for this to be over," he whispers, sliding us both off the bed, keeping my legs wrapped around him. "Care to join me for a bath?"

Keeping my back to the man, the water glides down my back, his hand pouring the water on top of my head, working all the soap free from my hair, massaging my scalp in comforting touches, trailing his fingers across my skin, he cleanses my body with gentle touches, kissing my back in sweet touches. Tuning around to face him, my hair smells of vanilla and spice, his gray locks falling into his face. Gathering me into his lap, he tucks my hair behind my ears, my hands gravitating toward his locks.

"What are you doing?" he asks with a smile, my hand reaching for the cup settled on the rim of the tub.

"Giving you the care you have always given me," I smile, dipping the cup beneath the water.

Wetting his hair, I push it back, gathering a small dollop of shampoo, and working it through his wild hair. Watching me with lovestruck eyes; his thumbs roll over my hips, my smile growing wider the longer he looks at me. Absolved in touch, he closes his eyes, allowing me to continue nurturing him, his body filled with pure bliss. Working until all the soap is out of his hair, I drag the soap across his body, kissing his chest as I do so, before washing his skin clean.

Turning me around to lean me back between his legs, I lay on his chest, enjoying the mass of bubbles surrounding us. Floating in peace, his head stays propped atop my own; his back settled against the tub.

"There's something I've been holding onto," Xavier whispers, digging into a nearby drawer, placing his hand over my eyes. "I figured you'd want to look at it in a new light."

Feeling his free hand hover in front of my eyes, he drops his hand, both of us observing the chain of rings, my eyes gravitating toward one in particular. Pulling it free from the chain, he clasps the necklace back on, Katiana and Andrew's rings settle above my heart.

A golden vinery band and a small stone, the ring stolen by the raven sits patiently in his hand, covered up by a facade I believed like no other.

"My ring," I whisper. "You grabbed it from the compound," I smile, a small chuckle leaving him.

"You have no idea how much I wanted to tear apart that ass for saying this ring was still his mother's," he whispers. "It ate him alive knowing the value it really held to you," he whispers, grabbing my left hand.

Gravitating the ring closer to my ring finger, he pauses, the promise of what the ring holds, one of my greatest values.

"I don't want this to be a promise any longer," Xavier whispers, my body filling with a second burst of energy.

Leaning upward, I look toward the man, my hand still in his.

Hazed with the presence of fear, his eyes are wide, his hands shaking.

"I am no longer willing to promise a life that could be stolen from us," he continues, leaning closer. "Forest," he whispers, holding the ring like a peace offering. "I don't want to promise you I may wed you once life gifts us an opportunity as I did in the past," he pushes, my heart racing. "I want you to marry me. I want you to be mine for as long as we may live. I want to live with you. I want to die with you. I want to grow so old, we may no longer walk. I want to cry with you," he pushes. "I want to laugh with you. Every good part of my life starts and ends with you. That is something I will fight for as long as I live."

Tears fall free from my eyes, years of torment buried in his words.

"I'm not promising you anymore," he gasps. "I'm asking you to let me love you for as long as we live."

Looking down at the ring, I release a sob.

"I became an Evermoore long ago," I whisper. "Becoming your wife would be my greatest honor."

Smiling like a fool, he pulls me close.

"No more promises?" he questions, gravitating the ring closer.

"I've always wanted to be married in the fall," I smile. "Let's drown our demons, Xavier, and never look back."

Saying nothing else, he slides the ring over my finger, his lips meeting mine once more. Kissing him so vigorously, water rushes over the sides of the tub, his laugh fills the space, my heart filling with joy.

"You give me a reason to fight," he whispers.

"And you give me a reason to live," I whisper.

Guided by night, his touch was nothing short of addictive.

Kissing me until my lungs scream for air, and holding me so tight, I wonder if I may pass out, the feeling of his love consumed me, giving us both our first peaceful night of rest in what seems like years.

CHAPTER THIRTY-EIGHT

KAIDEN

"Hey," Aaron's voice mutters, all of my focus shifting to the doorway he lingers in.

Having decided to settle into bed for the night only moments ago, Bekah and Valerie eagerly took one of the guest bedrooms, leaving Aaron and me to decide between sharing a room or taking the couch and risk hearing whatever it is Forest and Xavier plan to get up too. Staying seated on the floor, I wave him in, watching him awkwardly make his way inside, being careful not to do anything to make me uncomfortable.

Still filled with pain from the events over the past few days, the painkillers Xavier convinced me to take have only really been effective in making me drowsy, making it that much harder to stay awake despite my active mind.

"How are you feeling?" Aaron questions, joining me on the floor, his arms tucked in his lap, being sure to stay as far away from me as possible.

"Like I was tortured and thrown into water," I sigh, closing my eyes, a small laugh of defeat exiting his throat.

"I had a feeling the Cure-All wouldn't do much for the pain," Aaron sighs, doing his best to stay light-hearted despite all that has happened.

Barely able to process all the truths that have unfolded, every moment of silence in my mind feels like another tipping point, just begging to implode.

"Sometimes, I wonder if I am being punished for the way I treated the Unfortunates and anyone else the Untouchables deemed inferior," I sigh, Aaron's brows pulling inward.

"Why would you say that?" Aaron questions, a genuine look of sorrow riding his expression.

"Tell me I'm wrong. There were so many instances I could have made a difference. Do you know how many times Forest begged me to step up and aid her in her defiance, and I just stood back and watched all the atrocities unfold," I mutter, holding my hands to my face.

Shielding my eyes from the moonlight, a silent sob escapes my throat, my emotions no longer able to be suppressed well enough to hide them from Aaron.

"You know I wanted to kill you?" Aaron mutters, all of my focus shifting away from my spiraling emotions.

Taking an unsteady breath, I pry my hands away from my face, glancing in his direction.

Already looking at me, he holds my attention, his body just a few inches closer.

"You wanted to kill me?" I clarify, his head slowly nodding.

"I was so pissed off that Fallan and Hunter had gotten involved with the kids of an upper leadership Official. Looking back at it, I suppose that's what Fallan always wanted. You acted as if everything in the world came down to rules and, more often than not, looked at me as if I was beneath you."

Feeling immense guilt, I close my eyes, trying my best to see the silver lining in all of this.

"So what stopped you?" I question, shaking my head in defeat.

"The way you looked at Hunter," Aaron mutters. "You looked at him as something other than an Unfortunate, and when I realized you actually cared for him, something inside of me shifted towards you," Aaron pushes, my throat going dry.

"How could that possibly make you look at me differently?"

"You were not avoidant of Hunter because he was an Unfortunate. You were avoidant of him because you loved him. You loved him so much, you were scared you would never be enough for him. You were scared you could not be what he needed. Anyone willing to love anyone that much is someone worth looking at differently," he says, looking at me with genuine sorrow.

"I'm sorry he's gone, Kaiden," he whispers, a hateful thought slipping into my mind.

"No," I hiss. "You're not... and I want to know why."

Clamping his mouth shut, he looks at me blankly, my hands shaking in light of my nerves.

He can sit here and tell me all the ways he misses Hunter, but, deep down, I know it's the farthest thing from the truth. He loved Hunter, yes, but the way he grieved the man was different than all the rest. He felt a relief he would never be willing to admit. One more deep-rooted than any of us could anticipate.

"I am-"

"You're lying," I push, poking my finger into the man's chest. "Stop lying to me, Aaron."

Grabbing my hand, he begins to drag it off of him, his eyes wide.

"Damn it, Kai, I'm not lying-"

Here goes everything.

Moving forward before he can stop me, I lean into the man, allowing my lips to graze his, his body tensing up at the touch, his hand staying placed within my own. Feeling almost foreign to the feeling of another's lips on me, I immediately regret the action, wondering if my pointless theories on why Aaron has been so defensive might have been unjust. Ready to pull away, I feel something on the back of my neck, his hand cupping the back of my head, pushing me further into the kiss.

Pulling away only briefly, our breaths become a mix of heat, his words shakily exiting his throat.

"I won't apologize for wanting something that is not mine-"

Silencing him again, I go in for another kiss, this time cupping his face, allowing myself to feed into the touch as much as I can. Letting the feeling of his touch linger, my face becomes flush with heat, my mind coming to no rational conclusions on why I have allowed this. Letting several seconds pass, I embrace his touch, only pulling away when I need a moment to breathe.

Gasping and sitting with our foreheads touching, we swallow nothing, our eyes hazily watching one another.

"I'm not asking you to apologize," I whisper, my head shaking. "I'm asking you to not leave me like everyone else."

Saying nothing else, his arm wraps around me, my body leaning into his, as we both sit side by side. Resting my head on his shoulder, he places his head atop my own, his warmth radiating through my body.

"Fine," he whispers, his hand landing on my own. "Then here is where I stay."

CHAPTER THIRTY-NINE

ELYON

T he mangled bodies of my men lie in front of me; their ears torn clean from their bodies, gashes, and lesions spanning across the entirety of their bodies. Displayed in front of me like a lineup of animals hunted for the kill are the men who found the bodies, none of them willing to speak.

Focused solely on Josh's worn and abused body, I take a deep breath, wondering at what point I was naive enough to believe his lack of communication derived from any form of success. Touching my temple, the bind tethered to Xavier and Forest is non-existent, void of any light as if they have both passed on. Crouching down to be more level with the bodies, I look them over as I speak. □

"Where did you find them?" I question, one of the men finally clearing his throat.

"Outside of New Hope. A group of our Shifters brought them to us, turning away as quickly as they had arrived. There was no submission toward us left in them. Had they not feasted on our men, I'm sure they would have come for us next," the man says, my eyes hyper-focused on the scratch marks lining Josh's arm. "They left us with the gift of our men's chips. Nothing more, nothing less."

"Did he kill her?" I question, a mix of desire and disdain for the answer to be yes swirling inside of me.

"Initially, one of the Shifters had dragged her under the water, she was beaten to all hell and barely able to take a full breath. It was in Josh's notes you asked him to take," the man says, pulling a mangled notebook from Josh's jacket, tossing it my way.

Flipping through his accounts of the torture he inflicted toward Kai and Forest, the entries end after he tossed her in the water, giving little clarity to what followed.

"The Shifters told us their kind was keeping her under the water, waiting until her heart had stopped before moving to retrieve Kaiden. Forest had managed to set her brother free, sacrificing her life in the process."

"That all sounds an awful lot like death to me," I snap, waiting to hear the punchline to this whole fiasco.

"Her group managed to pull her out of the water. The Shifters dragged Xavier down and forced him to bear the same fate as Forest. Their hearts stopped seconds apart. Once one of their own managed to wake Xavier up, his only goal was to resuscitate Forest-"

Raising my hand, I close the man's throat, taking several seconds to process this newfound information. □

Those damn fools died nearly in unison.

They severed my bind the only way they possibly could.

A unified death.

One that they were not supposed to come back from.

"So what you're telling me," I hiss, taking a step closer to the man, pointing my finger deep into his chest. "Is that Forest Evermoore, my rat, is awake?" I question, none of the men willing to say yes or no. "And I have no way to keep a hold on her or the blonde twat?" I push, the men's heads slowly nodding in agreeance.

Taking a deep breath, I take a step back, glancing toward one of the Officials.

Hiding the lingering presence of a mark under his sleeve, he stays the quietest, his face flush with nerves.

"You," I point, urging him closer with my Hold. "Come closer," I ask, watching the man take a cautious step.

"Sir-"

Thrashing out my hand, the taloned ring fashioned to my finger slashes the man's throat, my hand reaching toward the array of glasses set out for my choosing. Grabbing the largest one, I position the cup under the man's throat, watching his red fill the cup, my hand holding up his collar before dropping him to the floor. Letting his blood pool around him, the other men stay utterly still, my body taking in the rich liquid, letting the energy soothe my horrific thoughts.

Lingering in the doorway, one of my closer followers watches me, their silver mask reflecting back the dreary image in front of me.

"Don't be a stranger," I hiss. "Come in."

Stepping over the bodies, they move past the petrified Officials, stepping on Josh's body with little to no remorse. Reaching their hand out, I offer them the rest of my blood, watching them devour what's left in the glass with ease. Nodding their head, they lower their body, kneeling at my feet, patiently awaiting my next command. Placing my hand atop their hooded head, I sigh, glancing at the pile of bodies before me.

"If only there were more like you," I whisper, staring down my shaking men.

"Take care of the bodies. Get a few of my more desirable-looking Marked women up from below. Have them wash up the blood," I smile, dismissing the men with a wave of my hand.

Watching them scramble to work, they drag the bodies as quickly as they can, holding back gags once they make eye contact with their fallen comrades. Sighing deeply, I look over the display of party favors ready for my choosing, prompting my loyalist to rise. Watching me with an observance so few care to have, I run my finger along the tops of each glass and napkin, tugging at the ones I find more visually pleasing.

"Josh failed me miserably," I whisper, questioning whether or not chopping his body to pieces would bring me any peace. "Can I guarantee you will not fail me as he did?" I question, their silence one of the few things I hate about their demeanor.

Saying nothing, they raise their gloved hand, holding something tightly. Concealed in a black envelope, I take the letter, anticipating what lies beneath the red wax seal.

"Each day those deviants are alive is another day my resources are at risk. I am not willing to play any more games," I warn, grasping the letter with all of my might.

Nodding their head forward, they urge me to open the letter, my hands ripping open the paper.

Printed on black paper, and coated with gold ink, the invitation is beautiful, the message it delivers one most would see as an honor.

For Forest and her companions, it is a threat.

Attached to the invitation is numerous photos of the group's deceased family members, the pictures a variety of happy portraits, to gruesome images. Taking it all in, I smile, patting them on the shoulder with glee.

"You got all the preparations done?" I question, feeling their body grow tense beneath the robe.

Again, only nodding, I smile, holding the invitation up with a smile.

"And her dress?" I ask, once more receiving a nod.

"Will it all be sent out in the morning?" I ask, knowing the answer well before it is given.

Taking a sigh of relief, I smile toward the display of party embellishments for my picking, easily isolating my favorites in light of the good news.

"I want as many of these outside that rancid cabin in the morning, along with her and Xavier's attire. If they do not attend, we burn their home to the ground and slit the throat of the old man, the old woman, and all she cares about until she is forced to slice the knife over Xavier's neck herself," I smile, reveling in their silence.

Entering the room, weak and feeble, the Marked slaves move in quietly, their hands carrying large buckets of soapy water, their skin bruised from lack of nourishment. Taking in the sight of their defenseless figures, I grab a chair, taking a seat with a grin.

Shaking as they clean the floor, they avoid my gaze, my loyalist barely looking in their direction.

"Pour us a drink, and enjoy the show," I urge, not posing the offer as a question.

Moving quietly, they grab a neighboring chair, settling on grabbing the whole bottle of vodka from my bar cart, popping off the lid with ease.

Taking a large swig, they shove one of the slower women to the floor with their boot. Pouring some of the liquor over her body, her voice trembling as the liquid seeps into her open wounds. Working quicker now, they take a seat, handing me off the bottle, my smile moving higher along my face.

"You have such a hatred for the Marked," I whisper, my grin wider than before. "You'd think you were not one of them."

Anything but a smile lingers under their mask.

CHAPTER FORTY

XAVIER

N o nightmares.

No pain

For the first night in what seems like forever, the shadows did not win.

There were no screams. There was no fear. The bleak realization that when I awoke the horrors of what were in my dreams were far better than my reality was something I had grown used to. Now, waking up has never felt more blissful.

Curled up and asleep, the sunrise casts rays across her peaceful state, her body tucked into me, the white of her scars illuminated by the sun. Casting down her spine, the ink molds to her body, her lips parted, her hair a wild mess. Holding onto me with the ring clung to her finger, her cheeks are rosy, the love bites I left after the tub trailed across her skin in all the places she chose not to focus on healing. Cupping her face, I roll my thumb over her cheeks, lingering on the way her skin feels beneath my touch, questioning if any of it is real to begin with.

Kissing the top of her forehead, I work my way down her face, taking extra time on her lips, before carefully moving her off of me. Sliding free from the bed, I tuck a pillow under her body as a replacement for me, pulling up her covers higher despite how beautiful she looks so bare. Yanking on a pair of soft pants, I decide on the use of a shirt, unsure of how many looks I might get from our companions over the deep nail marks tethered to my back.

Sliding out the bedroom door, Aaron's fire barely stays roaring, the two guest room doors still closed. Taking a glance at Aaron and Kai's room as I walk by, the door is slightly ajar, both of the men asleep on the floor, their backs pressed to the side of the bed. Covered with a blanket, their heads lean on one another as if they fell asleep talking. Giving them a little more privacy, I close the door, happily smiling as I make my way toward the kitchen.

Tossing a few more logs in the fire, the chill morning air from the forest is no joke. Despite being some of the warmer months, mornings were always the coldest here, making it easier to find the time to create as much skin-to-skin contact as possible.

Gravitating toward the kitchen, a thought enters my mind, one foolish in nature.

Sitting peacefully unbothered by time, the singular jar of pancake mix sits on the pantry shelf, barely used, just waiting to see me once more. Grabbing the jar, all the mornings spent in this kitchen come rushing back, the smile she wore every time she would see me cooking, only to end up seated on the counter, wrapping herself around my waist.

Tossing the jar back and forth in my hand, I roll my shoulders, wondering if there is still any culinary touch in me.

"It would be rude not to feed the house guests," I rationalize, twisting the knob to the gas stove.

Flipping the delicate breakfast food, a stack of pancakes lingers on the plate next to me, my face and hands streaked with batter. Varying from burnt to underdone, I hyperfocus on getting at least one perfect, wondering at what point I forgot how to simply toss a pancake.

Too focused on the food to notice her presence behind me, a pair of arms wrap around my sides, her front pressing against my back, the warmth of her cheek settled against my shirt. Turning off the stove, I smile, ditching my hyper fixation on creating something perfect.

Turning around, she wears one of my shirts, her legs bare, her eyes observing my act of love with delight. Hiding a laugh, she wipes away a streak of batter from my face, landing it in her mouth.

"A bit behind on your culinary touch?" she questions, her grin encapsulating her face.

Letting my arms wrap around her waist, I pull her onto my feet, locking her lips with mine.

Kissing me hard and long, her hands wrap around my neck, her body instinctively moving to wrap around me. Taking the opportunity to grab her legs, I carry her closer to the counter, setting her down on its cool surface, watching her body cling to me the moment the cold counter touches her skin.

"Too cold?" I question, placing my hands on her thighs.

"Just right," she whispers, her fingers trailing across my face, creating as many mental notes as she can.

Gravitating back toward my project, I finally get a good flip, feeling slightly more encouraged than I did moments ago.

"It's almost sinful I could not remember mornings like these," she whispers, toying with the spoon covered in batter. "You, in our kitchen, cooking without a care in the world," she whispers, her voice one of the most calming presences in the room.

Smirking, I focus on my task, fighting the urge to carry her back to our bedroom and give her another taste of what she felt last night.

"Shit," she mutters, my eyes finally glancing her way, the batter streaking her front, touching her thigh. "I really thought I was going to be able to help," she smiles, looking around for a towel.

Switching off the stove, it's impossible to look away from her as she is right now.

Wild hair, the soft material of the shirt pressed against her beautiful frame. More present in light of the cold, her breasts show through the shirt, my eyes gravitating toward the mess she has managed to make on herself.

"Wanna hand me the towel?" she questions, a more enticing idea swirling in my mind.

Grabbing her off the counter, she stifles her yelp, letting me hold her close, her back meeting the surface of our sofa. Yanking up her shirt enough to expose the bottom of her breasts, I stay leaned over her, gravitating toward the batter on her thighs, watching her eyes grow wide.

"They will wake up at any moment," she whispers.

"I know," I grin, silencing her protests the moment my lips meet her skin.

Trailing kisses up her thigh, I stop at the batter, licking it clean, her hips moving upward, my hand keeping them down. Letting the point of my tongue dance across her skin, I move higher up, kissing along her lower stomach placing my hand over her warmth, already eager to feel my touch. Feeling her through the material of her underwear, I begin a slow massage, working my mouth up the middle of her stomach, trailing to one of her aching breasts.

Squirming with pleasure beneath my touch, she hisses through clenched teeth, wanting nothing more than for me to enter her with my fingers. Pausing at her breast, I take my time with my mouth, swirling my tongue over her nipple, her hands landing in my hair.

"I think I am all clean, Xavier," she whispers playfully, wanting nothing more than for me to keep going.

"Not yet," I whisper, moving her aside, allowing my back to meet the sofa, as she crawls on top of me.

Straddling my legs, her hair falls into her face as she looks down at me, her eyes wide with lust. Positioned on top of my length, the strain in my pants is unbearable, the flush of her cheeks enough to get anyone going. Running my hands along her body beneath the shirt, she begins to pull up mine, the tattered torso under her one I prefer she sees in the night.

Grabbing her wrist, her eyebrows raise.

"It's a lot worse in the daylight," I warn, her head shaking.

"You are the one thing in my life the daylight makes that much brighter."

Saying nothing else, she waves away my hand, allowing herself to raise my shirt, the scars along my skin deep and uneven. Taking it all in, she runs her hands over my front, lowering her head and body to meet my waistline. Kissing a deep scar along my lower stomach, she whispers.

"I will never allow your skin to be scathed like this ever again." Trailing higher, she kisses a hash of scars, her lips delicate and soft. "No one will touch you like this again so long as I live," she continues, working higher up my front. "The day I met you, is the day I found a reason to fight for something other than the Prophet's downfall," she continues. "Every scar, every cut, every drop of blood, all fuel to the fire burning within me," she pauses, her eyes glancing up toward me. "You are my infinite always, Xavier Evermoore, the reason my world found purpose," her voice wobbles. "Don't ever forget how much love I have for you."

Trying to keep it together, I drag her closer, letting her body sprawl atop my own, my hands holding her as tight as humanly possible. Gravitating toward my lips, I latch her into a kiss, cupping her face with great care, the feeling of her ring gliding across my skin enough to make any man weak in the knees. □

"I want to leave this place and marry you the first opportunity I get," I whisper.

"Is that a promise?" she questions, her smile wide.

"It's a guarantee."

Startled, something heavy shakes the cabin, both of our eyes snapping to the front door. Casting shadows through the window, the presence of bodies swarms the perimeter, both of us quickly standing, a feral rage coming over us. Hearing three loud pounds meet the surface of the door, the whole room seems to shake, urging the doors of our companion's quarters to open, each one of them petrified, pushed into the living room with knives positioned close to their backs.

Wearing head-to-toe tactical gear, Officials shove our companions forward; their mouths snapped shut, their bodies still decorated in their leisure clothes. Feeling a cold draft, the windows to their guest rooms are wide open.

Despite yesterday's bloodshed, they still had the nerve to waltz in here, begging for something to happen.

"I love the smell of pancakes in the morning," one of the men says, his beard peppered with age.

Keeping Aaron and Bekah held back with daggers, the pair thrashes, anticipating a fight.

"Elyon was right in assuming these two are the ones we should be wary of," the man says, his blood buzzing with the energy of a Marked.

In fact, all of their blood has the presence of Marked DNA.

Swinging open the door, and closing it with a loud thud, a figure in silver steps into the room, their walk different than that of the Prophet. Keeping my focus on them, Forest's eyes narrow on the two Officials holding our friends, her fists clenched to avoid bringing down the whole room.

Straightening her shoulders, her eyes gravitate behind her, focusing in on the mask of silver.

"I know you," she whispers, their shoulders tensing up. "I can smell it in your blood."

Saying nothing they remain still, throwing a sign toward the men holding our friends.

"We are not here to draw blood," the Official sighs, letting go of our companions, all of their bodies swarming toward us.

Huddling into a group in the center of the room, we all stand watch, anticipating what is to come.

"We've simply come to remind you what is at stake and extend an offer to both Xavier and Forest," the Official smiles. "No plus ones."

Saying nothing else, the men around us Winnow, leaving nothing but a group of fast heartbeats.

Stepping away from the group, I surge toward the front door, ready to bring down anyone willing to come here like this.

Nearly tearing the door off of its hinges, I pause my rampage, staring outside, the litter of what has been left behind making my stomach sink.

Joining next to me, she says nothing, her eyes sticking to the message they have waved in our faces like a red flag.

"There is no escaping him," she whispers, her voice cold with fear.

A quiet cabin and a life with a wife I admire endlessly.

All nothing but a dream, so long as Elyon is alive.

The problem is, to end him, I must lose her.

That is a sacrifice I am never willing to make.

CHAPTER FORTY-ONE

FOREST

Hugging my brother as tight as he may allow it, our hands wrap around one another, his back unscathed by the blade of the Marked who had managed to Winnow in here. Taking shallow breaths, his heart races against his chest, sounding off in my ear like a drum. Cupping his hands around my head; his body shakes beneath my touch, all our eyes on the gift left for us outside, equally disturbed by the message it brings.

Hundreds of pictures swarm the grounds, some happy family portraits, while others are horrid shots of certain loved one's deceased corpses. Scattered amongst the photos are numerous black invitations, each one sealed with New Havens' emblem, one ripped open, settled in Xavier's hand.

Pulling away from Kai, I avoid the pictures of my father or the family portrait we took the night before the new year. Gravitating toward one of the older photos, I see a younger, smiling Xavier, his parents, and Lily in the shot, all clueless about the life that would be in store for them the minute they left the compound's front door. Biting back vomit, the picture of Bekah's mother swinging from a noose rests in her shaking hand, Valerie and Aaron's parent's morgue shots the next to meet my eyes. Holding Xavier's family portrait tightly, I tuck away the photo in my pocket, watching the man look over the invitation with disdain.

"Elyon has invited me and Forest to a New Year's celebration meant for all of New Haven," Xavier whispers, all of us avoidant of the two boxes left behind on the porch. "He says he is looking forward to a night filled with surprise," Xavier continues, guilt swarming in my stomach the longer I look at the photos.

His family is dead because of me.

He has only ever felt pain because of me.

Grabbing the invitation from him, his jaw stays clenched, his arms crossed as he glares at the array of photos.

□

New Haven cordially invites you to a night of thrill, surprise, and elegance.

Let's welcome another year of prosperity, order, and longevity with our youth.

Come dressed to impress and hidden by a mask.

I expect to see you both dressed in what I have picked up.

Attendance is not optional.

I'll be seeing you, my devils.

- Elyon Morgan

Dropping the invite, I try and keep my calm, trying to control my anger. Kneeling down toward the boxes, Xavier pulls free one of the tops, a suit made of black satin and gold thread waiting patiently for him. Settled on top of the suit is a mask, one like the ones worn the night of the Lottery. Crouching down with him, I pry open the top to the second box, met with nothing but black feathers weaved together to create a dress meant to turn heads. Filled with jewelry and a mask much darker than the rest, the dress is a target on my back, its feathers a sick reminder of what has been lost.

"Raven feathers," I scoff, cramming the dress back into the box.

"When is it?" I question, keeping my focus on the dress, unable to look at anything but the mask resting before me.

"Tonight," Xavier whispers, my eyes darting to the man. "The party is tonight."

Tuning out the clamor of the others as they question what is to come, the noise surrounding me goes quiet, my focus on nothing but the water before me. Pulling away from the conversation, the chill air slaps my legs, my body moving, stepping over each and every photo beneath my feet. Barely hearing Xavier try and formulate a plan, the water before me calls to me, the forest surrounding us void of life. Watching something creep along the tree line, Mason emerges from the shadows, his body now almost entirely a man. Curled dark hair and a scar working down his right eye, ink travels across his skin, his golden-brown eyes watching me with curiosity. Feeling the rise of energy collecting in my palms, heat traps itself in my face, my hands shaking with adrenaline, fear, and anger pouring into my soul.

Feeling the ground beneath me rattle, my breaths become shallower, the surface of the water shaking the longer I struggle to dictate my emotions. Taking large, raspy breaths, I coil my hands into my hair, wondering at what point I will implode.

"Forest?" Xavier's voice questions, the weight of the situation all becoming too much.

Forcing my hand out toward the water with my Hold, the ground rattles as the waters rise up from the pool, hitting the tree line in a massive wave, seeping into the Earth, leaving something closer to a small pond in the divot before us. Forcing my hand forward again, multiple trees break at the trunks, crashing to the ground, the sound thundering through the wood, only making it that much easier for Mason to move away from the shadows.

Unable to hear anything but the scream of defeat leave my throat, my body crumples to the ground, surrounded by the dozens of photos of those crossed by Elyon and the society controlling mankind. Gasping and shuddering as I take breaths, I focus on my ring, feeling Xavier's arms surround me, his lips pressed to my ear as he pulls me into his lap, letting me hyperventilate against him until the Earth no longer shakes.

"I'm going to lose everything," I shudder, the guilt of all I have allowed to happen eating away at my very existence. "All because I couldn't follow through with my very reason for existing."

Running his hand through my hair, he says nothing, allowing his fingers to trail over my face, touching my skin until I have calmed down.

Brushing away his hand, a mask of coldness casts over my face, my body forcing itself up into a standing position, my focus on no one but Mason. Looking over the very visually pleasing man, he crosses his arms, watching me with a lack of sympathy I need to see right now. Following my movements, Xavier lets the interaction we shared on the ground stay behind us, keeping his focus on me and my sudden attention on Mason.

"Why are you back here so soon?" I question, his eyes wary, hiding truths he does not have the courage to lay before me.

"Mason?" Xavier pushes, growing significantly more impatient the longer the man lingers before us.

"Elyon and his servant in silver came to visit my people before they stopped here. They were furious about the bodies you all delivered and were hoping to use the deaths of our brainwashed kind as leverage to gain an alliance," Mason whispers, something red blotching the side of his shirt.

"Why are you alone? Were you not creating talks of peace with your people?" I question, sensing the bad news before he had even had the chance to say it.

"Elyon had the remains of my people with him, some old, others whose throats he surely slashed moments before. He blamed the deaths on all of you. If there was any chance for a union before this mess-"

"Then the Prophet took the opportunity away," I hiss, putting the pieces together.

Trying to suppress my anger, I take a step back, racking my brain with a million possibilities and even more negative outcomes.

"What are you saying?" Xavier questions, wanting to hear the man lay it out before jumping to anger.

"There will be no union with the Shifters. They have already chosen to back Elyon in whatever it is he needs. They are too blatantly foolish to understand he cannot turn them into the humans they want to be. Elyon parades his Paradoxes around, feeding my people the lies that he had created them, knowing full well your blood is what was needed in the first place. I tried to warn my people of Elyon's deceit," Mason whispers, glancing to his side. "Elyon's men saw to it I didn't make it within 100 feet of my people's refugee. It didn't take me long to piece together where their next pit stop would be," he mutters, looking around the tattered space.

"And what were you doing when you were supposed to be swaying them to back Forest? Have they not seen how you look now?" Xavier questions angrily, grabbing the man by the shirt.

"They will not choose the losing side, Xavier," Mason snaps, shoving the man's hands away. "They will not fight a war that will cause them to lose the life they barely have to begin with." Mason seethes.

Reaching into his mind, I sense something else, the real root of his distractions.

"You've been trailing a Marked?" I question, anger bubbling within me. "That is why you've been so distracted."

Saying nothing, his mouth snaps shut, his eyes averting to me.

"It's some kid I saw leave the compound the night Fallan and the others passed away," Mason hisses, justifying his absent mind. "She left without a trace, leaving nothing in her trail. There was no sign of her in New Haven or anywhere close to this portion of the New World Order. I have never seen anyone leave Sanctum's borders so easily. I needed answers-"

"And because of it, we have no fucking Shifters," I snap, my voice shaky.

Taking a step toward me, Xavier places his hand on the man's chest, both men toe to toe, his breath brushing his face as he speaks.

"We are not a populous who will be dictated by yet another unhinged Marked-"

Forcing my hand forward, Mason's body is forced backward, colliding with what's left of the water. Drenching his body in the healing liquid, I flare my arms away from anyone's grasp, standing at the water's edge, my eyes narrowing at the man now wading in the shallow pool of reflection.

"I am not Elyon!" I yell, the energy buzzing within me something I have yet to feel. "You want to know why I stood back and did nothing as they threatened me in my own home?" I question, my voice carrying well beyond this small area. "I was willing to sacrifice Aaron and Bekah's lives in order to kill them all in one clean sweep, and I would have done so happily, savoring the taste of every single one of them," I seethe, pointing my finger at Mason. "Do you realize what it means to have nothing you love left on this planet?" I question, snapping my attention toward the group. "Do any of you realize what it means for me to allow the people I care about to suffer in order to win?" I push, getting nothing but blank stares. "This war is one I can win. I have no doubts about that truth," I shudder, giving Xavier a long look. "The only way to do so is to allow the people I love to perish." Glancing back toward Mason, I snap my hand up, forcing him into a standing position. "The woman I am now is a woman who is fighting for the people she loves, Mason Veron," I grovel, fishing his last name from the depths of his mind. "Take the people I love away from me, and force me to win this battle, and I will become something so much worse than the Prophet."

Tears roll down my cheeks, my hands shaking.

"And Elyon knows that. He knows I will not sacrifice what I love most," I whisper, finally locking eyes with Xavier. "Which is why we must go. This only ends in more bloodshed the longer we avoid his word," I say, silently moving past Xavier.

Laughing like a crazed fool, Mason sounds mad, his voice a mix of humor and fear.

"You think this end when Elyon is gone?" Mason questions.

"Mason, enough," Xavier growls, getting nothing but a scoff as a response.

"You know better than anyone what the cost of defeating the Prophet is. Do you not see what he is doing? What he has already done? It doesn't matter who dies or how many times he has slain us; there will always be another. At least accept that the only way out of this is to run far away from all of it-"

"Like you did?" I question, glaring in his direction. "How has running treated you so far, Veron?" I question, years of torment and abuse clouding his mind. "Did you finally outrun your monsters?" I question.

Letting the group fall into silence, I scoff at the man, grabbing Xavier's hand without another word.

"I froze," I whisper, looking over Xavier, his arms crossed as he watches me.

Saying nothing, he shakes his head, wrapping his arms around my body.

"You know better than anyone how quickly Elyon would have seen to it that all of the people outside pissed at you, would be dead if you had acted when his forces were here. They need to see your fear. They all need to see your fear." Xavier says, his body guiding us closer to the edge of the bed.

Taking a seat, I join him, letting him gather me in his lap.

"Do you think I convinced them? Do you think they will stay behind?" I question, his thumb rolling over my cheek.

"Snapping at Mason like that and giving me the cold shoulder. I'd say if confidence is what they were hoping to have in you, they were sorely disappointed," he whispers, making me smile despite the meaning of his words.

"They had to think they got the upper hand on us," I whisper.

"Well, I'd say Mason was convincing. The less everyone knows, the better. So long as Elyon's men believe they have the Shifters on their side and all of us backed into a corner, we have an upper hand," Xavier says, his hand running through my hair.

"Was it true, about Mason and the girl?" Xavier questions. "Did she really make it out?"

"I had him following that lead after what happened in the compound," I sigh. "In between peace talks and conversion, he tried his best to keep tabs on her. It is like he said. She disappeared without a trace."

"Lucky bitch," Xavier sighs, my hands now the ones exploring his face.

"We have an upper hand, Xavier-"

"The servant in silver, you said you recognized their scent," Xavier says, bringing up the one point I knew he would. "How?"

Swallowing, I reflect on the familiar way their blood flooded my nose, hitting me like a vague memory.

"I can't recall," I say with full honesty. "It was like a childhood memory, not one of the altered ones either. Their presence was foreign, but their blood was not," I say, keeping myself tucked in his lap.

"Do you think the others will stay back?" I ask, listening to the sound of the man's heart.

"I'd say Mason's performance was telling. If anything, I'll convince Aaron to take himself and the others back to the compound. Mason will keep communications with the Shifters who will sneak their way into New Haven, and you and I will detain the Prophet," Xavier says, reaching into his pocket. Pulling free a vial filled with swirling liquid, I look it over.

"It's a mix of your blood and the waters. Exactly what is needed to create a bind to the Prophet. I wasn't sure why Josh had taken you here, now, I know," Xavier whispers, pulling free a page from his pocket.

Looking it over, I see the old text, the writing familiar to that of Elyon.

"It would seem the Prophet was eager to create us new binds. All he needed was the water. Who knew that's what was in our IVs when he was torturing us."

"That's all I'll need to create a bind?" I question, his head nodding.

"So long as you will it."

"I'm sure I can think of a few ways to torment his soul," I smile. "Lesions across his eyes?" I ask, a devilish grin pulling across our lips.

"So long as you're walking out of that ward with me by the end of the night, I am pleased," Xavier smiles, his lips pressing to mine.

Pain enters my chest.

The guilt of his sorrows are still so deeply wound to his soul.

"Do you love me?" I question, needing to hear it from him.

"For as long as I draw breath, Forest Flower," he whispers, his lips devouring mine. "And even after the stars have burned out."

CHAPTER FORTY-TWO

XAVIER- THE DARK DAYS

Listening to the crackle of the fire, I watch her pencil drag across the sketch-book; her eyes determined to capture my image, my body rigidly still. Seated between my legs on the floor, I run my fingers through her long locks, the grey now chased away by the presence of a dark brown dye. The image of her like this is something that has grown challenging to get used to. So focused, her eyebrows are creased inward, her hands shielding the sketchbook from me, her eyes a mix of green and gold as she watches me.

Smiling once we make eye contact, her face grows red, her eyes darting away as if she were a shy schoolgirl. Settled along her ring finger is the promise ring, the ring my father bought my mother from the Unfortunate sector, one of the few things I kept from my parents before giving them the burial they both deserved.

"Why do you look away like that?" I question with a grin, her eyes darting up toward me.

"You still make me incredibly nervous," she says, keeping her focus on the drawing. "I never understood the whole concept of getting butterflies. Then, you looked at me as you do now, and it all made a lot more sense," she grins.

The plan is foolproof really. The Prophet has no idea what she looks like and is itching to have me start bleeding my way into society. Given the face of the Commander, an elder had finally decided to step down, the Prophet wanting nothing more than to begin using their pawn piece. It's simple. I'll explain I found disgust and disloyalty with their rat, begging for their forgiveness. Then, I will take up my rightful duties as acting Commander, leaving her to live out her Untouchable act in peace, giving us both an opportunity to come together again under the ward. Her memories of me might be hazy, feeling like distant recollections. The Prophet is many things, but they would not deny a man love. I do my job, and Forest stays safe.

If I do my job well enough, I may have the opportunity to leave, giving both me and Forest a chance to leave New Haven in the ash behind us.

"You're spiraling again," Forest whispers, her eyes not fully focused on me.

"I don't like the idea of the woman I love having suppressed memories," I whisper.

Cupping my face, her thumbs roll over my cheeks, her body only moving that much closer.

"I have no doubts you could make me fall for you once more," she whispers. "The less I know of what I am capable of the better. The memories are not suppressed, rather, tucked away. One kiss from you, and all these good moments come flooding back." Pressing her lips to my nose, she continues. "I need time to adjust, believing I am a subservient, perfect little Untouchable. That way, when I see your handsome face again, I will have become accustomed to the lifestyle and can only focus on you," she whispers, my arms wrapping around the woman.

"Will it be odd? Having Andrew as your father and parading around as his son's sister?" I question, her nose scrunching at the comment.

"Kaiden is older, twenty, as far as I know. I think for me, the hardest part will be keeping up the act of having been in the family for years, hence suppressing some of my finest memories," she frowns, glancing down at my hands now running under her shirt.

"I almost forgot," she says with a smile, dragging her hands over my eyes. "Keep them closed.

Not wanting to protest, I sit in solemn wait, feeling her body move away, my smile only returning the moment I feel her warm skin once again. Buzzing with excitement like a child, I hear the sound of metal, my eyebrows raising with curiosity.

"Open," she commands.

Prying open one of my eyes, her palms are open, a circular metal watch resting in her hands. Looking at the chain dangling from the device, I grab the watch with curiosity, looking over its shiny front over and over.

"A watch?" I question, unsure of how to react.

I never really have been a watch man.

"Look inside," she says sarcastically, nudging my arm playfully.

Flipping open the watch's top, I observe it closely, feeling the corners of my mouth rise up. The picture inside is one I will hold onto tremendously.

A day ago, right before she dyed her hair, I caught an image of her outside the cabin, one that would make any man's heart flutter. Smiles and all, she looked as beautiful as an angel, the look of joy in her expression one I could stare at every day and never get bored of.

Looking down, an engraving runs over the rim, the words solidified in my heart.

Do you love me? For as long as I draw breath.

Saying nothing, I glance up at her, my heart filled to the brim with love for the woman.

"I had someone in the Sanctuary craft it," she smiles. Awaiting my reaction, she looks embarrassed. "Do you like it?"

Smiling at the comment, I grab her chin, pulling her lips to my own, devouring her mouth in a kiss.

"I love it almost as much as I love you."

Running my tongue along her bottom lip, I hold it between my teeth, feeling her smile the longer I tempt her with the touch. Wrapping her arms around my neck, she brushes the sketchbook off of her lap, prompting me to explore her with my mouth, giving us a moment together I will cherish so deeply.

Standing as I hold her, she glances toward the bedroom.

"It's not even sunrise yet," I tease, ready to hear her rebuttal.

Hearing a large crash, four large canisters come barreling through our windows, her body quickly moving off of mine, our eyes frantically searching around the space, seeing nothing but the large swirls of white smoke filling the space. Grabbing onto me, I hold her close, forcing her to cover her mouth with her shirt, my own hand reaching for mine. Feeling something force my hand down, both of our wrists stay at our side. Holding our breath before the smoke can touch our noses, paintings, and portraits fall down from the walls. The sounds of boots drag across the hardwood floor.

"Forest, Xavier, run!" Andrews's voice screams, both of us gasping the moment hands collide with our torsos, forcing air out of both of us. Sucking in a deep breath, the smoke has us on our knees nearly instantly. Feeling my vision begin to spot, Forest's eyes roll into the back of her head, my arms catching her, slowly lowering her to the ground, preventing her from hitting her head.

Trying my best to get a good look at who has disturbed us, the gleam of silver sends me into a panic, my arms thrashing out, ready to attack.

"Bad move, Xavier," they say, glee ridding their voice. "Consequences."

Forcing their leg forward, their boot hits my jaw, darkness quickly clouding my vision.

Waking up to the smell of cheap latex and linen, a painful wave of discomfort rolls through my jaw, the feeling of strain around my wrists more than enough to make anyone go into a panic. Feeling my back pressed against a wall, the room around me spins, taking several blinks to fully adjust. Focusing on the movement ensuing around me, a slow green light flashes across my vision, a brunette in a lab coat the source of the light. Working with her chip at full blast, my stomach drops the moment I realize who she is peering over. Forest's lifeless state is plastered across the medical chair.

Trying to force my legs to move, it is as if I am paralyzed, nothing but the neck up able to move from its limp state.

"Trying to get one of my own doctors to work behind my back," the Prophet's voice taunts, my head turning to see their figure leaning against the wall. Andrew blankly stares at his wife form beside the Prophet as she silently works on Forest. "I thought you were smarter than that," the Prophet whispers, shaking their head in disgust.

"W- what, what are you doing?" I question, panic flooding my chest.

"Getting a good look at my rat you have gotten so cozy with," the Prophet says, scoffing at the sight of her. "To think, I have been cowering from such a frail, insignificant Marked," they snap, glancing toward Andrew. "I should snap this one's neck for his treason."

"No!" I yell, swallowing dryly. "Damnit, just let them all go, I'll do whatever you need-"

"I know you will," the Prophet interrupts. "You, her, and everyone else associated with all of you will do exactly what I want."

"What are you doing to her?" I question, tears streaming out of my eyes, blurring my vision.

"Well, you see, I liked the idea of her not remembering you. I liked the idea of you both suffering even more. Katiana, sweetheart," the Prophet says, reaching into their coat pocket, pulling free a vial mixed with a clear liquid swirled with the rich red nature of blood. "Go ahead and put this in her."

Trying to move, none of my limbs work, my body begging to be rid of its paralyzed state. Grabbing the syringe from the Prophet, Katiana works with a blank stare, my eyes glancing toward Andrew.

"Andrew!" I hiss, receiving not even a blink from the man.

"He can't hear you. Once he has left this room, it will be as if he never even met you," the Prophet beams. "In fact, Andrew, why don't you send in our guest?" the Prophet questions, my body sweating in a panic.

Saying nothing, Andrew walks out of the room, Katiana's hand plunging the syringe into Forest's neck.

"Now you both are bound to me, as well as one another. Try and end it, try and let death be your escape, and you only take her with you. Try and tell her who she truly is, or allow your lips to meet hers, and you both meet a world of pain you might not be able to come back from," the Prophet says with pride, a deep-rooted, sinister nature lingering in their tone.

Watching Katiana work diligently, she holds a scalpel in her hand, keeping it far away from Forest's ear.

"While you have been playing house, I have been designing a new chip. One that I'm almost certain will kill Forest if she ever tries to remove it. I have forced the chips into any of her followers lingering under this ward. I'd say if death does not take them after removal, the suicidal thoughts surely will."

Looking at Forest's lifeless state, all the fears come flooding in.

"Why are you doing this?" I question, filling with pain.

"You disobeyed me, Xavier. You harbored the one woman I feared the most-"

"Why keep her alive then?" I question, snapping before they can finish.

"I wanted to kill her, but I need to observe her before I do so. I would hate to see perfectly good resources go to waste, all because I was too fearful of what she might be capable of," the Prophet gripes, the door to the room opening once again.

Stepping into the space, my eyes grow wide, his set of deep blue eyes landing on me before gravitating toward Katiana.

"Fallan Markswood," the Prophet beams. "I knew you would be able to track them down." The Prophet smiles, a look of regret plastered over Fallan's expression.

The boy whose parents the Prophet had me sick Andrew after.

Dove's partner.

Saying nothing, Katiana extends the scalpel toward the man, his hands already knowing what to do.

"What is he doing here?" I question frantically, watching the man slide the scalpel over his finger, before handing the device back to Katiana.

"Fallan was a bit unnerved after your fiancé killed his partner," the Prophet states. Fallan's head hangs low, not able to look in my direction.

"So, I thought up something quite brilliant."

Sliding the blade over Forest's finger, Katiana draws red. Her hand moves the scalpel away from the injury, only to create a new one on the back of Forest's ear.

"What are you doing to her?" I question, Fallan's eyes on no one but me.

"I am giving her the suppressed memories you so desperately wanted her to have of you, and replacing them with the image of him," they exclaim. "This will make it that much easier for her to come running to him, in light of the false bond they now share."

Piecing together the need for the blood, I shake my head.

"You will do what? Seduce her-" □

"Torment her," Fallan states. "Unlike you, I can keep my word. The moment she comes crawling to me, wondering why she can't seem to shake me, all of the memories she thinks she has of me will come flooding back. Once the opportunity is right, I will murder her as she murdered my Dove and deliver her to the Prophet as you should have done long ago. Perhaps tampering with her food delivery routes will be my first step in getting her addicted to my blood," Fallan states, my jaw taut with anger.

"Your bind to her will falter," I snap, my voice livid with rage.

"So long as I slip my blood into her food's delivery routes, our connection will remain stronger than anything you could have had with her."

"I will find a way to tell her. I won't let you touch her-"

"You'll have no choice. Your bind to me has come with some... additions. Think defiantly, act defiantly, and you will only feel the pain. You will suffer trying to keep your shared memories suppressed from her," the Prophet says, my eyes gravitating toward Forest.

Watching the spindles latch to the back of her ear, Katiana inserts the chip, my stomach dropping the moment I watch it settle into the back of her head. Closing the wounds up with Cure-All, I feel a pain in my chest, one that I cannot be rid of.

"I'd say, come this afternoon, Forest Evermoore will be long gone. Forest Blackburn has a much better ring to it, wouldn't you agree?" the Prophet questions, Andrew's stare as blank as ever.

Unable to move still. I look around the space, trying to find a way out.

"You three can go, I'll see to it she is sent to her new home with no complaints."

Waltzing toward Forest, Fallan pries her ring from her finger, tucking it away in his pocket. Glancing toward me, he spits, kicking my leg as hard as he can.

"Insurance."

Moving out of the space, the Prophet grabs Fallan's arm before he can make it all the way out.

"She will be avenged, Markswood," the Prophet whispers, Fallan's only response a glare before leaving the space.

Kneeling next to me, I take in the sight of Forest like this, her body peaceful as if she is only sleeping.

"I admire the way you thought you could get the upper hand on me, I truly do," the Prophet gripes, tears flooding out of my eyes. "Given your marvelous track record, I'm surprised you thought there was any chance you would get to live with anyone peacefully," they sigh. "You are quite a fool, Xavier Evermore," they snap.

"And now you may live an eternity of suffering, knowing there is no way your Forest Flower will ever find true peace."

Shoving my head back into the wall, they laugh as they stand, my heart filling with dread.

"Enjoy your last few moments with her. Once you are done taking it all in, it's time to get to work."

Moving toward the door, they turn toward me.

"Don't ever cross me again."

Saying nothing else, the door slams shut, shaking the room with its movements.

Looking toward Forest, I try and move, my body as useless as ever.

"Forest?" I question nothing but an empty cavern in my mind, our lifeless connection running dry.

"Forest, baby, wake up," I cry, hitting the side of my head against the wall in frustration.

"Forest, please, please, wake up," I cry out, the pocket watch brushing against my leg inside my pocket.

"I can't do this. I can't watch you live a life I am not in," I whisper through gritted teeth. "I love you."

Waiting to see her eyes open, they stay closed, tears hitting my front.

"I won't leave you," I whisper. "I won't let them win."

Glaring at the camera, I yell.

"You won't win this war."

Snickering through the intercom, the Prophet laughs.

"I've already won, Xavier. Now pull yourself together and do your fucking job."

Death is peaceful.

I almost wish it would have taken me that day.

CHAPTER FORTY-THREE

AARON

"It's a trap," I snap, looking over the pair in confusion.

Having stepped out of their room only moments ago, the silence that blankets the space is unsettling. Staring out the window, avoiding looking in anyone's direction, Mason is clearly pissed, Forest's hateful words ones that stick with a man well after they are said. Looking over the two boxes positioned on the coffee table, the pair says nothing, letting us digest their insane plan once more.

"You are seriously considering going to the ball?" Kai questions, the first to break the silence.

Glaring at her brother, Forest looks at the man as if his question was the most outlandish thing to be said this whole conversation.

"I am running out of options here, Kaiden," she snaps. "Clearly, doing nothing and trying to stay out of it is not a possibility. If I run, he hurts one of you. If we stay where we are, we are just waiting for another attack. It doesn't matter how many resources we gather, Elyon is already five steps ahead," Forest gripes, Xavier now the one to clear his throat.

"Elyon would not have done all that he did if he wasn't serious. There are allies he has that we don't even know of. Elyon will not kill us, we both hold too much value in whatever larger picture he has formulated. At least this way, we know you are all safe-"

"That is if we benefit Forest," I whisper, her head snapping in my direction.

Growing silent once more, the air becomes suffocating.

"You want to repeat that, Aaron?" Forest questions, anger dripping from her tone.

"I heard it just as clear as anyone-"

"Aaron, don't," Kai starts, my hand swatting him away.

"No, Kai, I'm tired of you defending her every time she shows just how unhinged she really can be. You made it very clear how willing you were to sacrifice me and Bekah so long as it meant the others got out unscathed. A few more moments holding us at knifepoint and you would have gladly allowed the blades to pierce our backs-"

"I was angry!" Forest snaps, holding back her energy. "I was angry at the whole situation-"

"Right, and anger doesn't lead you to make deadly decisions?" I question, Kai's head hanging low at the reference to Hunter's death.

Taking several steps closer to me, Xavier adjusts my collar, his face cold, void of any clear expression.

"No one will stop you from lashing out," Xavier says, patting my front. "But disrespect my woman in her own home again, and I will do what her kindness has prevented her from following through with."

Swallowing dryly, I shove him back, barely getting a reaction from him.

"You both are willing to go on a suicide mission, knowing you both might be stuck under that ward," Bekah states, shaking her head in disbelief.

"Then let them," Mason chimes in, a scoff rolling off of his throat.

"It's clear Elyon wants them, and there's no end to any of this so long as he does not get his way. You can have faith in the fact that Elyon is a powerful force, or you can have faith that the both of them are stronger," Mason says, managing to force out admiration despite his anger. "At the end of the day, if only one person remains, I would rather it be someone on our side."

Casting the conversation with the looming presence of the sacrifice Forest would have to make in order to defeat Elyon, Xavier's smirk drops, his eyes darkening the longer he watches Mason.

"Don't look at me like that, Evermoore," Mason says, his eyes still gazing out the window. "You both know, the only way this ends, is with her and Elyon in a coffin. I'm not going to stand here and allow you to think there is any other solution," Mason says, Xavier's fists balling at the statement.

Grabbing the back of Xavier's shirt before he can move after the man, Forest clears her throat, her eyes wide as she observes the room.

"Aaron and Mason are right," she states, causing Xavier to face the woman. "I am unpredictable when angry, and it would take a sacrifice of both Elyon's and my own life in unison in order to stop his reign. The larger forces would never allow one to live without the other," she states, rolling her fingers over her tired eyes. "Which is why we will find a way to detain him, even if it means confinement ourselves. Elyon may be powerful, but he is the last thing from immortal. I have injured him before, gotten him backed into a corner. I can do it again."

"And if we don't?" Xavier questions, finally hitting the woman he loves with his first inkling of self-doubt.

"Well, I guess we better do everything in our power to not find an answer to that question," Forest whispers, letting her fingers coil with the man's.

"And you expect us to do what exactly while you both charge into that hell hole?" Kai questions, his hand scratching violently on his upper arm, something he has picked up over the past few months every time he is overwhelmed.

Keeping our hands concealed behind the back of the couch, I grab his hand the moment he has decided to stop violating his skin, feeling his body jolt at the touch, only urging me to grasp harder. Keeping his focus on his sister, he does not let on how nervous the grasp makes him feel. Still, I allow my fingers to entwine with his, squeezing a little tighter each time he takes a glance at his reddened arm.

Giving me one brief glance, I know he is silently thanking me, not allowing himself to read into the gesture.

I'm just comforting him.

That's all this is.

"I expect Bekah to take you all back to the compound. Talks of peace with the Shifters will be near to impossible now that Elyon has gotten in their heads. We need Marked, and we need them trained well. If we get stuck under that ward, we will need a way out, and the only way we are doing that is with the compounds unified," Xavier says, sounding more and more like the Commander he left buried in New Haven.

"I hate every part of this plan, Evermoore," Bekah says, crossing her arms in defiance.

"We don't have the luxury of being secure. There is no certainty in war," Forest whispers.

"And how do you plan on getting in?" Valerie questions.

"Elyon wants them," Mason says, finally looking back toward the group. "I would be surprised if they didn't have streamers and balloons waiting for you at the front of New Haven's gate."

Finally getting a smile from Xavier, Mason averts his eyes back out the window, hiding whatever shroud of humor the comment might have made him feel.

"I can train your Marked, get them ready for what's to come. I'll give you both two days under the dome. If we hear nothing by then, I'll utilize what allies I have left to seek you out, give me the intel I need to find you both a way out," Mason states, easing no one in the space.

"I am perfectly capable of training my own men. I don't need a Shifter-"

Winnowing before Bekah can finish her statement, Mason has the woman by the neck, his free hand extending out a blade, hovering it over one of the larger veins in Valerie's thigh. Staring me dead on, my hand is hovered near my dagger, his Hold keeping me from making another move.

"I am not some fucking monster you can keep shoved in the back of a closet," Mason snaps, forcing his face forward, inches away from the redhead. "Do not tell me you are capable of more than me. I am years older than you. Mind your mouth next time you speak. As far as I see it, you are as naive and clueless as any other Marked training under me. Keep your mouth in line, and you won't know what it means to see me as the monster you so desperately want to paint me as."

Pulling away from the woman, he releases his Hold, only prompting Xavier to let out a small laugh.

Glaring at the blonde, Mason cranes his head, Xavier's eyes lowered with amusement.

"What?" Mason questions, urging Forest to break a smile.

"I taught you that," Xavier smiles. "Your form is still horrid."

Lowering her brows at the comment, Forest clears her throat.

"And I taught Xavier that," Forest says, both men now wearing a set of frowns.

Feeling the tension build, Kai releases a bottled-up laugh of defeat, his hand clenching mine harder than ever.

Snowballing, laughs break free from everyone's throats, filling the room in hauntingly painful laughter, one that only fear and anticipation can create. Feeling a weight try and pry itself free from my shoulders, I let the sound of the laughter guide me away from my fearful thought patterns, allowing myself to finally take a full breath of air.

Gathering Forest in his arms, Xavier holds the woman tight, as if she is his only lifeline.

"If you both want to make it on time, you need to leave now," Mason utters, throwing us all back into our harsh reality.

Nodding for the both of them, Xavier examines the space, grabbing both boxes with a great deal of disgust.

"Take the car," Bekah sighs, tossing Xavier the keys.

Saying nothing, he nods toward the woman, giving her his own version of a silent thank you.

Pulling away from Xavier, Forest moves closer, my hand falling free from Kai's grasp.

Gathering me, Valerie, and Kaiden, she wraps her arms around our necks, allowing herself to feed into the touch, her brother's arms remaining wrapped around her well after Valerie and I have pulled away.

"I can't lose you," Kai whispers, his sister shaking her head.

"Keep Mark safe for me, Kai." She smiles, lightly kissing her brother's cheek.

"Hold onto the fact I love you."

Saying nothing else, she backs away before Kai becomes too emotional, keeping her emotions in line as best she can.

Nodding at Xavier, Mason moves toward the door, ready to guide us all as far away from New Haven as possible.

"Mason," Forest mutters, the man barely looking her way. "When all of this is said and done, I will help you track down the girl," Forest says, Mason's eye twitching at the offer.

"Tracking her down wasn't for my own self-gain," Mason utters. "She killed quite a few Shifters on her way out of Sanctum's boundaries. I wasn't looking for answers, I was looking for revenge. You know better than anyone why not to feed that drive."

Saying nothing else, he steps out of the cabin, his words feeling much heavier than anyone expected them too.

Letting the group file out of the space. I take in the smell of the outdoors. Leaning against the house, Mason moves toward Kai, his words silent, only meant for the brunette's ears.

Seizing up the moment the man moves away, Mason nudges to the front of the group, forcing us to trail behind him.

"What did he say to you?" I question, watching Kai blankly stare forward. □

"The only way this ends is with Elyon dead."

"You don't really believe that to be true?" I question, waiting for Kai's normal optimism.

Saying nothing, Kai looks away, sulking away from me, forcing his hand to his arm, scratching the skin raw once more.

CHAPTER FORTY-FOUR

FOREST

G rasping Xavier's hand, the drive that should feel like hours of sitting has only felt like a few minutes. Watching the mountains devour the lowering sun, the sky is painted in a variety of colors, each one more vibrant than the next. Taking it all in, Xavier holds the wheel as tight as he can, his hand resting in my lap, my thumb rolling over his knuckles every so often. Drowning my thoughts out to the sound of his rapidly beating heart, I flood his mind with nothing but the best memories I can think of, giving him all that I can until the thundering in his chest dies down to something much quieter. Glancing my way, he watches me for as long as he can before pulling his attention back to the beaten path and the potential debris just waiting to hit our tire at any given moment.

"Thank you for that." Raising my hand to his lips, he kisses gently, letting the touch linger for several seconds. "I'm fine."

"Stop doing that," I whisper, my voice breaking. Kicking the boxes filled with our ballroom attire, I grasp his hand tighter. "You don't need to pretend like all of this isn't terrifying. No one's around-"

"There's no point in making you feel my fear on top of your own, Forest. I'm not going to lie to you and say that I will make it out of there with you-"

"Why would you say that?" I snap, appalled by what he is suggesting.

Laughing in defeat at the comment, the man glances my way.

"You and I both know there is no scenario in which we both leave there unharmed. You are just now getting over the effects of the last time Elyon decided to cross us. I'm not pretending like I just walk away from any of this-"

"You did it again," I hiss. "You keep suggesting you stay back as if-"

"As if I'd stay back if it meant you were safe?" he questions.

"Yes."

"There is no other scenario. If we do not find a way to get Elyon in confinement, and things look bad, I will gladly push you forward and cut the throats of anyone who tries to follow after you."

Saying nothing, silence falls upon the vehicle once more.

"I'm tired, Xavier," I whisper, his focus falling on me once more.

"Tired of what?" he questions, his tone softening.

"I'm tired of you underestimating what my love for you really means," I hiss, yanking his hand up toward my heart. "Do you feel that?" I question, his mouth snapping shut. "Do you feel the way my heart beats?" I question, still receiving nothing but silence. "It beats because of you. It beats because I fight to live for you." Forcing my hold on the brakes, the vehicle comes to an abrasive stop, my hand forcing the vehicle into park, his eyes gleaming with the fear of this energy.

"Forest-"

Forcing off my belt, I slam my hand over his mouth, pulling myself out of my seat, and planting myself onto his lap. Getting him to look at me fully, I take the higher ground, letting his hands grab my waist, my arm wraps around his neck. Leaning into the man, our noses graze, his eyes filled with determination.

"Nothing will happen to you so long as I am breathing," I snap, keeping my hand over his mouth. "This was never your battle to fight, Xavier, and I will see to it the blood that is shed is not your own. I have spent years in the dark and even more fighting for our kind to find peace. Do not think for one second anything I have fought for means more than the life you deserve to live."

Widening his eyes, emotion momentarily cracks through his searing gaze, his hand quick to pry away my grasp over his mouth.

Grabbing the back of my head, he pulls me close, his grasp keeping me as close to him as he possibly can.

"The life I deserve to live is with you," he whispers, his lips inches away from mine. "I will not take any other outcome."

Unable to find my words; I try to speak.

"I-"

"No... I'm done listening. Just come here."

Slamming his lips into mine, my words are caught in my throat, any justification I can find for putting his life over mine quickly fizzling away at the feeling of his touch. Eating away at the very fiber of my soul, any reality without him at my side fades away, the need to feel him as I do now for as long as I may live something far greater than a want.

I need this.

I will always need him.

As he will always need me.

Gliding his tongue across my lower lip, I allow him entrance, feeling his tongue collide with my own, his lips working against mine in a hungry touch. Kissing him until there is no air left in either of our lungs, our foreheads press against one another, our cheeks flush with heat, the tips of our noses touching. Letting out a shaky breath, I close my eyes, letting the impending fear of what's to come eat me alive.

"You know I love you?" he questions, my mind hanging onto every one of his words.

"It's the only thing I know for certain," I whisper. "It's what I'm holding onto."

Saying nothing else, his head rests against my chest, my arms cradling him, letting him listen to my heart.

"You know I love you?" I question, wanting now, more than ever, to understand how true that statement is.

"It's what gets me out of bed every morning, even when I thought you hated me," he whispers. "Of course I know."

Saying nothing else, we hold each other like this for several more moments, embracing the blissful silence, before embarking into the great unknown once more.

Surrounding the entrance to New Haven like an unbreakable force, Officials of varying heights stand side by side, guns drawn and masks raised, each one of their identities concealed, hidden from the naked eye. Seeing Elyon's forces from a mile away, they make no effort to hide, and even less effort to stop our approaching vehicle.

Rolling back our shoulders, we both grip each other as hard as we can, slowly creeping closer to the place we were both forced to consider home. Feeling the car jolt to a stop once we are within twenty feet of the entrance, the gas meter quickly dwindles down to empty, my nose stinging from the smell of gasoline, now leaking from the bottom of the vehicle.

"One of the Marked in the lineup busted the tank," Xavier whispers. "I'd say they want us to get out."

Approaching the vehicle with a plethora of weapons strapped to them, eight Officials swarm our vehicle, making no effort to open our doors to try and pull us free from the vehicle.

Giving Xavier one final look, his lips press to the side of my head, lingering for a few seconds, before swinging open his driver's door. Following in his trail, I push my door open, kicking the boxes out of the vehicle, watching them collect with dirt. Scrambling to grab the gifts from Elyon, one of the men says nothing, grabbing the boxes with zero complaints.

Extending a hand out toward me to help me down, I glare at the Official trying to patronize me, shoving them back several feet with my Hold, raising my brows at every soldier willing to take a step toward me.

"Stay the fuck away from me," I hiss, lowering myself to the ground with a scowl.

Meeting Xavier around the front of the vehicle, he remains just as wary as I, glancing at every stagnant body surrounding us.

"They are not speaking," he whispers, clearly as unnerved as I am.

"They are not doing anything." Looking around at each unmoving body, chills run down my body. *"It's like a damn welcome home party."*

Watching the group step back, a clearing in the middle forms. A figure in silver moves toward us, their hands clasped in front of them.

Smelling the faint inkling of familiar blood, I take a deep breath, the mask more than enough to send me into a state of rage.

"Elyon?" I question, Xavier's head shaking.

"I thought you were ready to drop the mysterious mask act," Xavier barks sarcastically, the figure's head cocking with confusion.

Moving past the Officials, more masked figures emerge, each of their bodies concealed by dark satin robes.

"You are guests in New Haven," one of the Officials finally says, glancing toward the masked figures. *"However, Elyon's followers will not be disrespected."*

Unable to hide his laugh, Xavier shakes his head.

"I really hope you are not suggesting we respect any of you-"

As painful as it was that day of the fall solstice, an eardrum-shattering frequency blares in my ears, Xavier and I crumbling to the ground. Covering my ears immediately, the pain of this noise is more intense than the last time I heard it, jumbling my every thought. Feeling as if my brain is melting, I focus on anything I can, slamming my hand to the ground, feeling the ground beneath me shake.

"That's enough. Elyon wants them presentable and cooperative," the Official says, waving his hand in the air.

Feeling the noise die down, Xavier is the first to get up, his hands dragging me into his arms, holding me against him.

Pulling plugs from their ears, those who have the presence of Marked blood flooding through their body watch us, taunting us with the dozens of forces they have had the time to pit against us.

"Nice party trick," Xavier snaps, getting nothing but a smile from those around us.

"A reminder that you are no longer in your territory. Tread carefully, Evermoore; we'd hate a repeat of what happened the last time you didn't listen."

Taking a step toward the man, I place my hand on Xavier's chest, my frustrations growing more intense with each passing second.

"Is that a threat?" Xavier questions, his mind filling with violent thoughts.

"A threat?" the Official laughs. "It's a guarantee."

Drowning out the noise, every vile thing these people have done swarms my mind. A lifetime of murder and persecution, blindly following whoever ranks highest, no matter who they hurt in the process. Bloodshed, revenge, and evil blankets the group. Rapists, drunks, and murderers, all hidden by the facade of authority or faith to a man who knows only pain. Official or follower, every single person swarming this group is a part of the problem. Their minds are infected, not a single pure thought capable of running through any of their minds.

"Maybe your mother would have lived, had you not been a cowardice-"

"Shut your fucking mouth!" I bark, forcing the man backward, his body colliding with the men behind him, masked figures scrambling to pull on their concealment.

Ready to start up a new round of the noise, I focus on every one of their rotten minds, digging my talons into their rational thinking.

"Enough," I warn, keeping them still. *"We are not children you may taunt,"* I push. *"Do not treat us as if we are not deadly,"* I push. *"That mistake was fatal to ten of you."*

Urging all of those who spoke disrespectfully to grab their blades, Xavier cocks his head. Pushing the thought pattern, I allow every single foolish man who questioned our strength to drive the points into their necks, hitting the ground with dead weight. Watching the device fall from one of the men's hands, I slam my foot down on the device, watching it shatter.

Looking over what's left of the forces, they stay silent, taking a step back.

"Take our boxes to Elyon's quarters and leave them in our room," Xavier snaps to one of the closer men. "That is where we are needed? Correct?"

Only nodding, Xavier moves forward, taking my hand in his own.

Embracing the smell of human and Marked blood alike, Xavier glances my way, giving me his first smile of hope.

"He won't be happy we did that," I smile.

"He won't be happy about anything we do, the least we could do is show him who he has asked to waltz into his home."

Dirty and ridden with filth, the Unfortunate sector is worse than I remember. Crumbling, barely supported by the presence of Officials, we take our time making our way to Elyon's quarters on the Untouchable side of New Haven.

"It's like old times," Xavier smiles. "You, fighting every single one of the forces he throws your way," Xavier grins, a certain light filling his eyes.

"It would have been much better had you always been on my side," I tease, trying to make light of the situation. "You see how easily you took over my persuasion of those men?" I question.

"It did feel nice to watch them drop to the ground," Xavier sighs. "But this." Looking around the sector, life is the last thing to touch the souls of those who reside here. "This is genocide."

Lined up in body bags in the streets, those still managing to work look past the death, stepping over carcasses lining the sidewalks. Blinking green lights touch each person's ear, no one able to have a single free thought.

"It's all coming down," I whisper. "That's why he wanted us back. He needs us in line to maintain what stability he has left."

Smirking at the comment, Xavier says nothing, his hand guiding my focus away from him.

Plastered on the front of the building, a tarp hangs, burnt on the outer edges, a large black symbol painted across its front.

The symbol of the Marked.

Written in black paint, the words

Vivat Signatum

"Long live the Marked," Xavier whispers. "Welcome to our people's revolution, Mrs. Evermoore," Xavier smiles. "Now, let's bring this dictator to the ground."

Moving forward, we work through the sector, more defiant symbols of the Marked floating around the space.

Unable to stop myself from looking, Jolie's bakery is void of light, the windows shattered, the shop ransacked, stripped free of the memories it once carried. Creeping closer to the door, an old flyer remains on its front, Xavier the first one to grab it.

"I am sorry to announce the passing of...." Trailing off, he tries to tuck away the note. "We should just go-"

Grabbing the note from him, I Winnow away from him, taking in the information with a heavy conscious

I am sorry to announce the passing of Jolie Porter, one of the Unfortunate's long-time and most beloved bakers. In light of her grandson's passing by the hands of a vile Marked, Jolie saw to it to end her life on her terms, leaving behind a legacy with no heirs to continue her work. Thank you all for the support you gave Jolie throughout the years, and may Sanctum save us all from the poison that has infiltrated our people.

Long live New Haven.

Death to the Marked.

Dropping the note, I take a few moments to process what I have read.

"Forest-"

"She killed herself," I say coldly. "It would seem not everyone is thrilled with the idea of the Marked."

"Forest, that wasn't you-"

"It was. Let's not pretend it wasn't."

Creeping closer, the man grabs me, running his hand down my back.

"Fine, it was you. Jolie made her decision, as will everyone else in this society. War is coming, Forest, one that will force society back into the same problems it thought it eradicated. So long as free will is compromised, there will never be peace."

"And what side of this war do we stand on, Xavier? The side fighting for the greater good of our own kind-"

"The side that will bring freedom to all those tarnished by Sanctum's reign," he clarifies. "Look around, Forest, what do you see?" he questions, forcing me to look at what remains in this sector.

Looking around, the mindless bodies working through the streets drag along, their eyes barely blinking.

"Not them, Forest," Xavier smiles. "Look closer."

Craning my head up toward the crumbling buildings, dozens of eyes look down at us, watching us with genuine curiosity. Streaked with the black that paints the front of the banner, the bodies lingering above us watch us close, my Hold itching to drag them free from the buildings.

"Easy, Forest." he whispers. "I'd hate you to kill off our fighters."

Hearing it before my eyes can track it, I shove myself and Xavier aside, narrowly missing the dagger headed straight for my chest. Regaining our focus as quickly as we possibly can, a figure looms in the doorway of the building filled with the onlooking Unfortunates, their body covered in a plethora of layering, a white band wrapped around their upper arm, the black symbol of the marked painted on its front. Laughing with joy, they stay still, not even trying to run away in light of their attack.

"I heard you were a quick one," the raspy female voice whispers, her red hair tucked away beneath a tight hood.

Glancing up toward the onlookers, she frowns, another one of her mutuals stepping out from the shadows behind her.

"That's enough, Rowan," the woman utters, my eyes adjusting to the young girl's features.

Beautiful in ways that will carry out to her womanhood, she scowls at the woman, allowing her to pass her.

"Don't mind, Rowan. Corralling in some of the younger Marked in the Resistance has been tedious."

Saying nothing, Xavier and I hold our ground, narrowing our eyes at anyone daring to look in our direction.

Creeping closer, the woman's hair is as bright as Rowan's, clarity finally washing over me.

"Mrs. Auburn?" I question, shaking my head in disbelief.

"In the flesh," she smiles, all of my guards lowering.

Allowing myself to embrace the woman in a tight squeeze, her chip has been deactivated, still latched to her brain.

"How did you-"

"Rowan here helped me out once her group found me creeping within the Unfortunate sector. After you were taken from my classroom, I spiraled, wondering how a girl I cared for so dearly and a Commander I had seen on a few occasions could disappear from thin air so suddenly."

Taking it all in, she focuses on Xavier.

"So, you're the Commander that was in the shadows for so long?" she questions, ready to give him a piece of her mind for all the damage the chips have done.

"More like a poster child," he frowns. "And you," he says, glaring at Rowan. "I thought you made it far away from this shit hole's borders."

Kicking a rock, the girl scoffs at the man.

"Perhaps I felt the need to alleviate all of those still confined in the Prophet's grasp," she whispers. "Not everyone likes being locked away for his convenience."

Scattered with scars, despite being no older than twelve, her voice holds a trauma no child should carry. Raspy in tone, her voice comes out broken, as if it has barely been used.

"Big words for such a small child," Xavier pushes.

"How did things pan out for you and your group after I Winnowed out of confinement?" she asks. "Where is blue eyes?"

Feeling her presence in my mind, I am caught off guard, wondering at what point she had managed to slip in.

Sneaky little bitch.

"Hm," she scoffs. "Switching sides, Forest?"

Ready to pummel a child, Xavier cracks his neck, my hand on his chest.

"You are feeding right into it," I warn, her mouth curling into a smirk.

"I have better things to do than wade through your tormented mind-"

"You better watch yourself," Xavier snaps. "I have an angry Shifter hunting you down, ready to interrogate you in every way possible-"

"No," she smiles. "You don't. That man who thinks he's been following me is far from a beast," she sighs. "Idiotic, yes. But not a Shifter."

Saying nothing else, she waltzes back into the building, wearing a shit-eating grin most children would wear if besting an adult in argument.

Having nothing else to say, Xavier shakes his head, looking at me for some clarity on the situation.

"What is all of this?" I ask Mrs. Auburn, pointing to the clear divide among people regarding our kind.

"Some see your kind as poison, others like us see it as a way out of the control that has scathed society. The Unfortunate sector was the first to fall, run now by those whose souls are still trapped by the chips. Had Rowan not found a way to disorientate the chips in all of us from New Haven, we would be stuck in the very same situation-"

Clever girl.

"We are weening through this sector as best we can, taking what we can out of New Haven's borders. We've been confined here ever since the ward's protective measures escalated. Now I know it is just a way to keep you both inside. The Untouchable sector is as lavish as ever but held together by nothing but a fine thread. Chances are, if you're here, a collapse larger than I anticipated is on the horizon.... Why are you here Forest?" she questions.

Why am I here?

Killing Elyon can't be done without my own sacrifice. □

Sacrifice myself, and I have no guarantee Xavier, or anyone I care about, is safe.

Letting the guilt come over me about the plethora of decisions I have been forced to make over the past several months, I take a deep breath.

"To fight," I clarify. "To find a way to detain your lovely new dictator."

Smiling at the comment, Mrs. Auburn laughs.

"I do hope you accomplish what you are here for. The moment the wards are weak, we are taking the next group of people far from here. Rowan knows the quickest way out of New Haven's reach and I still have enough credibility on the Untouchable side to come and go as I please."

Looking over the woman, the part of myself she once knew is long gone, replaced by a soul that I now see was always there, just waiting to be seen.

"Where is Fallan and your brother?" Mrs. Auburn questions, Xavier now the one to speak.

"Elyon killed Fallan," Xavier explains. "And he will do the same to Kai if we don't find a way to keep him under wraps."

Nodding her head at this knowledge, she looks around.

"The ball. That's why you're here, isn't it?" she questions.

"How many people know of the ball?" I ask, curious how large of an event Elyon could have made this.

"Let's put it this way. Even the Unfortunates got invites and parcels filled with the nicest clothing."

"This isn't our homecoming," Xavier sighs, giving me a stern look. "It's a god-damn saving grace for this crumbling shit hole and you and I are the faces of its catastrophic downfall."

"You weren't our downfall," Mrs. Auburn sighs. "How do you get society to conform?" she questions.

"You take away their free will," Xavier retorts.

"And what happens when they want it back? "

"Rebellion," I whisper.

Elegant dresses and rich liquor aside.

This ball will end with bloodshed.

CHAPTER FORTY-FIVE

XAVIER

T reading more carefully than they did the first time, Elyon's guards guide us to our room without another word, the buzzing presence of Marked energy swirling within the depths of the elegant home. Knowing the layout all too well, I look past the study where my parents took their final breaths, the sound of the chains once confining my wrists now heavy with the presence of a new body. Holding my hand with a firm grasp, she tries to coax my emotions with anything but the feeling of fear.

For years, I carried the weight in my chest that came every time I allowed my thoughts to become too loud. It would suffocate me, making it hard to think rationally. The suffocation would quickly turn to panic, swarming me, threatening to break the cold facade I had been forced to uphold.

"You're safe," she whispers, her voice a gentle reminder that, no matter how many thoughts come crashing into my mind, she is never that far away.

Easing up at the sound of her voice, the void of loneliness I used to wake up dreading, is now just a small hole.

She's here.

She's really here.

You can breathe.

Feeling her own anxieties creep inside her mind, she holds them back as best she can, trying to hide the fears being here has forced onto her.

Waltzing through New Haven while blatantly unaware of her past here was manageable. Coming back here knowing damn well how much it took from her has to be nothing short of hell.

I know it is for me.

"So are you," I push, pulling her just a bit closer. *"I'm not letting you out of my sight behind these wards again."*

Smiling, we stop in front of one of the larger sets of doors in the guest wing, an arch of white lilies made up around its entrance. Glancing at the display of flowers with a coy smirk, the Official says nothing, his mind open enough to give me all that I want to know.

"I guess that's one way for his sister to be with him-"

Perhaps it was not in anyone's best interest for Elyon to educate his men on my life story.

Grabbing the man's hand, I yank him forward, Forest taking a step back to allow me to do what she would have no doubt done when hearing the snide remark in the man's mind.

"You should quiet down your thoughts about my family," I snap, bending three of the man's fingers backward, covering his mouth before he can scream. "You're lucky you didn't make a comment about her," I warn, glancing over at Forest. She watches the display of force with amusement, leaning into the doors with a look of satisfaction. "I would have broken much more than your fingers."

Grabbing his collar, and shoving him away, he runs away with no protest, holding his hand, doing his best to hide his painful cries. Rolling her eyes at the man, he grabs the knob to the door, allowing us both entrance to the over-the-top accommodations Elyon has made.

Sweet bottles of wine and luxury sweets meant for Untouchable events sit peacefully on a table in the center of the room. Decorated with more flowers than I can count, the sheer waste of a resource they take pride in cultivating here is now used as nothing more than decoration. Cleaned up and waiting on the bed, our boxes are wide open, both of our outfits ready to cling to our skin.

Moving closer, a note lingers on Forest's dress, its black inking standing out against the paper.

☐

Music starts at 6.

I expect to see you both there.

- E.M.

◻

"An hour of alone time before we are thrown into whatever it is he has planned for us," she sighs, rolling her eyes at the note.

Grabbing her dress free from the box, its details are beautiful, meant to make her stand out.

Coming up behind her, I kiss the sensitive point of her neck, letting her lean into me, savoring every moment of her like this.

"I can get dressed quickly. Let me help you," I plea, her only response a small smile.

Turning her around, I nudge aside the boxes, resting her back gently on the soft mattress. Watching her hair frame her head in a halo, my hand works quickly, unbuttoning and pulling her pants off her legs, my knees immediately hitting the ground, giving me the opportunity to land my lips along her skin. Working my touch from the lowermost part of her leg to her sensitive hip bones, I trail my tongue along her lower stomach, kissing her warmth through her underwear, her voice silencing any noise of pleasure.

This touch is not meant for arousal.

It is something meant for her mind to hold onto.

Something meant to feel safe.

Kissing up her stomach, I pull up her shirt, helping her yank the material off, her hands going for the clasp of her bra. Having no protests once she is left in nothing but her underwear, I kiss up her stomach, my nose grazing across her skin, her hands holding my head close. Kissing deeper, I make my way up to her breasts, leaning over her body, working as gently as I can across each tender bud, as much as I'd like to get more aggressive with it. Finally working up her neck, her lips finally meet mine, her legs wrapping around my waist, rolling me onto my back.

Both of us ignoring the strain in my pants, her arms wrap around my neck, my body leaning upward into a seated position, her body rested in my lap, engulfed by my arms. Staying straddled on my lap, her head rests on my shoulder, both of us clinging onto every moment of this tender connection.

"I sometimes forget how gentle you can really be," she whispers in defeat. "Behind all of that anger is this boy I so desperately want to protect."

Gathering my face in between her hands, she pulls back to observe me, her eyes scanning my face, before pressing her forehead to mine.

Taking it all in, there's no good way to ease either of us right now. This touch, these moments are the things that keep me going the most.

Reaching her hands beneath my shirt, her hands trail up my scarred back, taking time to gently graze each deep wound.

"Only with you," I sigh. "Only you are the one I have allowed myself to be this gentle with. Back at the med units here, when your mind was wiped, I held you between my legs and felt your presence for what felt like the first time in forever. At the time, I wanted nothing more than to toss Kai back into that hospital before he could interrupt us. You were so kind, so scared. It broke my heart to sense your pain and know there was nothing I could do about it."

"I wasn't even able to know your pain," she whispers, hiding a wave of emotion she has been carrying with her all day. "I wasn't able to protect you."

"You cannot protect everyone, Forest Flower," I whisper. "But you can sure as hell count on the fact that I will protect you," I push, holding her as close as I can.

"It's not just you who holds that mentality, Xavier. Your soul is mine to safeguard."

Saying nothing, I kiss her one last time, letting the touch linger for as long as humanly possible. Biting back her flood of tears, she pulls herself together, moving off my lap, her hands swiping the dress free from its box.

"I fucking hate parties," she snaps, pulling on the dress.

Clinging to her body perfectly, the outfit touches the floor, large slits working up the back and sides of her legs.

Decorated in numerous feathers, its front dips down significantly, reaching her sternum, her breast held back by the tight straps clung to her arms. Meant to show off her body, in every other scenario, this dress would be perfect. Marveling at the sight, I glance at my own box, allowing reality to set in.

"You look stunning, Mrs. Evermoore," I whisper, pulling her closer by the hips, her hand running through my hair.

"I look like bait," she whispers. "Now, let's see you in that tux, Mr. Evermoore."

Thirty minutes into changing, a fleet of Marked servants made their way inside our quarters, each holding the necessities needed to complete our looks. Had it not been for the fact these children had been tortured beyond belief, I would have dismissed them immediately, questioning why they thought it was a good idea to walk in here in the first place.

Sitting in front of a large mirror, two young Marked, shackled and drained, work on Forest's hair and makeup, painting her eyes in dark shadows. Her hair spans down her back in slight curls, a braided crown making up the top portion of her head. Covering her lips in a rich red, jewelry is draped across her skin, her eyes catching a glimpse of me in the mirror as the young male slaves make my hair as pristine as possible.

Hearing the grumble of the slave's stomachs, it's hard not to cover my ears to drown it out. Keeping my shoulders back, Forest struggles as hard as me, biting back the need to cover her ears.

"How long have you all been in his confinement?" I question, watching the heavy eyes of the boy drop down on me.

"W- we were all taken after our Expulsions. Our parents were told we passed, and we all became blood bags for him. Between the four of us, it ranges from three to eight years," the boy says, his voice coarse from screaming. "It's been three months since any of us have been allowed above, so please, forgive us if we are taking our time."

Saying nothing, Forest's gaze lingers on the youngest Marked in the group, a girl no doubt around the age of seven. Unable to watch her observe the girl like this, I dismiss the boy, approaching the girl with timid steps.

Cowering her head the closer I approach, pain swirls inside the pit of my stomach, Forest's hazy eyes gravitating up in my direction.

"Sit on her lap," I urge, seeing the bruises coating the young girl's skin.

Following my request with little to no complaint, Forest's arms widen, allowing the child to take an uncomfortable seat on the woman.

Looking around at the other three, I wave them over, grabbing the sheets from the bed to make the cold floor a little more tolerable.

"The rest of you, come here, take a seat."

All wearing the collars I was forced to make the Marked wear during the Lottery, they happily take a seat, shifting their weight off of their tired legs. Grabbing a rag filled with warm water, I move toward the little girl, gently working it across her skin, cleaning until the dirt has left her gentle face.

In the eyes, she has seen nothing but pain, her lids heavy with the presence of exhaustion. Grabbing a brush from the servant's supplies, Forest gently begins to work it through the young girl's hair, being sure not to tug too tight each time she gets a knot.

"Grab anything you'd like that isn't alcoholic; we will eat none of it," Forest urges the other three, waving her hand to the display of treats the Prophet had prepared for us.

Happily jumping at the request, they grab as much they can fill their arms with, gathering around the pile on the sheets, filling their mouths like starved dogs.

Waiting patiently on Forest's lap, the girl allows Forest to braid her hair, her face significantly younger once all of the dirt has been washed clean from her skin.

"Xavier, look in the drawers for a fresh set of clothes."

Moving with no protest, I grab the first set of smaller clothes I can find, settling on a large shirt, and a pair of pants with a chord to pull them tighter.

Picking up the girl, her small hands cling to Forest, the woman's hands grabbing the clothes with a silent thank you.

Moving themselves into the bathroom, Forest closes the door, leaving me to watch the starved children eat as if they have never seen food.

"You and your wife look stunning," the older girl in the group says in between mouthfuls of food.

"We're here to find a way to set you all free," I whisper, their eyes widening at my remark.

"That's not possible," the boy who did my hair says. "The Prophet's strength is otherworldly-"

"So is the woman in the bathroom with your friend," I smile. "He invited the wrong people into his home."

Saying nothing, the young boy's mouth curls into a smile, his teeth covered in brown from the sweets. □

Waltzing out of the bathroom, the girl looks much livelier, Forest's mind speaking to me quietly.

"Come here. She does not wish to eat right now," Forest smiles.

Moving toward the girls, I raise my brows, wondering what could be more important than having a full stomach.

Reaching her arms out toward me, the small child embraces the feeling of tender touch, her hands small, her eyes bright with fire.

"She told me you look like her father," Forest whispers. "She'd rather you hold her for the time being.

Unsure what to say, I allow the girl's arms to wrap around my neck, my arms easily supporting a body that should be pounds heavier. Feeling her settle into my grasp, there's something eerily comforting in having a child like this need me again, the faint memories of my sister swarming my mind, making it that much easier to hold her.

Crouching down toward the others, Forest grabs a piece of the sweets, nearly ready to land it in her mouth, her nose lingering on its smell.

"Xavier," she whispers, turning to me in confusion. "What does this smell like to you-"

Coughing, the three children begin to panic, each one of their faces growing purple, their hands grasping at their throats. Keeping the child in my arms, I force her face into my shoulder, making her cover her eyes, both Forest and I trying to pull free what could be lodged in all of their throats.

Picking up one of the sweets, I pick up on its scent, my heart dropping at the realization of what sweet berry lingered inside of each chocolate.

Baneberry.

Lethal if consumed when crushed.

Setting the girl down, I tell her to cover her eyes, working with Forest to try and find a way to get the sweets out of the children's system.

Hearing the door swing open once more, the horrendous sound from earlier sends us all into a panic, my arms immediately going toward Forest and the young girl, wrapping them both into my grasp.

Waltzing into the room, a fleet of Officials move forward, observing the children, and the display we had made with disdain. Stepping on the children with no regard for their well-being, each child's face grows purple, the Official's mouths scoffing as the noise forces my ears to ring.

"We should have suspected you'd be emotional enough to feed them," one of the Officials says, nodding their head to the children, their bodies no longer flailing in the ways they had when fighting for life.

Tucking her head into my chest, the young girl tries to get smaller, Forest's body positioned in front of her, hiding her from the fleet of men dragging her companions away by their ankles.

"It's time for you both to show face," the man says, the sound only growing louder, a new device held in the hand of a masked follower.

"Get up."

Gasping in between words, Forest tries to speak.

"L- leave them alone," she hisses, both her and I forcing ourselves to our feet.

"You missed one," the man says taking observance of the young girl. "Get your asses back over here-"

Running forward, Forest collides her body with the man, plunging her teeth into the depths of his neck. Placing the girl down, I watch as the masked figure Winnows away from the space, leaving just two other men, my fight finally kicking in. Running toward the other two men, a loud shot rings off in the room, my hands crushing the windpipe of both men before either of them can draw blood. Slamming them into the wall, both of their skulls crack, a streak of blood moving down the wall with their bodies, the room silent once more.

Taking in deep breaths, I turn around with fear, Forest's body on the ground, the little girl's figure draped across the floor.

Creeping closer, nausea clouds my stomach, the red blood of the Marked Official dripping down the sides of Forest's mouth. Holding the child in her lap, the realization of who the bullet was meant for settles, her wide eyes stuck in place, a large hole settled in the center of her chest.

"Forest-" I start, unable to see or feel anything but the deep-rooted pain of seeing someone so innocent taken so easily.

"I'm done," Forest whispers, standing up, her gaze as cold as ice.

Grabbing the sheet, she covers the child, avoiding my touch entirely.

Moving toward the entrance of the room, she grabs her mask, her voice dripping with rage.

"I've denied my birthright for too long," she warns, my heart dropping at the statement.

"There is only one way this night ends" she hisses, my words caught in my throat. "I'm done fighting the losing side."

CHAPTER FORTY-SIX

FOREST

S till trying to process the atrocious bloodshed left behind in our quarters, the mask aids in the concealment of my puffed eyes and flushed cheeks. Joining me seconds after I had left the room, Xavier knew better than to prod me right now, keeping his hand laced with mine as he tries to navigate his fleet of painful emotions. Hearing the shot ring through the air repeatedly, I run through every scenario that could have played out in order for me to stop what had happened. Pulling myself together, Xavier helps me wipe what's rest of the man's blood off of my face, two guards patiently at wait, ready to guide us into the ballroom of the home.

Buzzing with the loud chatter of conversation, the doors are a gateway to a night that only has a few ways of ending. Holding his hand tighter, other couples in gold masks linger further down the hallway, making their way into the home from the main entrance.

"He has been expecting you both all night." one of the men says, urging the doors a little further open.

"Enjoy yourselves," he says sarcastically. "You'll need it-"

Grabbing the man's arm, Xavier acts on impulse. Twisting it so hard, the man's shoulder is pulled free from the socket, I clamp my hand over the man's mouth before he can scream, his companion taking a cautious step back as the arm loosely hangs at the man's side.

"Watch your tongue around her," Xavier snaps. "If it wasn't for there being watchful eyes, I would have ripped it clean off."

Saying nothing else, Xavier pushes the doors the rest of the way open, both of us smiling, savoring what moments of victory we can before facing the biggest challenge of them all.

Surviving the night.

Decorated in a plethora of flowers and green and gold embellishments, the ballroom is grand, filled with people, all of varying classes. Holding trays and dressed pristinely, Elyon has ditched his Unfortunate service workers, replacing the waiting staff with Marked, all bruised in more places than one.

Looking past the fearful waiting staff, Unfortunates and Untouchables all graze upon the luxuries provided for all, chatting and conversing peacefully, acting as if there was never a divide to begin with. Hearing the lull of music fill the space, piano and violin drowns out the sound of conversation, adding an elegant touch to the already high-class event.

Glaring at the banner hung before the front of the room, I finally get an understanding of everyone's sudden civil nature.

"One New Haven. One solution," I whisper, Xavier's brows pulling together with focus. "It would seem Elyon has cooked up a solution to his crumbling authority," I scoff.

"No one's chips are activated," Xavier shudders. "They are all willingly here."

Filling the space with silver masks, Elyon's followers watch us closely, urging us to move further into the room. Now understanding Elyon's need for us to wear the clothing, all the other patrons wear white, including Elyon's followers. Embellished with golds and greens, each patron outfit is bright, making our outfits nothing more than something to gawk at, keeping us isolated from the rest.

Scanning the room for Elyon, I sense nothing, wondering at what point he will decide to show face, throwing the night into an event of madness.

Feeling the eyes around us begin to focus on our presence, I stay close to Xavier, keeping my head held high, feeling the energy within me threaten to break free.

"Drink, ma'am?" one of the Marked slaves questions, shakily holding up a tray of champagne.

Given the events in our room, the last thing we need is to indulge in anything Elyon has to offer.

"No, thank you," Xavier begins, the lingering presence of a chip behind the young man's ear calling to me. "I think we're fine-"

Focusing my attention on his chip, something inside of me urges me to pull it free, giving me the sense of control I so desperately crave. Keeping my hand lowered, I focus on the energy of the chip, feeling its spindles gently detach from the frontal lobe, before-

Watching the Marked's eyes widen, something wet and warm collides with my palm, quickly silenced with a crush from my hand. A small bit of red trails from behind the back of his ear, my eyes casually glancing down, his chip broken in my hand.

Raising my hand to the glasses, I drop the device in one of the drinks, lowering my eyes at the Marked with playfulness.

"Serve that to whoever is foolish enough to still administer Expulsion tests," I seethe. "Consider yourself freed."

Saying nothing else, I drag Xavier away from the man, watching his smile creep up along his face, his voice gasping with thrill.

"You plan on pulling stunts like that all night?" Xavier questions, the light-hearted boy trapped within the large man's body something so few see.

"We were clearly brought here to be a part of Elyon's show," I smile. "Might as well make it interesting."

Working through the crowds to look for Elyon, his followers in silver struggle to track us with so many moving bodies. Having pried the man's chip away from his head when no one was watching, I question how many of the Marked down here I can alleviate, bringing a whole new purpose to the night.

Locking eyes with dozens of mutuals Xavier and I encountered during our time here, the swarm of questions surrounding our presence escalates, some wanting to question Xavier as to where he's been, others fearful of the presence of a deviant like me.

Both consumed with gray locks, it's impossible to hide the differences we share from these people, making our presence that much more adamant.

Pulling me into the center of the room, Xavier's hands meet my waist, my feet instinctively landing on his own. Keeping me as close as he can, the man takes several seconds to observe me, ignoring the long stares from those around us.

"Those children's deaths will not go unnoticed," Xavier says, my mind focused on nothing but the bloodshed that has already ensued.

"I know that," I smile, wrapping my arms around the man's neck, pulling him just a bit closer. "What I have planned is so much worse."

Smirking, he wraps his arms around me.

"You could never be worse than him, Forest."

"That's the problem, Xavier," I warn, my voice cold. "I fear I am so much worse."

A smile has never left Xavier's face quicker.

CHAPTER FORTY-SEVEN

KAIDEN

"We left them behind to die!" I yell, letting the shame of our actions weigh down on every single person in the room.

Tapping her foot anxiously, Bekah crosses her arms, waiting for me to calm down before speaking.

"Kai, we will do what we can beyond New Haven's borders, but-"

"But what? Xavier and Forest need resources if they are going to make it out of New Haven. The only way to do that is refine the Marked here and have Mason-"

"Don't be foolish enough to think that the power this compound has is enough to liberate both of them," Mason scoffs, observing the room with as much disdain as he had at the front entrance. "Xavier and Forest made it clear what our purpose is, consider yourselves lucky you are out of the crossfires. Do you fail to remember you almost died when the Shifters and Elyon's guards got ahold of you? Thinking any of us have an upper hand on the man is how we found ourselves in this situation, to begin with," Mason snaps, his brows raised with curiosity.

Continuously prodding me, the man clearly holds a disinterest in most of us, only here out of loyalty to Xavier. If he had it his way, he would have been long gone from Sanctum's watchful eye long ago.

"Why is he here?" I question Bekah. Aaron lingers by my side, silently keeping a neutral stance despite the moment we shared back at the cabin.

As quiet as he appears now, I can tell Mason is the last person she wants to hear speaking. It may be easy for Xavier to look past the creature he once was, but to us, he is nothing more than another potential enemy just waiting to turn on us.

"I'm here, *Kaiden*, because I am trying to help my kind and an old friend in need. Why the hell are you here? No one is asking you to be involved in any of this. You can go back to your peaceful little dorm room, and cover your ears until it's all over-"

Shoving Mason away from me, something inside of me snaps.

It pushes me, feeding into the darkest thoughts swarming my mind. Baring my teeth at the man, a part of myself I hate to see makes a brief appearance.

"Stop fucking treating me like a child!" I yell, taking a step toward the man, brushing off Aaron's grasp ready to stop me. "Don't speak to me like I am a thoughtless fool."

Having gathered in my sister's room to look for anything that might give us any additional support, we met dead ends. Seeing the urns the moment I walked in, my mother's stood out, filling my stomach with a pit of shame and dread. All the years she nurtured me, giving me the life I may not have deserved, only to be reduced down into a pile of ash held in a shitty ceramic urn.

Cocking his head at me, Mason scoffs, holding his ground.

In this lighting, I can truly see the man he really is. Dark brown, loosely curled hair, stubble traveling up and down his jawline. A few inches taller than me, the height of his Shifter state easily reflected what kind of man he was. Marked up both arms with black ink, it travels up his neck, scars coating most places on his body in crosshatching. Sporting a pair of golden eyes, the man's age rests somewhere between twenty-five and twenty-eight, that is, if you're not considering the bloodlust that has kept him youthful.

"Lashing out is the last thing anyone wants you to do, but if it will finally get you to stop whining, and man the hell up, please, be my guest," Mason taunts.

He speaks authoritatively, no doubt used to telling others what to do to get his way.

Ready to fight my battles for me, I stop Aaron from taking another step.

"Fine," I hiss. "Fucking give me your best shot."

Watching the man's eyes slightly widen at my offer, he clenches his jaw.

"Kai-"

"Shut up, Aaron," I snap. "I do not need you fighting my battles."

Taking a step closer, Mason eyes are hot with rage.

"You don't want to do this, Blackburn-"

Forcing my fist forward, it lands on the man's jaw, his head snapping to the side. Barely moving his body, he eats the punch as if it were nothing, slowly popping his neck in response.

"You done?" he questions, superiority lingering in his tone.

Unable to hold myself back, I go for him again, this time feeling his fist collide with my side, the air knocking itself out of me. Doubling over, I let out a gasp, doing my best to stop Aaron from delivering the man his next blow.

"Aaron-"

Punching Mason again in the face, Aaron busts the man's lip, his tongue licking up the wound, his eyes lowered with amusement.

"Last time I checked, this was not your fight," Mason hisses, shoving Aaron back, my lungs taking in normal inhales once again.

"Guys, that's enough-" Bekah starts, trying to ease the tension.

Clamoring to get a good hit on the man, I collide my body with Mason's, thrashing my arms like a madman, releasing every ounce of anger I have allowed to stay stored within me. Hitting him as many times as I can, my mind becomes hazy, my thoughts consumed with emotion.

"I couldn't protect Hunter," I yell, feeling his hand grab my fist, stopping me from delivering another blow. Keeping his back to the nearest wall, his face is barely scathed, the cut on his lip already healed. "I couldn't protect my sister, and I sure as hell can't protect anyone here," I sob.

Shoving me away from him, I stumble backward, his hands brushing the front of his shirt, readjusting his clothing.

"Are you done feeling sorry for yourself?" Mason questions, prodding the fire once again.

Fuck this.

Barreling toward the man, I wrap my arms around his waist, forcing all of my weight forward, feeling his footing give out. Hitting my sister's dresser, the room full of people gasps, each one of them scrambling to catch the urns. Mason's back hits the floor with a thud, his hands dragging me down with him.

"Fuck!" Valerie yells, both Mason and I glancing to our right, watching as Fallan's urn slips free from her hands, plummeting to the ground beside our heads. Shakily holding my mother's urn, Aaron reaches out for Fallan's, mine and Mason's eyes widening as the ceramic safeguard of our friend's remains cracks before shattering entirely.

Screaming out, my voice trails off into the air, both Mason and I scrambling to sit upright, no longer focused on my pointless display of anger. Expecting a wave of ash to waft through the air, we stare blankly at the broken urn.

The sight in front of me is nothing short of petrifying.

"Is that...." I begin, unwilling to finish my sentence.

"Ch- check my mothers," I whisper, Aaron's body still working on autopilot, too focused on what lies before us.

Pulling open the urn's top, Aaron glances inside, his mouth dropping into a deeper frown.

"This one's ash," Aaron whispers. "It's sealed in a bag."

Wondering what hope I am trying to hold onto, I glance around, confused and overwhelmed by what is happening.

"Fallan's urn... it was filled with-"

"Sand," Mason utters, dragging his hand through the contents of the urn. "It's fucking sand."

Nudging me off of him, Mason grabs a handful of the sand. Watching it fall to the floor, Bekah finally speaks.

"What the hell is going on?" Bekah questions, all of us utterly silent.

"There were never any ashes in Fallan's urn," Mason whispers. "We just allowed Xavier and Forest into a trap much bigger than we anticipated."

"What are you saying?" I question, the man's hand wrapping around my wrist, helping me to my feet.

"Something tells me our raven was closer to the Prophet than we thought," Mason gripes, giving the room a cold stare. "We were all too blindsided to see it."

Grabbing his blade, Aaron moves toward the front door, looking back at us with pain.

"Then you better get your ass to work, Shifter," Aaron snaps, looking directly at Mason. "Because whatever happens tonight, there will no doubt be repercussions."

"The fight that is coming is not one anyone will be able to come back from," Mason warns. "Are you all prepared for what a war against the Prophet really means?"

"What other option do we have?" I question, grabbing my blade. Moving past Mason, I narrow my eyes at the man. "I've got nothing left to lose."

Grabbing my shoulder, he stops me.

"We are fighting a losing battle, Kaiden," Mason whispers. "If you were as smart as everyone makes you out to be, you would have run a long time ago."

"Is that why you're trying to find the girl?" I snap. "So you can find her way out and run like the coward you are?"

Backing away, Mason's gaze narrows.

"You know nothing about me."

Winnowing before I can rebuttal, Mason leaves the space, all of us a mix of shock and fear.

"If this is sand," Val starts, kicking aside the urn's contents. "Then where the hell is Fallan?"

Putting it all together, I take a shallow breath, shoving past the front door.

"We need to go," I snap to the others behind me. "Forest did know the masked figure in the cabin... we all did."

CHAPTER FORTY-EIGHT

FOREST

Working in perfect unison, Xavier guides me through the patterned movements of dance, our hands raised, his grasp tightly clutching my waist, keeping me well within arm's length. In theory, we should have switched partners five times by now but given the death stare he has given every man who has come near me, the opportunity to change partners has been slim.

Keeping up with the movements so easily, I am almost impressed by the grace Xavier is capable of exhibiting. Holding back a grin, the man raises his brows, a small smirk pulling across his lips.

"What?" he questions, spinning me for what feels like the millionth time.

"So, you really can dance?" I question, watching the wave of dresses flare each time the women are turned in a new direction.

"Spend enough time being forced to uphold the Commander's responsibilities behind the scenes, you find yourself needing to attend a few of these over-the-top events."

Lifting me with one arm, I stay pressed to his front, watching the feathers latched to my train sprawl every time he gives us a good spin. Keeping my arms wrapped around his neck, I hold my forehead to his, letting the moment stay our own.

"In another life, perhaps we could have met at one of these events," he smiles, moving us along with the rhythmic tunes of the violin. "After every Judgment Day, they host an event, letting the new wave of working-class dance the night away like this, and pick partners that they will choose to move onto their middle years with. Of course, I would have been your average Official, and I would be scared shitless to keep my composure around you." His grasp tightens. "But, I would still keep you away from every man's wandering eye and listen to your voice until it was engrained in my mind."

"I'd grab your waist as I am now," he whispers, pulling me just a little closer. "And feel your back arch into my hand as I dip you back," he pushes, leaning down with me, his hand fully supporting my weight. Leaning with me, his lips hover near my throat. "I'd brush my lips across your neck." Gathering my earlobe between his teeth, his words come out with a slight rasp. "And ask you how the hell no one has asked you to dance with them yet."

Pulling me back up, he nudges away one of the patrons ready to switch, keeping his focus solely on me.

"I'd already be mentally picking out our fancy house in the Untouchable sector, imagining every way to get down on one knee one day and claim you as my own for numerous lifetimes."

"All that from one interaction at a party?" I tease, completely enthralled by the man.

Pain is a feeling I have learned to shove down, one I have grown entirely comfortable with. In his presence, it feels as if a weight has been lifted from my shoulders, helping me see a future that seems so far from attainable.

"I wished so desperately for that life when you lost your memories. I thought, if I was close enough, perhaps I could give you a version of your life we never had a shot at."

"And what do you see now? What life do you envision now?" I question, still clouded from the pain of seeing such innocent lives stolen only moments ago, all because I was foolish enough to entertain anything remotely normal.

"Full honesty?" he questions, pulling me a little closer. "I have spent too long chasing you, envisioning every which way to spend life with you, yet there never seems to be enough of your soul to diminish my need for you."

"Seems like an impossible situation with only one of me," I smile jokingly, a serious expression casting over the man's face.

"I know." He stops dancing, his hands holding my face in his palms. Pressing his hand against her lower stomach, I feel pressure, something he has waited to say well before this night, threatening to breach his mouth.

Don't.

Don't give me more reasons to hold onto a life I can never have.

"I don't want it to just be us if we make it out of this. If we find a way out of here, if we find a way to make a home, I do not want to live knowing that a part of you does not carry on in the world well after we are gone. Aging may be slow for us, but death is inevitable. I wouldn't mind leaving this world knowing I did one thing right. The one thing I never got."

Widening my eyes, the proposition he has put before me eats me alive in every way possible.

"Are you asking-"

"Not now. God, not in the next ten years. Sanctum knows I would be terrible at it and fucking foolish for suggesting it in the first place."

All his life, he has only known loss.

Every good thing he has ever seen has been violently ripped away, taken in a way he inevitably blames himself no matter how hard he tries to rationalize why it has happened. Death of varying ages, all painfully showcased in front of him, forcing him to see the cost of a life that he was dragged into.

His sister, his parents, and any other innocent soul he has witnessed meeting death's hand, all because I am too weak to do the one thing that can end so many peoples suffering.

"I'm not telling you to agree to anything, or even agree with me-"

Gently pressing my lips to his before he can spiral, I silence the thought pattern he was set to fall down. Only easing up once I feel him kiss me back, his lips devouring mine, taking his time to savor the way I melt into his touch. Becoming a mix of silenced gasps and tight grasps, I kiss the man until his worries have faded, finally giving my mind the peace it needs.

"You deserve every good thing in this life, Xavier Evermoore. If a child is ever graced with you as their father, that would be their greatest gift. If this is your way of asking me if I think you can do it, then yes, I do."

"And you?" he questions, the answer hanging in the air around us.

"First, I keep you safe," I whisper. "Then, we may create any reality we want."

Feeling the worries swarm him, I take a shaky breath.

"Do you know I love you?" I question, holding him as close as I possibly can.

There is a moment of pause, his eyes watching me close, trying to read into my emotions further than what I have allowed him to see.

"I do," he whispers, resting his head against mine.

"Good-"

Feeling a tug on my dress, my body is yanked backward, hands of varying sizes moving me into the patterned dance line, the women spinning, the men handing me off one by one, making it impossible to keep track of Xavier through the chaos. Watching as women throw themselves onto the man, I am pulled further into the wave of bodies, numerous hands grazing across my body, Xavier's gray curls barely poking through the crowd, his body too surrounded to make leeway quick enough to close the gap of distance between us. Trying to focus on one individual person long enough to set my sights on who deserves to have their wrists snapped, a pair of cold hands grab onto me, working more forcefully than any of the hands I have felt previously.

Looking up at the partner that has claimed me long enough to catch my attention, my jaw is painfully grabbed, my cheeks squeezed, resting in the hand of the last person I wanted to see. Watching me with his gray streaked hair and golden eyes, Elyon's eyes are narrowed, his facial hair perfectly trimmed for the circumstances. Wearing a suit as dark as my dress, I glance around where I can, taking notice of the figures in silver, now lingering around the space, watching me with hands tucked inside their robes.

Sensing the presence before I hear it, each figure holds a device meant to create the noise, ready at any given moment to disorient me and Xavier if we decide to do anything foolish. Keeping my face in the man's hand, he drags me close, giving me a good look, his nose grazing down my cheek.

"A fetus?" he questions in a mocking tone, something cold touching my torso.

Forcing me to look down; the small blade he had tucked in his sleeve stays pressed against my lower stomach, my body one bad move away from having my intestines spill free from me.

"Should I poke you and make sure there isn't already one floating around?'

"I'm here, just like you wanted. You can keep Xavier out of whatever hell you have planned."

Trying to find Xavier once his hand has dropped from my face, he slaps me, forcing me to keep my focus on him.

"I'd say right now he has five women and three of my followers ensuring enough noise is ringing in his ears to keep him in his little dance circle for long enough for us to talk. Want him safe, then you will have a little respect," Elyon warns, tucking the blade back at his side. "Now wrap your arms around my neck and let us have a little father-daughter bonding time, you know, given you killed my favorite child."

Baring my teeth at the man, I bite back the urge to bring up Andrew, knowing damn well Elyon is already buried deep within my mind.

"Poor Andrew Blackburn," Elyon scoffs. "Had you not meddled in my affairs, perhaps he could have lived a full life with his lovely wife and raised that son of his to be significantly less useless."

"Lovely wife? Do tell me, did she ever fall for any of your advances, or did she continue to see you as the vile piece of trash you've always been?" I question, fully aware of the psychotic fascination he has always had with Lockland women.

Maybe if he had never sought out Katiana's mother, she would have never felt the urge to find a way to diminish a man with his abilities.

"I was foolish enough to share what I am with Katiana's mother. I should have known the Lockland women were nothing but filthy whores just waiting to bite when you least expect it," he grovels.

"Don't look so disappointed in my perception of them. You are, after all, an Evermoore, right?" he questions, grabbing at my hand with the ring.

Tugging it away from him. I suppress every urge to deliver him as much pain as I can before the noise can begin.

"What the hell are he and I *both* doing here?" I question, doing my best to find the real source of his lovely invitation. "I thought you had enough fun when you sent Josh to torture me in every way he could possibly think of."

"So you are really awake?" Elyon scoffs. "I should have known better than to trust that imbecile to do any of my bidding."

"You sound disappointed to see me," I grovel. "To think I was hoping to kindle a relationship with the man whose blood created me," I hiss.

"Do not act out because you are embarrassed of your lineage. Morgan is your true last name, whether you'd like to believe that or not. It took more than my blood to create your miserable existence. It's a pity Katiana's mother had to waste such a blissful night with me on something as useless as creating you."

"It's a pity even after all these years, she still haunts your mind. Enough for you to destroy her daughter's family, and lock Katiana away as if-"

"As if what?" Elyon prods, gathering the hair on the back of my head into his fist.

"As if anyone could see you as a being worthy of caring for," I hiss. "You may be in my mind Elyon, but I am in yours, and nothing but darkness coats your soul," I seethe.

"Is that so Forest?" he questions, baring his teeth for all to see. "And what do you think lingers in your soul?" he pushes, dragging his lips closer to my ear. "I'll give you a hint.... Your fiancé over there would not like the answer."

Tugging my head away from his grasp, I narrow my eyes, revolted by the way his laugh seems to bounce off of the walls.

Catching a glimpse of Xavier breaching through the group despite the noise they have forced onto him, I take a shallow breath, finally allowing myself some room to focus on the conversation at hand.

"Really, Elyon, why the hell am I here? Why the grand display of force with the children and a party to this magnitude? We both know your slipping control is not motivation enough for you to be foolish enough to drag Xavier into this as well, what the fuck are you not saying?" I question, his mouth curling into a smile.

"Perhaps I wanted to see if your skills were truly as impressive as so many have made them out to be," he sighs. "Or perhaps I am dying to kill off the only other person capable of creating my Marked." he pushes, my stomach swirling with fear.

"Cute talking points, now tell me why you really wanted us here," I push, his mouth dropping into a frown.

"I spent so much time envisioning what speaking to you like this would be like; I always imagined you'd be filled with much more fire," he pushes, shaking his head in disappointment.

"You'll know why I needed him here once the time is right," he smiles. "But I guarantee tonight will be a night you regret deeply."

"And why is that?" I question, keeping hold of my cold facade.

"You came here for answers," Elyon warns. "I brought you here to show people who my rat truly is."

CHAPTER FORTY-NINE

XAVIER

Hearing nothing but painfully disorienting noise, my body is grabbed in every way possible, hands of varying sizes slipping beneath the overlayer of my suit, swarming me like wild animals, every one of their faces concealed by a large masquerade mask. Turned every time I try and get a half-decent look at Forest, any strategic thought pattern on how to get out of this is washed away, my focus solely on whoever has taken the residency directly in front of me.

Face to face with a curvy woman, her chip blinks green behind her ear, her eyes glossed with the presence of coding guiding her every action. Catching a glimpse of Forest's gray locks, the imagery is quickly stowed away by the wave of moving bodies, the woman's hand grabbing my chin, forcing me to look at her.

"Are you scared yet?" she asks, her voice hauntingly cold. "Are you scared of the game you two have thrown yourselves into?" Her thought pattern dictated by the Prophet's word.

Shoving me away from her, a man takes her spot, his hand wrapping into my hair, keeping me still as his mindless companions swarm around us.

"You should be fucking petrified, knowing he has your sweet Forest Flower in his hands, dragging a knife across her soft underbelly as we speak," he warns, my blood running cold. Shoving past the pain in my head, I focus my Call on his mind, dictating and nuzzling my way as far in as I can, urging the man to take several steps back, leaving me the breathing room I need to turn my head.

Feeling a harsh slap across my face, one of the daintier women in the swarm smiles like an idiot, watching me catch my breath as I touch my pulsing face.

"Nice try. This room is filled with Elyon's followers and even more of his Marked slaves. It is awfully cute watching you try and wiggle your way out of this one." She laughs, my body buzzing, begging to release the rage swarming inside of me, no matter how many casualties are caused as a result of my unpredictable energy.

Forcing my head up, I grab the woman by the neck, tugging her toward me, too focused on Forest's safety to take notice of the light behind her ear.

"This whole room is filled with his mindless followers," I hiss. "You think I have enough morals to put your worthless, brainwashed life over hers?" I question. "You're merely a distraction."

Twisting her neck with ease, I shove her back into the next body, ready to take over, watching all of the eyes widen around me, the group too condensed to cause those who are free of their chip's control to take notice. Groaning and wincing, I block out the noise as best I can, setting my focus on the next person foolish enough to get near me.

"You think she will end up as lifeless as young Lily?" a voice questions from my side, ready to open the floodgates of pain I have in store for them.

"Perhaps Forest is next-"

"Keep my fucking sister's name," I start, grabbing the collar of the man foolish enough to speak. "Out of your goddamn mouth," I push, Tossing the man into the group, ensuring all of those around me close enough to touch my suit feel the weight of his body slam into them. "And sure as hell keep my woman's name off of your filthy tongue," I hiss. "Did you never learn it was a sin to utter the devil's wants?"

Watching the man flail, the noise from the device dies down, heads turning in my direction, the looming presence of Elyon's masked followers creeping free from the shadows. Baring my teeth toward every onlooking eye, people cover their mouths in confusion, chalking up the commotion to be nothing more than the cause of one too many glasses of the shitty champagne they have been serving all night.

Feeling a hand clamp down on my shoulder, I turn, ready to rip their head clean off their body.

"Xavier," her frantic voice gasps, her eyes wise with age.

Still wearing the same layers of clothing she often chose to wear in my presence, I take a few seconds to bring myself down, only truly registering her presence the longer I look at her.

The Teller.

Ready to ask her a million questions, she lands her hand over my mouth, silencing me before I can start.

"You need to go," she warns, the followers in silver taking a step closer.

Prying her hand from my mouth, I avoid the urge to look for Forest to give her the focus she needs.

"What is going on?" I question, wondering at what point she could have made it out here.

"I told you to never come back if you got out of here. She is awake. Why are either of you back here?"

"I thought-"

"There is something else at play here, Xavier."

Looking around, I finally find a break in the group.

"Forest-"

"Xavier," the Teller snaps, grabbing my chin with urgency, forcing me to look at her. "You don't understand, Forest-"

Watching as the bodies around me drop to the floor, every single mindless mutt groans in pain, their knees colliding with the marble in a loud thud. Snapping our heads toward the two bodies in the middle of the floor, she stands with a cocked head, her focus on Elyon, his wide grin threatening to tremble under the weight of his fear.

Holding Elyon by his neck, he grabs the back of Forest's head. Both powerful entities are locked into a stare down neither has any intention of breaking. Breathing shakily, I see their knife blades threatening to breach each other's lower stomachs, their eyes hot with rage, his eyes wide with amusement.

"Never speak to me like that again," I hear her snap, her voice low and cold.

"Big words for such a foolish girl," Elyon gripes, his eyes snapping up toward me.

"I suppose that is the end of our dance."

Saying nothing else, the pair steps away from one another, each one unharmed, left with nothing but a stare deadly enough to bring down this whole room.

Forest

"A rat?" I question, letting the humor linger in my tone. "All this time, and you couldn't come up with a better name?" I question, his eyes filling with amusement.

"What would you call yourself, then?" he asks, his eyes narrowing with hate. "As far as I see it, you have infested all that I deemed to be sacred in my world. You came in, infesting the minds of my Marked, who had the greatest potential. Now, you stand in my home, mocking me as if you have the upper hand in any of this when we both know that is the farthest thing from true."

Rolling my eyes at the man, I tug him closer, wondering what Andrew would think of the pathetic display Elyon has put on for all of us.

"Well, Fallan killed him," Elyon sighs. "No need to dwell on what daddy dearest might have thought."

Hearing something linger in the man's tone, I can't help but laugh in his face.

"Do not be jealous you are the last thing I would consider to be anything close to a father figure," I warn. "Last time I checked, all Marked derive from you in some way or another. I'm sure you have plenty of clueless mutts just begging to crawl under your wing."

"The two 'mutts' I took pride in are nowhere to be seen. Dove's head was ripped clean from her body, and you are the last woman I would consider to be one of my more impressive creations," he gripes.

"That is because I am not your creation. Taking away the Lockland's hard work in my creation already?" I push. "No wonder Katiana's mother sacrificed her life in order to make you-"

"Make me what?" he questions, grabbing the back of my head, my voice silenced by the sudden movement.

Smiling at his display of force, I find comfort in knowing I can so easily get into his head. So long as he focuses on me, the worst parts of his abilities are nowhere near Xavier.

"Suffer," I push. "She wanted to make you suffer."

"Are you seriously speaking to me as if you have any chance of besting me?" he questions, his fragile ego shattering at the idea of me having any advantage over him.

Reaching my hand out, I grab his throat, tugging him down on my level, his eyes inches away from my own. Feeling a sharp point touch my torso, the violent thought pattern we both shared now comes to fruition.

Gripping one another vigorously, our free hands point our blades toward one another torsos, the power display we now share, one many would find amusement in.

"You've learned well," Elyon smiles. "Sadly, whatever you think you are capable of means nothing in my presence."

"And why is that?" I challenge.

Barely able to glance up given my grasp, his eyes wander the space, his energy buzzing through the veins under his skin.

"Every single person in this space bends at my will," he whispers, his face nause-atingly close. "Even those who think their minds are stronger than my forces, sink into the grasp of my Call with something as simple as-"

Cutting himself off, I pull my focus away from him, nearly everybody in the space at a standstill. Still swarming Xavier enough to keep his focus off of me, the crowd surrounding the man is the only group of bodies in motion. Seeing the petrified expressions line every single person's face, I take several moments to register what has happened, fully aware of how little control anyone around us has. Stuck like statues, everybody once silently conversing is now stuck in place, awaiting the release of Elyon's Call and Hold.

Watching me with thrill, I take notice of a familiar face creeping closer to Xavier, the one person I wanted isolated from this whole event.

"She got out?" I question, my eyebrow twitching with annoyance.

"Perhaps if you weren't playing with fire-"

All at once, the energy inside of me bursts through the floodgates, each and every mind forced into the palm of my hand, including the moving patrons Elyon ensured would keep Xavier distanced. Wanting nothing more than to watch their heads bow as they cower on the ground, I force the thought of kneeling into every single person's mind, watching as the bodies drop to the floor, overcome by my presence. Too buried into every mind, any Call Elyon might have instilled is overpowered by my own, his voice gasping as his own knees threaten to buckle. Watching the Teller drop to the floor before she can finish her statement to Xavier, the man's eyes snap up in our direction, my focus back on Elyon's confused state.

Hearing people begin to struggle as they try and process how they ended up on the ground, I peer at the vengeful force in front of me, leaning my body into his knife, allowing it to slice straight through my skin, not giving him the satisfaction of a flinch. Tearing the knife from his hand, I drive my own into his side, watching him wince, His legs struggling to support him, our minds two drives of force fighting for the upper hand.

"Do not, for one second, undermine the evil you have allowed into your home," I warn, prying the knife free from within me. Letting it clatter to the ground, a splatter of blood surrounds it, the rich scent of my blood catching the attention of any Marked close enough to smell it. "Do not question who and what I am, Elyon Morgan, for that will be your most fatal mistake.... Never speak to me like that again."

Taking a step back from me, we both stare at the knife, the wound already healed. Pulling free the knife from his side, he tosses his own blade on top of my own, two of the richest Marked bloodlines mixing in a puddle on the ground.

"Big words for such a foolish girl," he smiles, a truth lingering in his tone that I can't quite decipher. "I suppose that is the end of our dance."

Feeling Xavier's large hands on me, I focus back on reality, watching him immediately touch my torso, finding nothing but a hole in the place where there was once a knife. Glancing at the floor, he quickly processes what has happened, glaring at Elyon, his body shifting in front of me.

"There is no time to play the hero now, Xavier," Elyon smiles. "It is time for the real fun to begin."

CHAPTER FIFTY

FOREST

Winnowing away from the both of us before either of us can attack, Elyon claps his hands as loud as he can, the entirety of the room going dead silent, my Call no longer embedded in the minds of those around us. Disoriented and confused, those around us try and recall the past few moments, wondering how and why their small talk over champagne turned into a dance circle they have no recollection of becoming a part of. Hearing whispers escalate the moment the blades are noticed, faint whispers turn into loud comments, each one asking who had managed to get hurt. Clapping once more, Elyon raises his brows at the mix of people, the followers in silver only that much closer.

Keeping one of his hands behind his back to keep hold of me in some way, Xavier's need for reassurance has skyrocketed, even if it means just a small clasp of my hand in his own. Glancing back at the Teller, we lock eyes, the spew of information ready to leave her tongue something she knows better than to repeat. Stepping into her mind, I hear her fearful thought patterns, each one ending with me in some way.

"Go," I hiss. ***"Before I reconsider allowing you mercy."***

Not arguing with me on the topic, I watch as she makes a run for it, shoving past anyone she can, her fear of me far greater than anyone else in this room. Too distracted by Elyon to notice her sudden exit, the followers in silver push people toward the center of the room, following along with Elyon's need to group his guests so close together. Waving his arms like a madman, Elyon places his finger over his mouth each time someone tries to speak to him, the room a mix of subservient Marked slaves, clueless Untouchables, or malnourished Unfortunates.

"If you would all just quiet down-"

"What the hell is going on?!" a man yells, silencing Elyon before he can start. "What the fuck are you doing to us-"

Slicing the man's throat clean open, one of Elyon's followers barely reacts as the man's body hits the floor, all of those around him screaming in panic, looking around frantically for a way out. Too petrified with fear to make a run for it. Elyon rolls his eyes at the panic, laughing with amusement at the pain he has created.

"I told you all to quiet down," Eyon gripes. "Clearly, I am going to have to take more extreme measures to get you all to listen."

"How long before we interfere?" Xavier questions, his interference the last thing I want right now.

"Stay quiet," I warn, squeezing his hand just a bit tighter. ***"He lives for the theatrics."***

Watching the pool of red collect our feet, clueless patrons stifle their cries, giving Elyon the full attention he so desperately wants. Keeping our focus on the man, Xavier and I silently anticipate his next move, keeping one another in line.

It doesn't matter what display Elyon puts on for all of these people.

Deep down, I know my little show scared him, rattling him enough to create distance between us.

Perhaps now he will begin to realize what kind of lines he has chosen to cross.

"Clearly, the night has decided to kick itself off," Elyon sighs, his supporters pushing in closer, the familiar presence I sensed once before burning my skin like fire.

Those not enthralled with Elyon are trembling, each one questioning whether or not they will make it out of this event alive.

"Tonight is not only a night to show you the true evils of our society, but it is also a night of rebirth."

Moving closer, I hear the faint whispers of the follower's thoughts, their need to draw blood insatiable.

Please, get closer.

I dare you.

"I have caused cities to crumble and built empires from the ash that settled," Elyon continues, the need to tear into every person around me eating me alive.

"Tonight, I did not only invite you into my home but also showed you the true face of power that lingers within this society," he gripes, clearly thinking highly of his rank at this moment.

Wagging his finger, the lights to the room become dull, nothing but the bright gleam of the candle stands lighting the space, the setting sun casting numerous colors through the large glass windows.

So many theatrics.

Is he prepared for the final act?

I know I am. □

"You have all come for retribution, for safety, to find a reason for your suffering. You are not only here as my guests, but also to witness the downfall of a formidable foe."

Feeling a smile pull across my lips, something within me darkens, the need to end this night eating me alive.

Glancing back at me, Xavier has a smile of his own, the drive to kill Elyon eating the man alive.

"The power that has ruined your society stands before you now," Elyon signals, his hand flying out toward us, every pair of eyes dead set on Xavier and me. "Time to watch it all burn down."

Show time.

Hearing a loud slam, the doors to the space fly open, Shifters of varying sizes creeping into the space, each one of their minds infested by Elyon. Grabbing and thrashing at any person they catch sight of the bodies once condensed in a small ring now all flee, taking a hit from one of the follower's knives or a sharp-edged talon from a Shifter. Smelling the accumulation of Cleansed and Tainted blood alike, Xavier and I move without a word, our hands tugging at our clothing, the blades we ensured stayed concealed under the layers finally coming out to play.

Sliding my knees across the ground, I slip under Xavier's legs, thrashing out toward Elyon, his body narrowly missing my blade's edge as his own blade barrels toward my front. Moving to the side before he can hit me, Xavier delivers a clean slice to the man's forearm, watching as the wound heals in seconds. One of Elyon's followers grabs Xavier, tugging him back as hard as they can.

Fighting much more aggressively than the other followers, the masked vigilante delivers multiple strikes toward Xavier, each one deflected, only giving the man the distraction Elyon wanted. Taking another strike at Elyon, I barely avoid a Shifter's talon from meeting my back, quickly forcing the creature away from me with my Hold, watching it collide with the marble wall surrounding the space.

Laughing with thrill, Elyon watches with delight, mine and Xavier's eyes meeting every so often, his need to get away from the follower heightened now more than ever.

"The fight has only just begun," Elyon snaps.

Tripping and stumbling over the dress, I tear away at its bottom, leaving me in nothing but the tight corset, and an underlayer meant to stow away the cold. Taking the parts of the dress I had ripped away, I stop Elyon's blade from colliding with my skin, wrapping the fabric around the edge of the blade and twisting it with all of the force I have. Watching it fly free from his hands, he narrows his eyes, using his body as his next best line of defense.

Colliding with me, we become a scramble of limbs and energy, each one of us trying to get the upper hand into the other's mind. Hearing his fleet of swarming thoughts, I tap into anything I can, delivering him a harsh blow to the face, feeling bones crack beneath the skin of my knuckles. Rolling away from his body, my energy begins to dwindle, my focus on Xavier and the follower now dangling in his grasp, lifted off the floor by their neck.

"Nice try," Elyon groans, the wound I inflicted already healing. "I'm not done with you yet."

Feeling a searing pain in my leg, Elyon drives a small knife into my thigh, my scream shaking the room, his body leaning over mine with determination. As if he is weightless, Xavier barrels toward the man, tossing him backward, hitting his face as many times as Elyon allows. Becoming their own swarm of tangled limbs, I force myself to stand, narrowly avoiding one of the follower's hands from grabbing my hair. Sensing their Cleansed blood from a mile away, I narrow my eyes at them, urging them forward with my Hold, ripping their mask clean from their face.

Petrified and confused, a young man looks back at me, someone no doubt still in their younger years at the Academy. Grabbing them by the neck, they beg for me to let them go. Looking back at Elyon, he forces himself on top of Xavier, glancing back at me with a look of malice.

"My father wants a show," I snap sarcastically. "And you are the main event."

Grabbing the man's blade, I slide its edge over my hand, forcing my palm against the man's mouth, holding the back of his head until he has consumed several drinks of my blood. Closing my eyes, I focus on the way the blood works through his system, feeling the way it changes the very fabric of his DNA. Groaning out in pain, his eyes flutter open and closed rapidly, the iris within the center of his eye gathering a new tinge of gold. Staring back at me in fear, his eyes are clouded with the presence of Marked energy, perhaps two traits lingering in his soul.

I guess he'll never know.

Tearing into his neck with my teeth, I clamp down on his larger artery, feeling the way his Marked blood rushes through my body. Watching Elyon as I do so, his shock is visible, visible enough that Xavier manages to shove him off of his body, his eyes wide once he looks at me.

Trying to fight against the grasp I have on his neck, the man tries to push away, fighting until there is not a single movement left in his body.

Tossing him to the floor once I am done, a new wave of energy washes over me, one so powerful, I wonder if I could bring down this whole building with one twist of my wrist.

Standing, keeping Xavier away with his Hold, Elyon shakes his head with delight, focusing his eye on me with a narrow look.

"It's that easy then?" he questions. "You make Marked in a blink of an eye?" he questions. "I'll need something better than that."

Saying nothing else, my mouth pulls into a grin, the swarming presence of something new approaching the building festers in my mind.

"Fine," I whisper. "So be it."

Shattering what's left of the windows, a fleet of black and white feathers dives into the space, pecking and clawing at every deviant individual they can find. Taking the moment of confusion to move forward, I force my Hold onto Elyon's chest, watching him collide with one of his masked followers, both scrambling to stand as I force Elyon's Hold away from Xavier. Consuming the space, ravens and doves scream out with joy, littering the space with bloodshed no one could anticipate as talons slash jugulars left and right. Giving some the opportunity to flee during the confusion, the swarm of birds Elyon had thought he kept locked away in his home for some grand act set their targets on him, his eyes snapping to me, a large grin playing across my face.

Taking a stand next to me, Xavier quickly grabs my face, running his thumb over my cheek, his eyes wide with confusion.

"When is this over?" he questions, his energy quickly draining.

"When I say so."

"Show me what your allegiance looks like," Elyon whispers, his focus toward us, neither of us having the time to react as the follower in silver once at his side, is now directly inf front of Xavier.

Ready to yank the person away from Xavier, Elyon is already behind me, his hands grabbing my waist as he turns me around, forcing me up and off the ground before slamming me to the floor. Taking a moment to catch my breath, the birds begin to fly away the moment my Call loses grasp, my head dodging to the side, Elyon's fist colliding with the floor rather than my face.

"Do you submit?' Elyon questions, the varying presence of multiple Marked bodies still swarming the space.

Anyone foolish enough to stay is either one of his followers or a brainwashed slave ready to bend at his will.

"Do you not see the truth, Elyon?" I question, focusing my Hold on every lingering party patron, prioritizing tearing at their skin, pulling it apart in a painful drag. "I always win."

Kicking him away, I turn on my stomach, extending my arms out, watching the bodies of all who remain drop to the floor, the follower in silver pausing, Winnowing away from Xavier and taking a stand next to Elyon. Watching me from his position on the floor, Xavier's eyes track the streams of blood now leaving every person's neck, its path leading to my hands, my wrists cut from my own doing. Letting their blood work directly into my system, the hue of gold surrounding my iris grows brighter than it ever has before, my legs moving for me as I stand. Surrounding my body with the blood of two dozen Marked, it floods my system, making it effortlessly easy to keep Elyon, his follower, and anyone else far away from me, Draining the bodies until they all stop moving, no one but the four of us remains, everyone beside me cowering, my hands clenching as I seal my wrists shut.

"Do you submit?" I question, something sinister touching my soul.

"How many children does it take?" I yell, taking a slow step, the room shaking at the sound of my voice.

"How many innocent Marked lives need to suffer, before you realize the truth?" I question, keeping Xavier on the ground.

"How many times must we come back here before you realize what allegiance to *me* really means."

Unable to recognize my own voice, Elyon blinks blankly, his body Winnowing. My heart drops once he has found his way behind Xavier.

Holding the man's head down, he points a blade against the side of his head, warning me to not take another step without speaking.

Fearful and in awe of my display of force, his follower in silver creeps closer, my focus solely on the man before me.

"Come closer," I whisper, now in the minds of every Shifter that remains, all of the creatures taking a stand beside me, the power play here undeniably gut-wrenching.

Holding the man I love in a deadly position, my ability to kill these men with little to no thought is prevalent, my forces far greater than anything Elyon can throw at me.

I can kill him.

I can kill Elyon.

Looking Xavier in the eyes, I see him rationalizing what that course of action would entail. Keeping my focus on his fearful eyes, his words touch my mind, the rage driving my actions coasting at a high level.

"Let him kill me, then stop him," Xavier whispers.

"I promise you, I will find you in the next life, and the one after that... the love I have for you is not confined to this life. Please, Forest, don't-"

It doesn't matter how much of an advantage I have.

Elyon has Xavier.

He can hurt Xavier.

I can't do this.

I won't do this.

Nodding my head down, I feel my knees buckle to the floor, the Shifter's heads lowering with me. Letting my energy settle down, I keep my focus on Xavier, letting the look of satisfaction wash over the Prophet's smug expression.

"Let him go," I whisper, Xavier's body thrashing.

"Clearly we both have exhausted all of our surprises for the night."

Laughing with a wide grin, Elyon shakes his head, his foot nudging Xavier's head away as he takes a full stand.

Stepping over Xavier, his follower in silver keeps the man's head down with their foot, watching as Elyon looms closer to my kneeled figure.

Crouching down on my level, the man scans me up and down, our eyes in a fight for dominance.

"Not quite," Elyon smiles, confusion closing my mind.

"You really thought killing Xavier was my final act?" he questions, cocking his head with delight. "You and I both know, that benefits no one."

Glancing back at his follower, he gives them a nod, snapping his focus back on me in a matter of seconds.

"You have impressed me tonight, sweet one," Elyon whispers. "Perhaps I was foolish to think Dove was my best child."

Shifting uncomfortably at the comment, the familiar presence of the follower eats me alive, Xavier's yells and shouts drowned out by Elyon's voice.

"A deal is a deal," he whispers, his tone so low, only my ear may hear his word. "Time to reap the rewards."

CHAPTER FIFTY-ONE

XAVIER- THREE YEARS AFTER HER EXPULSION

I have never found much pleasure in social events, let alone anything that requires me to dress up in a suit. Perhaps that's why I go out of my way to throw on this Official uniform, walking and talking like one of the military personnel, feeding the Prophet the excuse of getting to know my people as my reasoning for pretending to be Adams's inferior. In some way, I think Adam finds joy in pretending to dictate me, feeding into the delusion that when I am in uniform, I am nothing more than a talented Official, one seeking his guidance. On the surface, he dictates me like every other malicious asshole, feeding into his superiority complex like no other. Behind closed doors, he begs for my forgiveness, blatantly unaware that I am not the one calling the shots. The title of "Commander" means nothing so long as the Prophet lingers in the shadows.

Tuning out the sound of student's lifeless conversations, I follow the other Officials into the auditorium, narrowing my gaze each time a woman's eyes linger on me for too long. Toying with the watch in my pocket, I rub its top repeatedly, doing my best not to look for her in the crowd.

I shouldn't be here.

I know my place.

Elyon ensured her Expulsion would become my own personal torture.

One wrong move, one wrong word, and her life and mine may become forfeit.

But I have to see her.

I have to know she is okay.

I have-

Pausing, a familiar face clings to me, his conversation with his mutuals quickly becoming one-sided. Glaring at me with a blank expression, as if he can hardly process my presence in his vicinity, I glance behind me, half expecting his focus to be on Adam or another one of his mutuals he knows far better. Pulling away from his conversation with upper leadership, I take several steps away from the looming auditorium, giving myself the distance needed to gather my thoughts.

Exiting the same doors I came in from, I already start strategizing the best way out of here. The last thing I need is for the Prophet to catch wind of how much time I have spent at the Academy, attempting to steal glances at her in passing-

"Hey," his voice shouts out, my body going rigid at the sound of something so familiar.

Stopping dead in my tracks, I clench my hands by my side, pulling on the fakest smile I have ever utilized. Turning on my heels, I am met with the piercing green eyes I know all too well. Looking as if he has hardly aged in the past three months, avoiding him had been considerably easier when he was preoccupied running routes for Adam or worrying about his children in some way or another.

Now, he stands before me, observing me as if I am a stranger.

"You're that new Official... Xavier Hayes, right?" Andrew questions, crossing his arms with a cocked-head expression.

Nodding my head, the new name the Prophet has given me sounds like poison on the tongue of others. "Yes sir," I whisper, struggling to find my voice. "You're Andrew Blackburn, the one overseeing my training, correct?" I question, curious as to how the man knows my name.

"Adam has told me about you and covered for my ass every time I was supposed to report your progress. Every time I went looking for you, it was as if you disappeared before the workday was done. Though, given Adam's glowing report, I'd say you will end up being one of my most talented fresh new faces," he smiles, getting a closer look at me. "How old are you anyway?"

Readjusting my collar, I find it ironic to be having this conversation.

"Twenty-one," I lie through my teeth.

"Almost the same age as my daughter," he pipes up, my heart dropping. "Same age as my Kaiden."

Kaiden.

The young boy Andrew fought so hard to protect.

Staring at me with raised brows, it is as if the man is analyzing my face, trying to understand where I came from.

"Forgive me for staring, Xavier, you just look so familiar," Andrew whispers, puzzled by my presence.

"I get that a lot," I whisper in defeat, wondering how this conversation could impact me as much as it has.

Glancing toward the auditorium doors, the man checks his watch, anxiously anticipating the presentation he is about to partake in.

"Well, listen, my boy-"

Grabbing my shoulder, something inside me flares alive, both of our eyes widening the moment we feel the touch. Watching his eyes twitch, the light-hearted nature they once carried sinks into confusion. Narrowing his eyes at me once again, his free hand comes clamping down on my other shoulder, his eyes widening the longer he looks at me.

"Hayes?" he questions, sweat coating my forehead out of anxiety. "That isn't your last name-"

Grabbing hold of the man, I take a step closer, burying my Call within his mind. Wondering how his chip's functionality could have had a glitch, I sense the presence of suppressed memories, small droplets of the truth seeping through the cracks of his mind. Wishing more than anything I could open those floodgates, I put a stop to the leak, thinking of Forest and Forest alone.

No one can remember.

The only person I want to remember anything is gone.

I can't have anyone jeopardizing the truth.

"My last name is Hayes. It has always been Hayes," I whisper, feeding his mind a new thought pattern. *"You are Andrew Balckburn. You are Katiana Blackburn's husband and Kaiden and Forest Blackburn's biological father. You are my overseer, my mentor, you think of me as nothing more than a young and new Official eager to learn your ways. You do not recognize me... no one does."*

Saying nothing else, I let the man go, watching as his eyes blink away his confusions once more.

Taking a mental note of his faulty chip, I see the mental image of his finger prodding the chip from above the skin, pushing it, and poking it every which way over the past several days.

Mindwipe or not, the man remains curious about what he has allowed inside his mind.

Saying nothing else, Andrew rubs his eyes, looking around the space in confusion.

"Xavier?" he questions, glancing down at his watch. "Oh, shit, I have to go," he groans, giving me a slight nod.

Keeping the conversation light, the man walks away, slipping past the doors as quickly as he had left them.

Balling up my fists, the rage is the first to hit me, eating away at my every waking thought.

Wishing I could rip my own heart out, and let all of this suffering end for good, I clamp down on the pocket watch, fighting back the urge to open it, to give myself even an ounce of hope.

"What the fuck are you doing here?" his cold voice questions, every reminder of what I am fighting for rushing back into my mind.

Fallan Markswood.

Not even giving him the courtesy of a hello, I turn on my heels, grabbing the man with all the force I have. Indulging in the luxury of being an Official in an Unfortunate's presence, I drag the man away from the doors, pulling him closer to an isolated hallway, slamming him firmly into the wall. Watching his face grow red with heat, the man lowers his head at me.

"I'm going to have to ask you to rephrase your wording, you bastard," I hiss, imagining how nice he would look with his eyes plucked free from his head.

"Do I need to remind you who we work for?" Fallan questions, baring his teeth at me, his hands brushing off of his front.

Looking toward his pocket, something sticks out, my hand reaching out before he can stop me.

Shoving him away the moment he tries to reach for the vial, I look over the engraving on the side, taking notice of the initials.

F.B.

"You took her fucking Cure-All?" I question, watching the man's eyes roll.

"How else would you strike up a conversation?" he questions, a malicious smile spanning across his expression.

"You keep your filthy hands off of her-"

"For shame, Xavier," Fallan snarls. "Lay a hand on me, and the Prophet will know quicker than you can attempt to tell her how much you love her."

Filled with enough rage to rip his head clean from his body, I take a step back, watching him with lowered eyes.

"If you want to kill her so bad, why have you not just done it?" I question, his eyes rolling at the question as if the answer is obvious.

"What's the fun in killing her so quickly? I'd rather you enjoy watching her pretty little self fawn over me."

"If you lay so much as a finger on her-"

"You'll what?" he asks, taking a step closer. You'll hurt me?" he smiles. You'll make me suffer?" Shoving my chest, I hold my ground, letting him become eye level with me. "Last time I checked, Xavier, all the cards were in my deck."

Biting my inner cheek, I glare at the man, ready to leave this conversation.

"The Prophet loves your little Official act by the way," Fallan smiles, my body stopping in place. "In case you were wondering how sneaking around was going. He loves it so much, he wants you to befriend her, feed into daddy dearest's little mentor facade," Fallan smiles. "That way, when I deliver her to you, you may feel her hate as well as the pain her death will bring to the both of you. What better way to spend your final moments?" he questions, my throat dry, unable to find a response.

"They know?" I question, tugging on my uniform.

"Of course they do," Fallan whispers, readjusting my collar, his cold eyes stuck on my own.

"It's cute really, that you think you are capable of stopping any of this."

"Hey, Fallan," a female voice calls, a young blonde waving her hand to get the man's attention.

"Yeah, hold up, Valerie," he yells, his entire personality shifting in a matter of seconds.

Turning his head toward me, he smirks, my hand ready to smack the expression clean from his face.

"Perhaps I am curious how the sister tastes," Fallan smiles, all inner restraints within me snapping. "I know Dove was a real treat-"

Striking the man as hard as I can across the face, his body plummets to the ground, the blonde at the end of the hallway letting out a yelp.

Towering over the man, I press his head into the floor, ready to bash his skull in. Pulling my lips close to the man's ear, I poke my finger into his side, pressing down until I have surely bruised one of his ribs.

"They can't blame me for what they don't see," I warn. "Touch her, and you're a fucking dead man," I spit. "If Dove were here, I'd bury my Call in your mind, and make you be the one to rip her nasty head clean from her body," I seethe. "Tread carefully, Fallan Markswood, you're lucky my love for her triumphs my hate for you."

Letting go of the man, I give his head a good thump into the ground, fully aware of the cameras, now pointed in our direction.

Once watching the hallways, each camera, focuses on us, a deep-rooted pain running down my front, a lesion tearing away at my skin.

"Careful, Xavier. You do not touch what is not yours," the Prophet's voice whispers in my mind, a gentle reminder of how little control I have in any of this.

Marching forward, I ignore Fallan moving past me, giving the blonde a quick untruthful story revolving around my "Unfortunate harassment." Having felt every single one of his pockets for the ring while I was on top of him, I met nothing but dead ends, curious how many times I could encounter the man without pummeling his face in. Replaying his words in my mind, I watch as he and the blonde slip into the auditorium, a sick need to release my anger unhealthily creeping into my mind.

Perhaps I'm curious how the sister tastes.

I would rip his tongue free from his mouth.

I would hold her down and keep her in confinement.

I would do anything for him to never know what her vulnerability looks like.

Mind and body, her soul will forever be mine to safeguard.

Forcing down my bitter thoughts, I ignore the searing pain in my front, shoving past the auditorium doors, making one of my most foolish decisions yet.

What's another lesion if it means I see her?

What's the pain when the loss of her has made everything in my life miserable?

It doesn't matter what the Prophet may threaten me with.

They have already taken everything that matters.

They want me to play their game? Fine.

The problem is, I'm one hell of a cheater.

Joining the other Officials lined up against the wall, they watch the Unfortunates with hate, just itching for one of them to act up, ready to drag them across the floor.

The superiority complex the ones in uniform carry is appalling, something they pridefully showcase, as if they themselves aren't as easily manipulated as those below them. Taking a quick scan of the room, I see Andrew conversing on the sidelines of the stage, his focus on the school's leadership. Moving further into the space, I keep my body pressed against the wall farthest from the other Officials, letting my eyes hyperfocus on the crowd of students.

Like the air has left my lungs, a familiar scent clings to my nose, the rich presence of Marked blood swarming me, making my mouth salivate like a madman. Clamping my mouth shut, a faint mix of cinnamon and vanilla touches my nose, all of my senses rushing into hyperdrive, my body flooding with a warmth I thought to be lost long ago. Every so slightly turning my head, I see a head of dark brown locks, her hands fidgeting with her sleeves, her body isolated from all the others in the bleak, gray school uniform.

No.

This isn't happening.

Barely turning her head, every insufferable moment of my existence for the past three months suddenly becomes bearable.

Every scar.

Every cut.

Every night I allowed my screams to drown out in my pillows until the tears ran dry.

All for a moment like this.

A moment to see her again.

"F- Forest," I whisper under my breath, my voice breaking from the weight of my emotion.

Still as beautiful as ever, her vibrant brown locks stow away the gray, a certain innocence surrounding her expression.

Equally as clueless as Andrew, she cowers from the crowd before her, one she could so easily have kneeling at her feet with the use of her Call.

Watching the eyes of the Officials around her mentally undress her, I clamp down harder on my inner cheek, wondering at what point a brain bleed in one of these men could be played off as a freak accident.

Small and still, she smiles graciously at anyone willing to look her way, her eyes far richer in green than any other time I have seen her.

Walk away, Xavier.

Taking a step back, I try and rationalize.

Walk away-

Watching his eyes gravitate toward Forest, his blue eyes stare her down hatefully, her body going rigid at the interaction. Hearing the sound of her heartbeat pick up in my ears, the dull, faint whisper of our connection yearns for her touch, anything to spark the fire that has run on nothing but delusions for months. Gravitating his eyes toward me, the hand of the blonde grabs the man's chin, pulling his focus away from Forest, her body shaking from a mix of adrenaline and fear.

Walk away, Xavier.

Walk away-

"How insufferable is all of this to you?" I say before I can stop myself, her body jolting at the sound of my voice.

She's scared.

He has scared her.

Slowly turning her head, she pulls her chin up to look at me, every fiber of my being holding back the urge to grab her sweet face and kiss her until he cannot breathe. Widening her eyes at the sight of me, she takes a quick observation of my less-than-orderly uniform, her eyes stuck on my own. Taking a mental image of every little freckle painting her face, I scold myself for not noticing the ones she had along her nose, their color so faint, you almost have to be touching noses with her to see them.

Delicate dark lashes, and a set of beautiful plump lips. Her cheeks grow red the longer she watches me, her anxious fidgets now derived from something other than fear.

There's my girl.

Unable to find her words, she fishes for something in her mind, too startled by my words and my presence to continue on the conversation. In her world now, Unfortunates are outcasts and sympathy toward their kind is the last thing she knows how to entertain. Looking at her now, I question if this is the innocence Forest carried in her more youthful years. Tedious and wary, never knowing what to say or how to react.

"Because if you asked me, all I see is a bunch of pretentious assholes all having a reason to showcase their worst traits," I mutter, giving the room a hard look, focusing in on the group of students kissing ass to upper leadership. One of the curly heads sticks out in the group, his looks easily comparable to that of Andrew.

Kaiden.

"Overachievers," I whisper, dragging my finger to the blonde boy who has been licking the ass of every Official since I walked in. "A bunch of idiots wanting to sign their life away to be a glorified hall monitor," I continue, finally landing my finger on Fallan, my hate far greater than I can display at this moment. She needs to know her defiant thought pattern is not just her. "And people who never really had a chance at winning in this life," I admit, still uneasy every time I am forced to watch the Officials dish punishments to the lower-class citizens of this society.

Looking around as if I just uttered the world's greatest secret, she moves closer, whispering in fear.

"You- you just spoke about Unfortunates-"

"Like they are people?" I question, scanning my nail bed. "I won't tell if you don't."

Seeing the one thing I have been hoping for the entirety of this conversation, her mouth pulls into a wide grin, my heart fluttering at the sight of her sweet smile. Reminiscing about the way it felt to have that smile pressed against my skin as I held her to my chest, I take all that I can get, watching the woman in awe. Leaning my head into the wall, I cross my arms, challenging her to continue the conversation with my silence.

Come on, Forest Flower, let me hear all of those deviant thoughts.

"I think we spend a great deal of time making people feel seen when that's so far from the case," she says, a smile creeping along my lips.

Watching her cross her arms like me, I fight back every urge to grab her and kiss every square inch of her body, covering her mouth with my hand, letting my lips be a reminder of the touch we used to share.

"Do you not feel seen?" I question, knowing damn well her being seen is the last thing anyone needs.

"I feel like I don't fit in. There's a difference. Maybe it's because I am seen too much."

Pushing her further, I raise my brows. If she leaves this conversation with one thing, let it be that she is far from abnormal.

"And what's wrong with not fitting in with all of what I just pointed out to you? You want to be stuck in one of those bubbles?" I question, smiling like a damn drunken fool.

"Says the Official," she pushes, speaking to me as if I am not military personnel.

There's that fire I admire so deeply.

Even with her memories so far from her, the fire within her is brighter than ever.

"An Official who knows how to utilize the good parts of my job," I tease, wishing that this was truly the job I have been tasked with.

"And what good parts are there?" she questions, my eyebrows furrowing as I try and think of a response.

Seeing you.

The only good part of any of this is seeing you.

"Well, today I was supposed to be scanning the Unfortunate sector for contraband. Instead, I got to weasel my way into a conversation with you simply because of how awkward you looked pressed against this wall."

"Is that humor I am sensing in your tone?" she questions, my smile dropping.

If only you knew the way I could make you laugh.

"You seriously said that as if I am incapable of humor," I mutter, shaking my head in disbelief.

"You're the one who only speaks to me because of how I 'awkwardly stand,'" she says, quoting me as if she is trying to mock my tone. Unable to stop the noise that escapes my lips, my first genuine laugh slips free from my mouth, the sound foreign to both of us. Composing myself, I force out a hint of the truth.

"There might have been other motivating factors-"

Feeling the lesion expand, I snap my focus up to the other Officials, their hands waving me over, trying to get me to join the group of upper leadership on stage. I'm unsure how much longer I can keep up this conversation. Taking notice of my wandering eyes, she looks at what has grabbed my focus, staying silent as I begin to move past her.

"What's your name?" she asks, grabbing my sleeve. My heart breaks at these innocent questions.

My name is your name.

You are an Evermoore.

You will always be a part of me.

"Xavier," I mutter, her hand dropping its grasp.

Why couldn't she hold on for just a little longer?

Why does this all feel like my own personal hell?

"My name is Forest-"

I'm going to regret this.

"I know," I whisper, the lesion on my front expanding, warning me not to say anything else. Moving away from the conversation to join the other Officials, I keep my focus forward, fighting every urge to turn around and give her one last look. Guiding me closer to the stage, the other Officials begin to playfully shove me, my eyes averting to Fallan and his deep-rooted look of taunt.

"I don't know when, and I don't know how, but mark my words, Fallan Markswood; there will be a day you suffer for your sins," I whisper, his mouth pulling into a smirk.

"Careful devil," he hisses. "Your Forest Flower is now my Little Dove."

Feeling immense anger at the comment, I say nothing else, letting the pain of the lesion silence me, the bind constricting my throat enough to drive any man mad.

CHAPTER FIFTY-TWO

FOREST

S aying nothing else, he grabs me by the hair, dragging me across the floor, forcing me by Xavier's side. Throwing me into him, the follower lets up on Xavier, watching with a cocked head as he gathers me in his arms. Feeling a looming sense of guilt, I memorize the intricate details of Xavier's face, taking as much time as I can to observe the beauty in every aspect of the man.

"I love you," I whisper, pressing my lips to the side of his head, letting my voice trail off in a whisper next to his ear. "That's the only thing that matters."

Yanking my hair again, the follower pries me away from Xavier, both of us forced into a kneeled position with Elyon's Hold, our bodies constricted, barely able to move.

"Reap the rewards?" I question, my brows raised with confusion. "What the fuck are you talking about?" I hiss, not indulging in one of the many mind games Elyon loves to play.

"I must say, Forest," Elyon starts, ignoring my question. "You have not displeased me." Circling us as he speaks, his boot presses into my back, his hand just one movement away from slicing the back of my neck with his blade, paralyzing me with few movements.

I have to be careful.

I have to be diplomatic about all of this.

One wrong move and all that I have worked for comes crumbling down.

"You worthless pig!" Xavier shouts, peering at Elyon as he circles us. "You are a coward, just waiting for death to greet you." Xavier snaps.

Slapping him hard across the face, I thrash against the Hold, my eyes focused on the follower in silver.

"Yes, Forest, take a long hard look," Elyon gripes, grabbing the back of my neck, his hand forcing me to stay looking forward. "Get a good look at the reason for this whole night. I may be vindictive, but I sure as hell needed the extra support to come up with a ball like this," he hisses. "At the end of the day, what is a god without their loyal disciples?" Elyon questions, a scoff rolling off Xavier's tongue.

"Disciples you have manipulated and tormented like puppets. You are no god, Elyon Morgan; you are simply a fool."

Smiling at the remark, Elyon cocks his head at me.

"Fear the man who fears no god, Xavier Evermoore," Elyon warns.

"And who said you were our god?" I question, malice lingering in my tone.

"Gods do not kneel, Forest," Elyon smiles, a grin of my own working along my lips.

"She who kneels before god may face any foe."

Forcing my knees off the ground, Elyon and his follower brace for my actions, my hands outreached, ready to finish what I started.

"Careful, Dove," a familiar voice whispers from beneath the mask. My body immediately seizes up, Xavier's feral expression quickly dying down. "We wouldn't want more bloodshed than we already have."

Pulling up the bottom of the mask, every single noise goes silent, his deep blue eyes landing on mine, the slight sweep of his raven locks lingering on his forehead. Letting the mask drop to the ground, I am unable to find my words, Xavier's eyes wide, both of us stuck in a petrified state.

As if time itself had never moved forward, the past six months become non-existent, his lungs taking in full breaths, his heart beating rapidly within his chest.

The heart I saw ripped from him.

The heart attached to the soul I thought I loved.

Fallan. Running his hand through his hair, he yanks down his hood, giving Elyon a respectful nod, his arms crossing as he peers down at me and Xavier.

"Look at this," Fallan whispers, shaking his head with disbelief. "I'm gone for six months, Dovey, and already, you've allowed him to violate you," Fallan mutters, his voice so distant from the man I once knew. "How pathetic."

Yelling at the top of his lungs, Xavier tries to break away from the Hold, my face stuck in a blank stare, unable to look away from the man.

"H- how did you-"

"Deception, beautiful," Fallan smiles, Elyon grinning at the man with great pleasure. "It's funny what you can accomplish when two people so skilled with the mind come together. It was so easy to dump some sand into my urn before it was so carelessly handed off to you. You didn't even consider letting me rest with my parents-"

"You demon!" Xavier yells. "You filthy fucking Marked. You are a damn disgrace to our kind-"

"Watch it, Xavier," Elyon warns, raising his hand, the man's throat closing. "I don't like when you back talk."

"Stop it," I barely utter, my lip trembling as I speak.

Hearing Xavier's faint gasps, his lungs beg for air.

Silence it.

Silence them.

"What was that Dovey, I couldn't hear-"

"Shut your mouth, Fallan Markswood," I hiss, forcing my hand up, his hands immediately grabbing his throat, my eyes darting to Elyon. "Let him go or I snap his head clean off, just like his little bird."

Crossing his arms as he watches me, Elyon shakes his head, rolling his eyes with annoyance.

"Damn children," Elyon mocks. "Can't have any theatrics these days."

Watching him nudge his hand, Xavier gasps for air, his voice rasp.

"F- Forest, go-"

"Be quiet, Xavier," I hiss. "Just, be quiet."

Hearing the edge in my voice, Elyon raises his head, my hand releasing Fallan, his throat coughing, trying to get a decent breath.

"You fucking bitch-"

"That's enough, Fallan," Elyon gripes. "We are not here to hurl insults or taunt, Mrs. Evermoore. We are here to make a point, to show what real fealty truly means."

Kissing the ass of the man, Fallan closes his mouth, peering at Elyon, anticipating his next move.

"What now?" Fallan questions, staring blankly at both of us.

"Now? Now you get your reward."

Xavier

"For six months, I allowed Fallan to plot, ready to savor both of your demises, watching the way your blood may stain the floor," Elyon starts, waving his hand toward Fallan. Prying a knife free from his side, he hands it off to the man, his eyes wide with thrill. "Six months I have allowed him to fester with hate, ready to watch the way your eyes widen each time he speaks."

Trying to get a good look at Forest, she stands utterly still, her hands clenched, Fallan's focus solely on her.

"All this time you have spent running, trying to find a way to get an advantage on me, when in reality, I have always held the biggest advantage of all," Elyon pushes, my heart racing within my chest.

"All of this pain, all to avenge his sweet Dove," Elyon mutters, Fallan's jaw clenching at the comment.

Looking her up and down, Elyon glances down at his blade, Fallan's eyes hungrily devouring the sight.

"I suppose it is time," Elyon sighs. "I'm ready for the real work to truly begin."

Pointing the blade toward her from a distance, I try and force myself away from the ground, pulling at my shoulders violently.

"Forest, why don't you come here and get a taste of real pain," Elyon gripes, his eyes clouded with darkness.

Taking a step away from the Prophet, Fallan moves closer toward me, nothing but revenge scathing his mind. Holding up his head as Forest takes several uneven steps, my lungs struggle to find air, her body moving as if his Call is infiltrating her mind.

"Forest, don't-"

"Quiet," Elyon snaps, waving his hand, my mouth clamping shut, nothing but groans and yells stifled behind my sealed lips. "Your pain will be the best part of all of this," he hisses. "Watching the woman you love, ripped away from you in the blink of an eye."

Outreaching his arms toward Forest, the man smiles widely, the knife outreached toward her chest, her body only a few movements away from colliding with its point.

"You really did mean something to me," Fallan whispers as he moves past the woman, his hand coiled around her neck, holding her still. "I think I will always love you in a way that brings me nothing but conflict," Fallan continues on, her body rigid. "You were a better fuck than your sister."

Yelling as loud as I can, I cause more injury to myself than I do wiggle room to find a way out. Cocking his head as he watches me, Fallan shakes his head, taking a step closer, his body crouching down to my level.

"It is horrific, isn't it? Watching someone you love, moments away from taking their last breath?" he questions. "I never wanted any of this Xavier. I wanted a life of peace with the woman I loved. I'm sure that much you can understand. I found out quickly that a life of peace without Dove is not plausible. Perhaps now you will understand me a little better."

Forcing my head up to watch, Forest takes one final step toward Elyon, his arm surging forward, her body lurching into him on impact.

Finally allowing my scream to exit my lips, something violent rips through my throat, her hand wrapping around the Prophet's neck as she gasps for air. Watching him glance down at her with joy, Elyon twists his wrist. Fallan smiles wide, Elyon's eyes immediately snapping up toward us.

"Forest!" I yell, something wet touching my face, my tears spilling free from my eyes. "Forest, please-"

"Look how pathetic you are!" Fallan yells, shoving my head to the floor, his voice filled to the brim with glee. "Can you feel it now, Forest?" he yells. "Can you feel the pain my Dove was forced to feel by your hand?"

Letting my scream continue on, my voice has grown coarse from my yells, not one single rational thought entering my mind. My sobs nothing but hysterics.

My flower.

My light in this dark world.

I just need to get to her.

I just need-

"D- did you really think?" her voice questions, both Fallan and I going dead silent, our eyes snapping to Elyon. "That I was that naive?" she questions, her voice so very distant, her body no longer slumped against Elyon.

Holding the blade in her hand, her hand is clamped down around its edge, her back turned toward Elyon, her eyes lowered, filled with something malicious.

Taking a stand next to Forest, Elyon scoffs at the woman.

"Now you've gone and cut yourself, my dear," he smiles, turning the blade around in her hand, letting her hand wrap around the hilt. "We wouldn't want you getting hurt."

Too choked up, I can't find my words, the Hold still forcing me to my knees.

Sliding her eyes in my direction, the look she wears now is one I have never seen. Raising her chin in the air, she shakes her head at me, a grin spanning across her lips.

"Weak men," she whispers, gravitating her focus toward Fallan. "So weak you did all of this to avenge a narcissistic, vile bitch."

Patting Forest on the back, Elyon smiles, slinging an arm across her shoulder, pulling her in a little closer.

"I have no shame in picking my favorites," he smiles. "Your allegiance tonight was more than I could have ever asked for, my daughter," he smiles, my eyes growing wide.

"F- Forest?" I question, my voice shaky.

"You were fighting a losing side, Xavier," she whispers coldly. "I picked the winning one."

As if her tattered clothes and cut skin have melted free from her body, the outfit she wears shifts in front of my eyes, a cloak as dark as night clinging to her body, her hair wound up in numerous braids, her skin clean, untouched by any blood. Following her actions, Elyon wears something very similar, his cloak decorated with gold thread, their hands locking as they stand side by side.

"Y- you said-"

"That I'd kill her?" Elyon snaps at Fallan, my focus only on Forest. "I said I'd ensure that my useless daughter stays dead. Clearly, the daughter I value ensured that happened long ago," Elyon hisses. "You think I give two fucks about your pain over her death?" he questions. "I wanted my daughter to show me what she is capable of, what better way to showcase that power than an event as grand as this?"

"Forest," I say more clearly, her eyes barely looking in my direction. "You knew?" I question, my voice groveling.

"I know many things, Xavier," she smiles, barely looking my way. "Including when to swear my loyalty to my family," she continues. "I appreciate the ring," she smiles, looking over the part of me with delight. "But let's be honest. You are the farthest thing from my family."

Feeling my heart break, I struggle to breathe, wondering at what point my heart has broken enough to kill me on the spot.

"You're working with Elyon?" I yell, her eyes finally giving me a little more focus.

"I didn't know I was until my heart stopped. Turns out Josh's extravagant torture plan helped me in more ways than one."

"The conversation she and I had was very constructive back at New Hope. Sadly, it took all the best parts of her to reemerge before she fully appreciated them. I sent Josh out to torture her, knowing he was hot-headed enough to kill her. All that was left was giving her the reward of seeing you both like this after she found sand in Fallan's urn. It's a shame I don't have a camera. Both of your faces right now are priceless."

Yelling like a madman, Fallan tries to charge forward, Forest's hand already raised, forcing him into a kneeled position beside me.

"Pathetic," Elyon whispers, glancing down at his watch. "I suppose it is almost the end of our night, sweet one," he smiles. "I think it's time for our guests to get going."

Smiling at the man as if he has not tortured the both of us for years, she nods, taking several steps closer to the both of us. Crouching down on our level, her eyes finally meet both of ours, her hand raising to touch my cheek, my body instinctively flinching away for the first time from her touch.

Watching her smile drop, she grabs my face, forcing me to look at her, her voice dripping with malice.

"I was fighting a losing battle standing by your side," she whispers, her nose inches away from mine. "Love is strong, but nothing beats the feeling of sweet victory."

CHAPTER FIFTY-THREE

XAVIER- ONE YEAR AFTER HER EXPULSION

E very part of my soul is telling me to run away from this event and pretend as if it doesn't even exist. How pathetic must one be to crash a bunch of teenage Untouchable's social, hoping to get a quick fix of liquor and stir up enough commotion to cause a fight? Over the years, the idea of inflicting pain on others has grown considerably more tolerable, making the need to feed into human's sickest desires for violence that much more enticing. After hours of listening to the Prophet's critique of the work I've been doing and even more, staring at my wall, wondering at what point insanity will take over, I finally settled on crashing the event, knowing damn well this is the last place Andrew would allow her to be.

I have not seen her since her Expulsion let alone entertained the idea. Seeing her would be earth-shattering, forcing me to break rules that only put us both in danger. Learning the Prophet's ins and outs from the inside is the only way to get leverage. As long as they believe I am loyal, then I have an edge that Forest and I desperately need.

"Hey," a voice shouts, my head snapping up from the blank stare toward the fire. As cocky and arrogant as his father, a boy very similar to Adam stares me down, his cup filled to the brim with a liquid I'm sure gets him the attention of women he so desperately desires. Walking with two other thick-headed idiots, his thoughts surrounding who I am escalate, the foolish thought pattern of messing with me seeping into his mind. "All guests are supposed to stay inside for now until the Officials are done with their final rounds," Josh seethes, his face recognizable from the pictures in his father's wallet.

"I am sure if an Official wanted to bust your shitty party, they would have done so by now," I hiss. "So move along, I'm already in a shit mood," I admit, peering up at the man with anger.

"I think you are confused-"

Standing up, I grab the little weasel's shirt, tugging him forward, my face initially concealed by the mask and hood I chose to wear. Tugging down my mask, clarity washes over the man's expression, his eyes growing wide at the realization of who stands before him.

Unlike most of these idiots, Adam has felt no shame in sharing with his son where I truly stand in this society. Given I carry the facade of the Commander to some, it comes as no surprise Josh is debating whether or not to piss his pants in front of me.

"O- oh, sir-"

"Save it," I hiss, shoving the man into his friends. "Run along and entertain your party," I snap. "I'll continue drinking in peace," I mutter, toying with the flask settled in my pocket.

"Sir, I didn't mean any disrespect, you just looked like-"

"An Unfortunate?" I question, the hate these people carry, one I never thought could top mine. "Yeah, that's kind of the point."

Waving them away, they all look flustered, my eyes catching a glimpse of something spilling free from Josh's pocket.

Grabbing the chain with my finger, I tug it out of the man's confinement, watching it gleam in the fire's light.

"You big on jewelry Josh?" I question, fleeting thoughts of the name "Blackburn" passing his mind.

Suddenly much more interested in the item, I bury my Call into his mind, watching him with a cocked-head expression.

"Whose necklace is it?" I question, completely confused as to why I care so much.

"F- Forest Blackburn," he stutters, all other noises fading around me. "I stole it from her during homeroom, she is supposed to be coming tonight, and I figured I'd be able to get her a little drunk if-"

Up before he can finish the statement, I now bury myself in all of their minds, hearing countless sickening thoughts revolving around Forest. Clenching the chain so tight, my knuckles grow white; each boy finds humor in the ideology of getting her drunk enough to be taken advantage of. Biting back the want to kill all three of these idiots right on the spot, I take a sharp breath, doing the one thing I know I can do.

"You want to assault her?" I question, unsure of what an honest response will do to me.

"No, well, yes, just scare her-"

Forcing my hand forward, I strike the man as hard as I can across the face, watching him sputter as he hits the ground. Taking one look at his two pathetic companions, I make an executive decision, grabbing their necks before they can protest, squeezing until both of their windpipes have crushed. Hitting the ground with dead weight, both boys land beside Josh, his feet kicking away from his dead weight friends, his eyes glancing up toward me with fear.

"If you ever entertain a thought pattern like that again, I will rip you limb from limb and force your own hands down your throat. If you so much as think about laying a hand on her, so help me god, I will make what I did here today look like the pleasurable option."

Peering toward the woods near his house, I nudge my head.

"Now carry your useless friends into the woods, I'll report it as drinking gone wrong once I feel like their missing persons report has gone on too long."

Shoving her necklace inside my pocket, Josh shakily stands, his throat unable to swallow.

"W- what-"

"Move!" I yell, forcing one of his companion's arms into his hand, nudging him forward to begin dragging.

Taking a seat back on the log, the entertainment I have found in watching this pathetic idiot cover up his mess has grown considerably more enticing than any drunken fight could have been.

She is supposed to be coming tonight.

Perhaps I can stick around for a little while longer.

Quickly finding his rhythm again to entertain his guests, as if two of his friend's bodies weren't lying outside his house, Josh quickly excused himself, leaving me the breathing room needed to kill off most of my flask. Letting it settle in my stomach, I make my way around the fire, finding comfort in being concealed by the shadows the night brings. Watching the couples that had managed to make it outside leave once food was announced, the silence of the night brings me peace once more.

Staring at the lifeless bodies of Josh's companions, their faces are stuck in a look of shock, as if they are surprised their actions landed them where they are now.

What a damn pity-

Crack.

Startled, I snap my focus back to the fire, my hand resting on the hilt of my knife, ready to deliver Josh the blow he so rightfully deserves if foolish enough to waltz back over here. Looking past the flames of the fire, a body sits peacefully on the log, holding up a large hoodie close to the flames, before letting it settle on the seat next to them. Warming their hands, it's hard to make out their face from here. Shaking my almost empty flask, I tuck it away, letting the alcohol that has settled into my system guide my actions.

Perhaps messing with a few more elite Untouchables could sway my night in the right direction.

Tugging up my mask, I force back up my hood, keeping my eyes on the ground, silently working my way over to the clueless fool.

Taking a seat as quietly as I can, their focus is solely on the flames, completely clueless to the monster that has decided to take residency next to them. Watching the movement of bodies within the home, nearly every single person enjoys the lively chatter of the party, my curiosities growing on why someone would feel the need to be so isolated.

"Not big on parties?" I question, keeping my focus on the flames, not even bothering to look in their direction.

Sensing a stir, something in my chest aches to life, my smile dropping immediately at the feeling that has decided to enter my chest. Feeling a wave of anxieties that are far from my own, panic begins to settle in my system, my throat already feeling as if it is ready to close.

God, no.

Not here.

Please, don't be here.

"Not big with dealing with any of the assholes in there," her euphoric voice whispers, her hands raised, warming her chill body with the fire.

It's a voice I dream of every night.

One I would rip my own heart to hear say my name with familiarity once more.

Fidgeting with my flask, I can't help but laugh at the irony of the situation. Unable to fully look her way, it takes every fiber of my being not to grab her where she sits and kiss every square inch of her, avoiding her lips entirely.

Against my better judgment, I turn my head, her eyes locking with my own, her hair so dark, I would never be able to pinpoint her from behind. Looking at me with a blank stare, she finds no familiarity in me whatsoever. Clenching my hand around my flask, the urge to down what's rest and let myself feel whatever pain is sure to come becomes my only plan of action. Looking at her full cup, I try to think of a conversation to distract myself.

"Don't trust Josh's surprise in the punchbowl?" she asks, blatantly unaware of how uninvolved I am with Josh and his social events.

"As much as you do apparently," I smile, pulling the flask free form my pocket. "I like to come prepared. The strong stuff gives me the courage I greatly lack," I admit with full honesty, tugging down the mask, her eyes lingering on the sight of my face fully exposed.

Giving me that gorgeous smile, every moment of torture this brings me is worth a few seconds of seeing her joy.

Placing her hand on my chest, she tugs at my jacket, taking notice of the tidy Official uniform.

"What's with the getup?" she questions, her mind as sharp as ever.

Pulling my mask back up, I glare at the house.

"There are some people here I don't want seeing me," I admit, wondering at what point the Prophet realizes I have slipped away. Standing up, I make the decision to move closer, leaving little space between us, her warmth radiating through my clothes, extending the flask out to her, I have just enough to give her the buzz I'm sure she needs. Looking over the offer with wariness, I give the flask a few shakes.

"You aren't planning on drugging me, are you?" she questions, humor lingering in her tone.

"Do you honestly think someone would do that?" I question, ready to feed my justification for killing Josh's group of vigilantes.

"I don't put it beneath anyone."

"I drank first, I'll allow you to kick me in the head if I'm the first to go down," I joke, a larger smile creeping along her lips.

What I would give to run my thumb along that bottom lip and gather it between my teeth.

"What is it?" she questions, my mind racking itself to find a half-decent lie.

"Bourbon, I stole it from inside the house," I lie, the carts filled with fine liquor lingering in my room too complicated to explain.

"Stealing from upper leadership hm?" she questions, taking a large swig. "For shame," she taunts, lowering her eyes. "What about your scorecard?"

The way she would laugh if I ever told her she worried about something as trivial as the Untouchables and Unfortunates outdated grading system.

"Fuck the scorecards," I say without thinking, the alcohol guiding me. "Fuck this whole system." A pain lingers in my stomach, threatening for me to stop. "Sometimes rich assholes need to be humble, and those beneath us need to be saved."

Anticipating her Untouchable side to rain hell on me, she looks at me blankly, her cheeks rosy from the heat of the fire.

Come on, Forest, be smart. Tell me you'd report an asshole talking like this. Tell me your mind can stray away from deviance enough to not look past this.

I don't know why I want her to be wary of me.

Perhaps I hope it will keep the little raven-haired scum away from her.

Laughing with a smile, she breaks the tension, doing the one thing I hoped she wouldn't.

"This is generally the part where you should be contacting an Official for my deviance," I push, raising my brows at the woman. Smiling at the way her lips rise, I continue on with my lie. "The last time I came to one of these, some uptight asshole tried to report me to an Official, so, I've got to ask, why do you look so happy?" I question, reaching out without thinking, my fingers touching the corner of her mouth.

Expecting her to flinch away from the gesture, she stays still, closing her eyes momentarily, as if the touch could mean anything to her. Dropping my hand, I rub the back of my neck, mentally savoring every second I get to feel her gentle face once more.

"It's just... no one ever goes against the rules... it's nice to see. Plus, the asshole running this party has made my life nothing short of hell," she admits, the hate I harbor for Josh only growing. Pausing, she glares at me, her eyes narrowing. "What is your name?" she questions, looking at me as if I am the farthest thing from familiar.

I am walking a fine line talking to her like this.

One wrong move and it all comes crashing down.

"If I told you, would it even matter?" I question, selfishly letting her feel my frustrations over her lack of knowledge.

"Cryptic," she jokes, nudging my foot with her own, humor the farthest thing from me.

Closing her eyes, the music switches in tempo, the beat much more calming than the upbeat music being played moments ago. Gently swaying her body to the sound of the music, a thought infiltrates my mind.

Standing before she can stop me, I extend my hand out toward her, her eyes flying open, fixated on the gesture.

"What-"

"Dance with me. Everyone else inside the party seems to be enjoying the rhythm, so the least I can do is treat you to a dance," I smile, ready for her to finally back away.

Saying nothing, her hand gently places in my own, the feeling of her touch electrifying me. Pulling her up, her hands instinctively wrap around my neck, her cheeks only growing more red.

"I didn't say yes," she taunts, her eyebrows raised with thrill.

"Yet, you didn't say no."

Scrunching her nose, my heart melts on the spot, her hand dragging itself to my mask, tugging it down without asking.

"The least you can do is show me that smile while dancing with me," she pushes, her fingers trailing across my lips.

Filled to the brim with urges I can't explore, the alcohol in my system clouds my physical pain, my hand reaching up, cupping the side of her face.

Confused, she opens her mouth, my thumb dragging her lips closed, stopping her from getting a word in.

"I don't know how long I can be with you like this," I whisper, pressing my forehead to hers. "I am not from your sector, Forest, and it eats me alive knowing how little you know," I push, feeling the start of a lesion. "Please, Flower, just dance with me."

Watching her brows furrow at the comment, she relaxes, bringing her arms back around my neck, my hands lifting her onto my feet, allowing her the height needed to keep her focus on my eyes. Dropping my thumb from her lips, I slide my hands beneath her shirt, feeling the rough skin of her mark, before making my way to her waist. Surrounded by her energy, my heart beats rapidly, her head resting on my shoulder.

"W- what's going on?" she questions shakily.

"I'm allowing myself to be selfish and savor a few moments with you," I admit, her head pulling away from my shoulder.

Cupping my face in her hands, I lift her up, letting her observe me with those watchful eyes. Running her hand through my hair, something breaches her eyes, a smile cracking along her lips.

"Have we met before?" she questions, my heart racing, my focus solely on her.

"I've seen you in passing," I admit, feeling the lesion deepen. "But nothing more," I sigh. "Perhaps you're thinking of someone else."

It doesn't matter what I say.

The Prophet ensured she was hard-wired to gravitate toward Fallan.

An attraction built on the foundations of the love I have for her.

That little bastard is asking for the pain I have in store for him.

"I've seen you before," she whispers again, her focus deepening. Raising her hand, she touches her temple. "I can't explain it, and it feels so distant, but I've seen you in my dreams," she smiles, a sliver of hope entering my chest.

"Dreams?" I question. "You don't even know my name," I admit, her head shaking.

"Then tell me it," she pushes, both our bodies swaying to the music.

"Xavier... Xavier Evermoore," I admit, her eyes quickly widening, before closing once more.

"I'm-"

"Forest," I say without thinking, her head cocking toward me with confusion. "How did you-"

Giving her a look, I cut her off, pleading for her to not make me answer that question. Snapping her mouth shut, she stands still, letting her forehead press to mine.

"You're one odd Official," she whispers. "But I like it," she smiles, something flooding between us. It's the faint echo of what will always remain between us. A deep-rooted connection, one perhaps death himself could not take.

"You don't know the half of it," I whisper, feeling the chain of her necklace in my pocket. "That reminds me." Holding up her necklace in the air between us, her eyes focus on the pendant, her smile growing once again. "I figured you might want this back," I smile. "I'm assuming you're the Forest he stole this from."

Carefully grabbing the chain, her smile grows.

"Who the hell are you?" she questions again.

"Consider me your shadow," I smile, the irony in the statement unbelievable.

"Well, Xavier, you fancy helping me put this on?" she questions.

Nodding, she turns away from me, moving aside her dyed locks to her front. Taking a stand behind her, I take a moment to touch the skin of her neck, letting the chain rest along her chest. Clasping the back of the necklace, my hands linger near her neck, something coming over me.

Landing my lips on her neck from behind, I let the alcohol guide my actions. Pressing down on the places she loved most, small gasps leave her mouth, my hands on her waist, holding her as close to me as I possibly can. Expecting her to pull away in fear, she leans back, her eyes finding my flustered expression.

"Keep going," she whispers. "Something tells me there's a reason you spoke to me tonight."

There's my girl.

Covering her mouth, I pull her farther away from the house window, keeping her lips far away from my own. Backing her into one of the nearby trees, I press my forehead to hers, feeling our noses touch, before trailing my mouth to her ear.

"Hold onto this night," I whisper. "Hold onto me-"

"For shame, Xavier," their voice snaps, all of my senses going into overdrive.

Turning on my heels, my questions are quickly silenced by my yell, the small lesion once threatening my skin, now a deep cut across my torso.

Covering her gasp, Forest's eyes snap up to the Prophet, her hands shaking, her body ready to kneel by my side.

"What the hell is going on?" she questions, fully unaware of the power she holds.

Doubled over in pain, I try and tell her to run, my voice nothing but gasps.

"Well, you see, your fiancé here broke the rules, thinking that I would not notice," the Prophet sighs, Forest's head shaking.

"Fiancé?" she questions, running her hands through her hair. "I'm fucking nineteen-"

Bursting out in laughter, the Prophet grins, taking a stand over me, their body feet away from Forest.

"How are you not getting a kick out of this?" the Prophet questions, Forest's heartbeat ready to burst through her chest.

"Tell you what," the Prophet whispers, giving Forest a long look. "How about you remember tonight as a moment with Fallan, and you can recall it the first time you tamper with that little chip inside your head. Either way, the shittiest parts of yourself will stay buried, until death has claimed you as his own."

Shaking my head, I try and yell, my face being shoved further into the dirt.

"Shut up!" the Prophet hisses, kicking me hard in the back.

Sputtering, Forest surges forward, her hands colliding with the Prophet's body. Grabbing her wrists before she can give them a proper shove, they tug her closer.

Holding both of her wrists with one hand, they rest their hand on the top of her head, the presence of their Call in her mind eating away at every moment from tonight

"Say bye, Xavier," they whisper. "She had such a lovely night with Fallan."

"W- wait-"

"You danced with an Unfortunate, one that made you feel emotions you thought not possible. It was wrong, but the way he made you feel made it worth every second of deviance you partook in. There was no Xavier Evermoore. There was no man with the blonde locks. You danced a few minutes with the man who has given you the nickname Dove, and then he left, leaving you with nothing but a feeling of warmth in your heart, and the name Fallan nestled into your soul."

Watching her eyes take it all in, her grasp on the Prophet falters, her eyes closing before blankly moving past me and the Prophet. Giving the bonfire one last look, she swipes her hoodie, looking past both of us, her mind far from the moment we just shared.

Baring my teeth, the Prophet's hand comes over my head, entwining with my hair. Slamming my head as hard as they can into the ground, I take a shaky breath, letting her figure disappear beyond the back door of the house.

"Did you really fucking think I wouldn't catch on to your impulsive late-night rendezvous in this sector?" they question, digging their nails into my scalp.

"How the hell did you slip into her mind so easily?" I snap, thrashing against them.

"Maybe when all of her was intact, I would face trouble slipping into that mind of hers. Now that she is an empty, subservient, little Blackburn, I can alter her mind as many times as I like. So, if you think for a second you can make her see you differently or somehow push past the bind you and her both share, you're wrong. She will only know you to be the friendly Official working under her father. When, and only when, I require you to gain her trust, may you entertain any kind of conversation with her. Now, clean yourself up. You have two bodies to carry somewhere a little more private," they snap, shoving me down, their foot rising off of my back.

Turning onto my side, I anticipate the Prophet's silver mask, feeling unsettlement in the empty space around me. As quickly as they appeared, they are gone, nothing but the footprints of their boots in the grass around me.

Staring into the fire, I force myself into a standing position, grabbing the cup Forest had left behind before downing Josh's mystery liquid with a heavy soul.

After finishing what was left in Forest's cup and forcing myself to stay away from the house, I now stare down Josh's friends, both too large to be dragged without being noticed. Clutching my bloodiest lesion, I bite my lip each time the pain grows too intense, keeping my focus on the task at hand, my mind on high alert.

It doesn't matter what the fuck the Prophet said.

She remembered me. She knew she remembered me.

If there's a way out of this, I will find it.

I will do everything the Prophet says, so long as it means I am near her.

Perhaps one day she will think I am the very evil I set out to destroy, but, at the end of the day, I will always do what's best for her.

Even if it ends up killing me.

Lost in my train of thought, the sound of a body stumbling toward me catches my attention.

Turning on my heels, my vision is a bit hazy, my focus only on the man stumbling toward me. Grabbing my front, he looks all too familiar, his eyes blinking rapidly, his chip a dull red behind his ear.

Taking a closer look at the man, I wonder if the alcohol has gotten to me.

"How long have I been asleep?" the man questions, my head shaking with confusion.

"Are you fucking with me?" I question, glancing at the bodies the man has chosen to look past entirely.

"What the fuck is going on? I just hit my fucking head at this shithead's party, and it's like I just woke up. I don't know where I am, I keep getting these memories-"

Tuning the man out, his face becomes familiar in my mind.

This is one of Forest's followers.

One of the ones who believed in her cause to kill the Prophet. □

One who believed in the Apparatus.

It would seem the Prophet's brainwashing had no boundaries.

Glancing at the red marks surrounding his head, bruises form behind his ear, the chip most likely damaged, his thoughts too confused to pinpoint reality from a facade.

"Where is the Apparatus?" he questions, a scoff rolling off my throat.

"Clearly, I'm a little fucking busy," I hiss, shoving him away. The last thing I can handle right now is a conversation about the women trapped in Forest's mind.

"No," he gripes, grabbing my sleeve. "No, no, no, I saw her, I saw-"

"You really believe she is in there?" I hiss, anger rolling off of my tone. "Why don't you take this," I hiss, grabbing a knife off of one of Josh's friends, no doubt taken from the kitchen. "And go fucking pry that little chip out. I'm sure then you'll finally have some clarity," I hiss, sensing the mark painting his skin.

Saying nothing else, I shove the man away, no longer needing a reminder of my old life.

Grabbing one of the boy's limp arms, I begin to drag, my responsibilities to the Prophet the first step in getting the trust I so desperately need.

"The Apparatus is near, they will lead us away from this eternal hell."

Pausing, I glare at the man.

"Yeah?" I question. "And what happens if the Apparatus is dead?' I question, her blank stare painting my mind.

Saying nothing else, I ignore his quiet rambles, dragging the body further along, my mind too clouded with intoxication to focus on the potential consequences of my actions.

CHAPTER FIFTY-FOUR

XAVIER

"Y ou were right. He jumped on the opportunity to come here like a starving dog," Elyon hisses, his eyes dead set on Fallan.

"I told you all the lies he spewed about loving me were bullshit. All it took was a few simple whispers from you about avenging his Dove before he was biting at any opportunity to be involved," Forest smiles, speaking as if she has always had full clarity.

"Forest, please, baby, what the hell is the plan here?" I question, her eyebrows raising with curiosity.

"There is no plan here, Xavier," she smiles. "Fallan wanted to attempt his revenge, and I wanted to give my father a proper show of my force. You just happen to be collateral damage, once again," she hisses. "I was really hoping you'd stay back this time, give me one last thing to focus on. Perhaps it's best you see things for what they are. You love me, and I use you to get my memories back. Isn't that all just blissful?" she questions, not a single lie detectable under the thick layer of wickedness swirling through her mind.

"You fucking lying bastard, you were working with her?" Fallan questions, Elyon's shoulders shrugging.

"Blood before water, that's the saying, isn't it?" Elyon smiles.

"You're fucking lying," I hiss, glaring at Forest. "Elyon is the farthest thing from your father, and there is no scenario in which you would-"

"In which I would what?" she snaps, pointing her finger at me. "In which I'd side with my father. The one ensuring our kind finds its perfect balance. Do you think I like the lesser Marked walking this Earth? Lesser Marked like you and him?" she questions, pointing between Fallan and me. "No, see, your issue, Xavier, is you are too blinded by your love. It makes you brash and foolish and gets you into situations that you have no way of coming back from. That is why you will always lose. You will always have something that makes you weak. I am simply cutting off your poisonous tie to me. Perhaps, then, you will finally be capable of saving something or someone you love," she mutters, lowering her eyes at the both of us.

Thrashing like a fool, I try to get her to look at me. Her eyes avoid giving me anything but a brief glance.

"Do you really think I believe you?" I hiss, narrowing my eyes at the woman. "Do you really think there is any scenario in which I actually believe that you mean any of that?" I snap, her body Winnowing before me. □

Finally looking me in the eyes, she crouches down to my level, allowing her mind to be an open playground. Letting myself inside her thoughts, I find only dead ends, nothing but her allegiance to Elyon slapping me in the face.

"Love can be used in many ways," she whispers. "For comfort," she whispers, pulling her lips next to my ear. "Or for an advantage."

Giving me a cold look, she shakes her head, the woman in front of me entirely foreign to me.

"I love you-" □

"So did Fallan," she smiles, giving the man a glance. "The problem is, I didn't love either of you. You are both means to an end, part of a larger plan to serve a bigger cause. It's clear now, isn't it? I don't love you."

Nothing has hurt more than those four words.

Shoving me backward, my back meets the floor. The sound of shoes scuffing the marble floor fills the space, my head snapping back to take a look.

Funneling into the ballroom, some scattered Marked slaves, Officials, and guests take a step inside, their ages varying from young to elder. All housing a blinking green chip behind their ears, they frantically look around the space, cowering with fear at the sight of Elyon and Forest.

"How many?" Forest asks, speaking mentally to Elyon, my thoughts completely shut out from her own.

"All of them."

"Forest, take a minute to think this through-"

"God, how pathetic can you be?" she snaps, lowering her gaze in my direction. "Do you hear yourself now? Please, Forest, please, do the right thing," she mocks, rolling her eyes at me. "You fucking useless human being!" she seethes. "No wonder your whole fucking family died at your feet. Did you weep the same words to them when they lay bleeding out before you?" she questions with a grin, the pain in my chest only growing worse. "No wonder they fucking died."

Hit with a pain so deep, it's hard to breathe, my words are far from me.

Pulling her focus away from me, she narrows in on the citizens, each one cowering with fear.

As if they are all working in unison, every single neck snaps, each body plummeting to the floor. Their chips fly free from their heads, moving past my face before landing in the palm of her hand.

Thrashing and bloodied, the spindle from the chips is silenced by her clenched hand, her mouth pulling into a manic smile, her eyes peering at the chips as if they are rewards. Watching the blood begin to collect in puddles along the floor, I take a shaky breath, trying to piece together what just happened. Dead children and innocent men and women lay motionless on the floor, their faces stuck in a petrified state, their lives stolen with no remorse.

"What the hell did you just do?" I question shakily.

"I've made my point," Forest smiles. "Clearly, I've allowed myself to hold back a bit too much, don't you think?" she questions, glancing at Elyon.

"You won't just walk away from this," Fallan seethes. "You won't just walk away from the bloodshed you have created and Xavier-"

Laughing, she eyes the man down, looking at him as if he has said the most idiotic thing one man can say.

"Do you have any idea what I am?" she yells, her eyes glowing with the fire of a dozen suns. "Do you have any idea what is coming?" she grins, the very veins beneath her skin illuminating, like electricity running down a copper wire. "You crossed me, scathed me, and used me as if I am someone that would allow that to happen with no consequence. There cannot be perfection so long as your two's Tainted kind continues to run around the world," she whispers, filled with delight. "You should have never mistaken me as a woman who would fight for the losing side, Fallan Markswood."

With no warning, the blade the Prophet had handed her flashes through the air, both my eyes and Fallan's widening at the sight before us. Moving too quickly for either of us to react, the blood spills free from the man's right arm, his hand severed from the wrist up. Screaming out in pain, Fallan grips his hand, her hand grabbing his belt, forcing on a tourniquet, her hand grasped around his chin. Forcing him to look at her, she shakes her head, scolding the man like a small child.

"May that hand never touch another woman again."

Striking him across the face, he sputters, her hand licking her bloodied finger-tips clean.

"I should have cut your other off for Andrew."

Moving over to me, I shake my head in disbelief, wondering at what point I pass out from the betrayal seeping into my soul. Trying to move away from her, she holds me still, her hands cupping my face.

"It's been fun," she whispers, running her fingers along my cheeks. "You were always my favorite." Pressing her lips down on my own, despite what has happened, I hold onto every second of her sweet embrace, her lips lingering longer than they ever have before. "Remember that," she finishes, her eyes peering at mine. "Remember what I've said."

Watching something shift in her eyes, she Winnows away from me, taking a stand next to Elyon, his hand entwined with her own. Taking a large breath, he shakes his head at the both of us, giving us a malicious grin.

"If you expect to find us here if you return, you will be very displeased to see the result. Consider this mercy for the both of you," Elyon smiles, focusing in on me. "Thank you for returning my daughter to me. Both of your duties to me have been relieved, active immediately."

Trying to get her to look at me, I drown out the noise of Fallan's painful yells, her eyes locked with mine.

"Don't come back," she whispers, a grin moving along her lips. "Don't look for me."

Feeling the Hold release, my body finally gets some leeway, my legs scrambling to help me up, my body moving quicker than my mind can react.

As if I am back in that alleyway once again, I scramble to run toward her, ready to hold her down and question her true motive. Watching her body begin to Winnow, her hand pries something free from her finger, the small ring of gold flying through the air, stopping me dead in my tracks.

Catching it before it can hit the floor, the metal ring of her engagement band settles in my hand, her body slowly dissipating, one single thought from her entering my mind.

"Usque ad extremum spiritum meu."

Watching my hand pass through the air, I fall forward, feeling my knees hit the ground, nothing but empty space in the place she once stood.

Surrounded by an undeniable silence, the world around me grows quiet, the screams of pain surrounding me deafening, my eyes wide with confusion.

Shakily holding her ring, I stare at it in disbelief, her words clouding my mind, eating away at my every thought.

"Xavier," a voice yells out to me, my mind barely processing any noise.

Forced to face the frazzled expression of Kai, he wears tactical gear, his body crouched before me, his eyes as wide as my own. Shaking me over and over, I peer behind me at the group of our companions swarming Fallan, each one stuck in a state of shock, every single person moving as if they are in slow motion.

"Xavier!" Kai yells once more, his hand grabbing my face, the sound of his voice barely filtering to my ears. "Where is she?" he yells, nothing but pain entering my mind.

Saying nothing, I grab his hand, dropping the ring into his palm, blankly staring forward.

"She's gone," I whisper, something wet slipping free from his eye, shock consuming Kai's expression.

"Forest is *gone.*"

Ashes to ashes.

We all fall down.

End Book 3

A SNEAK PEAK INTO BOOK FOUR OF THE ORDER SERIES

Xavier

Nine months.

It has been nine months since she locked hands with the Prophet, turning her back on everything and everyone she loved, leaving nothing but death in the trail behind her.

I always craved a reality in which her bind and mine ceased to exist.

A reality where we may live peacefully, away from the treacherous grasp created by mankind.

Every day, I look at the cabin's door, waiting for her to arrive, ready to tell me her extravagant plan, ready to embrace me with the love they so heartlessly ripped away from us.

Now, my chest feels like nothing but an empty cavern, torn away from the one thing in this wretched life that made me believe I was anything more than a blood-hungry fool.

The Marked are falling.

The Order's reign is escalating.

There's no way to determine how this ends or how any of us make it out of this alive.

Countless warrants for our immediate arrest circle Santcumn's hubs, waiting for one of us to slip up, ready to drag us back to the demons that wait for us under the wards.

"Are you coming?" The raven-haired bane of my existence questions, my mind filling with disgust in his presence.

Two things are for certain.

Forest betrayed us.

Forest betrayed *me.*

"There's only one way to end this," I whisper, his eyes darting to me.

"Oh, Xavier," He mutters in a mocking tone. "This war is only the beginning."

ACKNOWLEDGEMENTS

I would like to express my heartfelt gratitude to my husband and my dad for their unwavering support throughout this journey. Your encouragement, patience, and belief in me have been the pillars upon which I've built this endeavor. I am endlessly grateful for your love and guidance.

To my best friend, Bekah, your constant presence and endless support have been invaluable. Your belief in my abilities has pushed me forward when doubt crept in. Thank you for being my rock and for always cheering me on.

And to all the readers who have embraced my work, thank you for making this dream a reality. Your support and enthusiasm inspire me to keep writing and sharing my stories with the world.

Love you all

ABOUT THE AUTHOR
Katerina St Clair

YOURLOCALWRITERZ

KATERINASTCLAIRAUTHOR

WWW.KATERINA
STCLAIR.COM

KATERINA ST CLAIR IS AN ACCOMPLISHED AUTHOR CURRENTLY PURSUING AN ACADEMIC PATH TOWARD BECOMING A CREATIVE WRITING INSTRUCTOR AT THE HIGHER EDUCATION LEVEL. RESIDING IN THE MIDWEST WITH HER PARTNER AND HER BELOVED LABRADOR SONS, SHE IS A DEDICATED PROFESSIONAL WITH A MULTIFACETED LIFESTYLE. WHEN NOT IMMERSED IN ORCHESTRATING HER NEXT LITERARY ENDEAVOR WHILE ENJOYING MUSIC, SHE FINDS SOLACE IN CULINARY PURSUITS OR INDULGES IN EXTENSIVE READING FROM HER EVER-EXPANDING TO-BE-READ LIST. HER LITERARY PREFERENCES GRAVITATE TOWARDS NARRATIVES CHARACTERIZED BY UNFORESEEN TWISTS, A QUALITY SHE ENDEAVORS TO INFUSE INTO EACH OF HER NOVELS.